Praise for
Finding Ida

'Elegant and illuminating about a less well-known but fascinating period of history. Marya Burgess takes a deeply personal story and makes it universal. The most memorable novel I've read this year.'

Tim Finch, author of *Peace Talks* (shortlisted for the 2020 Costa Book Awards) and *House of Journalists*

'It's an absorbing love letter to a family shaped by the often cruel twists of history.'

Fi Glover, writer and broadcaster

'Based on real events, this fascinating novel casts a light on a family caught in the crossfire of war and turmoil. An untold story, it is a salient reminder of the human cost of conflict and separation and the power of love.'

Di Speirs, Ex-Executive BBC Audio Books Editor

Finding Ida

Marya Burgess

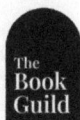

The
Book
Guild

First published in Great Britain in 2025 by
The Book Guild Ltd
Unit E2 Airfield Business Park,
Harrison Road, Market Harborough,
Leicestershire. LE16 7UL
Tel: 0116 2792299
www.bookguild.co.uk
Email: info@bookguild.co.uk

Map Illustration by Sarah McMenemy

The manufacturer's authorised representative in the EU
for product safety is Authorised Rep Compliance Ltd,
71 Lower Baggot Street, Dublin D02 P593 Ireland (www.arccompliance.com)

This work is entirely fictitious and bears no resemblance to any persons living or dead.

Typeset in 11pt Minion Pro

Printed and bound by CPI Group (UK) Ltd, Croydon, CR0 4YY

ISBN 978 1835743 454

British Library Cataloguing in Publication Data.
A catalogue record for this book is available from the British Library.

MIX
Paper | Supporting
responsible forestry
FSC
www.fsc.org   FSC® C013604

For the displaced and all who must find a new home.

Baltic Sea

Gdańsk

GERMANY
(EAST PRUSSI

Toruń

Poznań

Warszawa

Malinów

Pabianice

GERMANY

POLAND
1921-1939

Riga ↑ LATVIA

LITHUANIA

Wilno •

Białystok

Nieśwież

Zakątek

USSR

In later generations, everything is a story. History is surmises and good sentences.

Sebastian Barry, *The Guardian*, 21 Oct 2016

Family:
Ida (Idka) and **Luiza (Lou-lou)** Wolfer – sisters
Hugo and **Zosia** Wolfer – **Pappa** and **Mama**
Uncle Rafi Svenson – Mama's younger brother, **Aunt Wanda** (his wife, sister to Pani Aurelia, the bookkeeper at the mill) and **Kamila** (their daughter)
Aunt Ludmila – Mama's elder half-sister, and **Uncle Herbert** (her husband)
Aunt Rysia – Mama's younger sister, **Uncle Ryszard** (her husband), **Vera** and **Paweł** (their children)

❧

Zakątek:
House
Janek – steward
Anjela – maid
Marte, Beata, Katja – nannies to the sisters
Pani Marysia – cook
Vacek and **Pani Ewa** – replacement cooks

Mill
Pan Cholowa – storekeeper
Pani Aurelia – bookkeeper
Pan Graban – manager appointed by Korski Board

Neighbours

Pani Anna Grudzinska – friend (and Warsaw hotelier)
Pan Rubacz – farmer, and **Jurek** (his son)
Commissioner Petrowski, Wojtek (his son) and **Bożena** (his granddaughter)

Visitors

Uncle Stefan – family friend (and Luiza's godfather)
Stasia – Ida's school friend

Wilno:

Pani Jankowska – landlady (and mother to Pani Aurelia and Aunt Wanda)
Helena – Luiza's school friend

Warszawa:

Pani Rybicka – history teacher
Pan Garonski (Guzik) – maths teacher
Gosia (Bielska) and **Agnieszka** – two of the Three Musketeers
Isaak and **Sara Abel** – Hugo's former accountant and his wife (who teaches Luiza piano), **Elsa** (their daughter), **Dawid** (her husband) and **Misza** (their baby)

Malinów:

Waldemar – Pani Anna's son, **Grażyna** (his wife) and **Roman** (their baby)

Tadeusz (Zielinski) and **Dorota** (his sister)
Mirosław (Mirek) Timorecki – Ida's husband
Karol Wyczyński – Luiza's first boyfriend and **Wacek** (his
    friend)

Pabianice:
Pani Mathilde Krawcik – housekeeper
Oberleutnant Gustav Helfer – billeted in the apartment

Luneberg, Austria:
Uncle Georg – Hugo's brother, **Aunt Gretchen** (his wife)
    and **Helga** (their daughter)
Countess **Elena** Von Burg – Luiza's friend
Maria – Luiza's friend at the bank

Chapter 1

December 1955, Singapore

There's only the faintest draft from the ceiling fan. Luiza brushes back a damp lock of hair and weighs the letter in her other hand.

Amah left the post on the table this morning, and Luiza brought it through to the living room after lunch – the usual pile of bills, postcards and Club correspondence. When the pale blue envelope slipped from the stack, she had to squat to retrieve it, her full-term belly making bending impossible. She thought it was from Jack's sister in Rhodesia. But Kathleen uses aerogrammes, filling each flap with tightly typed news. And she addresses them to Jack; it's Luiza's name that's printed here. There's something about the quality of the paper, too: dull in colour, coarse in texture. And then there's the stamp. Her stomach lurches. *It's Polish.*

Reaching unsteadily for the arm of a chair, she sinks

carefully onto the seat and considers the flimsy paper. Too insubstantial, surely, to bear the weight of information she seeks. Ten years, now, since the war ended. And nearly as long since that final postcard. Her elegant sister, begging for a brown hat, for shoes, for underwear. Saying that the war had been hard, that she could no longer laugh or cry, that even though it was difficult for her to work she'd found a job in a restaurant. But no mention of the child. June 1947 the card was dated – Luiza was already married a month by then. She'd sent the clothes, but there hasn't been a word from Ida since.

Yet she's never given up. Letters to the Red Cross and to friends who could well be dead, at addresses that likely no longer exist. Those newsreels of Warszawa: the vanished streets where once she walked to school. Destruction and chaos throughout Europe. How could she hope to locate one woman among displaced millions?

She glances at her watch. In ten minutes, she must pick the boys up from school. Then a blissful respite from the heat – the children water-sleek and chattering like dolphins, Luiza and the other wives on the poolside, slipping languidly into the water between iced sips of lime and soda and lazy slivers of conversation.

Her fingers play with the envelope, teasing the place where the glued flap puckers. Unopened, it tantalises with possibility. Once read, the truth can not be unlearnt. Hidden words that have the power to eliminate all hope, to break finally the flimsy thread that connects her to her past. Without it, might she simply float away, insubstantial, un-historied?

She heaves herself out of the chair and hides the letter at the back of the bureau, behind the box of International Women's Club stationery.

That night, Luiza dreams of home. It's dusk and white pillars stand sentry before double doors opening on the tiled hall of a long, low house. The ceramic corner-stove is cool to her touch. On the left are the salon and her father's study, beyond them the dining room and kitchen. To the right lie the bedrooms.

Someone is playing the piano. Luiza opens the door to the salon, but the music stops, an abandoned coffee tray the only clue to recent occupancy. She crosses the parquet to the open French windows and scans the lawn as far as the lake. No one. The breeze stirring the curtains is heavy with the scent of jasmine.

She slides onto the piano stool and runs her fingers over the keys, seeking an imprint of the player's touch. Reaching for a coffee cup, she pictures her mother framed in the doorway, one hand raised, the small tray bearing the silver pot balanced on her fingertips. With her other hand she fans out her skirt and waltzes into the room to the rhythm of her own hummed accompaniment. Mama's eyes are closed, a private smile on her lips.

With the inexplicable logic of dreams, Luiza is transported to the warehouse of her father's mill and finds herself spread-eagled on bales of cotton. The hessian wrappings scratch bare arms and legs. Someone's calling her name.

It's Jack, trying to disentangle her from the collapsed mosquito net. With a gentle rub of her belly and a tickly brush of moustache across her lips, he heads for the shower. Luiza lies back, tracing with a finger the surge and ebb that ripples her belly as the baby flexes its limbs. When Jack returns, his black hair combed back severely, the scarlet comma of a shaving nick is written on his jaw. Her husband – his bony knees (to the twins' eternal glee, they were awarded first prize in a silly competition at the Club social) revealed beneath sand-coloured shorts – tall, with tanned arms emerging from sleeves emblazoned with the crown within a wreath that denotes his REME rank.

"Breakfast, Lou-lou?"

"I think I'll stay in bed for a while."

"Good idea, sweetheart. You must be tired after all that jabbering in your sleep."

"What did I say?"

"It was all in Polish. But I couldn't make out *kocham Ciebie*, so that's good – unless you were dreaming of me, of course."

Jack grins and plants a wet kiss, then grabs his beret from the top of the chest of drawers. He's fumbling to secure it under his epaulette as he leaves the room. Luiza hears him open the next door down, releasing excited yelps that precede the patter of her sons' bare feet, punctuated by Jack's military step. They disappear down the corridor to the dining room, where Amah will have breakfast waiting.

Luiza wonders what she said in her sleep and smiles at Jack's pronunciation. *Kocham Ciebie* – I love you – the only words of Polish he's learnt. She can't recall speaking to anyone in her dream – the salon was empty, as was the warehouse. But from the edge of consciousness, she retrieves the silhouette of a figure in the doorway. *Ida, was it you?*

She remembers the letter in the bureau.

Closing her eyes, she concentrates on the shadowy form, willing it to resolve into her sister. But Ida as she used to be, a smile lighting up her face until her eyes sparkled. Not as she last saw her – diminished, haunted. Luiza remembers keeping pace with the train, waving until she ran out of platform. But Ida kept looking straight ahead, seeing only the child she'd lost.

Over a solitary breakfast – she waited until she heard the front door slam before getting out of bed – Luiza returns to her dream. She's not dwelt on the past for so long. Her life now is Jack and the twins and this new child, due in a matter of days. Even in her search for Ida, she's never allowed herself to look back, other than to consider who might have news of her sister. It's been a relentless forging ahead, a systematic pursuit of one lead after another. Yet now that her search has finally elicited a response, she's hidden it away.

But her dream still took her there, to the place the word 'home' always conjures. Not this flat in the military sector, nor the apartment in Klagenfurt where they lived when first married. Certainly not that grim little two-up, two-down in Hollywood barracks when Jack was posted to Northern Ireland. No, home has always been Zakątek. The long, low house screened from her father's textile factory by a copse of silver birch. Set amid undulating fields near the village of Zapole, thirty kilometres south-west of Warszawa. Luiza sees it now as if she were a bird flying overhead: the lake and the tennis court, the lanes to Zapole and to the station at Grodzisk Mazowieck, choked with dust in summer and mud in winter. Mama at the piano; Pappa overseeing operations at his mill. And two little girls playing together, where they belonged.

Luiza's resisted such memories for so long, but now they're a flood. The residue of the dream washes over her and she's finally home.

Chapter 2

Summer 1927, Zakątek

*N*ow she wished that Ida would play with her at the mill, instead of sitting in the salon with the grown-ups. It was Ida who choreographed the games they played among the huge cotton bales in Pappa's cavernous storehouse. She clambered with just as much enthusiasm as Luiza, and her longer legs propelled her further. Sometimes their father appeared, back-lit in the mote-strewn sunlight that poured through the huge double doors. Stroking his black beard, he summoned the storekeeper.

"Pan Cholowa, will you look at these urchins? You'd better throw them in the tub. Here, I'll help you catch them."

Shrieking with terror and delight, the girls scuttled away. "Pappa, it's us!" Luiza squeaked. "It's Lou-lou and Idka."

But Pappa shook his head. "You can't be my little Lou-lou. She's got dark hair and a pretty blue dress – look at you, all covered in dust. And my Idka always has a clean pinafore – she's not a ragamuffin."

But Ida was nearly nine and would be going away to school in a few weeks. She said their warehouse games were childish.

Four years separated the sisters, and Ida never lost sight of her seniority. When she announced, "Lou-lou, that's a plain tile, so you're out", Luiza held her tongue, even though yesterday, crocodiles lurked behind the patterned floor tiles in the hall. Ida's years as an only child granted her impunity, and the ability to pinch hard.

It was not only their games that Ida had outgrown; the sensible clothes laid out by Beata, their current nanny, were no longer acceptable. At the dressmaker in Warszawa, she wheedled, "Mama, don't you think this would look much nicer with a ribbon around the neck, and perhaps pearl buttons?" When the new dresses arrived, Ida's were embellished accordingly, while Luiza's remained unadorned.

But Luiza was not bothered by this aspect of Ida's recent sophistication. While her sister paraded in the salon, she sprawled happily on the attic floor, where Pappa had laid out the complex network of Hornby track he purchased in England. Oblivious to the dirt accumulating on her ribbon-less dress, Luiza guided the clockwork trains with care. Pappa preferred the attic to the salon, too, but the bulk of his belly limited his reach, so it was Luiza who operated the engines.

"Oops, that one can't take the scenic route, Lou-lou,

it's much too long. The carriages will derail on the bends. You'd best return to the station, shunt the green engine in from the siding and split the load."

Luiza followed his directions, because Pappa knew about engines; his knowledge once saved his life.

Luiza's love for her father was clear and simple. She was a tomboy and happily filled the son-shaped hole in Pappa's life. The two of them were an easy match. But with Mama, things could prickle and rub. Though hungry for her affection, Luiza chafed at the constraints of the salon. She did her best to sit still while Mama played the piano or stitched her fine embroidery, but before long, her fingers marched down her lap or her tongue tried to touch the tip of her nose. Then Mama would shake her head and Luiza would soon slip out of the room, relieved but also a little sad.

Apart from the attic, Luiza's favourite place was Pappa's mill. As she skirted the lake, she thrilled to the growing rumble of machinery. Passing beyond the trees into the mill yard, she was engulfed by the clatter of the huge spinners and presses that transformed bales of Indian cotton into high-grade cotton wool. She didn't really believe that the mill was the lair of a fire-breathing dragon, but it was still best to be careful. Pappa and his foreman made a big fuss of the massive steam engine that powered the mill, and sometimes Pappa mused, "I don't know what's wrong with her today. Perhaps she needs to munch on a nice, juicy Lou-lou to lift her spirits." Luiza tingled with dread and delight in equal measure.

If she found her father in shirt sleeves, his hands stained with oil, she knew he was in a good mood. Which was why she always sought him first among the men who stoked the massive boilers for washing the cotton. Next, she looked in the shed where they transferred it from the spin dryers onto airing machines. Pappa was easy to spot among the village men; his white hair and fine lawn shirt, stretched tight across his paunch, stood out from the millhands' rough woollen clothes. He was not there, so Luiza crossed the yard to the pressing shed.

Here, women in kerchiefs and aprons combed out the clean, fluffed cotton and fed it into the presser, where it was digested to produce a matted sheet at the other end. The women reached to pinch her cheeks and tug her fringe as Luiza ran the gauntlet between the presser and the cutting tables, where they sliced the cotton wool into different sizes and thicknesses, ready for packaging. Still no sign of Pappa. She crossed the yard again to his office.

And there he was, at his desk, totting up figures he was tracing with a pencil. A frown brought his bushy eyebrows together into a single shaggy black line, mirroring his moustache and making a sandwich of his broad nose. The contrast with his white hair was startling. Glancing up, his grin parted his brows and lengthened his moustache as he beckoned Luiza to him. She held her breath as she passed Pani Aurelia's desk; Pappa's secretary was stick-thin and smelled of cigarettes and coffee.

Pappa swivelled his chair to accommodate her on his lap, and Luiza looked from the long list of figures to her father's face. Pappa winked.

"Lou-lou, thank goodness. I hope you've come to rescue me from these sums. It must be dinnertime, surely?"

There was a tutting sound from the desk by the door, and Pani Aurelia rasped, "Pan Direktor, we must get this order off. It really should have gone yesterday."

Pappa slid Luiza from his lap and eased himself upright. "No need to worry, Pani Aurelia. I'll be back after dinner, raring to go, I promise. Honestly, I might faint if I don't eat something."

The thin woman, whom Luiza had never seen swallow anything other than black coffee, grimaced, pursing her lips over small, yellow teeth that made Luiza shudder. Pappa shrugged on his jacket and queried, "What do you think the chances are that there's rum baba for dessert, Lou-lou?"

Holding her father's hand, Luiza skittered past the dark figure and breathed deeply once they were outside.

"Pappa," she whispered, conspiratorially, "Do you like Pani Aurelia?"

Her father's face became serious. "Pani Aurelia may not be the easiest person, but she has a good head for business and she's completely reliable."

"But why does she always wear black? Do you think she's a witch?"

Pappa chuckled before resuming gravely, "She wears black because she's in mourning. Poor Melina, such a bright girl. It's an unthinkable tragedy, to lose a child. Pani Aurelia's bound to be sad – sometimes even a bit cross."

Luiza considered this. "Pappa, if Ida or I died, would you get thin?"

Her father guffawed. "Not a chance! Just think of all the rum babas I'd have to consume to console myself. Now, let's get home."

Hand in hand they walked through the silver birches towards the white house. A portly, middle-aged man in a creased, linen suit with a small girl, her socks collapsed around her ankles and the pleats of her blue dress swinging as she skipped.

Chapter 3

September 1927, Zakątek

*L*uiza was about to snip when another pair of scissors appeared above her own and the feathery head of dill toppled into Ida's basket. There it crowned her sister's sizeable mound of herbs, while Luiza's trug was threadbare with a few sorry strands of chives. She glanced at her mother, who was sitting in the shade of the elm, but her eyes were on her embroidery. Ida stuck out her tongue and moved on to the mint.

A distant rumble rose steadily above the hum of bees in the lavender. Dropping their baskets, the girls raced to the front of the house as a glossy, maroon lorry nosed its way up the drive. Janek, the steward at Zakątek, was grinning through the windscreen and braying the horn insistently. He'd driven Pappa's new purchase all the way from Warszawa, and it was the first time a wagon without horses had come through Zapole. Clamorous, barefoot children swarmed after it, pursued by women in headscarves, loudly beseeching Our Lady and all the saints to defend them from this probable demon.

The monster gave a final belch and shuddered to a halt less than a metre from Pappa, who was waving his arms, impatient to inspect his investment. Janek jumped down and opened the bonnet. He'd driven an ambulance during the war, and now he introduced his employer to the internal combustion engine.

Ida climbed into the vacated cab and found the horn. Luiza clambered after her as Pani Marysia, the cook, appeared, wiping her hands on her apron to make the sign of the cross.

Pappa was circling the lorry now. He let down the tailgate to inspect the payload capacity, then hauled himself into the cab, nudging his daughters along the bench and squeezing behind the steering wheel.

"Give it a swing!"

Janek wielded the starting handle and Mama ordered, "You two, out!" Reluctantly, the girls jumped down.

"For goodness' sake be careful, darling," Mama cautioned. "Why not let Janek drive? Couldn't you just watch, to begin with?"

Pappa nodded absently, but his eyes were on the pedals at his feet. The lorry lurched and Pappa grabbed the wheel. Janek leapt out of the way, and the villagers backed into the trees as the vehicle weaved thunderously down the drive and into the lane.

The crash, when it came, was less startling than the deafening stillness that followed. Luiza had never seen her short, plump mother move so fast. How was it possible that she was already bending over Pappa, who was sitting on the ground with his head in his hands? The lorry was nose-down in the ditch, its tailgate flapping hopelessly over rear wheels that were suspended in mid-air.

"I couldn't find the blasted brake," spluttered Pappa, struggling to his feet with Mama's help.

Horses and ropes were brought from the mill, and in no time the lorry was upright again. With Janek in the cab, one of the millhands swung the handle. Eventually, the Ford coughed. Another swing and it growled, and Janek steered it cautiously into the mill yard.

Pappa had his arm around Mama as they walked back up the lane, the girls following.

"You know," they heard him say, "I really can't understand all the fuss about these infernal motors. Give me a steam engine any day."

"Does that mean you won't be driving it again?"

"Of that you can be quite certain, my love."

Ida took off at a run, calling over her shoulder, "Race you home, Lou-lou!"

A few days later, amid a final flurry of packing and farewells, her sister was gone. Mama, too. She'd taken Ida to the convent school herself. It was in Wilno, the city of her birth, and she had family to visit.

Luiza sips her coffee, but it's cold. Amah bustles in to clear the table and looks surprised to find her there. She should get on – so much to do before the baby comes. She shakes herself, trying to dislodge the hollow sense of homesickness that's lodged at her core. This is why she never looks back. Yet what she's been remembering didn't last. Ida left for school and everything changed.

Chapter 4

Autumn 1927, Zakątek

*I*t was as if daily life at Zakątek skipped a beat. Luiza would much rather the hurtful distance Ida had cultivated in the weeks before she left than her total absence now. All the familiar patterns had changed, and Luiza felt out of step.

She'd hoped, when her mother returned, that without constant comparison with Ida's neat embroidery and capacity for sitting decorously, Mama might find Luiza less disappointing. She certainly spent more time with her, working on her cross-stitch as well as introducing piano lessons. Luiza was left with little time for the attic or the mill. Even when she managed to escape, the twinkle had gone from Pappa's eye and he rarely resisted Pani Aurelia's instructions. Even mealtimes were subdued, the three of them finding it impossible to ignore Ida's empty place.

The only good thing to come from Ida's departure was that it was soon followed by Beata's. She was the nanny who had replaced pretty, blonde Marte, whose tummy had started to bulge behind her apron. Beata had a sharp nose and three moles on her chin, each sprouting a wiry hair. She smelled peculiar, too – like sour milk. She could not have been more different from Marte, who laughed a lot and was generous with cuddles. But now she was married to Stefan, who worked at the mill, and had a baby to look after. Luiza had visited her, taking a tiny coverlet that Mama had embroidered.

Since Ida never complained about Beata pinching or pushing arms roughly into sleeves, or raking the comb so it scratched her head, Luiza assumed it all had to be suffered in silence. In fact, the nanny never hurt Ida, but that only came out after the night when Luiza got into bed with her scalp stinging and her arm bruised and felt something cold beneath the quilt. She screamed. A long, dark shape slid onto the floor. One of Pappa's interns at the mill had shown Luiza a picture of a python, its middle distended in the shape of a small child. She kept on screaming.

It was a grass snake, not a python, and the nanny maintained that her joke was aimed at toughening up "the little miss". But Pappa did not find it funny, and the following morning Beata was gone. "The next nanny," said Pappa, "will be educated."

So Katja, whose father was a master at a school in Warszawa, arrived. She had serious brown eyes, which Luiza tried to catch blinking but rarely did, and wore her mousy hair in a bun. Ida would have called her plain, but

Katja was kind, and her voice, when she read to Luiza from the many books she had brought with her, was gentle.

One night, when the new nanny had been at Zakątek a few weeks, Luiza woke with a start as the bedroom door flew open. There was Katja, in her nightgown, a thin plait bouncing on her shoulder.

"Quick, Lou-lou, the mill's on fire. We have to get out!"

Katja picked her up and ran along the corridor and out onto the terrace. Beyond the silver birches the sky was lit up, the night illuminated in red and brilliant orange. Katja hurried down the steps and set Luiza on the lawn. The parched grass prickled her feet. It was nearly November, yet the lawn was still summer baked.

Luiza could make out a line of figures strung from the lake and disappearing into the trees. Crouching beside her, Katja explained, "They're passing buckets of water to put out the fire." Luiza spied Pani Marysia, comical in nightcap and gown, scurrying from the house with a tray piled high with the best dinner service. She wished Ida were here; her sister could mimic the cook's mountain accent perfectly, and her impression of tonight's startled waddle would be priceless.

Then Mama appeared, nearly as round as Pani Marysia, wearing her Chinese silk dressing gown. But there was nothing comical about the urgency with which Mama hurried from the terrace, a pile of embroidered tablecloths in her arms. Behind her, Anjela the maid wrestled with a rolled-up carpet.

"Mama!"

Her mother paused, before Janek's voice interrupted.

"Pani Zosia, is this the one?"

He was hidden by a large, gilt-framed painting of a deer, which he was struggling to keep upright. Mama flung the tablecloths in Katja's direction and hurried back as black smoke began to billow across the lawn, enveloping her and the terrace.

"The wind's changed. Move away from the house! Get to the other side of the lake!"

It was Pappa's voice, but Luiza could not see him through the surging cloud. It was making her cough so hard she could scarcely breathe. Katja threw one of the tablecloths over their heads and pulled Luiza down the slope to the jetty, where she dipped the cloth in the lake before tenting it over them again. But the air was clearer here, and Luiza pushed the sodden fabric away. Slowly, the house reappeared as the smoke thinned and drifted. Above the mill the sky still glowed, but it was no longer vivid with flames. Shadowy figures resolved, ghostlike in the pale light of dawn. Luiza, suddenly glad that Ida was not here, hugged the scene close; this adventure was hers alone.

The smell of burnt cotton hung over Zakątek for days. Then autumn finally arrived and wind and rain dissipated the stench, turning ash to sludge. Pappa often went to Warszawa. Even when home, he mainly stayed in his study, usually with men in dark suits whom Janek met off the Warszawa train. Sometimes they visited the mill and Luiza watched as umbrellas wavered and city shoes were saturated.

In the village, rain drummed on the wooden roofs, and yellowed leaves that had clung on through the extended summer were beaten to mulch. Luiza went with Mama on her welfare visits. Everyone wanted to know when the mill would reopen.

"God willing, it won't be long," was all Mama would say.

As well as the usual remedies for the sick, Mama had Janek load the trap with sacks of flour and kasha. And Pappa always sent tobacco for Pan Cholowa's untidy little cigarettes. Meanwhile, his wife gratefully accepted the other supplies and offered them bread and kefir, but Mama refused. On the way home, with the hood and apron of the trap raised against the rain and mud spatter, Luiza wanted to know why.

"I love Pani Cholowa's black bread."

"I know you do, but they don't have any to spare right now. Since the fire, your father's had to lay everyone off, so you can't go eating their bread, my love."

The only visitors were the men from Warszawa and Pani Anna, their neighbour and Mama's friend. She owned several hotels in Warszawa, and Pappa commented more than once that "Not many widows could take on their husband's business as she has." It always made Mama indignant. "So, you think I wouldn't be up to running the mill without you, God forbid?"

Kissing her hand, Pappa soothed, "Well, there's no engineering or manufacturing involved in the hotel business, my dear."

"There won't be any manufacturing, Hugo, if you don't get the mill back up and running soon."

Pappa sighed and returned to his study, where he greeted another dark-suited man from Warszawa.

Luiza, who was laboriously cross-stitching a daisy pattern that her mother had traced onto a square of linen, ventured, "Mama, I'll be able to take care of the manufacturing when I'm an engineer like Pappa."

But Mama clucked her tongue impatiently. "There are no women engineers, Lou-lou. If you want to be involved in the family business, perhaps you could train as a bookkeeper, like Pani Aurelia."

Luiza gaped at her mother. How could she suggest such a thing? But before she could object, Pani Anna arrived and was soon settled in a chair with a glass of tea.

"When do you expect the insurance money, then?" she enquired, her kind face creased with concern as she spooned jam into her tea. Mama sighed, stirring her own glass absently.

"Honestly, Anna, I have no idea. Hugo failed to update the insurance when he replaced some of the machinery last year, so now there's a dispute about the replacement value of the new pieces. Plus, they're questioning the cause of the fire, which appears to have started in the cotton store; they say it could have been a cigarette. Dear Pan Cholowa would never smoke in there, but the investigator has the poor man so terrorised that he can't think straight. If they can prove the fire was started through negligence, I'm not sure we'll get anything."

"Dear God, surely not!"

Luiza looked up; Pani Anna never raised her voice.

"What will you do if that happens?"

"Oh, we'll survive," said Mama calmly, the corners of her mouth turning up in an almost smile. "If the worse comes to the worst, we'll go back to Wilno. Hugo can always find a job there."

"But you can't leave! How would I bear it? You belong here. Hugo's done so well building the business. He can't just let it go. Is there anything I can do?"

Mama reached to pat Pani Anna's hand, which had a ring on every finger – more than one on some. Then she rang for more tea, and Pani Anna began an anecdote about someone famous who was staying at one of her hotels. Luiza quietly put down her cross-stitch and left the room.

In the attic, kneeling by the track, she assembled two Pullman coaches behind the red engine's tender and wound it up.

"All stations to Wilno. Boarding now, platform 4, all stations to Wilno."

She watched the train loop around the track. Would they really leave Zakątek? She could not imagine living anywhere else. In Wilno she could see Ida every day – but still.

A few days later, there was a break in the weather. Fluffy white clouds scudded across a blue sky. Wrapped against the chill, Luiza and Katja went on a visit. Pan Rubacz farmed the land around Zakątek, and his spaniel had a new litter. Luiza was bewitched and rushed to tell Mama about the puppies as soon as they got back. She found her at the piano, but she was not playing. She was watching Pappa, who was spilling out words as if he might run out of time before he could fit them all in.

"So, you see, they haven't been able to prove how it started. Everything was tinder-dry and a spark could have come from anywhere. Which means Cholowa's no longer under suspicion."

"Oh, he'll be so relieved." Mama smiled.

"Indeed. But the really good news is, while the insurers will only pay out to the value of the old machinery, the Korski board is happy to put up the rest, so I can replace the new machines and even upgrade some of the others. Thank heavens for Pani Aurelia and her meticulous bookkeeping – and that the fire didn't destroy the office. Korski was impressed by our recent turnover and could see that the profit margins are improving. They'll buy the mill and keep me on as director. It means things will continue pretty much as before, except we won't be taking all the risk, and I'll have more time for research."

Pappa took Mama's hand as Luiza squeezed herself between them.

"Pappa, does that mean we're staying at Zakątek? We don't have to move to Wilno?"

"Of course, we're staying at Zakątek."

With his free hand, Pappa raised one of Luiza's and danced her into a twirl under his arm.

"Now, I must get on; there's no time to lose. We need to be back in production in the new year."

He swung Luiza round one last time before leaving the room.

Chapter 5

Christmas 1927, Zakątek

Since the fire, Luiza was not allowed any closer to the mill than the silver birches. From here she watched as the charred timbers were removed and replaced. They were working fast to beat the snow. By the time it arrived, the roofs were in place and Pappa was confident that production would resume before spring.

"1928 will be a good year for Zakątek, I can feel it."

Everyone was smiling. It felt as if the household's proper rhythm had been restored now that Ida was home for Christmas. Luiza had so much to tell her.

"You should have seen Pani Marysia, Idka." Ida was brushing her hair while Luiza bounced on her bed.

"She was wearing her nightcap and walking so fast she was almost running with this huge tray of plates and things. Like this – look."

With her arms stretched in front and her bottom stuck out behind, Luiza scuttled about the room.

"Look, Idka, like this. Idka, look!"

Ida glanced but turned back to her reflection without missing a stroke. Deflated, Luiza joined her sister in front of the mirror. Ida's forehead was high and her nose straight, her golden-brown hair coiled over one shoulder. Luiza contrasted her own round face and dark bob. She scraped back her fringe – they had the same eyes, Mama's eyes. A murky blue-green – the colour of the Baltic in winter, Pappa said. His own were pale blue.

"I wish I had long hair like yours, Idka."

Luiza reached to stroke the glossy tail, but Ida batted away her hand with the brush. "You're too much of a tomboy for long hair."

Sucking her grazed fingers, Luiza tried again. "Idka, Pan Rubacz's spaniel's had puppies. They're so sweet. Shall we go and see them?"

"Why would I want to see a bunch of silly puppies weeing all over the place?"

Tears prickled and Luiza turned away.

"Alright," Ida relented. "We could go tomorrow, I suppose."

Maybe she had seen the tears, but now they were gone. "Oh, yes," breathed Luiza, "In the morning, though. Don't forget it's Christmas Eve."

"Mmm… Kamila might like to see them."

Tears threatened again. The puppies were her gift to Ida, but now the cherished visit would be spoiled. Their cousin was seven – midway between the sisters in age. She lived in Wilno, and it seemed that she and Ida had become great friends over the past three months, even though Kamila still played with dolls, for heaven's sake. It scorched Luiza's heart. She took a deep breath and made another bid for her sister's regard.

"Look, Idka, see what I can do."

Luiza turned a cartwheel.

"Did you see? I learnt all by myself. Did you see? Ida? Did you?"

"Yes, I saw." Ida's tone was grudging, but at least she had stopped brushing her hair. Encouraged, Luiza persisted.

"I'll do it again. Watch." But she had run out of space. Her feet rapped the shutter and she crumpled.

"Careful," said Ida, getting up. "Come on, Lou-lou, before you do any damage. I want to see if Pani Marysia's already made her poppyseed cake. It's the one thing that's better here than in Wilno."

Ida had travelled from Wilno with Kamila and her parents, Uncle Rafi and Aunt Wanda. Uncle Rafi was Mama's younger brother and a captain in the cavalry. In his tan uniform, spurs jangling against gleaming leather boots, Luiza thought he looked heroic. His blonde moustache was waxed, his fair hair clipped short, and his bright blue eyes twinkled with mischief. His surname, Svenson, was a reminder, according to Mama, of when Sweden invaded Lithuania in the seventeenth century. At that time, as now, Lithuania was part of Poland.

"Is it because you had a different mama from Uncle Rafi that you don't have fair hair and blue eyes, Mama?"

"No, we had the same mother, God rest her soul. So did Aunt Rysia. It was Aunt Ludmila who had a different Mama. Hers died, and then her father – our father – Pan

Svenson married again. He married our mama and first they had me, then Rafi, and then Rysia. So, all four of us were Svensons."

"But you're not Svenson anymore. Only Uncle Rafi is. Is it because he looks Swedish and you don't?"

"Dear Lord, no! It's because we three sisters all got married."

"But Uncle Rafi's married, too."

"He is. But women change their name when they marry and men don't. So, Aunt Wanda became Svenson and I became Wolfer. Do you see, Lou-lou?"

"Mm-hmm. Yes. But I don't think it's fair. I won't ever change my name. I'm Luiza Irena Wolfer – if I had a different name, then I'd be someone else."

Mama laughed and stroked Luiza's cheek. "Oh, Lou-lou, one day I'll remind you of this, when you've fallen in love and can't wait to leave home and take your husband's name."

"I won't ever leave home. The man I marry can come and live at Zakątek with us and he can be Pan Wolfer. But he'll have to be Pan Wolfer Second Class, because Pappa is Pan Wolfer First Class."

"You're spot on there, Lou-lou," chuckled Pappa, who had just entered the salon. Mama rose from her chair.

"I must see Pani Marysia – there'll be a lot of mouths to feed this Christmas. Won't it be wonderful to have Ida home? And I'm so glad darling Rafi will be here with Wanda and Kamila. And Stefan, too. Luiza, did you hear that? Your godfather's coming."

This was very good news. Uncle Stefan gave the best presents: Krysia, the doll whose eyes closed when you lay her down to sleep and who chirruped "Mama" when you lifted her upright again. (Luiza was fascinated by the mechanism that facilitated this, but that wasn't the same as playing with dolls.) Then there was the spinning top, with its snaking lines of blue and red and yellow melting into each other, and the interlocking bricks with which she had built a miniature Zakątek. And a box of paints in all colours.

Mama went on, "I hate to admit it, but I'm actually rather glad Aurelia's away while the mill's closed, or we'd have had to invite her, with Wanda being here. You'd never guess those two were sisters, would you?"

Pappa was sitting down with his newspaper. "Remember to lock away the best glasses. I'm not having your brother smash them again."

Mama kissed the top of his head, where the white hair was thinning. "Don't be such a grump, darling. It's a perfectly harmless tradition."

"Well, I'd rather he kept his traditions for the officers' mess. While he's in my house, drinking toasts from my crystal, I'd prefer him not to toss his glass at the wall. Poor Anjela was sweeping up for days."

"Oh, it wasn't that bad, darling. Don't be so hard on poor Rafi. You know how few soldiers get the Virtuti Militari – it's a great honour."

Pappa sighed.

"Come on, you were singing his praises after the Coup last year."

Straightening his paper, Pappa conceded, "Well, yes, we certainly needed the Marshal back."

Luiza knew that the Marshal was the man with a moustache as big and black as Pappa's. Pointing at his picture in the paper, Pappa had called him the saviour of Poland.

"Well then, are a few broken glasses such a high price to pay?" Mama placed a hand on Pappa's shoulder while he continued to frown. "Do cheer up, my love. Remember, Rafi's bringing Ida home. She'll be here tomorrow."

"Yes, yes, it's good of them to bring her. But broken glass is one thing. If he ever tries to shoot out the candles again, that's the last time he visits, do you hear? Firing a weapon in our home! What was he thinking?"

Luiza stared. "Did Uncle Rafi shoot somebody?"

Mama shook her head at Pappa. "See what you've done? Forget snakes, she'll be having nightmares about pistols."

Pappa grunted and Mama turned to Luiza. "Uncle Rafi didn't shoot anyone, Lou-lou. He just wanted to show us a special way of snuffing out the candles after dinner. It was a very long time ago, and it's all forgotten now, isn't it?" Mama glared at Pappa. "Rafi was young and high-spirited then. Now he's in a position of responsibility and acts accordingly. Why on earth did you have to bring it up, Hugo?"

Pappa sighed again, reaching for the hand that Mama had removed from his shoulder. "You're right, my love, of course. Your brother's a pillar of society and we'll have a wonderful Christmas together. But do make sure Anjela doesn't put out the best glasses."

Mama made to cuff his head, but Pappa caught her hand and kissed it. She was shaking her finger at him as she left for the kitchen.

On Christmas Eve, while the girls visited the puppies, Janek felled a fir tree and hauled it home on the sled. By the time they returned, it was in position in the dining room, the top lopped off so that the gold star would clear the ceiling. In the excitement, Luiza forgot to feel cross with Kamila. In any case, her cousin had been more excited about the puppies than Ida was. And when it came to the tree, without Kamila's help on the lower branches, Ida's promotion to the higher boughs would have left Luiza forlorn. It was the first year Ida was allowed to climb the ladder, and she made so much of her advancement that it nudged the younger girls closer. But once the tree was dressed, all three united in mutual admiration of their work.

It only remained, when evening fell, for Mama to light the candles. The girls waited out the interval impatiently, monitoring the sky through the salon windows. Would it never get dark? A pink glow persisted in the west, but at last Luiza whooped, "I see it!" Rubbing her breath from the glass with her sleeve, she pointed out a pinprick of silver: the first star of Christmas. The celebration could begin.

They raced along the hall, calling out the news as they ran. Impatiently they waited outside the dining room. When all were assembled, Mama opened the door. The tree radiated enchantment, a shimmering crop of candles reflected and multiplied amid the gleaming baubles.

"Beautiful," breathed Aunt Wanda.

"The magic of Christmas," murmured Uncle Stefan.

"Enough!" barked Uncle Rafi. "A man might starve amid all this wonder. Let's get to it." Standing to attention with a click of his heels, he ushered them through the door.

Mama approached the table to light the scarlet candles in their festive sconces. Once lit, more pinecones and flaming candles were revealed, these delicately embroidered by Aunt Ludmila. Her special tablecloth was spread only on this one night of the year.

When all were seated, Anjela brought in the first of the twelve Wigilia courses – one for each apostle. First came mushroom soup with *pierogi*, then jellied carp.

"Lou-lou, why aren't you eating?" queried Pappa.

"I keep thinking of Boris," replied Luiza.

"Who on earth is Boris?" asked Uncle Rafi.

"The carp, of course," said Ida and Kamila in unison.

"The carp!" exclaimed Uncle Rafi, "What the blazes?"

"I visited him every day," mused Luiza, "He seemed lonely."

Until yesterday, the large black fish with its ugly, whiskered face had been submerged in a zinc bath in Pani Marysia's scullery.

"For pity's sake!" exclaimed Uncle Rafi, "Lou-lou, you cannot go forming attachments with our festive fare."

The grown-ups all laughed, but Luiza continued to push her fork glumly around her plate. She was seated with her back to the tree and the mountain of presents piled around it. As each course was removed and replaced, her concern for Boris diminished and the glances over her shoulder increased. At last, the meal was done and it was time.

Ida and Kamila saw to the distribution, as Luiza could not yet read the labels. She was soon surrounded by a fine collection of toys and games, but then Pappa told her to shut her eyes. She heard the door open and a moment later felt something warm and furry deposited in her lap. One of Pan Rubacz's black-and-white puppies!

"Oh – is it really mine?"

Pappa was smiling. "She certainly is. What will you call her?"

"How about Boris?" quipped Uncle Rafi.

"I have an idea, Lou-lou," said Uncle Stefan. "She's such a contrast to all those colourful pictures you paint, she puts me in mind of a black-and-white photograph, as if she's in monochrome. So how about Mono?"

Chapter 6

Spring 1928, Zakątek

*W*hen Ida left this time, Luiza did not miss her nearly as much. Mono filled the gap. When she was not embroidering or learning piano with Mama, or numbers and letters with Katja, she played with the puppy, weather allowing, outside. From the silver birches, they watched as shiny machines were installed in the new sheds. After Easter, when the last of the snow was finally melting in the April sunshine, the lorry set off on its first delivery.

Romping home via the tennis court, the pair jumped the lowered net until Luiza's stomach growled dinnertime. She headed across the lawn with the spaniel stalking her. Alerted by a sudden clatter from the house, she saw Anjela burst from the salon and sprint towards the mill. Luiza started to run, Mono looping around her in excitement. From the terrace, through the open French windows, she spied her mother seated in her usual chair. But nothing else was as usual. On the floor, in a tangle of silks, lay her embroidery hoop, and Mama was tilted over the chair arm, with Pani Marysia trying to push her upright. Her face looked all wrong: one side drooped, as if weighted down. Then Katja appeared, blocking Luiza's view and steering her away, leaving Mono yapping disconsolately in their wake.

Over the days that followed, Katja read her stories, played counting games and set her letters to copy. She even proposed games with Mono. But Luiza could not stop thinking about the perplexing commotion in the salon and wondering when she would see Mama again. Katja's reassurance that it would be very soon grew less credible the longer the door to her parents' bedroom remained firmly closed. Pappa was no help; when not behind the bedroom door, he was in his study. If he appeared for a meal, he seemed so far away in his thoughts that Luiza could never think of a question that would travel the distance between them. Neither of them ate much, although Pappa regularly refilled his glass.

If Pappa was elusive, Pani Aurelia was unavoidable. She never used to come into the house – when not in the mill office she always used to stay in the annexe beyond the stable. But since Mama had disappeared, her black-clad figure materialised everywhere. If she was not firing instructions at a cross-looking Pani Marysia, she was skulking near Pappa's study with a bundle of papers. And whenever she saw Luiza, she reached out her yellowed fingers to stroke her hair. "Poor child, such a terrible tragedy," she muttered, while Luiza pressed herself into the wall, holding her breath until the Witch had gone.

After the mill and the attic, Luiza had always loved the kitchen. But the warm, bustling welcome had gone, with Pani Marysia intoning a constant litany of "Blessed Mary, in your mercy, heal Pani Zosia," while Anjela sobbed into her apron. They still sat her down with a slice of cake, but Luiza's appetite had disappeared along with the cheery sanctuary of the kitchen.

If she escaped Katja's attention, Luiza would wait in the hall for the tall, solemn doctor who attended Mama each morning. Opening the front door the minute she heard his pony's fast trot, she jigged impatiently from one foot to the other while he made his lugubrious descent from the trap. Although he nodded at her, he never spoke a word, even when she asked him directly when Mama would be better.

But this morning a horse with a much slower gait approached. It was a swaybacked bay that pulled up, the *drozhka* driver stepping down to help a slight figure in a grey coat and matching cloche hat from her seat. Luiza hung back, but Mono bounded down the steps. When the lady bent to pat her, the spaniel rolled over for a tummy tickle. The lady smiled at Luiza. "I had to leave my Ferdi at home. The journey from Riga's too long for an elderly dachshund."

Luiza stepped forward; Mama had told her about a dachshund in Riga. She scooped up her dog and peered at the lady uncertainly.

"You don't remember me, do you, Lou-lou? You were

still very young the last time I saw you. Not as young as the first time, though."

"I think I know who you are. Are you Aunt Ludmila?"

"Yes, dear, I am. You know I was there when you were born?"

Luiza nodded.

"Shall we go inside?" suggested her aunt.

But Katja swooped as soon as they were in the hall, and Luiza did not see Aunt Ludmila again until much later.

It was in the kitchen, where everything seemed reassuringly normal. Pani Marysia and Anjela were dry-eyed as they went about dinner preparation and discussed menus with Aunt Ludmila. And when Pani Marysia cut her a slice of *sernik*, Luiza found that she was hungry.

"I'll take my sister's meal to her," Aunt Ludmila was saying. "Can you prepare her plate half an hour before dinnertime?"

Pani Marysia, who was sprinkling dill on the potatoes, nodded. Turning to Luiza, Aunt Ludmila said, "Come, dear, it's time you saw your mother. I had no idea that you hadn't seen her since..."

Luiza, who had licked her finger to convey the last of the cheesecake from the plate to her mouth, paused, alert for the word that might explain the catastrophe that had befallen Mama. But Aunt Ludmila simply held out her hand. Luiza hesitated, remembering how unlike Mama she had looked that day in the salon. Now that the long-awaited opportunity presented itself, she was not at all sure she really did want to see her. But the hand Aunt Ludmila extended was so like Mama's that eventually, having wiped her finger on her pinafore, she took it.

Mama was propped up on pillows in her big bed, her face angled away from the door, and Luiza was reassured by what she could see. Her mother's dark hair with its sprinkling of silver threads was hooked behind her ear, and her familiar smile lifted this side of her mouth. When Mama reached for her, Luiza let go Aunt Ludmila's hand and took her mother's. Then Mama spoke.

"You-you," she said. And again, with effort, "You-you."

Luiza pulled back. A tear rolled slowly down Mama's cheek. Wiping it away, Aunt Ludmila took the hand that Luiza had dropped and spoke gently. "Zosia, don't fret, it's still early days." Turning to Luiza she continued, "And you, child, you mustn't be upset. Mama is ill, but she will get better. Slowly, but she will."

A week or so later, Janek swung the lorry up the drive to offload Mama's special chair. It had two large wheels in front and a smaller pair at the rear. By the time Ida came home for the summer, Aunt Ludmila had returned to Riga, and Anjela was wheeling Mama into the salon each morning, making sure to position the chair so that Mama's right side was in shadow before she applied the brake.

It was a lot easier, now, to understand Mama when she spoke, but her hands still could not ply a needle, nor play the piano. Yet the left one was never still, and its perpetual sequence fascinated Luiza. First, Mama touched the wedding ring on her passive right hand, then stroked the right side of her face. From there she moved on to pat her hair and smooth her skirt, finishing with a tap on the arm of the wheeled chair. Returning to her wedding ring, she began the whole uneasy cycle again.

It came as a surprise to Luiza that she missed Mama's visitors; if only she could see her dance in with her coffee tray again, she would never escape to the attic. But it was just as surprising that Ida, who had so coveted the lively salon, appeared not to mind its absence. She chatted cheerfully as she sewed, and Luiza noticed that Mama's left hand forgot its anxious routine. Instead, it stroked Ida's hair and directed her embroidery. Ida even made Mama giggle and seemed entirely untroubled by her disconnected face. Luiza still tried to stay on Mama's left side.

It was Ida who finally supplied the word for the calamity that had befallen them. "For goodness' sake, Lou-lou, Mama's had a stroke, that's all. She's still Mama."

And Pappa was still Pappa, only he was never there.

Luiza could smell freshly baked bread and the thought of it spread thick with golden butter and bronze honey drew her to the kitchen. She liked to dip her tongue in the honey puddles when no one was looking and lick the plate clean. She found renewed comfort in the busy kitchen, where Pani Marysia was always pleased to see her. In the salon, Luiza pictured her mother at the piano or her embroidery, but in the kitchen she remembered her brewing her special coffee, or mixing the yeast buns that were her secret recipe. With sticky fingers she reached down Mama's tasting spoon from its hook above the stove and pretended to dip it into the bubbling pot of ruby *barszcz*.

"Pani Marysia, I'm not sure the seasoning's quite right – a touch more salt, perhaps?"

Pani Marysia smiled and slid another slice of bread and honey onto Luiza's plate, just as Pani Aurelia's spectre appeared in the doorway. Luiza shrank into her chair as the thin woman advanced, discoloured fingers outstretched.

"Poor, poor child, how you need a mother's love."

Pani Marysia planted herself solidly between Luiza and the woman in black.

"Is there something you want, Pani Aurelia? Something to eat, perhaps?"

Pani Aurelia's small eyes widened; she glanced at Luiza's smeared plate with revulsion.

"No, no, nothing. At least, unless…"

She regarded the plate again, sucking in her narrow lips.

"Perhaps some bread and honey for Pani Zosia. Something sweet would give her solace."

Pani Marysia folded her arms.

"I have my instructions – Pani Ludmila was most clear – no sugar or fat for Pani Zosia."

"Oh, surely one slice would do no harm. You know what a sweet tooth the dear lady has, and she has so little pleasure these days."

Pani Aurelia's voice was less harsh than usual. Luiza wondered why she cared about Mama now, when she had never been her friend before. Even when Mama used to invite her, when she first came to work at the mill, Pani Aurelia never came to the salon.

"I have my orders," repeated Pani Marysia, immovable.

Pani Aurelia narrowed her eyes but said nothing as she turned to leave. Even the sharp tang of *barszcz* could not quite suppress the waft of stale tobacco that trailed in her wake.

Two years had now passed since the fire, eighteen months since Mama's stroke. Ida was back at school for the autumn term, and Luiza, at seven, was allowed to push the wheelchair. It was fun to propel it along the terrace in the sunshine. Mama laughed when Mono raced them, until they were near the steps and then she shouted at Luiza to stop.

Luiza found it hard to remember Mama walking. Or her face with both sides matching, though the weight that dragged at her mouth and right eye was not as heavy as it had been. Her right hand was still weak, but really, Mama was hardly lopsided at all anymore. Yet she still refused to receive guests. Except Pani Anna.

Pappa was rarely home because of something that was crashing in America. Most days he went to Warszawa and arrived home long after Luiza was in bed. At mealtimes, it was Luiza's job to cut up Mama's food, though she ate very little.

In accordance with Aunt Ludmila's instructions, desserts were no longer served, so Luiza went to the kitchen in search of something sweet after dinner. Pani Marysia was shaking her head at their plates.

"Blessed mother and all the saints, she barely touched it."

"Mama says potatoes don't taste the same without

butter. And she asked what was the point of mushrooms without cream? She's right. They aren't nearly as nice."

"But I'm only following the doctor's orders. Oh dear, if she doesn't eat, she'll waste away."

But that was the odd thing; Mama was not getting thinner, and Luiza had a troublesome inkling as to why. Last week, she had run into the salon to show off a new trick of Mono's and found Mama holding a box from Café Blikle – it was Pappa's favourite place for rum babas, which is why Luiza recognised it. Mama had tried to hide it beneath the rug on her knees, but it slid to the floor and Mono pounced.

"Leave it!"

Reluctantly, the dog backed off and Luiza retrieved the carton. Inside were three chocolate eclairs. As she returned the box to her mother, their eyes met and Luiza thought of when she had found Mono on the dining room table, wolfing down the cold meats that Anjela had set out for supper. Mama's eyes held the same, silent appeal.

But where had she got the cakes? She could not have bought them herself. Someone must have given them to her, yet everyone knew she should not have them. Who could have broken such an important rule? The entreaty in Mama's eyes made it impossible to ask. Luiza wished Ida were here, but Christmas was still a month away. And even when Ida did come home, Luiza found it impossible to divulge her concern; Mama's pitiful supplication was somehow too shocking to reveal.

The festival passed as quietly as the previous year. With Mama in her wheelchair, it was now Pappa who lit the candles on the tree. He was still very busy with the thing that had crashed in America and was apparently crashing in Poland, too, but he made them all laugh at Wigilia when he pretended to be Luiza's friend the carp (this year it was Bogdan).

By March the snow had gone, washed away by rain that fell steadily from a leaden sky. The mood in the salon, however, was lighter. Pani Anna was visiting.

"You know, Anna, sometimes I wish I'd married a cobbler. If I wanted to talk to him, I'd only have to open the door to the shop and there he'd be, hammering away."

Mama's friend laughed. "The only time that door would open would be when your cobbler wanted feeding. And there you'd be, stirring the cabbage soup with one hand and nursing an infant with the other, with four more hanging off your apron."

Mama frowned. "But at least he wouldn't be away all the time. I hardly see Hugo."

"Oh, Zosia, you know how hard it is to keep a business going these days. Goodness knows, we're having to create all sorts of offers to get bookings. Hugo must be struggling to keep his buyers, and the Board won't find new markets for him, for all their talk of 'freeing him up to concentrate on research'. They just don't have the same personal investment in the mill. He knows it's up to him."

Pani Anna paused, fiddling with her rings.

"But, you know, dearest, perhaps if you were—"

"If I were what?" Mama interrupted sharply, touching the right side of her face and fixing her eyes on Pani Anna.

"No, no, I didn't mean…" Pani Anna leant forward to pat Mama's knee. "I only meant that you should be less self-conscious. You're so much better, Zosia, you really don't need to hide away. See friends; open your house again. You'll soon find Hugo spending time at home if he gets a glimpse of the woman he married."

Mama looked away, then gave a sudden laugh. "Here's something that might remind him. Watch."

With her left hand she removed a cigarette from the packet on the table at her side and put it in her mouth. Then she wedged the matchbox in her right hand and struck a match against it. It took a few attempts for a spark to catch, but when it did, she raised the match to the cigarette and inhaled deeply. Shaking out the flame, she removed the cigarette and exhaled triumphantly, at which Pani Anna and Luiza both applauded.

"Impressive, my new party trick, isn't it? At least now I can do one thing without calling for help. Who knows, perhaps it's the first step?"

Pani Anna beamed. "Yes, and more steps will follow."

"Yet the tragedy is, the doctor says there's no real hope of improvement."

Pani Aurelia was standing in the doorway, shaking her head in morbid sympathy. It seemed to Luiza that the air had been sucked out of the room. The cigarette fell from Mama's fingers. Pani Anna quickly rose and propelled Pani Aurelia from the room. The door banged behind them and Luiza could hear Pani Anna's raised voice.

Rescuing the cigarette, she tried to replace it in Mama's hand, but her fist was clenched and tears ran down her cheeks. Luiza dabbed them with her handkerchief, but Mama shook her head.

"I need to rest, Lou-lou. Go and play now."

Luiza walked slowly down the steps from the terrace. The lawn was sodden but the sun had come out. Mono bounced and yapped, begging to play, but Luiza ignored her. At the lake she tossed a pebble and watched the water dimple, ripples spreading out over its silken surface. Again, she wished that Ida were here. Perhaps she should tell Pani Anna about the cream cakes? But she remembered Mama's pleading eyes and knew she would not.

A sudden shower pricked the lake and Luiza ran for the summerhouse, Mono barking ecstatically, thinking they were playing, at last.

Chapter 7

Easter 1931, Zakątek

*I*t was the third Easter since Mama's stroke, and the first to resemble the festival they used to celebrate. On Easter Saturday, Luiza's godfather arrived, bearing an enormous Wedel chocolate egg, a new box of paints and a suggestion that there might be an additional surprise in her room. There, on her bed, she found corduroy breeches; at its foot, a pair of glossy riding boots stood to attention. She stomped around in them until bedtime.

As Lutherans, the Wolfers' nearest place of worship was in Warszawa, but they sometimes attended the small church in Zapole; Pappa maintained that Catholics and Lutherans worshipped the same God. Besides, praying with his workforce strengthened his bond with them. Since Mama's illness, though, they had scarcely been to the village. When Uncle Stefan suggested Easter Mass,

Pappa declined, but Luiza and Ida set off with him early on Sunday in the milky, morning light.

The lane to the village was a tessellated tunnel of foaming blackthorn and gossamer catkins, its banks jewelled with primroses. But inside the wooden church, only the priest's white-and-gold vestments glowed. Even the women's colourful scarves were muted by the gloom. But not their voices; the congregation sang the hymns of resurrection at full volume.

Afterwards there was a cheerful exchange of Easter greetings outside the church, before the three of them walked home. They were in high spirits, hungry for breakfast and 'open house', which Mama had unexpectedly revived this year (though she insisted that she herself would remain in the salon and receive only close friends).

In the dining room, Pani Marysia and Anjela had spread a splendid buffet. The cook had outdone herself with the centrepiece: a huge chocolate and vanilla *babka*, moulded in the shape of a lamb with an Easter pennant declaring Alleluja! wedged in its crooked foreleg. It held pride of place amid the many dishes, which would be replenished throughout today and tomorrow, to feed the friends and neighbours calling in to celebrate the risen Christ.

Guests helped themselves from platters of smoked meats and herrings in cream, sweet and sour salads. There were soft, white, plaited loaves and dense, dark, rye and, as well as the special *babka*, *mazurek* tarts filled with fruit or chocolate or poppy seeds.

Before piling their plate high, however, each visitor

had to select, from a basket holding a careful assembly of coloured hard-boiled eggs, ammunition for the time-honoured Easter battle. Having chosen one, the challenge was to smash that of an opponent, while keeping the decorated shell of their own intact.

Luiza took egg selection seriously. After careful consideration, she chose a vividly stained red one, girdled in yellow. Gripping the rounder end, she confronted her father first and brought the tip down on the blue peak peeping from Pappa's plump fist. A crack immediately zagged across the shiny cobalt, and Luiza went on to vanquish Mama's yellow egg, then Ida's purple, before Uncle Stefan's (green with a swirl of orange tracery) finally shattered hers. Her godfather bequeathed her his champion. Wrapping it in a napkin, she stowed the egg carefully in her pocket.

At the buffet, Luiza was placing slices of kiełbasa on her plate when Pani Anna arrived with her son and his wife. Luiza told Waldemar about her new breeches and boots, which meant that she could start the riding lessons he had promised her. Then she guided him to the egg basket.

Uncle Stefan's winner quickly despatched Waldemar's egg, then that of his wife, Grażyna, and Pani Anna's, too. Luiza set off to update her godfather on his egg's triumphs.

He was not on the terrace, nor in the salon, where Pani Abel, the wife of Pappa's accountant, was chatting with Mama. Along the corridor, the door to Pappa's study stood ajar. Luiza could hear her godfather's voice, but something in his tone made her pause before rushing in.

"Oh, come on, Hugo – they're parasites. They hang around because you pick up the bill. Why on earth are you wasting time with them instead of coming home to your wife?"

"For God's sake, can't a man have a drink with a few friends after a hard day's work?"

"But they aren't friends, are they? They'll stay for as long as you're buying, but do you think they'll be there when the factory folds? You're drinking too much, old fellow, and it's affecting your judgement. Times are hard and you need your wits about you, not left behind in some Warszawa bar."

"Do you think I don't know how tough things are? Good God, Stefan, I've had to lay men off. How do you think it feels to see families suffer because I can't afford to keep them employed."

Pappa's voice had dropped, but Uncle Stefan's was raised in exasperation.

"They're not stupid. They know how difficult things are, but they also know you can't be at your best if you're drunk! Come on, Hugo, pull yourself together. You owe it to them, but most of all you owe it to Zosia. She needs you."

Pappa's reply was so low that Luiza could barely make it out.

"She doesn't need me, Stefan. She won't let me near her."

In the silence that followed, Luiza realised that she was holding her breath. Exhaling shakily, she remembered the loud crash that had shocked her awake a few nights ago. She had found Pappa slumped against the hall table and the silver tray that should have been on top was on the floor. Then Janek appeared and helped Pappa, whose legs did not seem to be working properly, along the corridor.

When Uncle Stefan spoke again his voice was gentle.

"It breaks my heart to see my two dearest friends in such pain, Hugo. Can't you see, Zosia's too proud to show how desperately she needs you – she doesn't want to seem weak in your eyes, when she's always been your support. She's terrified of losing your love, but she'd rather that than your pity. And you're so scared of letting her down that you stay away so you won't have the chance."

Luiza trailed back through the salon. Ida was on the piano stool, giggling with Jurek, the son of their farmer neighbour, Pan Rubacz. How could she laugh? Didn't she know that everything was falling apart?

Luiza made her way to the jetty and sat, swinging her legs over the water. Retrieving the champion egg from her pocket, she noticed a thin crack had snaked its way across the glossy green and orange shell. She flung it down and the egg rolled lopsidedly across the wooden boards, the pretty pattern now completely crazed. If only Mono were here, to nuzzle under her arm and lick away her tears. But, for the sake of the buffet, the dog was shut in the stable.

It was the thought of Pani Marysia's spectacular *babka* that eventually got her back on her feet. Wiping her sleeve across her face, Luiza set off for the dining room. But as she passed the salon, she stopped in her tracks. There was Pappa, his hand on Mama's shoulder, and there was Uncle Stefan, too, and Pani Anna with her family. And all of them were laughing. Even Mama.

Forgetting the *babka*, Luiza tucked herself in beside Pappa. He tousled her hair, but his other hand never left Mama's shoulder. Without Pappa's restraining hand on her head, Luiza thought she might just float away on a bubble of joy.

From then on, although Pappa still went away, when he was home, he and Mama chatted and laughed together, and it was Pappa who cut up her food. Pani Marysia exclaimed over the clean plates, and Luiza even forgot to worry about the eclairs.

Chapter 8

Summer 1931, Zakątek

*I*n September, Luiza would be going to school. But in the meantime, Pappa had a new intern at the mill. Piotr was tall and dark, with a brooding smile and a wispy moustache, and he was coming for tea. Luiza fizzed with excitement at the prospect of the sugar bowl trick. It was ages since one of Pappa's students had come to the house, and she could not wait to revive the prank of filling the sugar bowl with salt. Yet here was Ida saying no.

Nonplussed, Luiza persisted, "But why not, Idka? It's such fun, you know it is. I bet Piotr forces it down politely. I can't see him spitting tea all over the tablecloth, like the last one, can you?"

Ida swivelled her gaze from her reflection in the silver samovar to regard Luiza with disdain. "Why must you be so childish, Lou-lou?"

Later, spooning sugar from the unadulterated bowl into Piotr's tea, Ida was apparently enraptured by the intern's detailed description of a newly patented drying machine. Luiza, sneaking a macaroon to Mono under the table, caught her father winking at Mama, who stifled a giggle.

Luiza and Mono spent much of that hot summer in the lake. Ida's friend was staying and, while she and Stasia soaked up the sun on the jetty, Luiza floated nearby, listening to their tales of school. In less than a month she, too, would be a day girl at the convent in Wilno, lodging at Pani Jankowska's. The old lady was Aunt Wanda's mother and, consequently, Pani Aurelia's, but Ida assured her that it was absent-minded Aunt Wanda who took after their landlady and not her waspish sister.

Mono scrambled out of the lake and shook herself, spraying the basking girls. Stasia and Ida screamed, huddling against the wet spaniel's attempts at burrowing between them. Luiza pulled herself up onto the jetty, in no hurry to call Mono off. But suddenly she found herself describing an arc through the air and, with a splash, she was back in the lake. Surfacing, gasping, she spun round to find Uncle Rafi bobbing beside her, grinning brightly beneath his water-stained moustache. Three splashes followed in quick succession, and Uncle Rafi disappeared beneath the girls' united efforts, before coming up a few metres away, Mono paddling frantic circles around him.

Hauling themselves out of the water they collapsed, breathless, on the sun-bleached boards. Mono scurried from one to the other, intent on licking them dry.

"I didn't know you were coming, Uncle Rafi," said Ida, "Are Kamila and Aunt Wanda here, too?"

Their uncle tugged an ear, angling his head to displace the water.

"It's only me this time. I was on a mission close by, so I thought I'd pay my favourite nieces a visit before going home."

His recent promotion meant that Uncle Rafi had moved from Wilno to Warszawa. As he hoicked up a shoulder strap, Luiza noticed how slack the water-logged fabric was and recognised Pappa's rarely worn bathing suit.

"Mama must be pleased to see you." Ida smiled, bunching and twisting her hair to wring it out.

Uncle Rafi glanced towards the house. "Indeed, and now that I've cooled off, I'd better get back."

He set off at a run with Mono at his heels and Pappa's sagging costume flapping about his legs.

Uncle Rafi stayed for dinner and Mama sparkled. She was always more vivid when her younger brother was around.

"Rafi, no – it wasn't a bit like that, and you know it!"

"Wasn't it? From what I've heard, you had to agree to marry Hugo, or he'd have burst, he was buying so many rum babas as an excuse to see you."

Uncle Rafi winked at Stasia, who blushed.

"Perhaps it *was* the sweetness of more than just the cakes that made me such a regular customer at Cukiernia Svenson." Pappa smiled.

"Cukiernia Svenson?" Stasia exclaimed. "But we always buy our cakes there. I didn't know it belonged to your family, Ida."

"Not anymore, dear," said Mama, "It was sold after our father died, but they kept the name."

Helping himself to another *gołąbki*, Uncle Rafi queried, "Hugo, you do know that your appreciation of our father's skills as a patissier alone would never have won you my sister's hand?"

But before her father could answer, Luiza said, "It was because of the trains, wasn't it, Pappa?"

Nodding, Pappa addressed Stasia, "My father-in-law wasn't at all keen on his daughter marrying a foreigner, so it was only when he discovered that the foreigner in question shared a particular enthusiasm of his that his only son disparaged, that I had any chance at all."

Uncle Rafi nodded conspiratorially at Stasia. "I'm sure you'll appreciate, dear girl, that there are better ways to spend a Sunday afternoon than gawping at trains. The truth is that my brother-in-law the businessman is, at heart, an engine driver."

Stasia smiled uncertainly.

"And because my father would also have preferred the footplate to the pastry board, the two of them bonded at Wilno station, their mutual love of steam engines overcoming my father's initial distaste for having a German in the family."

Stasia looked sharply at Pappa.

"Oh, he's Polish now," reassured Uncle Rafi, "has been for ages. Though with some questionable political views." Having dabbed his moustache with a napkin, he carefully rolled its ends between his fingers.

"I have every right to object to military solutions

being imposed on a democracy," Pappa began, but Mama interrupted, "Poor Stasia doesn't want to hear you two debating politics. Tell her the Three Miracles, instead.'"

Ida sighed theatrically and raised her eyes to the ceiling. "Here we go – cue: The Heroic Escape from Bolshevism."

"You may mock," countered Mama, her tone sharper than usual, "but you might never have known your poor father if he hadn't made that heroic escape."

Pappa smiled at Ida and her friend and placed his hand on Mama's. "Ida's quite right, my dear. This is a story that's been told too many times and can be of absolutely no interest to anyone outside the family."

"On the contrary," said Uncle Rafi as he undid another of the buttons that travelled at an angle from the shoulder of his uniform jacket to its waist. Sliding a hand beneath the tan material, he stroked his chest thoughtfully and glanced pointedly at Pappa's paunch. "I think it's important to remember that this comfortable tycoon was once capable of heroic endeavour."

Stasia, seemingly mesmerised, nodded in agreement while Ida, tugging at her friend's sleeve, asserted, "All you need to know, Stasia, is that my father escaped the firing squad by stealing a train. And when he arrived home, even his own wife didn't recognise him, because his hair had turned white, and he didn't know the baby in her arms – me – was his daughter. There, that's the story."

With finality, Ida placed her folded napkin on the table.

"Well, perhaps the abridged version." Uncle Rafi chuckled.

"May we leave the table?" asked Ida, looking at Mama. But Luiza interrupted. "You've left out the ship, Idka, and the vodka and the thin commissioner with the big moustache and the snow and the horse and cart…"

She paused for breath, and Ida stared meaningfully at her friend. "Stasia and I are going for a walk."

Stasia tore her eyes from Uncle Rafi to protest, "But I'd really like to hear the rest of the story, Ida – your family's so interesting."

"It wouldn't be a walk to the mill office you're planning, would it, Idka?" queried Pappa. "I'm afraid Piotr has some urgent calculations to complete regarding the dryer capacity, so I'd prefer that you took your stroll in another direction."

Ida, her cheeks glowing, conceded with ill grace. "Oh, alright then, let's hear the famous story for the hundredth time as it's SO fascinating." She took up her napkin again and let her eyes follow her fingers as they traced the embroidered flowers, while Stasia's remained fixed on Uncle Rafi.

"Of course, I wasn't there, so I'm only telling the story from hearsay. But I'm sure we can rely on our hero to correct me if I get anything wrong."

Pappa, sighing deeply, pushed away his plate. From an inside pocket he drew a fat cigar and his special scissors and set about preparing the Cuban while Uncle Rafi continued, "In November 1917, the Bolsheviks seized power while my esteemed brother-in-law was conducting research at Petrograd Polytechnical University. He was arrested and deported to Siberia."

And so began the Three Miracles, the epic tale of Pappa's escape, which Luiza never tired of hearing.

Chapter 9

February 1918, Petrograd

The night before his execution, Hugo lay alone in the cell, his teeth chattering and sweat soaking his thin blanket. He tried to conjure his wife, but a line of men, their rifles trained on him, intruded. He mourned the dreams he would never accomplish, the children he and Zosia would never have.

Yet he had so very nearly escaped. It was barely two months since he had lain in another dank prison, anticipating this same fate. That cell he had shared with a fellow German, also charged as a bourgeois foreigner, and a Russian accused of counter-revolutionary activities. Their days were punctuated by rifle volleys – the firing squads were busy. Yet a miracle had saved him – a second miracle, in fact, because the first had occurred even earlier, after he was arrested at the Polytechnical University.

Put on a ship bound for Siberia, he had persuaded

the crew to allow him access to their potato store. And the vodka he produced ensured they did not leave him in Vladivostok with the other internees, but kept him on board for the return voyage. This was miracle number one, even if it did deliver him to that cell shared with his compatriot, Pauli, and the Russian, Alexei.

The second miracle occurred on the day Hugo was taken from their cell to appear before a selection committee. The commissar in charge was a thin man in a dirty, ill-fitting tunic. A yellowing moustache hung so far over his lower jaw that his mouth moved invisibly when he barked, "Well, Comrade Wolfer, are you in truth our comrade?" Pausing, he tugged thoughtfully at his moustache, from which his grimy fingers teased out a scrap of food. "We are here to determine whether you are a productive citizen or merely another bourgeois parasite."

Hugo swallowed hard, brushing greasy hair from his eyes with fingers as begrimed as the commissar's. He was doing his best to stand tall in his filthy clothes, but he felt faint, whether from hunger or fear he found it hard to determine. He prayed that the commissar could not hear his racing heart, which drummed so loudly that Hugo could scarcely make out the other man's words.

"So, Hugo Wolfer, we must decide whether you live or die. Show me your hands!"

Startled by the peremptory command, Hugo stared at the commissar in bewilderment before slowly extending his arms.

"Closer!"

Shakily, Hugo stepped forward and reached across

the open ledger on the desk. The commissar turned his hands palm up to reveal oil-stained calluses. He glanced enquiringly at his colleagues, who each gave a curt nod. Releasing Hugo, he dipped his pen in the inkwell and began to scratch laboriously across the page. Hugo clasped his hands together to contain their trembling.

At last, the commissar laid down his pen and fixed him with a final look of assessment. Hugo found it impossible to gauge how his judge inclined. The immense moustache hid any clue the man's mouth might provide, and his words, when he finally spoke, seemed to reach Hugo from a considerable distance.

"Well, it seems that you are, after all, a Comrade. You may go."

Hugo could not remember leaving the room, but somehow, he found himself outside the prison gates. Leaning against a wall he waited for his legs to find the strength to carry him away.

He was still reeling from this second miracle when he was again arrested. A fellow student at the Polytechnical University, a Russian whose poor research paper had been shown up by Hugo's, denounced him as a plutocrat. Those 'worker's hands' were the result of labour on the prison ship, he claimed.

So, now the day of his execution dawned, and Hugo despaired of a third miracle. The guards fell silent as he emerged from his cell, which he interpreted as the courtesy due a man's final moments on earth. Once his hands were secured behind his back, their conversation resumed, but Hugo paid no attention, concentrating instead on controlling the knot of panic unravelling in the pit of his stomach. With all his strength he sought to suppress the desperate pleas for mercy that rose within him.

"Dear God, let me not lose my dignity – grant me that, at least."

Once outside, Hugo joined a queue shuffling towards the wall at the far end of the prison yard. To avoid dwelling on the splashes of scarlet in the churned snow, he focused on the man in front. He seemed familiar.

"Alexei?"

The man turned. He was indeed the Russian from that first prison cell, but his eyes showed no flicker of recognition.

"So, Vladimir Ilyich has done for us both in the end, my friend," joked Hugo, surprised that his voice was steady and hoping that he might sustain Alexei, who was clearly in shock. "And Pauli? Is he here, too?"

Alexei, seemingly stunned, queried doubtfully, "Hugo?"

"Of course!"

"I didn't recognise you – your hair…"

But a blood-chilling cry cut off his explanation. A prisoner had broken from the line. A shot rang out, then another. Panic took hold and the condemned men scattered.

"Quick, over here!" called Alexei, inserting his foot in an iron ring, the snow having melted in a neat square to reveal a trap door. Pulling it open, he threw himself through the gap and Hugo plunged after him.

"Run!"

Their hands still tied, the two men raced clumsily through the dark cellar, scrambling over piles of coal, aiming for the outer wall and following it blindly until they stumbled upon a wooden supply chute. The rope binding Hugo's wrists had worked loose and now he fumbled with numb fingers to untie Alexei's hands. Gripping the splintered sides, they clambered up the chute and burst through another trapdoor.

Thick snow carpeted the lane, which was deserted apart from a single wagon. The horses' heads were deep in nosebags, steam rising from their shaggy coats in the weak winter sun. The carter was nowhere to be seen. The two men climbed beneath the canvas, wedging themselves between bolts of coarse cloth, their hearts racing. They could hear men shouting, then a rapid staccato signalled that the firing squad was back in business. They shrank down further.

A tuneless whistling heralded the return of the driver. His unsteady footsteps announced time spent in the tavern, and it was their good fortune that he failed to inspect his load. Gaining his seat on the third attempt, he snapped the reins and the wagon lurched forward.

Out on the boulevard, they could hear the cries of street vendors and the creak and jangle of horse-drawn traffic. Gradually the sounds of the city gave way to snow-muffled countryside. With the rutted cobblestones behind them, the wagon skimmed smoothly as the horses picked up speed. Eventually, cautiously, Alexei peered out. They were on a track with a ditch running along one side, beyond which loomed the shadow of trees.

"We'd better jump, before he gets to wherever he's delivering this cloth."

Raising the tarpaulin, Alexei leapt. Hugo held his breath, expecting the carter to pull up. But there was no change in pace, and Hugo lifted the heavy canvas and pitched himself through, rolling into the ditch out of sight. Alexei pointed at the forest, and the two men, crouching low, made their way towards its shelter as fast as thigh-deep snow allowed.

It was nearly eight hundred kilometres to Wilno – an impossible distance – so Hugo tried not to think about it. Instead, he concentrated on putting one frozen foot in front of the other, as his boots fell apart and his inadequate clothing soaked with snow, then froze. Sometimes he took the lead, sometimes Alexei. They rarely spoke, both shivering so hard that communication was difficult. Besides, they had to conserve their energy just to keep going. When Hugo caught sight of Alexei's grey face and icicle-hung beard, he knew that his friend was in the same hell he was and that the temptation to lie down in the snow and forget everything never went away. But each time it became overwhelming, Hugo summoned Zosia's smile. He had nothing left with which to wonder who or what kept Alexei from sinking into the snow.

Sticking to forest where possible, they kept going south-west, taking their direction from the sun during the short hours of daylight, eating snow to quench their thirst. They risked begging at isolated homesteads but steered clear of larger settlements. Some nights, flames painted the sky, but they never knew whether White Russians or Bolsheviks had lit the torch.

One day, they came upon an empty farmhouse. The residents must have left in a hurry; on the table was a loaf half sliced, the knife still lodged in it, and an open jar of bilberry preserve. The men fell on the food, and the sweetness of the jam released memories long buried, sending tears that stung chapped cheeks. The bed was a tangle of sheepskins and blankets, as if its occupants had just risen. Using the bread knife, they cut holes in the bed clothes and pulled them over their heads. On the look-out for anything useful or edible, they went into the yard, where the barn door stood open. In the gloom they made out shapes on the floor: two cows with their throats cut and a mess of dead chickens. Beyond the animals lay the humans. Hugo, gagging, turned back to the yard, Alexei close behind, and the sweetness of the bilberries spewed sour on the ground.

They walked on, until hunger made them reckless, and they approached a small town. In a siding near the railway station, swathed in clouds of steam, was a locomotive, primed and uncoupled. Hugo's cracked lips stretched into his first smile for weeks and he nudged Alexei. "I always wanted to be an engine driver."

Having made sure they were unobserved, the men climbed into the cab to find the furnace stoked and the dials registering satisfactory pressure; the driver and fireman would be back any minute.

Hugo, fingering the brass wheels tentatively, cast his mind back to Wilno station on those long-ago Sunday afternoons. On occasion, in exchange for a box of Svenson cakes, a coal-grimed driver would let the two amateurs have a go. Praying that he remembered aright, he spun the largest wheel and felt the locomotive roll with the release of the brake. He reached for a smaller wheel and adjusted the gear, beads of sweat glistening on his forehead, despite the freezing air. With a deep breath, he grasped the longest lever and pulled it firmly towards him. The engine choked into life. Hugo closed his eyes and gave thanks, before opening the throttle further and spinning the gear wheel again. As the engine gathered speed, he craned forward, straining to see what lay ahead in the darkness. Alexei had positioned himself between the tender and the glowing hatch beneath the boiler and was shovelling coal.

They drove the locomotive until the coal ran out, less than a hundred kilometres from Wilno and a lot further from the Bolsheviks. Their feet rested, they walked on determinedly until they reached the Svenson home.

The maid who answered Hugo's knock took one look before spitting, "Tramps, vagabonds, go away!" and slamming the door. Hugo called out weakly, "Gosia, it's me, Hugo Wolfer."

The door opened a crack and Gosia peered out, her usually ruddy face as pale as her white kerchief.

"Mary, Mother of God, save us – it's a ghost!"

Her cry brought Zosia to the door, a bundle in her arms. She stared at the men uncomprehendingly, but at last her face cleared.

"Hugo – oh, my love, it's you! We thought you were dead. But your hair…"

Hugo touched his head in confusion. Stumbling over the threshold, he confronted himself in the hall mirror. Unshaven for months, his beard grew black, and sooty eyebrows overhung eyes sunk in wells of fatigue and starvation. Above his raw and grimy face, though, his hair was a shock of white. He felt Alexei's hand on his shoulder and saw his friend's filthy, malnourished face reflected beside his own.

"It's why I didn't recognise you in the prison yard."

Not yet forty, the night spent anticipating his execution had left him an old man. Hugo turned back to Zosia, whose eyes shone with tears.

"Darling, I thought you were dead," she whispered. "Thank God, thank God. Here, hold your daughter."

Dumbfounded, Hugo looked down at the infant his wife had placed in his arms: Ida, the third miracle.

Stasia's eyes were wide. Even Ida, her napkin abandoned on the table, had lost herself in the drama of the familiar story and her central role in its fairy-tale ending. But Luiza was feeling left out, excluded from the happy homecoming that reunited the other three members of her family.

"So, I must be the fourth miracle?" she ventured.

Uncle Rafi laughed and raised his glass of plum brandy, "To the fourth miracle!"

"And now I'm going to school, I'm going to learn to be an engineer, just like Pappa."

Ida snorted, "Good luck with that. There are no engineering lessons at the convent."

Pappa frowned. "If Lou-lou really wants to be an

engineer, then we'll make sure she gets the education she needs."

But Mama shook her head. "Lou-lou's too young to know what she wants. And, Hugo, though you've certainly tried your best to make of her the son we don't have, remember that she's your daughter. It's enough for her to learn what the Sisters will teach her, and let's hope they can improve her embroidery, because it's beyond me."

Luiza slumped in her chair, dismayed at the shadow cast over her imagined future, the exciting prospect of school tarnished with disappointment before it had even begun. It was such a struggle to manoeuvre Mama's wheelchair over uneven ground that she wanted to invent something to make it easier. And she wanted to run the mill, so that Pappa could spend more time with Mama and keep her happy. But it seemed unlikely, now, that her plans would ever get off the ground.

Chapter 10

30 August 1931, Zakątek

"*L*ou-lou, are you ready?"

At the sound of her father's voice, she threw the tennis ball one last time before turning up the slope to the house. The grass was damp and slippery under the leather soles of her new shoes, and Mono soon caught her up. On the terrace, Ida's head was touching Mama's as they bent over a fashion magazine.

Pappa frowned, checking his watch. "It's time we were off. We don't want to miss the train."

The trunks had been sent ahead, and Janek had the landau waiting. Pappa wheeled Mama to the front of the house and Luiza walked beside the chair, but she was on the wrong side. Ida, on the left, held their mother's hand. Luiza eyed the other, limp in Mama's lap, and reached down to caress Mono's silky ears instead.

Mama smiled abstractedly amid kisses and assurances

that it would be no time at all before they were home for Christmas. Anjela and Pani Marysia broke off sobbing to deliver entreaties for the girls' protection.

Pappa climbed aboard last, causing the open carriage to tip alarmingly. The springs continued to complain as he settled into the forward-facing seat, opposite the girls. Janek shook the reins and they were off, Ida and Luiza waving to Mama until the bend in the drive swallowed her up.

Luiza passed her coins through the slot at the bottom of the mesh screen, and the cashier gave her a slip of paper in return. At the counter she exchanged this for a small parcel of *sernik*. She loved visiting Cukiernia Svenson and imagining Pappa buying cakes here, day after day, as an excuse to see Mama.

Outside the bakery, her new friend, Helena, picked up their conversation.

"But don't they change their underwear?"

"Well, if they're not allowed to see themselves naked, how can they?"

"They could shut their eyes."

Three weeks into the school year, the nuns remained a perpetual source of speculation. It was unnerving, the way they glided silently in their floor-length black robes. The occasional clack of rosary beads or a shiver from the white wings of their wimples were the only signs of propulsion.

"What about in the bath, though?"

"Perhaps they wash their underwear at the same time!"

Giggling, the girls came to the Franciscan Church, its arcaded porch straddling the pavement, the columns pasted with black-bordered death notices. The older posts had weathered to grey, but the lettering on this one stood out starkly. Silently Luiza mouthed the words: "Zofia Wolfer, nee Svenson. Born Wilno, 12 August 1884. Died Zapole, 22 September 1931."

The package from Svensons fell from her hand and crumbs spilled onto the pavement. Tentatively, Helena touched her friend's arm, but Luiza pulled away.

"It's a mistake. It can't be my mother – it's somebody else."

Helena followed her to Pani Jankowska's gate, where Luiza turned in without a word. The door to the spare room was open; a scuffed leather holdall stood on the table beneath the window. Uncle Rafi had one just like it. Through the window, she noticed the trees grow agitated in a strengthening wind. She flipped the catch on the holdall back and forth, matching the rhythm as she intoned, "It's-not-her-Mama's-not-dead."

"I'm so sorry, Lou-lou, but she is."

Uncle Rafi's blue eyes were clouded, and his moustache drooped. Beside him Ida, red-eyed, wove a sodden handkerchief through her fingers.

Prising Luiza's hand from his bag, her uncle led her, stiff but unresisting, to sit beside him on the bed. Ida perched on her other side. Between sobs, her sister explained, "Pappa asked Uncle Rafi to come and tell us about Mama, because he didn't want to leave her alone. She died the day before yesterday. She got ill in the night and died the following afternoon. Pappa was with her. Uncle Rafi came to the convent, but you'd already left."

Ida blew her nose, and Uncle Rafi stroked Luiza's hair.

Nine days later, when Pappa finally arrived, Luiza had still not wept. At school, the nuns prayed for her mother's soul, while her classmates eyed the black ribbon on her arm with curious sympathy. But Luiza maintained her silent mantra: "Mama's not dead. It's somebody else."

Ida's explanations barely penetrated the hushed space she found herself inhabiting. Only with effort could she make out words shaped by mouths that opened and closed around her. As if from a great distance, the news reached her that the post-mortem (what was that?) had delayed things. Until they released the body, Janek could not drive the lorry five hundred kilometres to Wilno with Pappa beside him and the sealed, lead-lined coffin in the back. Luiza nodded vaguely and wondered who or what was in the coffin. Because it was not her mother.

The night before the funeral it snowed and vibrant autumn was muted. In this monochrome, muffled world, Luiza felt at home. As in a dream, she walked beside her father from the Lutheran church to the cemetery. With each step she watched the toes of her black boots plant themselves in unmarked snow, careful to avoid the churn of the plumed black horses pulling the hearse.

The heavy coffin was finally lowered into the gaping black hole, and Luiza copied Pappa and Ida, taking a handful of soil from the white-capped mound beside the grave. When she let it fall, it covered the brass plate and hid Mama's name. The pastor's voice droned on, but his words did not interrupt her own litany, "It's not Mama; it's somebody else. Mama isn't dead."

It was eight months before the sisters returned to Zakątek. They spent Christmas with Aunt Ludmila in Riga. Pappa was there, too, and everyone tried their best to be cheerful, but conversations tended to die out and games were half-hearted. Luiza tried to play with Ferdi, but he was old and arthritic and she missed Mono dreadfully. At Easter, with Pappa away on business, the girls again visited Riga. But now it was the end of the school year, and they were finally going home. Luiza had not given up her silent chant, nor her belief that Mama was at home. But as they neared Zakątek, anticipation became fraught with foreboding.

Mama was not at the door to greet them, so she must be in the salon; she could not be in that box in Wilno. The grief that her incantation had kept at bay for so long now threatened to overwhelm Luiza. And the guilt. If she had not left for school, she could have protected Mama. If only she had stayed at home, she could have stopped Pani Aurelia giving Mama eclairs. She could have pleased Mama by working at her embroidery. Why had she not stayed?

Ida took her hand and led her into the hall. A black-and-white shape came barrelling at them in a yelping, licking frenzy. When Mono had calmed down, Luiza carried her down the corridor and opened the door to the salon. It was empty.

At the sound of voices, Luiza scrambled to her feet, brushing grass from her knees. Pappa rounded the corner with Stanisław, his current intern, to find Luiza among the fallen azalea blooms. Cheerily, he called out, "Mono lost her ball again, Lou-lou?"

Luiza smiled back. Once they were out of sight, she knelt again to meet the calm gaze of the woman in blue, a crown on her head and the babe in her arms. The statue was set in a stone alcove to the side of the path. On the ledge in front of it was a jar filled with poppies and cornflowers – Pani Marysia regularly visited the shrine.

As a Lutheran, Luiza knew better than to pray to statues or intermediaries. It was the woman in blue's Son she should be invoking. But in the Catholic churches of Wilno, Luiza had found comfort among the multitude of wood and plaster likenesses of this constant mother. When the ache of the empty salon became unbearable, this was her secret solace.

Her parents had discussed removing it when they bought Zakątek, before Luiza was born, but had decided against upsetting their Catholic staff. And besides, Pappa thought his mother would have appreciated it. Elżbieta was born a Catholic and had even become a nun. But her father – Luiza's great-grandfather – had made her leave the convent and renounce her faith – his own creed. All so she could marry the Lutheran son of another textile mill owner, thus merging the two businesses.

Luiza pitied her grandmother, having to exchange the sumptuousness of Catholic ceremony for the spare Lutheran liturgy. At school, she was excused Mass and benediction, yet she usually went. The candles reminded her of Christmas, and the mysterious Latin litanies made her spine tingle. She relished the colourful clutter of icons and statues; Lutheran houses of worship were so bare in comparison. There were times, at benediction, that the waves of incense left her with the feeling that she walked on air.

From the consolation of the shrine, she went to find comfort in the kitchen. But before she reached the door, a scarlet-faced Pani Marysia burst out, almost knocking her over. Luiza stood back in astonishment as she hurtled down the corridor, waving a serving spoon and shouting, "That's it! No more! If she thinks she can tell me what I can and can't cook – me, who's looked after this family all these years…"

Her voice faded as she stormed into Pappa's study without knocking and slammed the door behind her.

Through the kitchen door, Luiza spied Pani Aurelia. She was sniffing a simmering pot of *bigos* and wrinkling her nose, as if it smelled bad.

Chapter 11

Autumn 1933, Warszawa

"Shhh – he's coming!"

Leaving her post at the door, Luiza slipped back to her desk as fifteen girls in grey pinafores, their waists cinched by bottle-green sashes, sat up expectantly. A nervous giggle in the back row launched a wave of suppressed mirth, which surged towards the teacher's desk, where was placed a large cabbage. A mouth, eyes and nose were carved into the brassica, with wire-rimmed spectacles straddling it lopsidedly.

A similar pair rested on the narrow nose of the diminutive figure in the doorway. Pan Garonski wore an old-fashioned tailcoat and a silk cravat with a diamond pin nestling in its creamy folds. He consulted a pocket watch, nodded curtly and entered the room.

The mathematics teacher was the single irritation in Luiza's new life. For two years, Pappa had honoured his wife's wishes that their daughters attend school in her hometown, but the need to have his girls close grew implacable, and in September he had moved them to this secular school in Warszawa. Now they lodged with Uncle Rafi, Aunt Wanda and Kamila, and went home at weekends.

Ida had swiftly embraced life in the fashionable capital, and Luiza was also flourishing. At the convent she was the girl whose mother had died; her classmates were solicitous but wary and even her early friendship with Helena had dwindled. But here she was unmarked by tragedy and had quickly joined Gosia and Agnieszka as one of the Three Musketeers. The novelty of whispered secrets and private jokes among friends delighted her. She could scarcely believe that she, the outsider, shared such a coveted mutual identity: all for one and one for all.

Friends aside, the fact that needlework was not compulsory was another bonus. As was the availability of maths and science; her dream of becoming an engineer had revived. Yet it was history that she liked best, possibly because Pani Rybicka was her favourite teacher. With her bobbed hair and knee-length skirts, she was a world away from the enigmatic nuns, and her energetic style of instruction readily conjured the past into the classroom.

"You are such fortunate girls," she announced. "Who can tell me why?"

Luiza's hand shot up. "Because we were born into newly independent Poland. My father calls me and my sister the blessed generation."

"He's absolutely right," concurred Pani Rybicka. "After

a century's absence from the map of Europe, in 1918 our nation was at last redrawn as an independent state." Her glossy helmet of hair swung in time with each emphatic nod. "And your generation was the first for one hundred years to be born Polish." As Pani Rybicka beamed, each girl swelled with pride at her own personal good fortune.

It was regrettable that the teacher Luiza liked least taught mathematics, which she knew was necessary for engineering. Pan Guzik (Button) as they called Pan Garonski, after his frequent and idiosyncratic exclamation, could be cruelly sarcastic.

"I'm keen to see your workings for this calculation, Barbara Nowak, because you obviously know something the great Pythagoras did not. While he would have given this triangle an area of 40, you somehow make it 62. Should we perhaps bow to your greater knowledge? Guzik! You are nothing but a cabbage head."

Poor Basia's cheeks were scarlet. Pan Guzik regularly called them all cabbage heads, but Basia more than most. Even worse than his caustic rants, though, was the excessive amount of homework he gave. Last Friday things had come to a head.

"This is going to take forever! And we've got a French test on Monday – when are we supposed to revise for that?" complained Krystyna, who was generally acknowledged to be the best at maths.

"If it'll take *you* forever, what about me?" Basia was close to tears.

"And what about all the other things we're supposed to be able to do at the weekend, like actually not schoolwork?"

queried Luiza, who was worried that she might not have time for her Sunday visit to Pani Anna's stable.

"I suppose we could all just not do it?"

The girls stared at Gosia, who persisted, "Seriously, why stand for this? If none of us does it – absolutely *none* of us," she repeated, looking at Krystyna, "what can old Guzik do?"

"You mean, go on *strike*?" Agnieszka ventured.

The word resonated and the flame of rebellion, once lit, was fanned by The Musketeers. The cabbage on the desk had been Luiza's idea, which was why it was with a mixture of pride and terror that she watched Pan Garonski enter the classroom.

For a moment, his gaze rested on the cabbage, then he faced the class.

"Barbara Nowak, what interesting new trigonometric theory have you come up with this time?"

Basia stood, red-faced and silent.

"Pah – cabbage head." He turned to Marte Frinczyk. "Well, what answer did you get for question 1?"

Marte studied the floor.

"Guzik! Another cabbage head. Luiza Wolfer – let's try question 2."

Luiza stood, although it felt as if her stomach remained seated, her lips sealed.

"Guzik! At least I know there's one girl in this hopeless class who isn't a cabbage head – Krystyna Szymańska, the answers to questions 1 and 2, please."

When his star pupil failed to answer, Pan Guzik's eyes widened and his mouth narrowed. "Guzik! What is the meaning of this? Have you cabbage heads all lost your tongues?"

Gosia stood. The three of them had drawn lots to decide who would deliver their planned speech. "Pan Garonski, I'm afraid it's completely beyond a class of cabbage heads to manage the amount of homework you set."

The colour drained from his face. Slowly, deliberately he made his way to the front of the room and stood with his back to them. With a loud thump he brought his fist down on the desk. The girls flinched, and the cabbage rolled until it came to rest at a drunken angle, spectacles askew. The tension was unbearable, but at the familiar exclamation, "Guzik!", they could no longer contain their mounting hysteria.

When Pan Garonski turned to face them, red spots high on both cheeks betrayed his composure, and their hilarity subsided. Without a word he continued the lesson and made no further reference to the weekend's homework, nor any mention of cabbages. Before dismissing the class, he instructed them to revisit, for review next lesson, only the first three problems from their original homework list of twenty.

"Do you *have* to go out again tonight, Ida? Kamila's been stuck at home for days now, and she'd love to hear about Saturday's party. I told her about the green ice."

Luiza and Ida rarely arrived home from school together, but today they had met on the tram and were now walking down the tree-lined street in Saska Kępa where Uncle Rafi lived.

"Yes, I *have* to go out again tonight." Ida rolled her eyes. "We're seeing the new Gary Cooper film at The Atlantic."

The girls walked up the path to the grey front door, offset on one of the angular villa's white walls. If Luiza's new school was all but perfect, living here was the icing on the cake. The stylish house, which was not even as old as Luiza, had no association with Mama or the events in Wilno. There they had been boarders in an old lady's home; here Luiza felt part of a proper family, with their fun-loving uncle and warm, if absent-minded, aunt. Their cousin was frequently poorly (which made Aunt Wanda even more distracted), and Ida was often out with friends, but the villa felt like home. And now that Ida was too absorbed with her burgeoning social life to bother with her younger cousin, Luiza and Kamila had grown closer.

"Ooh, look!" Luiza pounced on an envelope, propped on the hall table and addressed to the Wolfer sisters. "It's from Pappa."

Splinters of light from the chandelier merged and swelled at table level, reflected in the silver that dipped and rose in the hands of the diners. Sparks pooled on the raised lid of the grand piano. Luiza recognised a Chopin sonata her mother used to play and stared at her plate, her veal cutlet unseen.

"Come on, Lou-lou, we're here to celebrate, not meditate. This dinner's costing me an arm and a leg – it needs eating, not committing to memory."

The envelope on the hall table had contained an invitation to join their father at the Hotel Brystol. Ida was reluctant to give up her cinema outing, so was here under duress. But this was Luiza's first grown-up evening out, and everything about it captivated her, from the starched napkin the waiter had snapped over her knees to the pianist in white tails.

Pappa leant over to spear a piece of veal from Luiza's plate, waking her from her reverie. She set about her meal again, her father regarding her with amusement from beneath shaggy eyebrows, still black even now that his shock of white hair was thinning. Ida regarded the incident with the pained disbelief that fifteen-year-olds reserve for their family's embarrassing habits. Pappa raised his glass to her in a placatory gesture, then spoiled it with a wink.

"It's time to toast your father, girls, decrepit though he undoubtedly is." Pappa smiled. Ida sighed, raising her eyes to the glittering chandelier. She proffered her glass casually, as if accustomed to champagne with every meal, while Luiza thrust hers forward eagerly. The splash, which fizzed hopefully up the sides of the shallow bowl, sank back into a disappointing amber puddle as Pappa continued, "This aged parent of yours may not be much to look at, but in here" – he tapped his broad forehead – "lurks the brain of a genius."

Ida examined the sleeve of her new bias-cut dress and ostentatiously stifled a yawn. Luiza was torn between devotion to her father and impatience for her first taste of champagne.

"I know I've been preoccupied recently, but I've been working hard on a very special project. Now it's done and, well, here's the result."

With a magician's flourish, Pappa pulled a document from the inside pocket of his dinner jacket.

"And that's what we're celebrating? That bit of paper?"

Ida's tone was carefully balanced between boredom and incredulity.

With a note of irritation Pappa continued, "This bit of paper, young lady, is a patent certificate, and it's what's going to pay for your increasingly expensive wardrobe. This bit of paper is what will keep Zakątek going while other factories are forced to close. This bit of paper—"

"But what does it say, Pappa?" interrupted Luiza, anxious to restore her father's good humour. Family outings were a rarity. "What is a patent certificate?"

Their father's desire to share his achievement overcame his annoyance.

"A patent certificate means that only the inventor – no one else – can manufacture his invention. This states that Hugo Wolfer, Director of Zakątek Mill, is the inventor of a new product, similar to cotton wool but made from flax. And this 'flax wool' – or 'lint wool' – can be manufactured only at his mill. So Zakątek is the only factory in Poland licensed to produce the new material that your clever father's invented."

Luiza struggled to grasp the significance of his statement. Zakątek already produced high-grade cotton wool – why should it make anything different? Ironically it was Ida, who demonstrated a studied indifference to all matters concerning the mill, who clarified the situation.

"Lint's used for dressings, isn't it? So why make wool from it?"

"Well, just think. If you combine the softness of cotton wool with the cooling properties of lint, then voila, you have the perfect wound dressing. According to your Uncle Rafi, the Ministry of Defence already recognises your father's genius and wants to explore the possibility of using it in field dressings. So, how about toasting your brilliant father, then?"

Luiza raised her glass in imitation of her father and sister. Before she could drink, though, Pappa added quietly, "And your wonderful, much-missed mother."

Ida shot Pappa a smile of great tenderness. "To Mama *and* Pappa," she said, and took a sip. Luiza felt unsettled, the high spirits of a moment ago overshadowed by Mama's absence. She raised the glass to her lips, but the magic was gone. And when she finally tasted it, the champagne was not at all the sweet nectar she had anticipated. With a grimace she swallowed a mouthful, before turning her attention to the dessert menu.

Chapter 12

December 1933, Warszawa

The maths strike had been a success. Pan Garonski now set them acceptable amounts of homework and had not called anyone – not even Basia Nowak – a cabbage head since. In fact, the girls had become quite fond of their only male teacher, and there was a Christmas surprise for him at the end of the final maths lesson of term.

When Gosia placed the enormous parcel on his desk, the little man disappeared behind it. Even when he stood, they could only see the top of his bald head. But more of him was revealed with each layer he removed. Luiza, who had supplied the treasure at the heart of the parcel, jiggled her foot in anticipation.

At last, Pan Garonski removed the final sheet to reveal a matchbox. This he slid open and carefully tipped into his hand. Staring in bewilderment at the tiny silver button glinting in his palm, he innocently queried, "Guzik?" When the class erupted, he peered at his giggling students in confusion. Slowly, he smiled and raised his prize in triumph.

"Guzik!" he proclaimed, grinning disarmingly at the class.

Soon after, the girls went home for Christmas. Pani Marysia was gone, replaced by Vacek, who used to be the chef at the Rumanian embassy in Warszawa until he almost caused a diplomatic incident. When a dinner guest left the pastry shell of the chef's trademark *boeuf en croute* untouched, Vacek had stormed into the dining room, demanding that the philistine who did not appreciate his culinary art identify themself.

"And it was the German ambassador." Pappa laughed. "It was getting a bit fraught, so I said I knew a place where every plate Vacek served would be scraped clean. Because, honestly, those weeks after Pani Marysia left, when Pani Aurelia and Anjela were managing the kitchen between them… well, let's just say that I ate out a lot. So Vacek's improved things in the Zakątek kitchen no end – though we have to make allowances for his artistic temperament!"

Luiza missed Pani Marysia's warm welcome and her abundant kitchen. Vacek tolerated neither visitors nor snacks. Anjela had already informed them of Pani Aurelia's first and last kitchen inspection under the new regime.

"She was fussing as usual, telling him to avoid rich ingredients and only cook simple dishes. And Vacek chased her out! Honestly, he even threw a spoon after her – it's lucky he was only stirring when she came in, not cutting something up."

Pani Aurelia always spent Christmas with her mother in Wilno, yet there she was, dressed in black even at Wigilia, waiting outside the dining room after the first star had been sighted. And when they went in (it was the first time that Ida had been charged with the lighting of the tree), she actually made for Mama's place at the table. Incensed, Ida rushed to claim it for herself.

"Imagine the old witch thinking she could take Mama's place!"

The languorous demeanour Ida had cultivated since seeing Greta Garbo in *Grand Hotel* had vanished; her cheeks glowed, even though she had started to wear powder.

"She's trying to get her claws into Pappa, Lou-lou, and we have to stop her."

Luiza almost whooped for joy. Ida had always dismissed her anxieties about Pani Aurelia, but at last she recognised the threat she posed.

"The problem is that we're not here to keep an eye on things. Pappa always believes the best of people, so he can't see that she's a scheming witch. We mustn't leave him alone with her."

But Ida's expanding social life meant that Luiza was often left alone with her, and the thin woman assumed an authority that she never attempted with Ida.

"Goodness me, child, what would your poor mother say if she saw you in such a state?"

She had materialised in the hall as Luiza arrived back from Pani Anna's, where she had enjoyed a long, muddy hack on Nutmeg, the pony Pani Anna let her ride.

"I can't think why you're allowed to roam wild like this – your poor mother would be beside herself."

Pani Aurelia pursed her thin lips until they disappeared, while Luiza clenched her fists. How dare she presume to know how Mama would have felt (although she suspected that her mother would not have relished seeing her quite this dishevelled).

The thin woman opened the door, hugging her black jacket close against the biting March wind. Stepping outside, she said, "Go and tidy yourself and meet me in the dining room – I'll be back in thirty minutes."

When Luiza presented herself, Pani Aurelia pointed at a pile of stockings and socks. "Darning those should keep you busy until supper," she snapped and left the room. Luiza sighed, then stared at the door in disbelief. Surely the woman had not locked her in. She tried the handle – she had.

Ida had stayed in town that weekend, so she was not there to share her indignation, but Luiza was determined to bring her grievance to Pappa as soon as she was released. At supper, however, he was engrossed in a paper covered in figures, so she just glared at Pani Aurelia, who was picking at the food on her plate and narrowing her eyes at Luiza. When Pappa disappeared into his study afterwards, Luiza hurried to her room before further outrage could be inflicted.

The next morning she woke with a sore throat. By evening she was streaming with cold and could not return to Warszawa. Over the next few days, miserable in bed, she regretted Pani Marysia's departure more than ever. The old cook would have sent Anjela up with regular supplies of comforting chicken soup and fortifying *kogel-mogel*.

By Thursday she felt better. She knew that Pani Aurelia was taking some samples to a prospective buyer in Warszawa, so now was her chance to make the point forcibly to Pappa that his secretary should stick to her office duties and leave his daughter alone.

She did not look for her father in the production sheds as she used to. These days he was always in the office. She could hear him as she approached, and he sounded angry.

"I expressly said that this order should be prioritised, Graban. Yet now I discover that it has *still* not been fulfilled. The Goldfarbs are among our longest-standing customers – I will NOT have them kept waiting in this manner."

"In your absence, I had to prioritise in terms of capacity."

The second voice was thin and rather high and made Luiza shudder. Pan Graban had been installed as manager by Korski, the company that now owned the mill. She had only met him once. Much younger and taller than Pappa, he seemed embarrassed by his height and slouched awkwardly as if to disguise it. He always sounded apologetic, but not in a sincere way. When he first arrived, he had been invited to tea at the house. It proved uncomfortable, and the invitation had not been repeated. He complimented everything excessively – their home, the furnishings, the cakes… It made them squirm. When he left, Ida complained, "That vile man – he positively oozes – I'm surprised he didn't leave a trail of slime as he slithered away. And slobbering all over my hand with those disgusting fat lips, ugh."

For a thin man, Pan Graban did have very plump lips, which he was always licking. Ida's comment had fixed an image in Luiza's mind and now she imagined his unnaturally high voice issuing from those slug-like lips.

"The Goldfarb account may be old, but you have to admit it's not very substantial. Whereas this new order from Mannheim is, and it required immediate attention."

"Not at the cost of an existing client," Pappa exploded. "Zakątek Mill has always prided itself on customer loyalty. We rely on good relations with small accounts like the Goldfarbs. They stick with us through hard times, when large orders can fall away. Besides, Chaim Goldfarb is a friend."

"Well, Pan Direktor, as the manager appointed by the Board, I must insist that such business decisions are mine to make. Which leaves you free to concentrate on the research and development that is your strength, sir, without distractions. And perhaps it is better that my decisions are not influenced by the bonds of friendship, but simply by good commercial practice."

There was a pause before Pappa spoke again. His voice was quieter now, but Luiza recognised that as a danger signal.

"Good commercial practice? And that includes letting down reliable customers? Let's just hope the accounts bear out your position, Pan Graban, because, I have to say, the figures I've seen so far don't appear to."

"Ah, but a new regime always needs time to bed in.

I'm sure the Board – and you, Pan Direktor – will see an improvement very soon."

"Pan Direktor," Pappa was muttering as he came out of the office. Luiza held back, judging that this was not the time to approach him with her problems.

"Director of what, exactly?" Pappa's head was down, his shoulders hunched as he crossed the yard and disappeared into the engine room.

Chapter 13

Spring 1935, Zakątek

A whole year had passed and Luiza had still not reported her problems with Pani Aurelia to Pappa. He was so caught up in his work that the right moment had never presented itself. Besides, she had learnt how to avoid the Witch when she was at Zakątek. Which was less frequently, anyway, as her life in Warszawa developed and their father's insistence on regular visits relaxed. But this weekend, she and Ida were both going home, at Pani Anna's request. Their mother's friend would soon be exchanging her country retreat near Zapole for another, further west, and this was one of the last opportunities for a neighbourly gathering.

It had been raining when they caught the train at Warszawa Central after Saturday morning school. Yet just thirty minutes later, when they alighted at Grodzisk Mazowiecki and joined Janek in the landau, the sun was shining and he had taken down the hood. Luiza craned her neck to see the end of the rainbow, which arched over the lane, brushing aside catkins that dripped in her face.

"You can be sure I won't be doing *this* once Pani Anna's gone," Ida grumbled, irritably wiping the drips from her sleeve. "When I think of what I'm missing in town."

Luiza felt torn. Zakątek was home, but she had come to appreciate all that Warszawa had to offer, especially when shared with the Musketeers. In winter they skated on courtyards specially flooded for the purpose. The first time Gosia and Agnieszka had steered her through the archway of an apartment building after school, she had gaped in disbelief to see skaters within the walls. In summer they played tennis or swam from the Vistula beach. When it rained, there was always the cinema or a museum, or even one of the art galleries that Mama's younger sister, Aunt Rysia, had introduced her to when she visited from Riga. And then there were the cafés, all of them serving excellent cakes and ice cream.

Yet Pappa, however distant, was at Zakątek, as was Mono. So was Nutmeg, though not for much longer. After Easter, Pani Anna would be taking the pony with her to the large estate she had bought near Kutno. Waldemar and his wife, who was expecting Pani Anna's first grandchild, were going to live there, too.

Aware of how little time was left, Luiza took Nutmeg out straight after dinner. They were cantering along the edge of one of Pan Rubacz's fields when she recognised the approaching rider. He was Wojtek Petrowski, the son of a neighbour, a retired commissioner of police. Wojtek lived in Warszawa but kept his horses stabled at his father's. Last summer, Luiza had made friends with the commissioner's granddaughter when she came to stay, and Bożena had shown off her uncle's horses: Aurora, an exquisite Arab mare, and the magnificent chestnut thoroughbred, Prince.

And now here was Prince, being brought to a reluctant halt beside her. Dancing impatiently, he shook his fine head, while Nutmeg sampled the hedgerow and stubbornly ignored Luiza's best efforts to keep him facing forward.

"Good afternoon." Wojtek was grinning down at her from Prince's lofty back. Red-faced from the struggle to make Nutmeg behave, Luiza looked up at eyes of a deep, velvet brown. There was a dimple in Wojtek's cheek, just like Clark Gable's – his moustache was like Gable's, too. Attempting a casual "Hello", her voice betrayed her with an embarrassing squeak.

"Tell me, how's that delightful sister of yours?"

"Ida's fine, thank you," replied Luiza, primly. "How is Aurora?"

Grinning, Wojtek mimicked, "Aurora's fine, thank you," and winked, before touching his spurs to Prince's flanks. Giving the horse his head, he called back, "Do tell your sister I was asking after her."

Luiza watched them gallop up the field. At the top, Wojtek stood in his stirrups and turned towards her, his blonde hair bright with sunlight. He raised an arm in salute before horse and rider disappeared into the trees.

Having finally got Nutmeg to stop munching, she made him trot on as she re-lived her humiliation: "*'How is Aurora?'* Oh, you stupid, stupid idiot!"

Urging the bay pony to canter, Luiza's embarrassment subsided as her imagination transported her to a place where an unconscious Wojtek lay on the ground, Prince having thrown him. Managing to catch the spooked thoroughbred, she galloped for help. Wojtek's injuries proved serious enough to prevent him riding (though not too serious); so impressed was he by her handling of Prince that he asked her to exercise both his horses until he recovered, when they rode them together…

"Wojtek Petrowski was asking after you," announced Luiza at supper. Ida shrugged dismissively but could not conceal a smile.

"What were you doing with Wojtek Petrowski?" asked Pappa, sharply.

"I met him out riding. He was on Prince – he's SO gorgeous."

Pappa's eyebrows almost met his receding hairline as he thumped his hand on the table.

"I do NOT want you talking to that young man, do you hear?"

"It's alright, Pappa." Ida laughed. "It's the *horse* Luiza thinks is gorgeous."

Pappa sat back and took a sip of water.

"But why shouldn't I talk to him?" Luiza asked, anxious about the impact that her father's edict might have on their outings on Prince and Aurora, once Wojtek recovered from his riding accident.

"He has a reputation. I don't want either of you alone with him. Do you hear me?"

Luiza nodded.

"Ida?" Pappa's blue eyes bored into his elder daughter.

"Oh, for goodness' sake," exclaimed Ida, dramatically, "Honestly, I don't understand what all the fuss is about. *Alright!*"

"Why can't we be alone with Wojtek?"

"I'll tell you later, but as there's clearly no danger of that at the moment, I'm going to make the most of it," announced Ida and promptly joined the group clustered around Wojtek, leaving Luiza by the door. They were at Pani Anna's farewell gathering and the girls had entered the salon, leaving Pappa with their hostess in the dining room.

Wojtek held his audience (mostly women) rapt, but he broke off when Ida joined the circle. The pair were soon absorbed in conversation and the others drifted away, one or two of the women glancing resentfully at the newcomer. Luiza was still watching when Pappa arrived from the dining room. She threw her arms around him enthusiastically, doing her best to block his view, but he spotted Ida and made a strange, harrumphing sound, taking a determined step in her direction. Just then, Ida peeled away from Wojtek with a dismissive wave of her hand. Pappa stopped, and they both watched her weave her way to join Grażyna, Pani Anna's pregnant daughter-in-law, who sat by the window. Perching on the arm of her chair, Ida launched an animated exchange. When she looked up, laughing, her eyes found Pappa's and her apparent surprise nearly convinced Luiza that her sister had not noticed his arrival.

Later, Luiza faced Ida on the train back to Warszawa.

"It's lucky you left Wojtek when you did."

"Luck had nothing to do with it," Ida responded, enigmatically. Luiza waited for clarification, but Ida was examining her reflection in the night-dark window. When it became clear that nothing more was forthcoming, Luiza changed tack.

"What did Pappa mean about Wojtek's reputation?"

"Well, let's just say the girls he knows aren't *convent* girls." Ida smirked.

"But neither are we, anymore. I'd hoped I might be able to ride his horses once Pani Anna's gone."

"Well, that's not very likely," snorted her sister. "He's hardly going to let a twelve-year-old loose with his precious horses, is he?"

"I'll be thirteen soon," Luiza offered, hopefully.

"Makes no difference. Those horses are the only thing Wojtek Petrowski loves more than women – at least, it's between them and his cars. If only Pappa weren't so old-fashioned, I could be driving back to town with Wojtek now, in that sports car of his."

Ida peered out impatiently. The train had come to a halt in the suburb of Ochota. Steam swelled beyond the smeared glass as they began to move again.

"We'd go dancing at Café Adria," she mused, stretching her arms dreamily above her head.

"Café Adria? Isn't that where they've got the chimpanzee? Oh, could I come? I'd so love to see it!"

"Trust you to want to visit Warszawa's most exclusive bar just to see the novelty chimp. The Adria's got a rotating dance floor, and the best orchestra in town. But, no, Luiza Wolfer just wants to dance with a chimp!"

Deflated, Luiza sat back, muttering, "I didn't say I wanted to dance with him, just that I wanted to see him."

Ida sighed. "Anyway, there's no Café Adria for us, chimp or no chimp. We have to go back to boring Saska Kępa. Honestly, I can't wait until I leave school and start to live."

Chapter 14

Spring 1935, Saska Kępa

*I*t was a few weeks later, on a Saturday evening, that Pappa turned up at the villa. Ida was out, and Aunt Wanda was with Kamila, who was unwell again, but Luiza was sketching in the salon. She hugged him happily as he explained that, after a meeting with a visiting German manufacturer, he had been overcome with a need "to see my girls before going home." But when Uncle Rafi emerged from his study and set up the chessboard, it became clear that there was another reason behind her father's visit.

"Tell me, Rafi, what do you know about this order?"

"Mmmhh?" Uncle Rafi's hand was hovering between his bishop and his knight.

"This, I think we can call, 'substantial' order from the Ministry of Defence, Major Svenson? Why so many field dressings?"

Uncle Rafi moved his bishop and sat back.

"What's the problem? Surely it's good for business?"

"Of course, it's good for business. I'm just not sure it's good for Poland. What's the old man planning?"

The smoke from Pappa's cigar drifted over them. This salon was nothing like Mama's at Zakątek, with its colourful *kilims* and dark, polished wood. Here, all was pale and stream-lined, the latest styles from Paris and Berlin. Pappa and Uncle Rafi sat in matching low-backed, dove-grey leather chairs, their broad arms thrust confidently forward. Luiza leant against Pappa's chair, cushioned from the gleaming parquet by a thick, cream and grey rug. She was drawing spring flowers that were arranged in a black and grey, sunray-patterned vase.

"Is it the insurgencies? For a man who prides himself on his nationalism, why the Marshal can't see that Belarussians and Ukrainians are also patriots is beyond me."

Uncle Rafi looked up sharply. "Ethnic Belarussians and Ukrainians living on Polish soil are Polish citizens and should behave as such."

Leaning forward, Pappa tapped the ash from his cigar into an onyx ashtray and made his move.

"Just as Poles were Russian, or Prussian, or Austro-Hungarian citizens for over a century?" he mused. "Should we have given up our nationhood?"

Uncle Rafi's frown deepened as he contemplated the board, but he made no comment.

"So, I ask again, why stockpile dressings?"

Pappa had pushed himself back in the deep chair and

his feet barely reached the rug. Puffing on his cigar he persisted, "Come on, Rafi, you must have some idea?"

Thoughtfully, Uncle Rafi combed back a wayward lock of blonde hair, his other hand hovering above the board.

Pappa tried again, "Our revered leader isn't feeling unnerved by Herr Hitler's Luftwaffe, is he?"

Uncle Rafi moved a pawn before sliding back in his seat. His long legs ensured the manoeuvre was more dignified than Pappa's awkward shuffle. Her uncle braced his elbows on the arms of his chair and steepled his fingers, tapping them against pursed lips, as if signalling his mouth to remain shut.

Pappa shifted forward again and peered at the board. "Or is it because, now that Herr Führer's reinstated conscription, he's threatening us with an army five times the size permitted by Versailles?"

Uncle Rafi countered abruptly, "You know perfectly well that we signed a non-aggression pact with Germany only last year."

"Ah yes, of course, Herr Goering's hunting trip. Well, I for one don't believe the wild boar he bagged is the only piece of Poland his boss is interested in."

"I believe it's your move," Uncle Rafi said, stonily.

For a few minutes, the only sounds were ruminative puffs from Pappa's cigar and a steady tock-tock from the timepiece on the cabinet. Luiza loved this clock, with its strangely distended, rectangular face forever separating an impossibly long and slim, half-clothed woman from a wolf-like dog. A squeak of leather signalled that Pappa had made his move.

"Of course," he continued caustically, "it can't be that we're preparing for serious injury from Comrade Stalin, because we've signed a pact with him, too."

Uncle Rafi's eyes were on the board, his lips tightly compressed. Pappa stubbed out his cigar and reached for Luiza's pad.

"You know, that's really very good, Lou-lou. I tell you," – he waved the sketch at his brother-in-law, – "I'd give you more for this than for either of those treaties with all their fine signatures."

"Don't be ridiculous," Uncle Rafi exploded, finally. "They're our security."

"No, *that's* ridiculous. Do you seriously believe that either of our neighbours will honour an independent Poland for a moment longer than it suits them, treaty or no treaty? The dear Marshal's under the illusion that Poland's still a Great Power – what a hopeless romantic he is."

Uncle Rafi's fingers drummed the arms of his chair. When he spoke, he sounded weary. "Hugo, you know how vulnerable we are. Poland's stuck in the middle. We need to be strong, but we also have to maintain good relations with our neighbours."

"But it's not only Poland's geographical position that's vulnerable," Pappa retorted. "Unemployment's at 40 per cent and the situation in the countryside is desperate. How does that make us strong? What's going to keep Herr Hitler's aeroplanes in their hangars with their tails between their legs? A cavalry charge?"

Uncle Rafi sprang to his feet, and Luiza thought he might haul Pappa up by the lapels. Instead, he executed a precise about-turn and marched to the cabinet, where he poured himself a shot of vodka, then another.

"The problem with your beloved Marshal," said Pappa, addressing his brother-in-law's back, "is that he's so concerned with what's happening beyond our borders that he can't see what's staring him in the face at home. Which of his treaties is going to save him from being attacked within his own borders? The unemployed aren't going back to the land as ignorant serfs. They've had experience of direct action in the factories. Piłsudski ignores them at his peril, mark my words. If he doesn't sort out the economy – and fast – the Peasants' Party will over-run him before the National Socialists or the Soviets get a chance."

"But we're not the only ones with economic problems," said Uncle Rafi, turning to face Pappa. "The whole world's in trouble. Even America."

"America's got its New Deal. But we don't even have to look across the Atlantic for ideas; we could do worse than copy Hitler's economic policy. Those new roads, and the trains all run on time – it's a pleasure doing business there these days. As soon as I'm across the border my blood pressure falls. Of course, it comes at a price. That zealous little man appears to have hypnotised the entire population. All they can do is raise their arms and shout 'Seig Heil!' They seem to have lost the capacity for independent thought. And the few that haven't simply disappear—"

"Are you going to respond to my bishop to rook six, or not?" Uncle Rafi interrupted, having resumed his seat. Pappa examined the chess board, dismayed to find his queen threatened.

"Since you're obviously not engaged with the game," Uncle Rafi continued, "why don't you concede defeat? You'll miss your train."

He reached to dismantle the board, but Pappa raised a hand.

"Defeat? Not likely. Checkmate."

Uncle Rafi stared in disbelief, then shook his head. "I never learn, do I?"

Catching Luiza's wary look, he laughed. "Your father uses highly questionable tactics to maintain his competitive edge, Lou-lou."

Pappa smiled briefly before stubbing out his cigar and continuing, "But seriously, Rafi…"

"No!" Uncle Rafi threw up his hands. "Get off now, Hugo, and catch your train. I've got an early start – back to Białystok first thing."

"Really? Poor Wanda scarcely sees you these days. Give her my love, by the way, and dear Kamila, too."

Uncle Rafi nodded. In the hall, Luiza embraced her father. Watching him walk down the path, it occurred to her that his coat seemed too big for him.

The following morning, Luiza drew back her curtains to see the cherry tree outside her bedroom, so recently weighed down with blossom, was brilliant again, this time with snow. She ran down to breakfast, buoyed with plans for sledging, but found her aunt pacing the dining room; her satin dressing gown billowed at each turn.

"Has Uncle Rafi already left for Białystok?"

"Białystok?" Aunt Wanda regarded her blankly.

"Yes, last night he said—"

"Uncle Rafi's at the Belvedere," interrupted Ida from the table. "He left a note."

She slid across a piece of paper: *The Marshal has been taken ill.*

When the telephone rang, Aunt Wanda rushed from the room, returning a few minutes later with tears streaming down her face.

"He's gone. The Marshal's left us."

It was a strange day. Luiza met Gosia for a walk in the snow, but it was already beginning to melt. They watched people greet each other in tears and disbelief; strangers embraced. Returning to the villa, Luiza took her sketchpad to the salon and switched on the wireless. But only martial music played, interrupted by a solemn announcer repeating the news that the Polish nation had lost its father.

The funeral was the following Saturday. Uncle Rafi was part of the guard of honour, but Aunt Wanda stayed home with Kamila. Ida, Luiza and their father stood among thousands in the rain on Krakowskie Przedmieście and watched Marshal Piłsudski's final journey through Warszawa. His coffin, draped in the red-and-white flag with its crowned eagle, proceeded on a gun carriage from St John's Cathedral to the railway station, from where it would continue south by train for burial with the kings in Kraków.

Luiza had never seen such crowds. They packed the wide pavements, and Pappa had to squeeze through, towing his daughters, until they reached the steps of the Church of the Holy Cross. From its raised porch there was a better view. Squashed between Ida and Pappa, Luiza glimpsed the white surplices of the priests who walked in single file on either side of the road. Between them marched the infantry, with the cavalry at its centre.

A wave rippled towards them as men removed their hats at the approach of the gun carriage, replacing them once it had passed. A cry of 'Attention!' made Luiza turn; behind them an old man snapped a salute as the coffin drew level. The empty sleeve of his worn jacket was neatly pinned. Luiza wondered how he had lost his arm and whether it still hurt. A row of medals weighed crookedly on his breast pocket, while tears coursed down his wrinkled cheeks. She became aware of sobbing all around her. Ida dabbed her eyes with a lace handkerchief, and even Pappa's were wet. Why, she wondered, when he was always so critical of the Marshal? She considered the man with the big moustache, whose black-ribboned photograph was everywhere, but she felt no urge to cry. If she had not wept for Mama, why would she for this stranger?

The evening was subdued. Uncle Rafi was not back, and Kamila was in bed. Unusually for a Saturday, Ida was at home; Warszawa's restaurants and entertainment venues were all closed as a mark of respect. It was long past Luiza's bedtime, but no one had pointed this out and she was certainly not about to. They were playing a half-hearted hand of rummy when the front door slammed.

Footsteps approached, clipping the parquet, and Uncle Rafi went straight to the cabinet. He seized a bottle of vodka and flung himself full length on the chaise longue, his spurs scoring the pale leather. Aunt Wanda winced but said nothing. Uncle Rafi gulped straight from the bottle, contrapuntal to the steady rhythm of the clock.

"What a goddamn mess," he muttered.

Pappa coughed and gathered up the cards. "It's late," he began, but Uncle Rafi continued regardless, his voice thick. This was clearly not his first bottle of the evening.

"Have to be off first thing – damned Belarusians. Can't let them destabilise things now."

Luiza noticed the skin around Aunt Wanda's nails turn white as her fingers pressed into the green baize. Pappa placed the cards in their wooden box and nodded to Ida, who took Luiza's hand.

They were about to say goodnight, when Aunt Wanda asked quietly, "I suppose you're going to Białystok?"

Uncle Rafi swung his feet to the floor. Without looking at his wife he sketched a shallow bow, then strode out, still gripping the bottle. Pappa gestured for the girls to leave.

Upstairs, Ida began a complicated routine involving various creams and lotions. Luiza, perched on the kilim-draped divan, which served as a spare bed when Ida had a friend to stay, flicked blindly through a magazine. Eventually she threw it down and inspected her nails, before starting to excavate them.

"Will you stop that! You can be really disgusting, you know, Lou-lou," admonished Ida, regarding her sister in the mirror through a mask of cold cream. Luiza sat on her hands and contemplated the red-and-green weave of the kilim, as if she might find there an explanation for the evening's events.

The lengthy business at the dressing table finally complete, Ida joined Luiza on the divan and sought her grubby hand with her own manicured fingers. Luiza was reassured by her touch. In a world that was again threatening change, one thing remained constant: Ida was still her sister. There would always be the two of them.

Chapter 15

May 1935, Saska Kępa

There was no sign of Uncle Rafi or Aunt Wanda when Luiza came down for breakfast on Sunday. But her father and sister were absorbed in a familiar debate.

"I am certain, though," Ida stated, peevishly. "I've known for ages, yet I've waited, as you asked. But I really don't see why I have to wait any longer."

It was an argument the pair had rehearsed many times. Ida, encouraged by Pani Anna, wished to convert to Catholicism. But Pappa, even though he frequently stated, "It's the same God, so we must follow the path that brings us closest to him", was steadfastly opposed.

"Yes, you have waited," he agreed now, spooning sugar into his coffee, "but I want you to wait a while longer. You need to be an adult before you take such an important step." As he stirred his coffee, Luiza was struck by how old he looked. His face was creased where once his cheeks were full. And his waistcoat hung slack – when had his paunch disappeared?

"But it's what I want to do. What I need to do." Ida was not giving up. "Pani Anna says—"

But Pappa interrupted, his voice firm, "For the time being, you're still a member of this family, and you're my responsibility." Spearing a slice of ham he continued, "I'm sure Pani Anna wants what's best for you, but so do I. And I don't think you're ready to make such a serious commitment yet. Wait just one more year."

"Or two or three! I'm nearly seventeen, and I leave school next month. When are you going to stop treating me like a child?" Ida demanded.

Pappa gave a tired smile. "Perhaps when you stop acting like one."

Luiza flinched, anticipating an explosion. But no doors slammed. She glanced at her sister. Ida's face was set as she cut a small corner from a white slab of *twarog* and, with meticulous care, transferred it to a slice of rye. Balancing a piece of tomato on top, she delicately conveyed all three to her mouth. Then, having drained her cup and dabbed her mouth with her napkin, she stood, wished them a stiff 'good morning' and closed the door quietly behind her.

Luiza peered up from her roll, which she was spreading with her favourite combination of *twarog* on honey. The sweetness of one was a delicious challenge to the tartness of the curd cheese. Searching Pappa's face, she noticed that his moustache and eyebrows had turned almost as white as his hair. He caught her eye and winked as he rose from the table. "I must be off; I've got a meeting."

"But it's Sunday."

"I know. No rest for the wicked." But Pappa's smile failed to make his eyes crinkle in the usual way. "I'm off to see Pan Abel, but I'll be back. Aunt Wanda's kindly putting me up again tonight, because I have to get to Świętokrzyska early tomorrow."

This was where Korski had their offices. And Pan Abel was on the Board, so why did Pappa need to see him today if there was a meeting tomorrow? Before she could ask, her father was gone.

He was away all day and Ida, who had gone to meet Pani Anna, and no doubt attend Mass, stayed out, too. Uncle Rafi must be on his way to Białystok, and Aunt Wanda was nowhere to be seen. It was another wet day, so Luiza played Ludo with Kamila. Her cousin wanted to hear all about the funeral and whether Luiza had spotted her father in the guard of honour.

"I do wish I could have seen him. Poor Pappa, he's very unhappy – he loved the Marshal so much."

Luiza would have liked to ask her cousin if it really was the Marshal's death that was upsetting her uncle. Last night was the first time in ages that she had seen her aunt and uncle in the same room. Surely Kamila had noticed how her mother blanched whenever Białystok was mentioned? Perhaps not, being ill and in her room so much. Should she tell her? But Luiza worried about how she might react. She thought of what Uncle Stefan had said to Pappa the Easter before Mama died. If only Uncle Rafi had someone to tell him that he should stay at home with his wife before it was too late.

On Monday morning spring returned. The snow and rain of the previous week were banished by warm sunshine. Pappa walked to the tram stop with Luiza.

"Uncle Rafi really loved the Marshal, didn't he?"

Pappa gave that tired smile again. "He did. Sadly, sometimes when you lose something that's dear to you, everything else that's important gets lost, too. There's always a danger, when you devote yourself to a single cause, that you fail to notice what's happening elsewhere."

Pappa squinted into the sun along Waszyngton Avenue. A red blur was drawing closer and taking on the definition of tram.

"It's so easy to put our all into what we *think* is central to our lives and not what really is."

He paused, stroking his moustache, before he added, "But sometimes we get the chance to set things straight before it's too late."

The tram had rattled to a stop, and they ascended the steep steps. Pappa found a seat near the back and Luiza stood beside him. With a shrill whine the tram took off again, rocking and swaying down the centre of the broad avenue towards the Poniatowski Bridge. The din made conversation difficult and Luiza, legs braced against the uneven pitch and roll, held on to the back of Pappa's seat as she struggled to make sense of his words. She thought again of that last Easter with Mama at Zakątek and of Pappa's hand on her shoulder. But this was swiftly overlaid by the disturbing image of Mama trying to hide the chocolate eclairs. If only she had told Pappa about her suspicions, could he have done something before it was too late?

The racket changed pitch as the tram crossed the bridge, the river diamond-glazed by the early morning sun.

With the Marshal gone, would Uncle Rafi realise that Aunt Wanda was the most important thing in his life? Or would he miss his chance because of Białystok?

They were nearing Luiza's stop on Nowy Świat. She dipped her head to kiss her father goodbye, but he signalled that he was coming, too. Together they waited for the tram to clatter off towards the Old Town before Pappa steered her across the street. Horse-drawn and motor-driven vehicles vied for space, and he hurried her through the gaps before they closed over again. Once they had turned off the main thoroughfare onto quieter Foksal, Luiza queried, "Won't you be late for your meeting?"

Pappa's hand was still on her shoulder. He squeezed it, nodding. "Perhaps I will. But you've reminded me, Lou-lou, how important it is to make time for the things that really matter."

Straightening the white beret that was part of her summer uniform, he planted a whiskery kiss on either cheek. "Goodbye, dearest. I think you and Ida should come home more at weekends – your aunt's got enough on her plate, and we shouldn't impose."

"But will you be there, Pappa?"

Her father, frowning, looked into the distance. "Oh yes, I'll be there. I've been away too much, it seems."

With a visible effort he drew his attention back to the present, carrying on with a wink, "And then we can both keep an eye on that sister of yours and make sure that she doesn't run off to a convent."

Luiza, giggling at the improbable image of Ida in a nun's habit, watched Pappa retrace his steps along Foksal. Once he had rounded the corner, she turned and was immediately caught up in the white-capped, green wave that surged towards the school entrance.

Chapter 16

May 1935, Zakątek

*I*da was not at all happy about going home that weekend, but Pappa was adamant. Once they were there, she recovered her spirits. Perhaps she was as relieved as Luiza to be away from the villa with its strained atmosphere. Aunt Wanda rarely emerged from her room; when she did, her satin dressing gown was stained and her hair unwashed. Kamila was clearly distressed by her mother's withdrawal and repeatedly asked her cousins about the funeral and her father's role. It was as if she was searching their account for the key to what was going on.

Ida suggested that they visit Zapole with supplies, as Mama used to do. Luiza suspected that her sister's display of charity was mainly aimed at convincing Pappa that she was sufficiently mature to become a Catholic, but she was still delighted. She had not been to the village for ages.

Pani Cholowa welcomed the girls warmly. "Just look

at you, Pani Ida, the picture of your dear mother. Oh, how we miss her."

Luiza felt a pang of guilt as she accepted the kefir and black bread Pani Cholowa offered. She was acutely aware of the earth floor and the sparsity of furniture in the dark cottage. When she was younger, she had not recognised how different this small, dim space was from the salon at Zakątek, but now she could hear Mama's voice in her head: "They have so little, and yet they insist on sharing. We cannot offend their hospitality, but we must not exploit it."

She politely refused a second helping, and they left to visit Marte. Their one-time nanny now had four little ones of her own. The baby Luiza remembered was a sturdy boy of seven, with his father's shock of blonde curls and his mother's high cheek bones. Wide blue eyes stared curiously from the doorway, until he ran off to play with the other barefoot children. Marte wanted to hear all about life in Warszawa; the capital was only thirty kilometres away, but it might as well have been across the ocean as far as the villagers were concerned.

"Is it true that women wear trousers?" she asked, blushing.

When Ida replied that she had seen this in American movies, Marte made the sign of the cross. Luiza told her about the chimpanzee that hung round the neck of the maître d' at the Café Adria, but Marte shook her head, refusing to believe something so outlandish. Olga, who used to help in the kitchen at Zakątek in the days when guests were frequent, had joined them and her eyes and mouth described perfect circles as she listened.

"But what about Pani Aurelia?" she asked, when Marte's giggles over the chimp had subsided.

"*What* about Pani Aurelia?" asked Ida, sharply.

"Well," Olga looked uncomfortable, "it's just…" She hesitated, then plunged on. "Anjela says she's always making eyes at Pan Direktor and he'll find himself married to her before long."

"And," Marte continued, "Stefan says Pan Graban's changing everything at the mill and pushing Pan Direktor out."

Ida protested mildly, suggesting a misunderstanding, but she had turned very pale. Before long, she thanked the women for their hospitality and stood to leave. Luiza followed, echoing thanks and goodbyes.

Janek had driven them to the village, but they had told him not to wait. Leaving the dusty lane, they cut through the mill yard, silent this late on a Saturday, and on past the silver birches to the lake. Ida sat on the bench and unpinned her hat. Her silk-sheathed legs were neatly parallel and her gloved hands in her lap. Luiza flung herself down on the grass and inhaled deeply, happily sniffing the damp earth. Rolling onto her back, she gazed up through a lattice of foliage, watching flashes of blue change size and shape as the boughs that framed them swayed in the soft breeze. After a while, she sat up and began threading a daisy chain, glancing at her sister from time to time, waiting for her to make sense of what they had just heard.

Ida had regained her colour as they walked, but her mouth was set, and vertical lines creased the smooth skin above her nose. Eventually, she shook her head and breathed deeply, as if something had been resolved. Then she pronounced, "So, we have to watch out for Pappa on two fronts: the Witch and the Slug. Regarding the first, we need to get him to spend more time with Pani Anna."

"I think he's a bit annoyed with her," Luiza ventured.

"Annoyed? Why?" Ida looked surprised.

"Well, she's been pushing so hard for you to become a Catholic."

"Hmmm." She furrowed her brow again. "Perhaps we should pull back on my conversion for a bit, just until Pappa remembers how much he really likes her. Pani Anna's invited me to Malinów once term's over. If you came, too, then he'd have to visit; otherwise, he wouldn't see us all summer."

Luiza's initial joy at the prospect of being reunited with Nutmeg was short-lived. "But if Pappa's there with us, then what about Graban? Pappa needs to be at the mill if he's to keep an eye on the Slug."

"Yes, you're right," Ida mused. "There *has* to be a way to get that odious man to slither away for good."

"Remember I told you about the time Pappa was so cross with him for not fulfilling the Goldfarb order? Well, Lotte Goldfarb is in my class, and she won't speak to me now. Gosia says it's because there was such a delay that Goldfarb almost went out of business."

"I'm sure the delay didn't help, but I think Goldfarb's probably struggling like a lot of Jewish businesses at the moment."

"But then surely that makes it even worse. Pappa

would hate for Zakątek to add to their problems. How could he have let it happen?"

Ida shrugged. "I'm sure Pappa had no idea this was how it would turn out when he sold the business to Korski. It was fine while Pan Trawnik was manager – he and Pappa got on well. Graban only replaced him after Lemski became chairman of the Board, didn't he? I don't think Pappa rates Lemski, and presumably he appointed Graban."

Luiza was taken aback. Ida gave the impression of complete indifference to mill business, yet she had identified this connection. It seemed obvious now, but it had completely escaped Luiza, even though she was the daughter who planned to run Zakątek.

"And I bet Lemski's behind Pan Abel leaving the board, too," Ida mused.

Luiza gaped at her. "Pan Abel – what do you mean?"

"Oh, Rilke at school is his niece, and she mentioned that he's probably leaving Korski. But I didn't get the impression it was by choice."

Luiza recalled the previous Sunday, "Pappa visited Pan Abel. Then the next day he had a meeting at the Korski offices, and he seemed, I don't know, thoughtful – a bit sad. Do you think he was worried about Pan Abel? I wish I'd asked him what was wrong. But all I could think of was Uncle Rafi after the Marshal's funeral. What was that about, Idka?"

Ida sighed. "Oh, Lou-lou – who knows what goes on with men? Uncle Rafi drank too much so as to drown his grief over the Marshal. When he's back from Białystok everything will go back to normal again, you'll see. As for asking Pappa what was wrong, honestly, when has he ever talked to us about his problems?"

She picked up her hat and straightened the ribbon. Turning it in her hands, she gazed beyond the lake to Pan Rubacz's land. Splashes of scarlet signalled poppies clustered among the rye, which was on the point of turning from green to gold.

"Lemski couldn't get rid of Pan Abel on his own," Ida speculated. "I wonder who the other anti-Semites on the Board are."

Just then Mono arrived, trotting purposefully across the lawn. Snuffling appreciatively at Luiza, the spaniel burrowed into her lap while Luiza buried her fingers in the silky coat.

"But we're still not getting anywhere with the Slug problem," Ida continued briskly, straightening her skirt. "We'll just have to keep thinking. Come on, let's get back."

She pulled Luiza to her feet. Mono loped ahead as they walked up the slope towards the house, Ida smoothly poised, Luiza wrinkled and grass-stained.

On Sunday afternoon, Pappa treated them to ice cream in Grodzisk Mazowiecki before they caught the Warszawa train. Seated on a worn velvet banquette in an alcove at Marynka's, they waited for their order to arrive. Their imminent return to the troubled villa was weighing on Luiza, and Pappa and Ida both seemed lost in their own thoughts. Eventually Ida broke the silence.

"Pappa, we've been... I've been... wondering – is

everything alright? This Pan Graban, he doesn't seem... well, is the mill... are you...?" Her voice trailed off.

Gently, Pappa removed the spoon she was gripping and covered her hands with his own. Even now, when he complained of being office-bound, the creases on his stubby fingers were still etched with machine oil.

"Listen, you're not to worry, do you hear?" He looked from Ida to Luiza. "In business there are always ups and downs, but I'm taking care of things. There's absolutely nothing for you two to concern yourselves with. Understood?"

The girls nodded and the timely arrival of their sundaes was a welcome distraction.

Chapter 17

Summer 1935, Saska Kępa

*I*da's prediction that things would return to normal in Saska Kępa was proved wrong. Although Aunt Wanda was up and dressed again, she was vaguer than ever and barely acknowledged her nieces. Kamila seemed even more frail, and there was no sign at all of Uncle Rafi.

As planned, Ida invited Pappa along on several outings with Pani Anna, but he was never available, and Ida was soon caught up in a flurry of end-of-term social events. These kept her in Warszawa, while Luiza spent most weekends at Zakątek, with no escape from her worries about Pappa. When he was not at the mill he was locked in his study, frequently with Pani Aurelia. The pair only emerged at mealtimes, continuing to pore over dense columns even at the table.

At least Pani Aurelia had no time to bother Luiza, but

this was small compensation. Everything she loved about Zakątek, everything that made it home, had vanished: Pappa's grin and his bear hugs, Pani Marysia's welcoming kitchen, Nutmeg, too. Even Mono had changed. No longer a mischievous puppy, she had her own, independent agenda.

At least Luiza got to ride Gem, a retired plough horse belonging to Pan Rubacz. He was such a long-term favourite that he had been granted a final summer among the bees and wildflowers in one of the farmer's water meadows, before winter feed costs sent him to the glue factory. Luiza straddled him bareback, and the two of them ambled along the stream and up the willow banks.

By late June, when Uncle Rafi finally returned from Białystok, Aunt Wanda had already taken Kamila to her mother's in Wilno for the summer and soon Ida would leave for Malinów with Pani Anna. Luiza would have loved to join them, but she knew that Pappa would not leave Zakątek, and she would not leave him.

"He'll be fine, Lou-lou, you really should come. What on earth will you do there all summer?"

They were in Ida's room at the villa while Ida prepared for an evening out. "Pappa told us he has things under control, remember? There's nothing you can do. And he'll never visit Pani Anna unless you're at Malinów, too."

"He won't come anyway. You haven't been home for ages, so you haven't seen how hard he's working. He never lets up. And he's got so thin!"

"Well, surely that's to the good? The doctor's been on at him to lose weight for ages."

Ida's words were not easy to decipher through the tissue with which she blotted vermilion lips.

"He's looking really tired – and old," Luiza worried, spiralling a lipstick in its gold tube, until Ida placed it in her sequinned bag. Smoothing silver-grey silk crepe over slender hips, she checked in the mirror for wrinkles and exclaimed, "For goodness' sake, Lou-lou, he is old. He's nearly sixty!"

"He's fifty-five," Luiza interjected.

"Nearly sixty," repeated Ida with emphasis. "Of course, he's tired. As he said, there are ups and downs in business, and this is one of the downs. It'll be fine, though – you know how clever he is. But we really should get him to Malinów." She smirked, "He might benefit from Pani Anna's all-over sun cure."

"What do you mean?" asked Luiza, curiosity supplanting anxiety for a moment.

"Pani Anna sunbathes in the nude!"

"No!" Luiza was scandalised.

"And she's invited me to."

"Ida, you haven't!"

"Not yet, but I plan to. She says the sun is healing and we should let it reach every part of our body. Her bedroom window opens onto a flat roof, so she can sunbathe without being overlooked. I'm sure it would do Pappa good."

The sisters giggled at the thought of their father, whom they had rarely seen even in a bathing costume, stripped to the altogether in Pani Anna's company.

"That should get the romance going!" Ida was laughing

so hard that she toppled backwards onto the bed, and Luiza, gasping for air, fell on top of her. Eventually they calmed down and Ida returned to the mirror, exclaiming, "Oh no, my mascara's run. Blast, I'll be late."

Brooding again, Luiza played with a glass stopper and asked, "But what about the Slug?"

Ida replaced the stopper in a bottle of scent. "Pappa will squash that creepy Graban in the end. And if not, if he doesn't like the way Lemski's running things, well, Pappa doesn't have to stay."

Luiza stared at her sister. "What do you mean? Leave Zakątek?"

The blast of a car horn sent Ida rushing to the window, one end of a cerise chiffon stole floating behind her.

"It's Jerzy, I have to go."

At the door she paused, "Really, Lou-lou, don't worry. It'll be alright, you'll see."

She blew a kiss, sending it on its way with a flourish of crimson nails, and was gone.

Luiza remained at the dressing table, her fingers absently exploring the various bottles and jars. Picking up a discarded lipstick, she exposed the waxy pink nub and drew it across her lips, watching her reflection in the mirror as she pouted and grimaced, then blew herself a kiss. With a sudden shiver of distaste, she scrubbed at her mouth with the back of her hand.

At the top of the stairs she paused, listening for Uncle Rafi. All was quiet. With a sigh, Luiza walked slowly to her own room and opened the window. Snatches of laughter and conversation drifted from the suburban street to accentuate her loneliness. The comfort of family life that she had embraced so hungrily when they moved here had vanished. She lay on her bed. Tears leaked from her eyes and pooled in her ears. The prospect of summer at Zakątek offered no solace. Yet worse, far worse, was the possibility of losing Zakątek altogether.

Luiza turned on her side and drew her knees to her chest. She regarded the scarred face of the Black Madonna on the small wooden icon at her bedside. A present from Pani Anna, Luiza had grown to prefer this dark, mysterious representation of the divine Mother to the sweetly bland, pink-and-blue plaster figures she had turned to after Mama's death. The sad eyes returned her gaze and, slowly, Luiza grew calm. Eventually she slept. Her dream transported her to Zakątek, the sound of Mama's piano playing wafting from the salon to Luiza in her bed. The music stopped; her bedroom door opened. Luiza held her breath as her mother brushed her lips across Luiza's cheek and whispered, 'sleep tight, Lou-lou'.

Once the holidays began, Gem was Luiza's only consolation until Commissioner Petrowski's granddaughter, Bożena, arrived. In the light of Pappa's stern injunction, Luiza worried about bumping into Wojtek, but when Bożena said that her uncle was on a driving holiday in Italy, there was nothing to stop her visiting the stables. Aurora offered a velvet nose for stroking, while Prince simply rolled his eyes. Luiza and Bożena played tennis or dressed up in her mother's clothes and make up. But the dark shadow louring over Zakątek did not lift, and Bożena was not

Agnieszka or Gosia. Luiza missed the Musketeers and all they got up to in Warszawa. And she missed Ida.

A chill in the air was already presaging autumn, when Pani Aurelia failed to appear in the dining room one evening. Pappa was scanning a document and Luiza had to ask him twice if they should wait for his secretary before Anjela, who was fidgeting with the tureen, served the soup.

"What? Oh, no. She won't be joining us," he said, without raising his eyes from the paper. Anjela ladled out mushroom soup, which Luiza ate despondently. Even the food at Zakątek had lost its appeal. Vacek had not lasted long. Pappa entertained so rarely that the chef had soon left for somewhere his skills were more widely appreciated. So now, while Anjela looked after the basics, Pani Ewa came in daily from Grodzisk Mazowiecki. She cut an eccentric figure on a large black bicycle, her hat secured against the wind by one colourful scarf, with another worn bandanna-style against the dust. But Pani Ewa's menus failed to live up to the vivid promise of her appearance. Her dishes were unimaginative and lacked flavour. Pappa seemed not to notice, but Luiza mourned another of the former pleasures of home.

Pani Aurelia's absence failed to lift the mood in the house. Pappa was still preoccupied. When Ida blew in like a whirlwind for the final week of the holiday, Pani Anna having cleared Malinów of guests as her daughter-in-law's confinement drew near, he nodded vaguely at her stories of tennis parties and dinner dances, while Luiza hung on every word. Ida would turn seventeen this month. Her hectic, end-of-term party schedule had been in celebration of leaving school, but now Pappa was insisting that she go back for a final year. Luiza anticipated resistance, yet Ida appeared resigned to her fate.

They were in Luiza's room, her sister helping her pack for their return to Warszawa, when Ida asked, "So, what have you done with the Witch, Lou-lou?" Luiza was dredging her chest of drawers for warm underwear and woollen stockings, discarded there since spring. "I didn't do anything. She just didn't show up at supper one evening."

"Hmmm…" Ida was measuring a navy-blue dress against Luiza. "I don't think this can be considered decent – you've really shot up. We'll have to arrange a visit to the dressmaker."

Dropping the dress on the floor, she took another from its hanger. "And I'll be coming with you. Enough of these sailor dresses – you're thirteen, not eight."

Luiza shrugged. "But it makes no sense. Why would she just stop coming to the house? She was never out of it before. She can't be ill, because she's still at the mill every day."

The following afternoon, Luiza was throwing a ball for Mono when Ida appeared. She led them to the bench by the lake, where the September sun threw its golden light beyond the water, burnishing Pan Rubacz's ploughed fields all the way to the horizon.

"Well, that's the mystery solved." Ida grinned triumphantly.

"What do you mean, what mystery?"

"The Witch's disappearance. *That* mystery – remember?"

"Oh – how did you solve it?"

Ida tapped the side of her nose. "Who knows everything that goes on here? Who is the oracle of Zakątek?"

"The oracle? What do you mean?"

"Oh, for goodness' sake, I asked Anjela! I can't believe you didn't think to ask her yourself. She was positively bursting to tell the story."

"What story?"

"Well…" Ida paused, tantalisingly. Then, in a close approximation of Anjela's husky voice and local accent, with an eager expression that was remarkably like the maid's when she had gossip to impart, she began.

"That afternoon I was dusting in the salon when I heard Pan Direktor shouting in his study. I knew it was just him and Pani Aurelia in there – he didn't have visitors. So, I went into the corridor, just to make sure everything was alright." Ida lowered her voice, conspiratorially, "And I was just in time to see Pani Aurelia flying out of the study. She ran out in such a state – her face all flushed, no jacket, hands clutching her blouse together."

Shocked at the ostensible reason for Pani Aurelia's disarray, Luiza searched her sister's face for reassurance. Ida, maintaining Anjela's delivery, smiled and patted Luiza's hand reassuringly.

"Oh no, don't you worry, no, no, not Pan Direktor – he would never! No, it was all that Witch's fault."

Luiza found her voice. "What do you mean, Idka? What did Pani Aurelia do?"

Ida was clearly enjoying herself. "She must've thrown herself at him, mustn't she? What I heard – the shout from the study – that was Pan Direktor saying: 'Good God, woman, what are you doing?' And then" – Ida paused, dramatically – "there was the note."

"What note?" Luiza still felt weak.

"The one Pan Direktor asked me to take to Pani Aurelia, along with her jacket. Of course, if it'd been sealed, I would never have read it. Never!"

Ida folded her arms and paused, assuming an expression of utmost probity, before rushing on in eager justification, "But it was only folded. That was deliberate, wasn't it? Pan Direktor must have wanted the truth to be known."

"But what did it say?" Luiza whispered, fearful of complicity with such questionable ethics, yet desperate for confirmation of a palatable truth.

"It said…" Ida paused for effect. "It said: 'I sincerely regret the misunderstanding earlier today, and, in particular, anything in my conduct which may have given rise to it. As far as I am concerned, this unfortunate incident never happened, and tomorrow I shall expect you at your desk at the usual time. From hereon we shall only work together at the mill.'"

Chapter 18

December 1935, Warszawa

That autumn, Luiza and Ida mostly stayed in town, and Pappa visited whenever he had business in Warszawa. On these occasions, they always tried to include Pani Anna. Pappa was still thin, but he seemed slightly less preoccupied. Ida was convinced that the debacle with Pani Aurelia had shaken him into an awareness of Pani Anna's appeal. The old twinkle could be seen in his eye, and most of the time, he actually listened to what you were saying. So, Luiza found herself worrying less. She became absorbed in her Warszawa life. With winter approaching, she was particularly looking forward to skating again.

The University of Warszawa was on Krakowskie Przedmieście, the broad and stately continuation of bustling Nowy Świat. The Musketeers would pass the entrance on their way to Old Town cafés after school.

Usually they caught the tram, but this afternoon large flakes were flurrying from a steely sky as the first snow of winter muffled Nowy Świat's bustling commercial pageant. Even the clanging trams were hushed by the snow, seeming to glide over the deepening white carpet. The novelty of the blanketed spectacle was such that the girls decided to walk.

For a while they threw snowballs, pausing only to catch tumbling flakes on their tongues. But soon their green coats and velour hats were rimed in white and woollen gloves were frozen, so they trudged on, hands thrust deep in pockets and heads bowed.

Luiza sensed the rhythm of the chanting before the meaning of the words punched through. A crowd shouting "Jews out!" blocked the wide pavement outside the university. Their smudged placards provided more detail: 'Stamp Out the Jewish Conspiracy', 'Beware the Enemy Within' and 'Stop Jews Corrupting Polish Youth'.

The demonstrators were mainly young men. Some were scruffily dressed but most wore smart, military-style jackets with a green-and-white badge on the sleeve. Pedestrians were forced to the kerb, where a line of policemen, keeping the road clear for traffic, barred their way. Turning back, the girls were trying to thread between the agitators when a shout went up. The mob surged towards the gates, jostling Luiza away from her friends. When the tide ebbed, she found herself deposited at the university entrance. She could see a small group of students approaching from inside, the men flanking the women protectively. All were staring ahead as they made for the open gate, yet Luiza sensed that their impassive expressions masked raw fear.

The demonstrators grew quiet. The snow and the fading light lent an unreal quality to the scene, and Luiza, trapped between the two factions, felt as if she were watching a film. As the small column came through the entrance, one of them lunged at an offending placard and threw it to the ground. He wore a long, red scarf and the scant beginnings of a beard. With a howl of animal rage, the crowd surged again, propelling Luiza forward. The students closed together. They had no hope of retreat, for the gatekeeper had swung the tall gate shut behind them. A boiling wave broke over the huddled band, and Luiza was pressed against the elaborate ironwork.

"Sweet Jesus, how did you get there? Quick, in here, child!"

The gate opened a crack and Luiza was pulled through before the barrier clanged shut again. The uniformed gatekeeper rammed the iron bar home.

The crowd had torn the small knot of students apart. In the snow-lit gloom, fragmented by the gate's ornate scrolling, Luiza watched clusters merge and separate. Arms were raised and briefly silhouetted, before falling back to fuse with shapes huddled on the ground. Legs, clearly outlined for a moment, melded, with each kick, into forms slumped on the pavement.

A figure materialised and seized an iron leaf to pull himself upright. It was the boy who had snatched the placard. His scarf was gone, his lip swollen. Blood poured from a cut above his eye. Slumped on the other side of the gate, his dark eyes were level with Luiza's. She screamed at the gatekeeper, "Let him in! Open the gate!"

But the bull-necked little man in his over-sized greatcoat did not hear. His eyes were fixed on the student draped on his gate, and his face was distorted with loathing. The boy's head suddenly jerked back, to be thrown against the iron curlicues with a sickening crack. Luiza turned and slid down the gate, wrapping her arms around her legs and burying her face in her knees.

After an eternity, the cries and thuds behind her subsided. When the gatekeeper pulled her to her feet, the naked hatred was gone, his round face showed only concern. "Are you alright, miss?" he asked. "Mother of God, you had a close shave – I hate to think what might have happened if I hadn't got you in here."

"Why…?"

"What's that, child?" The man cocked his head attentively.

Luiza rallied her voice, "Why didn't you let him in?"

"Who? Oh, you mean the Jew-boy? Got what was coming to him, though, didn't he?" He chuckled. "Teach him to come strutting through here like he owns the place. Think they're so high and mighty – Christ killers, the lot of them."

"Lou-lou! *Lou*-lou! Are you alright?" Gosia and Agnieszka were on the other side of the gate. "Thank goodness we found you."

"If you're this little lady's friends, you'd better take her home."

The gatekeeper removed the bar and gently pushed

Luiza towards them. She shrank from his touch, her teeth chattering, while Gosia and Agnieszka gabbled on excitedly. "Did you see what happened? We got shoved to the outside, and all those policemen were in the way. Oh, look, isn't that blood?"

Gosia pointed to a patch of churned snow that showed dark beneath a streetlamp. Luiza turned away. A tram was stopped on the other side of the road. She ran across and pushed her way on board, leaving her friends gaping in bafflement.

The tram took off, and Luiza, swaying amid the steaming press of overcoats, felt utterly alone. Her fellow passengers were intent on the comforts of home, oblivious to what she had witnessed. And soon the falling snow would cover the blood and wipe out the horror and they would never know. But she knew – how would she ever forget? Tears came. She wanted the sanctuary of home, too. To be at Zakątek with Mono, with Pappa, with Ida – and with Mama.

Chapter 19

December 1935, Saska Kępa

The next day was Saturday, and Pappa was waiting for her when she came out of morning school. Salt and shovels had done their work overnight, and on Nowy Świat the traffic ran over slush, between blackened mounds. They walked south, in the opposite direction from last night, and caught a tram to Marszalkowska, then made for the porticoed entrance to the Hotel Mazowiecki on Nowogrodzka. A uniformed doorman swept them in and they climbed the broad, curved staircase to Pani Anna's private apartment on the mezzanine floor.

Ida, who no longer had lessons on Saturday, was trying on hats. Pani Anna's milliner had delivered a selection, and the floor was littered with hat boxes. Turning from the mirror to greet them, her sea-green eyes sparkled beneath an arctic fox cloche.

"Pani Anna's with the chef – she'll be back soon. What do you think of this? Isn't it gorgeous?"

"Fabulous," agreed Pappa. "As I'm sure is the price."

"How about this, then?" she queried, pouting behind black net that poured from a satin pillbox.

"Very sophisticated but, perhaps, a little old for you, my dear?"

"Oh, honestly, Pappa, I'm seventeen—"

"Just," interrupted her father.

"…as good as eighteen, so when will you realise I'm not a little girl anymore? I suppose you'd be happier with me in this?" She jammed on a hat with a brim, very like the school velour Luiza had just removed.

Pappa smiled. Ida plucked a long feather from a pile of trimmings and tucked it into the hat band. Having achieved the desired angle, she tilted the hat provocatively over one eye. Laughing, Pappa picked up the newspaper and Ida returned to the mirror.

Luiza drifted about the cluttered room. Amid the ruby velvet drapes she felt cocooned against the unpredictability of the outside world. Familiar objects were reflected and multiplied in the abundance of polished mahogany. Pani Anna's husband, dead before Luiza was born, looked out sternly from a silver frame. One hand rested proprietorially on the shoulder of his young bride, who gazed at him adoringly. Her face was smooth and her body slight, the familiar plumpness and wrinkles swallowed by the retreating years.

Most of the photographs featured Waldemar. A small boy, face solemn, unruly hair severely slicked down.

Older, in tennis whites, running a hand through curls. Solemn again, with Grażyna on his arm, and here on Mitzi, his beloved black mare. Luiza was tracing the arch of the horse's neck with her finger when Pappa exclaimed, "Dear God! What have we come to? Students beaten up – for heaven's sake, there were women there. That wretched ONR – they're nothing but fascists. It's an illegal organisation, so why didn't the police put a stop to it?"

Ida, still appraising herself in the mirror, enquired laconically, "What's the problem, Pappa?"

Slapping the newspaper with the back of his hand, he continued, sharply, "Perhaps if you spent less time trying on hats, you might be aware that anti-Semites are attacking Warszawa's students. God save us, it's spreading from Germany."

"As a matter of fact, I did read about that demonstration, and I suppose we are still allowed free speech? I thought you detested dictatorships that imprison people for their beliefs – that's what you're always telling Uncle Rafi."

"Of course, everyone has the right to demonstrate, but not violently." Pappa tapped his paper again. "If all they were doing was demonstrating, how is it there was blood on the snow?"

"The account I read said that it was a Jewish student who started the trouble," said Ida, removing a velvet cloche and smoothing her hair.

Pappa turned the page, shaking his head. "What hope for our Jewish friends? Criticised for being gutless cowards if they do nothing and accused of fomenting violence if they stand up for themselves."

"It *was* a Jewish student who struck first, but he only broke a placard. He didn't hurt anyone." Luiza turned back to the photographs to hide her agitation.

Pausing in her deliberations, Ida viewed her sister's reflection in the mirror. "And how do you know, Lou-lou?"

"I was there. I saw it – saw him."

"What are you saying, Luiza?" enquired Pappa, fixing her with a penetrating look as he folded his paper and placed it on the table at his side. Luiza, her legs suddenly weak, sank onto the nearest chair.

"We – Gosia and Agnieszka and me – we were walking to the Old Town for hot chocolate after school. We tried to get past the demonstration, but I got separated from the others, and then the Jewish students came out. They looked so frightened, but one of them grabbed one of the horrible banners and then the crowd… they started to…"

"Were you hurt?" asked Pappa.

Luiza shook her head. "No, the gatekeeper pulled me inside. But it was horrible." Tears put a stop to words, but not to the pictures inside her head: the dark, shifting shapes in the half-light, the boy's dark eyes, the churned and stained snow.

Pappa regarded her with concern.

"The gatekeeper helped *me*, but why didn't he open the gate for the student? Oh, Pappa, he was bleeding, but the gatekeeper just watched. And he said such horrible things. Why wouldn't he help him?"

Pappa sighed while Ida, her forehead creased, declared, "Oh, come on, Lou-lou, you know why. It's because the student was Jewish, and that ignorant peasant believes all the Jewish conspiracy rubbish he's peddled."

Luiza sniffed, wiping her nose with the back of her hand.

"Ugh, use this," said Ida, holding out a small, laced-edged square.

"What in heavens use is that?" Pappa exclaimed, waving a large handkerchief. Luiza slid from her chair to perch on the arm of his, and her father held the cloth for her to blow her nose. Just like when she was little. Then he took her hand in his.

"Lou-lou, your sister's right. People always a need a scapegoat. The gatekeeper wants any hardship in his life to be someone else's fault, and Jews have always borne the brunt of bigotry. You'll hear lots of lies, but when you do, just think of the Abels, the Kleinmans – our friends."

Luiza nodded slowly. "I know, Pappa, but I still don't understand why people tell those lies."

"Oh, Lou-lou!" Ida sounded exasperated. "There's no rational explanation, so stop looking for one. They tell them because they're stupid!"

"Well, my dear, there you have it." Pappa smiled, nudging Luiza. "A dialectic on antisemitism, as delivered by Ida Wolfer." Luiza, her breathing still fitful in the aftermath of tears, managed a faint smile.

A rustle of tissue paper preceded Ida's next proclamation. "Oh, this has to be the one – don't you think?" She had on a crimson felt hat with a fan of black net at the back. "Or no, perhaps this really is more me," she reconsidered, putting on the original fur cloche instead.

"Oh, I can't decide! What do *you* think?" She viewed them expectantly.

"The red," said Pappa, as Luiza asserted, "The fur."

Ida giggled. "Well, I suppose I'll have to take both, then. And now, let's choose one for Lou-lou. How about this?" She was holding a Tyrolean-style hat with a feather on the side. "Come here, let's see what it looks like on."

Encouraged by a gentle push from Pappa, Luiza was surprised to see how the hat changed her face. She looked older, prettier.

"My, doesn't that look lovely," crooned Pani Anna from the door. Pappa rose to greet her, bringing her proffered fingers to his lips. Pani Anna clasped his hand affectionately and declared, "It's good to see you, Hugo. And such perfect timing! You can't deny how lovely your daughters look in these hats."

Pappa laughed. "Yes, perfect timing to bankrupt me."

Pani Anna winked at Ida, her kind face creased into a jolly smile. Then her eyes rested on Luiza, who was still exploring her changed image in the mirror, and the smile faded. "But what's this? Lou-lou, have you been crying?"

Luiza tore herself away from her reflection to drop a polite curtsy, but Pani Anna tilted her chin with a forefinger and searched her face.

"Poor Lou-lou got caught up in the demonstration at the university yesterday and saw things she shouldn't have," Pappa explained.

"Oh, how dreadful. My poor, dear girl." Pani Anna's hazel eyes had a way of melting with compassion, and Luiza stifled an urge to burrow into her arms. Instead, muttering "I'm alright", she turned back to the mirror, where she caught Pani Anna exchanging a meaningful glance with Pappa, before announcing brightly, "Well, I don't know about you, but I'm starving. Meetings about menus always make me hungry. How about dinner? And then, that film?"

Chapter 20

December 1935, Saska Kępa

The next morning a fresh fall of snow cloaked the garden. Under Kamila's supervision (her cousin mimed directions through the salon window), Luiza built a lopsided snowman. Later, when a staff car arrived to take Uncle Rafi to a meeting at the Belvedere, Luiza and Pappa begged a lift to Łazienki Park.

Their breath clouded the sharp air as they crunched over the hilly paths, the trees dazzlingly white against a cloudless sky. Luiza, elated by the clarity of the day, chattered enthusiastically about school and new clothes and plans for Christmas. Pani Anna had suggested the three Wolfers come to Malinów.

"But I'm not sure," Luiza mused, jumping from the path to plant both feet in a temptingly pristine expanse of snow. Its depth came as a surprise, over-topping her boots. She giggled as she tried to regain the path, reaching for

Pappa's outstretched arm for support. Back on the path, she concluded, "I think I'd miss Christmas at home too much."

The only Christmas they had not spent at Zakątek was the one after Mama died. *Yet it might do Pappa good to be away from the mill*, she thought. Although, bundled up in his winter coat, his weight loss was not so evident, and he seemed happy. She followed his gaze across the lake, where the Łazienki Palace, framed by snow-hung trees, had been transformed into a scene from a fairy tale. The statues on the roof and atop the colonnades to either side were clad in white, the balustrades and balconies frosted. Rosy darts from the westward-dipping sun set the silvered tableau a-shimmer with jewelled lights.

"It's like magic," breathed Luiza.

It was Pappa who eventually broke their spell-bound silence. "We'll freeze to death if we don't get moving," he said, and Luiza realised that she could not feel her feet. "Let's warm up," he exhorted, setting off up the path at a trot as Luiza, laughing, sped past him.

They took a taxi to Blikle, where Uncle Rafi met them. The men ordered brandy while Luiza chose a doughnut and hot chocolate.

"Why haven't you put a stop to these demonstrations, Rafi? It's getting as bad as Germany."

"Don't be ridiculous," replied Uncle Rafi, glancing up from his pipe while continuing to tamp down the tobacco. "There's no comparison. Germany has antisemitic laws. All we have is a few protests. Anyway, I thought you were all for tolerating different opinions?" he commented, striking a match.

"What about the Jewish opinion? And you don't need laws to sanction discrimination; simply create a suitable climate through inaction and you've legitimised brutality."

Absently, Pappa picked up a spoon and scraped the final portion of jammy dough from Luiza's plate. As she watched in dismay, Uncle Rafi chuckled, pointing the pipe he had been trying to suck into life at her empty plate. "Such high-minded talk, Hugo, and yet you steal the last morsel from your own child's plate."

Pappa threw Luiza an apologetic look and rang the spoon against his glass until a waiter appeared. Luiza was soon in possession of a second doughnut, while Pappa prepared a cigar and Uncle Rafi, sipping brandy, queried, "Hugo, you know it's the fact that Jews are over-represented in commerce that lies at the heart of this dilemma? Poles should be running Polish businesses – surely you can see that?"

Pappa groaned. "I've made this point countless times before, but our Jewish citizens *are* Poles."

"Then they should assimilate better; if they want to be considered Poles, they should live as Poles."

Pappa, making a visible effort to refrain from escalating the argument, stroked his moustache before commenting, "I saw Isaak Abel the other day. You know he's off the board at Korski? Well, he's talking about joining his brother in America – says he can only see things getting worse here. You heard about the demonstration at the university?"

Luiza glanced up to see Pappa incline his head towards her while looking pointedly at Uncle Rafi. She considered her plate, but the doughnut had lost its appeal.

Uncle Rafi puffed thoughtfully before pronouncing, "The violence was regrettable, of course, but it was a small demonstration, well contained. You can't stop the odd eruption, but as long as we keep the overall situation under control—"

"You mean like a safety valve?" interrupted Pappa. "Give them the chance to let off a bit of steam to prevent the whole caboodle going up in smoke?"

Uncle Rafi shrugged. "Not how I'd have put it, but basically, yes."

Pappa exploded. "This misguided, gutless government! I never thought I'd miss the Marshal, but he had no time for anti-Semites, and he never sanctioned violence against Jews. Since he's gone, you're so anxious to appease the National Democrats that you might as well have Dmowski as Prime Minister. When will you realise?" – he went on, stabbing the air with his glowing cigar – "that capitalising on nationalistic bigotry won't help Poland. Creating a sound economy is the only way. If men like Abel leave, God help us."

"Hugo, keep your voice down, for heaven's sake."

Luiza noticed that customers at neighbouring tables were looking their way. She concentrated on her doughnut.

"Rafi, I'm serious," Pappa continued more quietly. "In God's name, I should know what I'm talking about, trying to run a business in this superstitious nation."

"Exactly." Uncle Rafi paused while the waiter delivered more brandy. "Then you know what we're up against. It's the Church and the peasants who hold the power, and we have to keep them happy."

"Rubbish!" Heads turned again. Pappa lowered his voice and continued, "You have to educate the peasants out of their superstitions, and you have to keep the Church where it should be, tending souls, not agitating against Jews."

"Oh, come now, that's not quite fair."

"But the Catholic hierarchy supports the National Democrats. On the one hand, they're colluding with the ignorant, 'Christ-killer' antisemitism of their peasant flock, while on the other they're supporting the so-called 'intellectual' arguments of the economic scapegoat model – they're guilty twice over! Anyway, you're Lutheran, so why do you defend the Roman Church?"

"I'm only trying to keep a balanced perspective. Antisemitism may not be what we want, but you can't deny that it's tough for Poles who are struggling, when they see Jews doing alright."

"Which Jews doing alright? They're suffering as much as anyone. This myth of Jewish invulnerability is ludicrous. If there's less money around, how can Jewish businesses not be affected? And now there's talk of boycotts, it will be even worse for them." Pappa sounded dispirited. "What I don't understand is why we're talking about Jews in the first place – Jewish traders, Jewish businesses. They're Polish – have been for generations."

"Of course, they are," agreed Uncle Rafi. "And when the economy picks up this will all blow over. They're an essential part of the fabric of Polish society."

"Yes, the essential scapegoat no society can be without," Pappa concluded, bitterly.

Chapter 21

January 1936, Saska Kępa

*I*n the end, Luiza was pleased that they spent Christmas at Malinów. Not only was she reunited with Nutmeg, but Waldemar introduced her to rabbit shooting, which she took to with enthusiasm. Pappa was less keen.

"I simply don't see how killing God's creatures can be considered sport."

"You're obviously not a farmer, Hugo," Waldemar countered. "We'd have no crops left if we didn't cull the little pests. Instead of being squeamish, you should be grateful your daughter's putting food on the table – she's got a good eye and a steady hand."

Luiza glowed in Waldemar's approval and thrilled with every shot that found its mark. The soft, warm weight of each retrieved body caused her only a moment's disquiet before she found herself excitedly taking aim again.

But the very best thing about Christmas at Malinów was that Pappa was his old self. He ate well and seemed content in Pani Anna's company. The pair took brief excursions each day to benefit from the brisk air, but they seemed happiest ensconced by the stove, chatting and playing cards. The sisters congratulated themselves. It seemed that their scheming had paid off, which left Luiza to work on her marksmanship while Ida gravitated to the nursery. Four-month-old Roman was all dimples and smiles.

As 1935 became 1936, Luiza celebrated her first *Sylvester*. She had never stayed up for New Year, but Pani Anna insisted that she was old enough at thirteen. Her small glass of champagne was not the disappointment that her first – in honour of Pappa's patent – had been. This time, she knew better than to expect sweetness, and she enjoyed the way the bubbles in her mouth and nose ended up in her head. Pappa joked that the champagne enhanced the visual effervescence of the fireworks that Waldemar set off at midnight.

Once the festivities were over, the girls returned to Saska Kępa for the start of term. The mood in their uncle's house had improved in the months leading up to Christmas. Aunt Wanda was dressing elegantly and smiling vaguely again, while Uncle Rafi seemed to have got over the Marshal's death. It was a relief to have her funny, dashing uncle back, but Luiza still worried about the distance between him and her aunt. At least equilibrium was restored and Kamila, though still frail, was no longer distressed.

When Luiza went to bed the night before her maths test, Ida was still out. Aunt Wanda, too, and Uncle Rafi had been away for days. In her dream, the bell signalling the end of the exam was ringing and she was staring in horror at the paper on her desk, which remained blank, even as she continued to write. The bell kept on ringing and, eventually, sleepily, she struggled into her dressing gown and pattered down the wooden staircase to the telephone.

"Hallo?"

"I'm connecting you – go ahead, caller."

The operator's words faded into the hiss of the line as a female voice emerged, "Pani Svenson?"

"She's not here. I'm her niece."

"This is Sister Teresa from the Holy Cross hospital in Białystok. Major Svenson has been admitted with pneumonia. Pani Svenson should come at once."

"She'll be home soon – I'll tell her. It's her bridge evening."

"It's important – she must come. You will tell her?"

"Yes, I will. Thank you."

"Who was it?" Kamila stood on the landing, tousled fair hair framing a pinched, white face.

"The hospital in Białystok. Uncle Rafi's got pneumonia. We must let Aunt Wanda know."

Leaning heavily on the banister, Kamila started down the stairs, but Luiza leapt up, two at a time, to grasp her cousin by the arm. Kamila was breathless, her lips blue.

"What are you doing, Mila? Let me help you back to bed."

Kamila pulled her arm away and descended another step.

"Hang on, then, I'll get your dressing gown – before you catch pneumonia, too."

By the time she returned, Kamila had reached the hall and was slumped in a chair, the telephone receiver in her hand. "They're playing at Pani Padowska's tonight," she wheezed.

Luiza was draping the robe around her cousin's thin shoulders when the front door opened. Aunt Wanda entered, together with an icy blast. She peered short-sightedly at the girls as she unbuttoned her coat.

"Why on earth are you two still up? It's gone ten! Mila, darling, you're shivering. Here." She wrapped the fur around her daughter and scrutinised her pale face.

"There was a telephone call," Kamila whispered, "Pappa's in hospital."

Aunt Wanda blanched. "What?"

"He's got pneumonia," said Luiza, acutely aware of her responsibility. She alone held all the information. It was essential that she conveyed it correctly. "Sister Teresa from the Holy Cross hospital said you should come at once."

Aunt Wanda repeated, "Holy Cross... where?"

Luiza paused; the name had assumed such monumental proportions that the syllables now snagged on her tongue. She took a deep breath and let them tumble out. Aunt Wanda nodded vaguely.

"I'll take the early train. I must pack. You two should be in bed. Get along, Lou-lou. Here, darling, let me help you up.'

"I'm coming to Białystok, too," stated Kamila.

"Don't be ridiculous, darling. You can't possibly travel in this weather."

"I'm coming." With that, Kamila rose and made her way slowly upstairs, Luiza following. She heard Aunt

Wanda pick up the telephone and ask for Zakątek. Luiza wondered why her aunt wanted Pappa, before realising that she must be calling her sister. Back in bed, determined to stay awake until Ida came home, she was soon asleep.

In the morning, the maid told her that Kamila and her aunt had taken the six o'clock train with Pani Aurelia. Ida had apparently made them breakfast before they left and was now back in bed. Luiza felt the familiar pang of exclusion on hearing that Ida had taken over while she, the original guardian of the dramatic message, slept. But she felt guilty as soon as she remembered the cause of the crisis. Poor Uncle Rafi. She left her breakfast unfinished and went to her room, where she knelt in front of the icon of Mary and her divine son and offered up a prayer for her uncle's recovery. It was hard to believe that Uncle Rafi could be gravely ill. He was always so very much alive.

The maths test distracted her, as did the Musketeers, so it was only on her way home that Luiza remembered the drama in Białystok. Ida was in the salon, looking tired but poised on the chaise longue. She was embroidering an intricate panel.

"Have you heard anything?" asked Luiza from the doorway.

"Pappa rang after Pani Aurelia updated him. Uncle Rafi really is ill. He…" Ida bit her lip as she looked down at her fine stitching. "They think he might die." Her lovely face crumpled.

Luiza was stunned; how many times had she seen Uncle Rafi stride into this very room, his spurs jangling? He could not die.

"Are they sure?"

"He had a really bad cold and then he was on an unheated train for hours. It made him dreadfully ill. Last night he had some kind of crisis. He should have turned the corner after that, but..."

Ida wiped a finger across her eye and folded the embroidery. She swung her feet to the floor and patted the grey leather beside her. Luiza curled up against her sister, pressed close by the tilt of the Corbusier seat.

The winter dusk crept about them as the girls sat in silence. Long after the room was consumed by darkness, the telephone rang. Ida went to answer it while Luiza remained curled on her side, her eyes shut and fists clenched, as if through sheer will power she could hold bad news at bay. Ida's terse responses reached her through the open door.

"Yes, I see. No, we're alright – really. Yes, I'll tell her. When will they be back? Oh, I see. Where will it… Yes, alright. Goodnight, Pappa."

Luiza opened her eyes. "Is he…?"

Ida's nod was barely discernible in the gloom. She went to the window, where the shutters were still open. Arms tightly folded, she stood with her back to the room. The yellow pools of light cast by the streetlamps showed Ida in sharp relief. Her shoulders shook. Luiza went to her and they wrapped their arms around each other. *First Mama, now Uncle Rafi*, Luiza thought, numbly. Ida and Pappa were all she had.

"But I don't understand. Why didn't Aunt Wanda let us know about the funeral?"

Marya Burgess

It was a week later, and Ida and Luiza were in Pani Anna's rooms at the Mazowiecki. Their mother's old friend had swept into the villa soon after Pappa's telephone call and found the sisters huddled in darkness. Going rapidly from room to room, flicking switches until the house was ablaze, she had chivvied them into packing a few essentials, then scooped them into her waiting car and deposited them in her cosy apartment.

Seated at the table, Luiza was doing her art homework – a pastel still life of a jug with grapes – while Ida leafed through the latest imported French _Vogue_ and related today's telephone conversation with their father.

"Pappa said she didn't want us there."

"But why?" Luiza was belligerent. "He was _our_ uncle."

"Pappa thinks she was embarrassed. She just wanted the whole thing over as quickly as possible."

Luiza gaped at her sister. "What do you mean, embarrassed? Embarrassed that her husband died?" Her voice climbed perilously.

"Calm down, Lou-lou," said Ida, moving to the table and continuing quietly, her eyes on Luiza's unfinished drawing. "You see, Uncle Rafi caught pneumonia travelling on an unheated train—"

"Yes, I know," Luiza interrupted impatiently. "He had a cold, and because he was on that freezing train all night, he got ill and died. What's embarrassing about that?"

Ida sighed. "He wasn't supposed to be on that train. He was supposed to catch one the following morning, direct to Warszawa. Instead, he took the night train, so that he could stop off for a few hours in Białystok."

Luiza breathed in sharply and waited. Ever since the night of the Marshal's funeral, those four syllables were imbued with menace.

"You see, Uncle Rafi was in love with somebody else, and she lives in Białystok."

"Somebody else? Not Aunt Wanda?" Luiza's eyes were wide. This was a concept that belonged in a film, not in her life.

"She's the daughter of a colonel," Ida continued.

"Is she married?"

Ida shook her head. "She's… well, she's only a year or two older than me."

Luiza stared at Ida incredulously.

"Anyway, he caught the night train so that he could meet her. He was planning to travel on to Warszawa, but he became too ill."

Luiza selected a blue pastel and began to shade in the jug. "But I still don't see why we couldn't go to the funeral."

"Aunt Wanda was worried that the girl – the colonel's daughter – might come…"

"But the funeral was in Wilno, and she's in Białystok!"

"…and she did. She made an awful scene, apparently. They had to drag her off the coffin. Poor Aunt Wanda – and poor Kamila."

Luiza was still shading in the jug. "When are they coming home?"

"They're not, Lou-lou," said Ida gently as Luiza paused in her colouring. "Aunt Wanda's decided they'll live with her mother in Wilno."

Luiza was now carelessly raking the pastel beyond the jug's outline. "Where are we going to live, then?"

"Well," Ida's tone brightened, "that's the good news. We're going to live here!"

Luiza looked up, "Here? At the hotel?"

"Yes!" Ida nodded, laughing. "Won't that be fun?"

And it was. Every time she came home, Grzegorz, the doorman, saluted her as he set the revolving door turning. She never tired of the magical transition from the noisy hubbub of traffic outside to the hush of the foyer, with its deep carpet and deeper sofas. And now she lived in the heart of Warszawa instead of a suburb, she could skate as long as she wanted every afternoon. And there was a café downstairs that served cakes and hot chocolate at all hours. The hotel soon became the Musketeers' favourite place to meet. But after school today, Luiza had an appointment with Ida and Pani Anna at the dressmaker.

"You're nearly fourteen, Lou-lou. I can see Ida's style isn't right for you, but I think you have your own," said Pani Anna, holding a swatch of Irish tweed up to her face. "Yes, the heather colours bring out your eyes. What about a suit in this one?"

"Proper huntin', shootin' and fishin' style." Ida laughed.

"Sporty, yes," mused Pani Anna, "but the cut can still be feminine. What do you think, Mireille?" she demanded of the dressmaker.

"Perhaps in an A-line skirt and a belted jacket?" mused Mireille.

"We need to get you some brogues, too – they'll look the business," continued Pani Anna.

"Brogues? Why don't we get her some trousers, while we're at it?" Ida exclaimed.

Luiza glanced hopefully at Pani Anna.

"Heavens, no. It's enough that she spends half her life in breeches; she certainly doesn't need an excuse to wear trousers when she's not on horseback."

"Tweed's all very well now, but what about the summer?" queried Ida.

"Gaberdine," pronounced Pani Anna. "Mireille, let's look at a gaberdine demi-saison coat or jacket. And then some simple cotton blouses and dresses."

"She can't wear brogues with those!"

"Of course not. We'll order sandals and court shoes, too."

Chapter 22

April 1936, Warszawa

"My word, Lou-lou! Where's my little girl gone?"

Luiza was at Warszawa Central to meet her father off the Grodzisk Mazowiecki train. So preoccupied was she with her reflection in the train windows – she was not yet used to seeing herself in the skirt and jacket Mireille had styled for her – that she had missed him. But now there he was, standing on the platform in front of her, and she could see that the old worries had returned. His face was creased; even his moustache drooped. He wrapped his arms around her so tightly that she squeaked, "Pappa, I can't breathe."

Releasing her with a watery smile, he commented, "I hope you're not too sophisticated for hot chocolate, because it's what I need right now, to chase this wretched damp from my bones."

It was a wet Sunday morning at the beginning of April.

The last of the snow from this particularly vicious winter had finally been washed away by days of continuous rain. It was only the second time Luiza had seen her father since Uncle Rafi's death. He had visited them at the Mazowiecki soon after she and Ida moved in, and she had found comfort in his embrace. Yet, just as when Mama died, he did not refer to their mutual loss.

It was Ida who had voiced the unspeakable. "I'm glad Mama isn't here. It would have broken her heart to lose her little brother." Pappa had patted her shoulder and blown his nose loudly, while Luiza pursued the train of thought Ida had set in motion to an uncomfortable destination: If Mama were still here – if she, Luiza, had not left Mama alone – then Uncle Rafi might not have fallen in love with a girl barely older than his daughter, because his elder sister would have instilled some sense in him.

In the cab to Blikle, Luiza could not help but remember the last time she had been there with Pappa, to meet Uncle Rafi after their magical walk in the snow-jewelled Łazienki. And when Pappa steered her away from the booth where the three of them had sat, she knew he remembered, too.

They ordered chocolate (Pappa's with a shot of brandy) and a doughnut to share. This time, Luiza had no competition from her father's predatory spoon; Pappa barely touched a mouthful.

"Right," he said, salvaging a smile and rubbing his hands. "Now I'm ready for anything. Shall we go?"

It was the week before Easter, and Pappa had given in to Ida's request that they attend the special Catholic Palm Sunday service. Walking up Krakowskie Przedmieście with arms linked under Pappa's large umbrella, as they joined the slow-moving column entering the Church of the Holy Cross, Luiza was confronted by another memory. They had climbed these steps together almost a year ago, for the Marshal's funeral. It was raining then, too. She recalled Pappa's tears as the gun carriage passed and wondered whether he had shed any for Uncle Rafi. Surely he had loved his brother-in-law more than the Marshal, despite all their arguments.

At the top of the steps stood a life-size figure of Christ, bent under the burden of the cross on his back. Luiza brushed her glove against the statue's straining shoulder and prayed that no one else in her family be taken, then immediately felt guilty for asking, for had not He willingly undertaken much greater suffering?

Inside, once their eyes adjusted to the gloom, they made for the pew where Ida had saved them seats. Pani Anna handed each of them a woven wand of catkins and sprouting hazel, picked at Malinów. The palms had been blessed during this morning's procession to the church.

The alchemy of candles and incense, of mysterious Latin chants and voices raised in unison, wove its habitual spell on Luiza. Soon she was brimming with good intentions. Determined to be virtuous, she yearned for official inclusion in the promise of salvation that encompassed her. When the bell rang and the priest in his purple vestments raised the host on high, Luiza bowed her head and fervently whispered, "Mea culpa, mea culpa, mea maxima culpa."

The three Wolfers stayed in the pew when Pani Anna

answered the summons to communion, joining the throng that shuffled towards the altar rail. Luiza watched avidly as the priest passed back and forth before the kneeling communicants, declaring "Corpus Christi" over each miraculous wafer he dispensed. "Amen," responded the recipients, presenting tongues eager for the sacred white disc.

She scanned their faces as they returned to their seats, searching for a glow of consecrated piety, a mark of newly sanctified status. Pani Anna, squeezing past to resume her place in the pew, caught her probing eye and beamed beatifically. Satisfied, Luiza screwed shut her eyes and sent up a prayer: "Dear God, please make Pappa let me be a Catholic soon. I know I'm not always good, but I promise I'll try harder, and I know I'd do better with you in my heart. So please, please change Pappa's mind."

Opening her eyes, she caught sight of Ida's bowed head, the long feather on her hat pointing straight up into the lofty vault of the frescoed ceiling. Luiza closed her eyes again and added a second clause to her prayer: "Ida's been waiting longer, and she's holier than me, so please make Pappa let her become a Catholic very soon. And if you could make it so he lets us both convert, that would be absolutely perfect. Amen."

When she opened her eyes this time, she noticed how drawn Pappa's face was as he leant forward, elbows on knees and hands clasped. Once more Luiza prayed. "Please, God, make Pappa happy again. That's the most important thing. We can both wait to become Catholics, if only you can make him how he used to be. Perhaps not as fat, but not this thin. Amen."

After Mass they had dinner at the Brystol, their four blessed palms displayed in a vase the waiter provided. Pappa had ordered wild boar, but he left most of it. He even turned down dessert (and the sweet trolley featured some fine-looking rum babas), in favour of a cigar.

Luiza was looking forward to their afternoon treat, *The Thirty-Nine Steps*, which had received a glowing review from Gosia. But Pappa's plans had changed. "I need to see Isaak Abel, and I so rarely get into town these days, I really must take the opportunity. I'm sorry, but you can tell me all about the film at supper. You know I'd probably fall asleep, anyway."

Luiza, her own mood plummeting, noticed that Pani Anna's face had fallen. She quickly recovered, though, and commented cheerily enough, "Of course, Hugo, dear, you must go and see Pan Abel. We'll still have a fine time, won't we, girls?"

"Pappa, may I come with you?" Luiza was almost as surprised to hear her request as were the others.

"But Lou-lou, you've been going on and on – Gosia says this and Gosia says that," exclaimed Ida. "Why would you miss the film now?"

Luiza could not explain the silent appeal of dark eyes amid blood-spattered snow that the mention of Pan Abel had elicited from the darkest corners of her mind. Instead, she mumbled, "I just… it's a long time since I've seen the Abels."

"Of course, you can come, Lou-lou," encouraged Pappa, with a warm smile. "They'll be delighted."

They left the others on Senatorska and caught a

northbound tram. Getting off at Gęsia Street, they turned right up Karmelicka and came eventually to Mila. In this part of town, the shops were open on a Sunday and the streets bustled with men and boys, twin ringlets hanging in front of their ears and white tassels below their waists. Lamplight leaked from shop windows, causing the dismal drizzle to glisten on black coats and broad-brimmed hats.

Passing through a pair of tall doors, they entered a large foyer with wooden letterboxes ranged on one wall. Ahead was a stone staircase. The broad, shallow steps were bordered by a wrought iron balustrade with a polished banister, the stairs wrapping around the elaborate ironwork of a lift shaft.

Chequered tiles announced each step as they approached the lift door. Luiza pressed the button, and somewhere in the bowels of the building a mechanism wheezed into action. The grinding grew louder and looped coils of cable writhed and stretched into life within the iron cage. Peering upwards, Luiza watched the base of the cabin descend.

They got out on the second floor and rang the bell above a gleaming brass plate: ISAAK ABEL, Chartered Accountant. The door was opened by a plump girl in maid's uniform. Frizzy dark hair escaped her white cap and her face flushed pink, as if embarrassed by her role. Pappa gave their names and asked if Pan Abel was at home, but she did not reply and the three of them continued to stand there awkwardly until a woman's voice called, "Who is it, Branka?" Still the girl said nothing, while her face turned crimson.

Pappa cleared his throat and called, "It's Hugo Wolfer."

The whisper of silk announced Pani Abel's approach. Short and squarely built, she conveyed an impression of dignified assurance, even as her hands fiddled behind her back with the ties of a large apron.

"Hugo! What a lovely surprise. Oh, but my dear, how thin you are – you've clearly not eaten at our table for far too long. And who's this? Surely not Luiza? You've grown up, dear. But why are you still at the door? Branka, what were you thinking? Take our guests' coats – and here, this, too," having finally extricated herself from the pinafore. "Then fetch us some tea."

Pani Abel led them down the corridor to a large room, turning on lamps as she went. A grand piano stood by the window, and the walls were lined with paintings ranged in tiers. Some were murky oils in elaborate gilt frames, but these were interspersed with more simply framed canvases that were brightly slashed with colour. Beneath the pictures stood polished cabinets. On one of these stood the sloping branches of a menorah with its crop of candles. Richly upholstered chairs were grouped in clusters, as if this one room could be used simultaneously for separate gatherings. Pani Abel steered them towards four chairs with gilded arms and legs, arranged around a small marquetry table of gold and blond wood.

"I must apologise for Branka; she's painfully shy. I'm training her – hence the apron." Pani Abel laughed. Her fingers, on which large stones sparkled in the lamplight, played with a necklace of even bigger gems. "We were making chicken soup – can you believe she doesn't even know how to do that? What can her mother have been thinking? It was such a shock, Hanna leaving after all these years, but her son was emigrating to America and simply would not leave her behind." Pani Abel sighed. "So many going, Hugo. Such strange times."

Without waiting for a response, Pani Abel eyed Luiza and continued brightly, "How sweet of you to visit, dear. You know, when I first saw you, I thought you must be Ida – it's such a long time since I've seen you both. Your poor, dear mother… such times we had at Zakątek." Pani Abel patted her neat chignon. Her hair was dark, apart from distinctive bands of silver on either temple, and her eyebrows arched over eyes that appeared black.

"Such wonderful times. I'll never forget Zosia waltzing into the room with her delicious coffee – how often did I ask her secret? And now… well, I'll never know."

She paused, lost in her own reverie and apparently unaware of the effect of her reminiscences on her guests. Luiza had not heard anyone speak so openly of her mother in years. Her own memory had snagged on Mama after the stroke, but now she found herself filling in Pani Abel's sketch, and Mama as she used to be was suddenly, vividly present. Glancing at Pappa, she saw him fumble for his handkerchief and quickly dab his eyes.

Oblivious, Pani Abel continued, "You know, I can see her now, sitting at this piano, singing Schumann in that wonderful contralto of hers. Nobody's played that piano as well since. Neither Elsa nor I can pretend to have her touch." Back in the present again, Pani Abel looked directly at Luiza. "And what about you, dear, have you inherited your mother's talent?"

Luiza shook her head.

"Oh, come now, don't be modest. Play something."

Pani Abel rose and opened the piano seat to take out some music.

"Ah, yes, this was a favourite of Zosia's – the 'Moonlight Sonata'. Here you are."

She positioned the sheets on the stand and Luiza froze. Pappa, his voice gruff, interjected, "Lou-lou doesn't play."

"Doesn't play?" Pani Abel gave an involuntary snort of disbelief. "What do you mean?"

"Just that." Shifting uncomfortably in his chair, Hugo examined his fingernails. "I suppose I didn't think at the time, what with… And later, well, I supposed it would be too… too…"

"Too painful?" Pani Abel chided him gently. "Come now, Hugo, that's not the attitude. You should rejoice in your memories, not run away from them. What about Ida? Does she play?"

Seeing her father's discomfort, Luiza stepped in. "Ida never really took to the piano. Neither did I. Mama tried to teach us both. Ida embroiders beautifully, though – just like Mama."

Pani Abel smiled, "Good, that's good. Now, dear, how old are you?"

"Fourteen in July."

"Well, it's not ideal, but it's not too late, provided you're prepared to work hard. Are you?"

Luiza nodded politely, uncertain as to the conversation's direction.

"Good. Then we'll start with two lessons a week – you'll have to practise hard in between – and see how we go. After school on Mondays and Thursdays, would that suit you?"

As Pani Abel's meaning became clear, Luiza exclaimed, "You mean, for piano lessons?"

"Of course, for piano lessons."

"It's most generous of you, Sara, but really…" Pappa's voice had an edge to it, yet still Pani Abel ploughed on.

"But really nothing, Hugo. It's settled. Tomorrow at four, Luiza. And now," Pani Abel turned to Pappa with a winning smile, "I know you didn't come to see me, Hugo. Isaak should be home any minute. He's out pushing a perambulator to show off his grandson."

"But of course, congratulations! I heard Elsa had a child."

"In February. He's nearly seven weeks."

"And mother and baby are well?"

"Oh yes, they're fine. She should be back soon, too. She and Dawid have taken advantage of the doting grandfather to have a quiet coffee on their own. Speaking of which, where is that girl with our tea? Please excuse me."

Pani Abel swished from the room and Luiza regarded her father, uncertain where he stood regarding the piano lessons. He had risen from his chair to examine one of the brighter canvases, a haphazard, multicoloured jumble of slabs and streaks. A landscape caught her eye: poplars on a riverbank. She got up for a closer look, but the trees seemed to disintegrate. When she stepped back again, they re-formed into recognisable shapes. She studied the brushwork. Instead of stroking the paint onto the canvas, the artist appeared to have dotted it with repeated jabs.

"Ah, Luiza, you're admiring Isaak's Pissarro," Pani Abel commented as Branka, flushed and sullen, trailed in her wake, carrying a large tray. "So, you like the Impressionists?" their hostess continued, while directing the maid to distribute tea glasses and poppy seed cake.

"Yes, I do, but I've not seen one like this before – the dots, I mean."

"Lou-lou's a dab hand with the paintbrush herself," observed Pappa. "And her subjects are recognisable. Which is more than can be said for that." He waved one hand at the colourful canvas as he accepted a glass in its silver filigree holder with the other.

"Now don't let Isaak hear you criticising his Malevich – he'll accuse you of being a philistine. It's his pride and joy. Though," Pani Abel lowered her voice conspiratorially, "I can't say it's my cup of tea."

Luiza had just accepted some cake when the loud wails of a baby reached them. Pani Abel hurried from the room. Moments later, her husband entered. His clean-shaven cheeks were pink and his yarmulke nestled, almost hidden, amid a startlingly white and luxuriant tumble of curls. Isaak Abel approached her father with outstretched arms and the two embraced warmly.

"Hugo, my old friend, what an unexpected pleasure. But can this elegant young lady really be Lou-lou?"

Luiza smiled and dropped a perfunctory curtsy, but

Pan Abel took her hand and raised it to his lips, causing Luiza's cheeks to flush as pink as his.

"Last time I saw you, you were so high," he said, stroking the air at waist level, "and still in pinafores, and now look at you." He released her hand and shook his head at Pappa. "The more our daughters blossom, Hugo, the steeper our decline. Look at me – a grandfather! It'll be your turn next."

He punched Pappa playfully on the arm and Pappa, grinning, spluttered, "Hold on, Isaak, they're not married yet. But mazeltov, my old friend – I can hear that your grandson has a splendid pair of lungs."

Pan Abel grimaced. "Yes, and the whole of Mila knows it." The doorbell rang and he excused himself, but soon returned, relief written on his face. "Elsa's back and she thinks the baby's just hungry."

"Then there's every chance you'll be allowed to take him out again," teased a dark-haired young man who had followed Pan Abel into the room. He wore wire-rimmed glasses, corduroy trousers and a diamond-patterned sleeveless pullover, and it struck Luiza that he could have stepped out of a film.

"Dawid, you met my dear friend, Hugo Wolfer at the wedding – you remember? And this is his daughter, Luiza."

Dawid shook Pappa's hand and, to Luiza's surprise, hers too. Branka arrived with more tea as Luiza searched Pan Abel's round face for some sign of hardship associated with being ousted from the Board. Like Pappa, he was dressed in a dark suit, but he filled his, testing seams and buttons to the limit, just as Pappa used to.

"Well, and how's life, my old friend?" Pan Abel enquired. "You're looking tired. Working too hard, as usual."

"And you're a picture of health, as usual. And, judging by your new purchase," Pappa nodded at the Malevich, "you're managing to keep your head above water. Not missing Korski too much, then?"

"Not at all," laughed Pan Abel, helping himself to cake. "There's always work for an accountant."

"Really?" Pappa frowned. "You've not been affected by the boycotts, then?"

"Oh, it's easy enough to boycott shops – there's usually a Christian somewhere who sells bread that's almost as good, or who can make shoes that wear nearly as well. But Poles can usually overlook their prejudices where money's concerned; they'll always come to the person best able to keep the taxman from their door."

"So, what about America? Will you be joining Jakob there?"

"What, and leave my grandson? I've been trying to persuade Dawid that we should all go, but he won't even consider it."

Dawid smiled. The flash of straight, white teeth transformed his serious face to match his film-star clothes.

"Isaak woos me with promises of a new life in New York," commented Dawid. In what Luiza had been taught was an unforgivable lapse of etiquette, he fished the lemon slice from his tea and peeled the flesh from the rind with his teeth. "The streets there are, he assures me, paved with gold."

"But does he jump at this opportunity?" asked Pan Abel in a tone of affectionate exasperation. "No, instead he lectures me on what lies beneath those golden pavements. 'Somebody's blood will have paid for the gold,' he tells me, and I tell him, 'Dawid, I'm an old man. I've learnt that you can't right all the wrongs of the world. All you can do is your best for your family.' And do you know what he says?" Pan Abel looked enquiringly at Pappa, who shook his head. "My son-in-law says, 'I know I can't go through life without stepping in somebody's blood, but at least here I know whose blood it is.'"

Luiza stared at the red-and-gold pattern on one of the rugs and saw blood on snow.

Pan Abel pressed on. "'Even if it's the blood of your own people?' I ask him. '*Especially* if it's the blood of my own people,' he says."

Dawid cleared his throat and, wiping his hands on a napkin, said, "Luiza, would you like to meet my son?"

She followed him out of the salon and along the dark corridor. When he paused outside a closed door, Luiza asked, "Why do you want to see the blood?"

Dawid released the door handle and turned back to her. "I don't *want* to see it, but if it's there, I don't want to turn a blind eye."

"Why not?" she persisted.

"Because I may be able to do something about it. I'm a lawyer; I see it as my duty to defend those who can't defend themselves."

Luiza watched her fingers pleat the hem of her blouse. "Outside the university last winter, there was blood."

"You saw it?"

Luiza nodded. "It was after school. We couldn't get past the demonstrators, and then…" Her voice faltered. Gently, Dawid stilled her busy fingers.

"You'll crease it," he said. "I heard about what happened there. It must have been very frightening to witness."

"No, well, yes, it was frightening, but what was worse… what was awful was not to be able to do anything."

"Of course, you couldn't, then. But *now* you're doing something, simply by being here, by being our good friend. So, come and meet the handsomest, most doted-upon baby on earth."

Dawid flashed another heart-stopping smile and opened the door. With his hand on Luiza's shoulder, he steered her into the bedroom, where Elsa was seated on a low chair, nursing the baby. Pani Abel was bustling about, folding away tiny garments.

"I've brought another admirer to pay court to his imperial majesty." Dawid bent to kiss his wife and stroke the baby's head. Pani Abel stopped folding for a moment to watch the young parents watch their baby. Elsa had her mother's colouring. Her dark hair was gathered loosely at the nape of her neck, but some escaped strands hung over her face. Shaking them back, she smiled warmly at Luiza. "Hello, Lou-lou – I'd never have recognised you. Do you want to come closer?"

Luiza approached tentatively, embarrassed by Elsa's state of undress. At Malinów, Grażyna nursed Roman in private, but Elsa smiled encouragingly and Luiza, looking down at the baby, exclaimed, "Oh, isn't he just like Pan Abel."

The baby stopped sucking and opened his eyes to gaze intently at Luiza. Elsa and Dawid both laughed. "Yes, he is. That's why Pappa so loves taking him out." Elsa slid the baby to her lap and leant him forward over one hand. With the other, she covered herself. "I think he's had enough. Your turn."

Dawid placed the baby on his shoulder, patting the tiny back. He was soon rewarded with a loud belch and smiled at Luiza. "You'll have to excuse our son's appalling manners. But he should be quite happy now. Would you like to hold him?"

Luiza nodded apprehensively. While Ida adored Pani Anna's grandson, she had always felt too clumsy to touch him, and this baby was even smaller. The compact little body was heavier than she expected. Dawid guided him onto her shoulder, where he settled, warmly moulded to her shape. She rubbed her chin against the velvety fuzz on his head and breathed in milk and talcum powder.

Pani Abel had visibly held her breath during the manoeuvre, but now she commented, "You'll be a fine pianist, Luiza. You have feeling, which is the most important thing. Technique, anyone can learn, but feeling – you either have it or you don't. Now, I'd better see if I can avert that girl's next kitchen catastrophe, or we'll never eat supper."

Dawid looked at Luiza with amusement. "So, you're a musician with feeling, are you?"

Luiza flushed and turned away. Elsa was unselfconsciously buttoning the front of the camisole over her breasts, which strained against the cream silk.

"I don't play…" Luiza stammered in confusion, thrown by such easy familiarity in the presence of a man.

"Luiza's mother played beautifully – didn't she, Lou-lou?"

Luiza nodded agreement. Having turned her back on the couple, she found herself confronted by their reflection in the dressing table mirror. Elsa's arms were raised for Dawid to pull her dress down over her head, and Luiza saw him release his wife's hair where it had caught. Stroking it back, he placed his lips on the side of Elsa's neck. She shrugged him off and walked around Luiza to pick up a hairbrush.

"Sadly, her stroke prevented her from passing on her skill. So now Mama's browbeaten poor Lou-lou into lessons." She smiled at Luiza in the mirror while skilfully coiling her hair and skewering it in place with pins that Dawid handed her.

"Let's join the others. Are you alright carrying Misza, Lou-lou? We'll show him off to your father while he's being so well-behaved."

Chapter 23

June 1936, Warszawa

*L*uiza looked forward to her piano lessons. Now that it was summer, snippets of conversation in Polish and Yiddish floated through the open windows to punctuate her attempts at stringing notes together. There was comfort in the press of Pani Abel's body on the piano stool and the scent of lavender that rose from the keys (Pani Abel insisted they washed their hands before touching the Bösendorfer). Luiza's were larger than Pani Abel's, yet the older woman's ringed fingers danced over the keys, alighting gracefully and moving on, like jewelled insects in search of nectar. Their deftness and precision contrasted starkly with her own stumbling efforts to connect the black-knobbed stalks that marched across her score with the anonymous ivory and ebony battens beneath her fingers.

Today's lesson over, Luiza visited Misza while Pani

Abel disappeared to torment poor Branka, calling as she went, "I hope you're staying for supper, Lou-lou?"

The baby lay in his crib beneath the open window, his mouth describing a perfect 'o' as his eyes tracked the undulations of the paper birds Luiza had painted and hung from the canopy. Elsa glanced up from her book. Following Luiza's gaze, she smiled tenderly and reached to stroke her son's bare legs, which kicked erratically in appreciation of the flying birds. Luiza felt herself subsumed in the orbit of love around the infant.

As usual, supper was a noisy affair. At first these heated discussions, where each comment, no matter how inconsequential, had to be scrutinised and challenged, had confounded Luiza. At home, arguments were rare, yet at the Abels' disagreement was commonplace and vociferous. But Luiza learnt there was no menace in the differences so loudly expressed. Exasperation, yes, but with affection. It still astonished her how everything and everyone merited consideration.

"I saw Jerma Majer at the dressmaker's today, having a suit fitted – pale green. Can you imagine? She looked bilious."

"Jerma? Oh, but surely it brought out those striking eyes of hers? I'd have thought green would suit her."

"Not pale green."

"Not green at all – she needs dark reds and violets."

"But it's summer! Surely the poor woman is allowed to wear pastels in summer?"

Only Dawid remained silent, absorbed in a newspaper folded beside his plate.

"Oh, Lou-lou," exclaimed Pani Abel, with the abrupt

change of subject that no longer took Luiza by surprise. "I meant to tell you. *Der Rosenkavalier* is on in the autumn. Your dear mother loved it so – we must take you."

Pan Abel beamed, enquiring, "When will we be attending your first recital, then, Lou-lou?"

Luiza blushed and fumbled for an excuse, but Pani Abel interjected firmly, "It'll be a while, yet. It's more than just her playing that needs work. Luiza's musical knowledge is abysmal. I can't think what Zosia would say – her daughter doesn't know Bach from Chopin. What can they be teaching her at school?"

"Maths, French, geography, science, history…" listed Dawid, looking up from his paper. "What's the topic for your latest history essay, Lou-lou?"

"How did the 1926 Coup restore moral health to Polish public life?" Luiza recited.

"Ah," began Pan Abel, rubbing his hands. "Note the interrogative adverb at the start. Its absence would perhaps allow for a more balanced argument."

"Come now, Pappa, Lou-lou's beloved Pani Rybicka is never going to allow that the great Marshal Piłsudski did anything short of save our nation," responded Elsa, mildly. The Abels had discussed Pani Rybicka's views at some length over the weeks, contesting facts that Luiza had believed indisputable. But their arguments made sense, and Luiza had incorporated some in her essays, with the result that her marks for history – previously her best subject – had dropped. Her marks for literature, mathematics and French, however – subjects upon which the Abels also deliberated with her – had improved.

"Well, you can't deny that he at least kept the anti-Semites under control," said Dawid. "Since he died things are a lot worse."

For a moment, Luiza was back in Blikle, a depleted doughnut on her plate and Pappa arguing with Uncle Rafi. The memory brought with it a sharp stab of loss; so much that was familiar and linked with Mama had vanished along with Uncle Rafi and his wolfish grin. Yet it was also true that, through the Abels, she had discovered an alternative connection with her mother.

Elsa unfolded Dawid's newspaper and Pan Abel exclaimed, "What's this? *The Worker*? Come now, Dawid, you realise you're feeding the conspiracy that all Jews are Communists by bringing the organ of the Socialist Party into this house?"

Levelly, Dawid replied, "We need to keep abreast of things – including the Comrades' views. Which are, this week, that Poles are imprisoned by the foreign element in their midst, namely the Jews, who control 90 per cent of commerce and prevent the army getting the equipment it needs. So, Jews are both traitors and misers. Yet, such hyperbole should not be seen as incitement to riot and boycott," he continued, "because, apparently, attacking Jews 'diverts the attention of Polish society from its true difficulties.'"

"That's what Pappa said to Uncle Rafi," Luiza commented. They all turned to her. Embarrassed, she regarded her plate while Pani Abel reminisced, "I remember how fond of her brother your dear mother was." She sighed. "Another one taken much too young."

"I can imagine those two had some heated debates," observed Pan Abel. "Your father never was the Marshal's biggest fan, whereas your uncle…"

"He was in the guard of honour at the Marshal's funeral," Luiza declared, eager to have Uncle Rafi's importance recognised by her new friends.

"You must have felt very proud of your uncle that day," said Elsa, and reached to cover Luiza's hand with her own.

"But I really don't think it's safe for Lou-lou to be in Mila," protested Pani Anna. She was not at all happy about the piano lessons. Having failed to persuade Pappa to stop them, she was now insisting that her car should convey Luiza to and from the Abels'. But this would mean giving up time with Misza, as well as the energetic debates over supper, and Luiza was fighting her corner hard.

"Either Dawid or Pan Abel always sees me to the tram. Dawid even brings me all the way to the hotel sometimes. Honestly, there's no need for the car," she pleaded.

Fortunately, Pappa stepped in. "Really, Anna dear, Isaak would never allow Lou-lou's safety to be compromised."

"But these days, how can he guarantee it? Such dreadful things are happening."

"Indeed they are. Which is why it's more important than ever that we stand by our friends." Pappa's tone indicated that the matter was closed and Pani Anna said no more. In his absence, though, she quizzed Luiza about the food and the conversation at the Abels' table, all the while fingering the gold cross at her neck.

"They do, they do! And then they use the blood to make their funny bread."

"For goodness' sake, Marja, don't be so stupid."

"But it's true! Our maid was visiting her family, and a baby disappeared from the village. Everyone knew it was the Jews that took it."

With barely two weeks before the summer vacation, the fine weather had broken, and students were confined to their classrooms at break. The Three Musketeers had gathered around Luiza's desk to discuss alternative after-school plans, now that a swim in the Vistula looked unlikely. The rest of the class, except for Mirjam Libenbaum and Lotte Goldfarb, who appeared to be engrossed in the colourful illustrations of a large book of natural history, were grouped near Marja Kiszczak.

"But Marja, how did they know it was Jews who took the baby?"

"Because the cradle was empty on Friday morning."

"So?"

"So, the old crows could sit nodding over fresh blood matzos on Friday night," Marja concluded triumphantly. There was a loud click as the door shut. The illustrated book lay abandoned on Lotte's desk.

"How's that for an admission of guilt?" Marja sneered, then sniffed ostentatiously. "At least the pong's left with them."

Some of the girls giggled, but Krystyna Szymańska, frowning, queried, "It doesn't sound very plausible to me – where's the evidence? It's all just peasant superstition. Tell me where the Torah calls for the blood of Christian babies?"

"How should *I* know?" Marja responded irritably.

"You don't expect *me* to read their filthy books, do you?" Her round face took on a sly expression as she lifted her voice. "You should ask Luiza Wolfer."

Luiza, Gosia and Agnieszka raised their heads.

"Come on, Luiza," needled Marja, "tell us why Jews need the blood of Christian babies."

Flushing angrily, Luiza retorted, "You must be sick in the head, Marja Kiszczak, if you believe such evil lies."

"Very well, Miss High and Mighty, prove that they're lies, then."

"I refuse to dignify such obscenity with debate."

It was something Luiza had heard Dawid say, but she was surprised by its effect on her tormentor. Lost for words, Marja soon lost her magnetism, and the group broke up.

The following afternoon, Luiza went shopping with Gosia. She needed buttons for a gaberdine jacket, while Gosia had to run an errand for her mother. Luiza found the exact style and shade she wanted at Baumgold, then went to meet Gosia on the corner of Nowogrodzka. They were going to Lardelli's for ice cream. Waiting to cross Marszalkowska, Luiza turned to watch a fine pair of chestnuts pulling an open landau.

"Ugh, Lou-lou, there's something on your back."

Craning her neck, Luiza caught a putrid whiff. She struggled out of her blazer and met the dead eye of the herring that was pinned to the cloth.

"How on earth did that get there?"

"Someone put it there, you dolt! They saw you coming out of a Jewish shop and put the mark on you. Get rid of it, for goodness' sake – people are staring."

Luiza grappled with the pin, while trying not to touch the herring. The fish dropped into the gutter and she sniffed her jacket. "Yuck – this needs cleaning."

"Just fold it inside out for now. Come on."

The policeman directing traffic at the junction was signalling for them to cross. Gosia seized Luiza by the arm and pulled her across the street. It was true, Luiza realised, people were staring; she felt hot inside. Gratefully, she slipped into Lardelli's cool foyer and handed her bundled up blazer to the cloakroom attendant, who shook it out, wrinkling her nose as she placed it on a hanger.

When they had placed their order, Gosia regarded her narrowly before cautioning, "Perhaps you should avoid Jewish shops – things are getting nasty."

"What do you mean? I can shop where I want."

"Not at the moment, you can't. Next time, it might not just be a herring. This is a warning – they're probably watching you because you're always at the Abels."

"Who's watching me? Don't be ridiculous, why would anyone watch me?"

"Oh, come on, Lou-lou – remember the demonstration at the university? Things aren't getting any better, and those barbarians don't like friends of Jews any better than they like Jews themselves."

"So, I should give in to a lot of ignorant bullies and desert my friends? Is that what you're saying?" challenged Luiza, her cheeks pink. The waitress glanced at her as she placed their sundaes on the table, and Gosia waited until she had gone before she spoke again.

"There's no point getting angry with me. I feel exactly

the same, but you have to face facts: This is not a good time to be friendly with Jews – in fact, it's dangerous. You just have to be careful until things change."

"How will things ever change, if all anyone does is *be careful*?"

They sat in silence, staring at the dishes in front of them. Neither girl picked up her spoon. Then Gosia snickered, "That woman's face – in the cloakroom."

Luiza tried to maintain her sense of injury, but a giggle escaped. Soon they were both doubled over, helpless with silliness.

"I walked the length of Nowogrodzka with a herring on my back!" Luiza chortled.

"And you didn't find it fishy?"

"I was in too much of a pickle…"

Their sundaes were melting before the friends were sufficiently restored to tackle them.

"Well, here she is, the Jews' best friend," Marja Kiszczak announced, cutting through the buzz of cloakroom exchanges regarding homework and the forthcoming holidays. Luiza was changing her shoes and reciting French irregular verbs in her head for today's test.

"Luiza Wolfer," said Marja, appearing from the other side of the bank of pegs and lockers, brandishing a thin newspaper.

"Have you seen this?"

Luiza recognised *The Friends of the Jews*, a freesheet which published photographs of non-Jews who patronised Jewish businesses. Marja spread it on the bench and pointed to one of the grainy photographs. Luiza recognised herself, emerging from Baumgold.

"*Such* a good friend to the Jews," Marja sneered. "She's almost one of them. She certainly *smells* like one of them." She sniffed. "Yes, a definite hint of eau de herring!"

There was a ripple of laughter and Luiza clenched her fists, hoping that her face did not look as hot as it felt. The assembly bell launched a general scramble to hang up blazers and hats and buckle indoor shoes and then Gosia and Agnieszka swept her into the hall.

That afternoon, the three friends went to the beach between the Poniatowski and Kierbedź Bridges. They saw Ida at once – not in the water but lounging on a deck chair, wearing a pair of wide, sailor trousers she had copied from Chanel. She was surrounded by admirers and was, without doubt, the most glamorous person there.

"She's SO beautiful, Lou-lou," Agnieszka remarked as the three girls spread their towels. Propping herself on her elbows, she watched hungrily as Ida laughed and shook her head, playfully tapping with her fan the muscled shoulder of one of her devotees. "She reminds me of Claudette Colbert," she mused. Luiza had her eyes closed, basking in Ida's reflected glory, although she knew better than to display their sibling connection in public. Ida could be particularly scathing when she was working on her allure.

"What do you want?" she had asked coldly, the last time they coincided on the beach. Agnieszka had pushed Luiza into placing her towel close to where Ida was holding court, the plan being for her to invite her two friends over, so they could all be part of the most enviable group on the riverbank. So Luiza had dripped her awkward way through the adoring young men, only to be rewarded with her sister's surly enquiry. Mumbling a hastily concocted message concerning Pani Anna's whereabouts that evening, she had retraced her damp steps, mortified.

"She's waving at you!" Agnieszka shook Luiza's shoulder.

"Of course, she is," muttered Luiza.

"No, she is, honestly, Lou-lou. Look."

Luiza kept her eyes screwed shut until Gosia confirmed, "Actually, Lou-lou, Ida *is* waving at you. It looks like she wants you to come over."

Opening her eyes, Luiza was astonished to see that it was true. Indeed, one of Ida's bare-chested acolytes was just then loping towards the trio.

"Come on, little sis, big sis wants you," he drawled, pulling her up and towing her back to Ida. Sliding her sunglasses down her nose, her sister bestowed one of her most dazzling smiles.

"Well, it's not *Vogue*, and it's a shame you were in school uniform, but it's clearly you, Lou-lou," Ida said, holding up a copy of *The Friends of the Jews*. "Congratulations! I'm pleased to see that you're shopping at Baumgold – they definitely have the best haberdashery selection in Warszawa."

A couple of the young men nodded their approval and smiled at Luiza. Her sister, meanwhile, winked affectionately, before pushing up her glasses and turning her attention to her messenger. Luiza stood for a moment, stunned, before returning to her friends. She led them back down the beach at a run and plunged into the water, weightless with joy at Ida's public commendation.

At the Abels' that evening, Luiza noticed the photograph from the freesheet was tucked into the frame of the mirror in Elsa's and Dawid's room. She was cuddling Misza and Elsa caught her looking at it over the top of his head.

"Dawid spotted it." Elsa laughed. "Not the most flattering image of you, but we do appreciate the context."

Luiza smiled weakly, as Elsa took Misza and placed him in his cradle, then sat on the bed with her.

"I don't understand it." Luiza sighed.

"What?"

"Why people hate you so much."

Elsa shrugged. "They don't really hate *us*. They're frightened, but it's easier to claim hatred of us than face what they really fear."

"But doesn't it scare you?"

"Sometimes," Elsa admitted, glancing at the cradle. "I'm scared we won't be able to protect him."

"Right, final question. Who said to whom: 'You have in your fingers an orchestra of butterflies?' No conferring – you have thirty seconds from now."

Dawid checked his watch as the others scribbled. School finished the following day, so Luiza had just had her last piano lesson until September and had been invited to a special farewell supper, for which Pani Abel had made her favourite, *naleśniki*. Even Pani Marysia's crêpes had not been as light as the ones served at the Abels', nor the curd cheese so fragrantly sweet. Having eaten, they were now engaged in a quiz that Dawid had formulated. All the questions were harvested from subjects they had discussed while helping with her homework.

"Right, time's up. Let's start with the last question. Can I have your answer, Lou-lou?"

"Adam Mickiewicz, to Fryderyk Chopin."

The marking of the quiz caused much hilarity, with Pan Abel coming last. When the laughter finally died down and Luiza prepared to leave, she felt sad that it would be months before she visited again.

"Now, be sure to practise every day, dear," admonished Pani Abel.

"Misza will miss you," said Elsa, hugging her.

"Be sure to stay out of trouble, our good friend," smiled Pan Abel.

Dawid walked her out, saying that he would see her to the hotel. Unlike his father-in-law, Dawid did not wear a yarmulke, and his smart suit was what any young professional would wear. Guiltily, Luiza recognised her relief that no one need identify this man beside her as Jewish.

Dawid joked with her all the way, posing silly supplementary questions to the quiz he had devised. But as the two of them stood on the pavement in front of the Hotel Mazowiecki, he regarded her solemnly.

"Take care of yourself, Lou-lou. These are strange times."

"But surely it's you who need to take care?"

"I'll certainly do that," replied Dawid, with a sardonic smile. "Besides, haven't you heard? The Communist Party has proposed that trade unions form units to defend Jews against antisemitic attacks. They even want an international conference about the issue. So, we'll be able to rest easy in the hands of Polish workers."

The grin disappeared and he became serious.

"You're a good friend, Lou-lou – we'll miss you."

Gravely, he shook her hand, as he had on their first meeting, and Luiza watched him walk away, until he was lost in the crowd of window shoppers and flâneurs who were making the most of the fine evening. Turning to face the revolving doors, she smiled expectantly at Grzegorz, in his braided uniform. But the doorman's gaze was cold and he made no move to set the door in motion, remaining 'at ease', with his hands resolutely behind him. Luiza felt her face grow warm – a sensation that was becoming familiar. She pushed against the brass bar, but the door would not move. She tried again. Confused, she stood back as an elderly couple – he in a crumpled linen suit, she sporting a fox stole in spite of the heat – approached the door. Grzegorz snapped smartly to attention, and Luiza saw him flip the switch to unlock the door, before placing his gloved hand precisely where hers had just been. With a slight push, he set the door in motion. Quickly, she slipped in behind the pair and ran up the carpeted stairs to Pani Anna's apartment.

Neither Ida nor Pani Anna was in. They had travelled east that day, together with Roman and Grażyna, to introduce the baby to Pani Anna's family in Nieśwież.

Luiza sat on her bed. Despite the warm evening, she felt chilled and climbed beneath her eiderdown. Staring at the scarred face of the icon on her bedside table, she tried to formulate a prayer, but only one word came: "Why?"

Chapter 24

July 1936, Malinów

A week later, Luiza arrived at Malinów. With Ida and the others in Nieśwież, only Waldemar was at home. He enlisted Luiza's help in tackling the rooks that threatened his golden hectares of barley.

It was thrilling to track the bird's flight and judge the precise moment at which to pull the trigger. The black shape hung in the air for a heart-stopping moment before plummeting in a diminishing spiral to earth. In her head, Pappa's voice asserted: "If God had meant us to maim and kill his creatures for sport, he would not have created them things of beauty with a capacity for fear" and she fired again to silence him.

When she was not shooting, she was riding. Having outgrown Nutmeg, Waldemar had promoted her to Rumi, a fifteen-hand dapple-grey mare with a zest for life that expressed itself in a brief bucking frenzy when given her head. Caught unawares the first time, Luiza had come off, but now she was prepared for the ritual and enjoyed the challenge.

Today she had kept her seat and Rumi had settled into an easy canter when Luiza caught sight of a landau turning in at the park gates. She adjusted the mare's pace to fall in beside it. "How was Nieśwież?" she called.

Pani Anna responded with a tired smile. "Lovely, but it's such a long way. We're exhausted – all except Roman."

The little boy was using his mother's hands to lever himself upright on her lap, bouncing and crowing with delight. Grażyna, her mother-in-law and the nursemaid regarded his antics indulgently, but Ida seemed mesmerised by the dust rising in their wake.

She was still distracted at supper. Luiza had to ask her three times to pass the butter. With a wink Waldemar announced, "Your sister's got something on her mind. Or should I say someone?"

Ida flushed but her gaze soon drifted back to the casement window, open to the mild evening air with its delicious scent of stocks.

"So, who is he, then?"

Luiza lay on her front on Ida's bed. Her chin in her hands, she watched as Ida dreamily brushed her hair. The private smile that played on her sister's lips made her want to pinch her.

"For goodness' sake, Idka, stop looking so unbearably smug. What's his name? How old is he? How did you meet? When are you getting married?"

The final question broke Ida's trance. Brandishing the hairbrush more vigorously, she protested, "Don't be ridiculous." But the mildness of her tone rendered the objection unconvincing.

Luiza knelt, wide-eyed. "Ida, you *have* spoken about marriage, haven't you?"

For the first time, Ida looked directly at her, and her eyes danced.

"Oh, Lou-lou! He's so... wonderful! You can't imagine." She sighed, before crimping her lips again in that exasperating smile.

"Ida!" Luiza shrieked. Seizing her by the wrist, she pulled her sister onto the bed. "Stop being so completely impossible," she ordered. "Tell me his name."

"Mirosław Timorecki. Oh, Lou-lou, you've no idea! He's so... so..."

"Wonderful. Yes, I know. Age?"

"Twenty-two. He's an engineer. He's doing his national service, but from next year he's got a job with the railways."

"O-ho! Well, he should get on well with Pappa, then."

"Oh, yes, he..." Ida's smile faded into a puzzled frown. "Why?"

"Because of The Three Miracles, of course." Her sister still looked bemused. "Pappa's Sunday afternoons with our grandfather at Wilno station, remember?" Luiza exclaimed. "And his escape from the Bolsheviks on the locomotive."

Ida nodded then, vaguely.

"Anyway, how did you meet?"

"At a party in Nieśwież. That's where he's from. He

asked me to dance. We danced all night. Oh, Lou-lou, he's..."

Ida's gaze wandered again, so Luiza gave her a shake. "When exactly are you getting married?"

"I don't know – soon, I hope. Although I can already hear Pappa: You need to wait a while, Ida. Oh," – Ida's glowing face crumpled – "I can't bear it. He'll never let me marry Mirek. I'll be an old maid before he says yes, and Mirek won't want me anymore."

"Don't be ridiculous. When you're twenty-one you can do as you like."

"But that's over three years away," she wailed.

"Elope, then! Why look for problems before they even exist? How do you know Pappa won't think Mirek's absolutely right for you and give his blessing? They'll have trains in common – it's a promising start."

"Pappa had trains in common with Dziadek Svensen and he still had to wait thirteen years," Ida lamented, her mood shifting from ecstasy to despair.

"Yes, but there was the minor detail of Pappa being foreign. Do you have a photograph?"

Ida took one from her handbag, a studio portrait of a handsome young man in infantry uniform. With one foot propped on a chair and his wrists crossed on the raised knee, he leant his weight forward. His cap dangled from one hand and he held a half-smoked cigarette in the other. His face was broad, with a fine nose and a high forehead, overhung by a lock of hair. The stylised pose generated a raffish look, a hint of a smile in the self-assured look he aimed at the camera. Luiza could see why Ida was smitten.

"Well, he's certainly good-looking. But I don't think this is the photograph with which to introduce Pappa to his future son-in-law. It has Wojtek Petrowski written all over it – Pappa would see a playboy, not an engineer."

"What do you mean?" demanded Ida, plucking the photograph from Luiza's fingers. "He doesn't look anything like Wojtek; he's much more handsome."

"Well, he's differently handsome, but he looks every bit as much the ladies' man. Pappa would have you locked in a convent in no time if he saw this. When you arrange for them to meet, make sure you brief Mirek very carefully on how to behave. Tell him to concentrate on the engineering and switch off the charm." It was a novel situation, thought Luiza; she had never before given Ida advice.

Ida deliberated. "You're right. Yes, he'll need to show his serious side. Oh, Lou-lou!" Ida's eyes sparkled as she hugged her sister. "I want to introduce them right away – I'll ask Pani Anna to invite Mirek over when Pappa comes. Pappa will love him. You'll love him! When we're married, we'll live in Toruń – that's where his job is. You can come and stay. We'll have such fun."

"Only two days – please, Pappa. Surely you could manage two days?"

"I'm sorry, Lou-lou. I honestly can't." Her father's sigh extended over eighty kilometres of crackly telephone line. "Things here are complicated. I'm truly sorry to miss your birthday, but we'll celebrate again once you're home."

"It won't be the same," Luiza responded, aware

that she sounded peevish but unable to swallow her disappointment.

"I know, Lou-lou, but it's the best I can do."

He sounded so tired. Guilt made her relent.

"Don't worry, Pappa. It will be nice to have another celebration to look forward to."

Luiza thought she heard him blow his nose. And when he finally spoke, his voice was muffled. "Good, good. That's what we'll do, then. I have to go now. Goodbye, Lou-lou."

"But, Pappa, we'll speak on my birthday? You'll call again?"

The buzz on the line ceased.

"I'm sorry, Miss, but the other party has disconnected the call," said the operator. "Shall I call them back for you?"

"No, thank you."

Pappa did call, though he said little beyond 'Happy Birthday' and was nonplussed when Luiza thanked him for the racquet, even though Pani Anna had told her it was from him, specially for her tennis party.

Waldemar partnered Luiza in the mixed doubles, while Ida played with an adoring Tadeusz Zielinski, from the farm abutting Pani Anna's estate. When they lost and Ida chided her partner for watching her more than the ball, Tadeusz maintained that it would have been unchivalrous to beat the birthday girl.

Returning from the stables a few days later, Luiza spotted a familiar valise in the hall and found her father in the salon.

"Pappa! You did manage to get away…"

Her voice died. Pappa seemed like a child seated in a

grown-up's chair. It was not just that he was even thinner, but that he looked so vulnerable. Luiza had never felt this protective of him before. All she wanted was to gather him in her arms.

His face was grey, and the hand he reached towards her shook. Stooping to embrace him, she felt it flutter against her back. When she withdrew, her cheek was moist with his tears.

"What is it, Pappa? What's happened?"

He shook his head.

A hand was on her shoulder, and Pani Anna's voice, soft with sympathy, in her ear. "It's alright, Lou-lou. Your father's had a shock. There was an accident at the mill. But there's nothing to worry about. He needs a few days' peace and quiet and he'll be right as rain."

"An accident?" Luiza's voice rose in alarm. "What happened? Were you hurt, Pappa?"

"Nobody was hurt," Pani Anna soothed. "But your father is very tired. Why don't you go and change and let him rest?"

"Pappa?" Luiza implored. Her father smiled weakly. In a hoarse whisper he said, "I'm alright, Lou-lou, really. Do as Pani Anna says."

Reluctantly, Luiza left the room.

Ida was swimming with friends at a nearby lake, so Luiza was alone with her anxiety. She bathed and changed quickly, but when she returned to the salon Pappa was no longer there. He did not appear at supper and neither did Ida, who had telephoned to say that she would be staying on at the Zielinskis', where an impromptu party had been arranged. Luiza should come. Pani Anna encouraged her, but she did not have the heart.

Instead, she spent the evening in her room, the scent of jasmine wafting through the open window. She watched the red ball of the sun descend to the horizon's golden line and rest awhile, before sinking slowly beneath it. In its place rose the moon, a perfect sickle, and Luiza counted the stars as they gathered in the darkening sky. The pinpoints of light soon grew beyond number, yet still she sat, unable to contemplate sleep as she rehearsed different scenarios for the accident at the mill. Her knowledge gave her scope for varied and detailed possibilities, involving spinners, driers and combers. But mainly steam. Yet she had seen no evidence of physical injury, and while Pappa's debility was distressing, Luiza was more tormented by his unprecedented abandonment of Zakątek. Whatever had happened had clearly pushed him beyond endurance, yet Pani Anna claimed that he would recover. How could she know? A tide of terrifying questions threatened to overwhelm her, until a throaty roar intruded upon the stillness of the night. Luiza watched her sister accomplish a graceful exit from the low-slung car, even while twisting her body to elude the driver's attempted embrace. With a wave of her hand, Ida skipped up the steps as Tadeusz Zielinski rammed the car into gear and thundered off.

Luiza was waiting on the landing.

"What, still awake? You should have come, Lou-lou — it was a laugh."

Luiza followed her sister into her room, Ida humming

a tune as she waltzed around the room, kicking off her shoes and undoing her dress.

"I couldn't. Something's happened."

"Mmm... what?" Ida was in her slip now, admiring her reflected dance in the mirror. "Honestly." She giggled. "That Tadeusz Zielinski. He just won't take no for an answer. I used to find him charming, but now I've met Mirek, well, he's just a foolish boy, really."

"Idka! Pappa's here."

"Oh, but that's marvellous. Now I can invite Mirek."

"No, you can't. Something's wrong; he looks dreadful. Pani Anna said there was an accident at the mill, but no one will tell me what happened. They keep saying there's nothing to worry about – if that's true, then why does Pappa look so awful?"

"Oh, honestly, you old worrier," Ida said, tweaking Luiza's nose affectionately. "You know he's been working much too hard for ages now. I expect it's finally caught up with him, and Pani Anna's prevailed at last and he's here for a rest."

"But what about the accident?"

"It's probably just a bale of flax that got wrongly processed. You know how Pappa gets in a state with anything short of perfection at his precious mill," said Ida, yawning. "Goodness, I'm tired. Now, go to bed and let me get my beauty sleep. You'll see, in the morning things won't look half as bad."

Somewhat reassured by Ida's words, Luiza slept. But in the morning Pappa did not appear for breakfast, and when Ida came from his room looking shaken, the terror returned. As did the familiar sense of exclusion; she was not invited into Pappa's room, nor to Pani Anna's study, where Ida went next.

Waldemar suggested a ride, or perhaps taking the guns out – he had spotted some rabbits on the lawn earlier. But Luiza shook her head. She did not want to leave the house while the answers she sought were concealed behind doors which might open at any moment. Eventually, Waldemar left for the stables. As she lingered in the salon, Luiza was reminded of another time she had waited for closed doors to reveal the secrets behind them, after Mama's stroke.

Eventually Ida, pale and agitated, beckoned her into the study. Pani Anna began in soothing tones: Things had not been going well at the mill for a while; Pappa had been working too hard and needed rest. He might need to give up Zakątek...

Ida interrupted. "Lou-lou must be told everything. She has to know the truth, or she'll just be left worrying."

So Pani Anna took a deep breath and began again, going all the way back to the Ministry of Defence's lucrative order for Pappa's patented invention. It was then that Korski's chairman, Lemski, had set about ousting Pappa, so that he himself would be left in control of the patent and the profits. To that end, he had engineered the appointment of the unctuous Graban as manager.

Pappa's suspicions were aroused, which was why he so rarely left Zakątek. He had worked himself into the ground, overseeing operations he would normally have left to his manager. Minor disruptions having failed, Lemski ordered more extreme action and two days ago, during the pre-switch on inspection, Graban said one of the spinners was overheating. Pappa went to have a look, while the manager made an apparently urgent telephone call.

Pappa was at the top of the ladder, about to step onto the platform to look into the huge metal basin, when there was a rumble deep within the machine and the hiss of steam entering its network of pipes. He knew instantly he was in danger; the valve was not yet open for operation, which meant that, as pressure built, the machine could explode. He scrambled down a few rungs before launching himself into the air and landing, just as the valve blew, in a vat full of soaking flax.

"Thank God the valve gave, or the whole spinner could have blown up," Luiza exclaimed.

The wet flax protected Pappa from the scalding steam, and Pan Cholowa and the others pulled him out before he drowned. No one knew how the lever in the engine room came to be switched so that steam was sent to the spinner. Graban, back from his phone call, looked shocked and oozed concern.

The doctor was sent for. Remarkably, Pappa was unscathed, and the only prescription was rest. Pappa intended to go back to work the next day but, on reflection, had finally determined to let go. His life was worth more than this dirty fight.

"But what will he do? Can he really give up Zakątek?" Luiza found it hard to imagine.

"Nothing's decided yet, but he's thinking seriously about going to Łódź," Ida explained. "He's got a friend there, remember, the one with that big factory in Pabianice? He's been pressing Pappa to come and set up production at Bauer and Lande for ages, but Pappa would never leave Zakątek."

"Łodź?" Luiza looked aghast. "Would we have to live there?"

"How should I know?" Ida's irritation revealed her own misgivings, but Pani Anna interjected, equably, "Let's not rush ahead of ourselves, dears. The first thing to do is to get your father back on his feet. He's had a bad shock, and he's going to need all our help to recover. Whatever he decides to do, he needs your support. He's been struggling on his own and he needs his daughters."

Both girls looked shamefaced and Luiza asked, earnestly, "Tell us what we can do, how we can help."

"Just give him time to recover – keep him company when he needs you. But it's probably best not to ask a lot of questions. I don't think he wants to talk about it yet. He'll tell you as much as he wants in his own good time. And, when he's ready, he'll also inform you of his decision."

Pani Anna rose from her chair and approached the sofa. She squeezed her plump bulk between the sisters and hugged them to her.

"Don't worry, my dears, everything will be fine, you'll see. And, anyway," she added, with an impish wink, "Malinów is closer to Łodź than it is to Warszawa."

Chapter 25

August 1936, Malinów

*P*appa's resilience surprised them all. His hands stopped shaking within a couple of days and he began to eat, tempted by dishes Pani Anna knew were his favourites. He took long walks in the park, turning down both girls' offers of company with a smile. "Thank you, but I need time to think." He slept each afternoon and retired early in the evenings.

Less than a week after his dramatic arrival, his valise was back in the hall and Luiza found him in the salon, taking tea with Pani Anna and Ida.

"Ah, Lou-lou. Good. I was hoping you'd be back in time – I don't want to miss my train."

"What train, Pappa? Where are you going?"

"To Zakątek."

Luiza gasped. "But Pappa – are you sure? Is it safe?"

"Oh, yes, it's perfectly safe. Don't worry."

With that he put down his glass and picked up his Panama hat and the brass-topped cane he had taken to using on his daily walks. The coachman had brought the landau to the front door. Pappa looked back only once to wave.

They heard nothing from him. Luiza was busy riding, swimming and playing tennis, yet a stubborn knot of anxiety persisted in the pit of her stomach. Ida, meanwhile, thought only of Mirek, whose letters arrived almost daily.

"Lou-lou, do stop worrying. You saw how much better Pappa was when he left."

"Yes, but we don't know what's going on at Zakątek. He almost got killed, remember?"

"Well, you can be sure we'd hear if that happened – no news is good news. Now, go and shoot something and let me get on with my letter!"

At last, a phone call: Pappa was in Pabianice and he wanted them to join him.

He met them at Łodź station, in one of Bauer and Lande's cars, driven by a chauffeur in a peaked cap. He seemed more solid, more elementally Pappa than he had in a long while. But Luiza's relief turned to dismay as the built-up streets sped past the windows of the long, black Mercedes.

The Bauer and Lande factory lay ten kilometres southwest of the city, in Pabianice. Here things were slightly better; the buildings were lower and Luiza felt there was room to breathe. The car bumped over the cobbles of a wide, tree-lined street with tramlines running down the middle, before turning off through an arch beneath a clock. It was in the middle of a crenelated white wall, which stretched the length of the entire block. The yard they found themselves in felt familiar: Bales of cotton were stacked along the walls, and men were loading Hessian-wrapped rolls onto two lorries, while through the open door of one of the sheds came the steady hum of machinery.

"Here, follow me," Pappa called, leading the way through another door into a large, cavernous space.

"You see, the boilers and spinners can stand here, then there's room for the dryers over there, and in that corner we can put the combing machines. They say the Bauer and Lande steam engine can supply the power, but I'm not so sure – I may have to install my own, which would mean building into the yard. Anyway," Pappa stopped pacing to gesture expansively and grin at his daughters, "what do you think?"

Ida, who was using a lace handkerchief to rub dust from her handbag, eyed the empty shed with distaste, but Luiza was enraptured.

"You could make the whole process far more efficient here – you wouldn't have all that carrying to and fro, the way it is at Zakątek, with the boilers so far from the spinners. But how big can their steam engine be?"

"Well, it does rather make ours look like a toy. Come, I'll show you."

Pappa was through the door and striding across the yard with Luiza close behind, but Ida had had enough. Standing in the doorway, she raised her voice. "Look, I haven't come all the way to Łódź to admire a steam engine."

Pappa smiled sheepishly. "I'm sorry, my dear. I only wanted you to see how ideal all this is for our purposes."

"It may be for ideal for your purposes, but mine have very little to do with a grubby shed and a pile of machinery." Ida's voice was climbing. "What am I going to do? Where will Luiza go to school? And where are we going to live? "

"Oh, but it's all arranged, my dear." Pappa grinned. "Come along and see our new apartment."

"All arranged? You've arranged our lives without even consulting us?"

Pappa reached for her hand. "Just come and see, please Idka."

The word 'apartment' alarmed Luiza. Surely it was insane to give up all of Zakątek for an apartment. She fell in behind Ida and Pappa, who had tucked her sister's arm under his so she had no choice but to walk with him. Striding past the waiting car, Pappa dismissed the driver with a wave of his hand. They were through the archway and out onto the street, Luiza hurrying to keep up. Pappa led them to the end of the block and turned into the next street, an avenue of nineteenth century, four-storey apartment buildings. They crossed the road, climbed the steps of the third house and Pappa held open one of the tall, narrow double doors. Inside it was dark, with a strong smell of polish. They climbed a flight of stairs and their father unlocked a door.

The gloomy landing had filled Luiza with foreboding, but once the door was open, a stream of light set the dust motes dancing. She had expected a dimly lit hallway, like the Abels'. Instead, she found herself in a large, square lobby, with regularly spaced doors and a broad passageway leading off. Sunlight poured through the open double doors of a large salon, where the French windows were flung wide onto a small, flower-decked balcony.

"Ah, Pani Krawcik!"

At her father's exclamation, Luiza turned from the window to see a tall, slender woman enter the salon. She wore a simple but well-cut dark dress, partially concealed by an apron on which she was wiping her hands. She extended one to Ida, who shook it in bewilderment. The woman repeated the gesture with Luiza.

"So, you're the lovely daughters I've heard so much about. Delighted to meet you."

She spoke fluent Polish, but with an accent.

"Pani Krawcik is our housekeeper, girls," announced Pappa. "She's going to keep us in order."

The woman smiled. Dark curls framed fine, strong features and Luiza found herself smiling back. Pani Krawcik continued, with her delightful inflection, "But you must be starving. Come, lunch is prepared. Well, to be more accurate, a picnic is prepared."

In the dining room, a tablecloth was spread on the floor. There was a single chair, which Pappa finally took, at Pani Krawcik's insistence. Luiza noted this victory on the housekeeper's part; Pappa rarely conceded. The rest of them sat on cushions as they ate from a colourful spread of cold meats and salads and drank a refreshing berry compote. Ida had recovered her composure, and having discovered that Pani Krawcik was from Paris, she quizzed her about fashion houses.

"I'm afraid I never spent much time in the Eighth Arrondissement – the Eighteenth was my neighbourhood – Montmartre."

Luiza opened her eyes wide. "Did you know any artists?"

Pani Krawcik gave her slow smile again. "Well, yes, a few you wouldn't have heard of, including my husband. But I used to see Picasso and Marc Chagall around, and Rene Magritte, occasionally."

"Not any of the Impressionists, then?" Luiza was disappointed.

Pappa laughed. "Pani Krawcik is much too young to have seen them, Lou-lou."

"Yes, the proponents of the later 'isms' were more my time – Cubists, Surrealists. And, of course, there was jazz – I even saw Josephine Baker! There were some wonderful clubs. We danced all night."

Ida sighed. "How marvellous. I love dancing – there are excellent places in Warszawa."

"Here in Łódź, too."

"Really?" Ida looked doubtful.

"Oh yes, I only agreed to move to my husband's hometown on condition we could still go dancing. Of course, since he died, I haven't had the opportunity. But I heard that the Karasiński and Kataszek Orchestra played here not long ago."

"Really?" exclaimed Ida. "I saw them at Café Adria."

Pappa raised an eyebrow. "Well, now we've established that the nightlife meets with your approval, Ida, I assume the move can go ahead?"

The girls returned to Malinów that evening, leaving their father to the complex arrangements involved in moving his business. It was the final week of Luiza's school holiday, but she was perturbed as to Pappa's plans. Though hugely relieved that he was so fully himself again, she was acutely aware of impending loss: of her school friends, of the Abels, of Zakątek. Ida's feelings, on the other hand, were less ambivalent.

"It's ridiculous! How can he expect us to just up sticks and move to some god-forsaken hole?"

"Well, Łódź is Poland's second city, so I don't really think you can call it that, dear," Pani Anna attempted, but Ida would not be mollified.

"I don't care! It's drab and horrible. And I don't know anyone there. For goodness' sake, I've finally left school, my life should be beginning, and he wants to bury me in Łódź. Has he even asked what I want? Has he considered me for just one second?"

"Ida, dear, try to remember how bad things have been for your father and for how long. Now he's found a way out, a way to get back his health and happiness, and his family. He's doing this for you."

"Well, I wish he wouldn't." Ida sobbed. "If I elope with Mirek, it will be Pappa's fault."

Luiza could not help pointing out the lack of logic in this argument. "But Toruń's much smaller than Łódź…"

"Oh, don't you start!" exploded her sister. "I don't care if it's a village. I'd rather live in a hovel with Mirek than in Pappa's wretched 'apartment' in Łódź."

"Here, dear – come sit by me and calm down." Pani

Anna patted the couch. "You're bright red. All this shouting does your complexion no good at all."

Ida threw herself down, her face in Pani Anna's lap. The older woman stroked her hair. "You know, I remember your dear mother once said something very similar – though in a much calmer manner. That she'd rather your father were a cobbler and they lived in a cottage, because then at least she'd see him every day. If she were here now, she'd leap at the chance of you all living together in an apartment around the corner from a factory where your father is well supported, where he'll be happy and safe."

Ida sobbed harder, while Luiza tried her best to see that the benefits of the move outweighed the losses. But then, "Oh, no!" she exclaimed, and Pani Anna looked up.

"What is it, dear?"

"Mono! She'll hate living in an apartment."

Luiza began to cry. With her free hand, Pani Anna patted the couch again, and Luiza came to lean against her. Stroking both their heads, Pani Anna consoled, "It will be alright, you'll see. Everything will turn out for the best."

Chapter 26

September 1936, Zakątek

*L*uiza was perched on the stone parapet of the terrace outside the dining room at Zakątek, fondling Mono's ears as the spaniel lay in the sun beside her. She was saying goodbye to Zakątek, and to Mono, who would be going back to Pan Rubacz.

From behind her came the clink of china and rustle of paper. Anjela was packing the dinner service into boxes, pausing frequently to blow her nose. Luiza had been helping, but needed a break from Anjela's repeated, tearful hugs and Janek's unrelenting glumness. He was taking down pictures and rolling up kilims. At least there was no Pani Aurelia. According to Anjela, she had become hysterical after Pappa's accident. The men had to drag her off him. Now she was in Wilno, living with her mother, sister and niece.

Pappa had secured employment for Anjela and Janek

on neighbouring estates. But they had been at Zakątek longer than Luiza and could not imagine leaving it any more than she could. She tried not to think that she might never see them again. They had known Mama. And Zakątek was the only place she could remember Mama. She worried that the faint memories she had would fade even faster without Zakątek as reference.

Luiza turned to face left, where the bedroom wing stretched, partially obscuring the silver birches on the way to the mill. The grass disappeared down the steep bank to the lake – she could see the tops of the alders and willows at its edge. She remembered the night of the fire, when smoke had obscured the trees, and Mama, in her silk dressing gown, had supervised the removal of valuable items from the house. Now she looked straight ahead, where the graceful sweep of lawn was bordered with rose and acacia, and the azaleas which hid the Marian shrine. She had visited it earlier that day and left a jug of pink and mauve hydrangeas – Mama's favourite – on the ledge. Having taken in each element of the vista before her, she now closed her eyes to fix it behind her eyelids.

Opening them again, she panned to the right, where the salon and Pappa's study hid the tennis court. She imagined piano chords wafting through the window and pictured the lane beyond, the rutted track to Zapole, which she had travelled with Mama to distribute provisions. But her musing was interrupted by voices coming from the study.

"But why can't we stay on in Warszawa with Pani Anna?"

Ida sounded close to tears.

"Because I want my family with me," stated Pappa in a tone that was reasonable but definite. "I've been without you for too long. See how you've grown? – what I've missed. You're a woman now; soon you'll be leaving me for good. I want my daughters with me until then."

"What about Luiza, though?" Ida tried a different tack. "You can't just take her out of school. What about her education?"

There was a pause, and when Pappa spoke, he sounded less sure. "I know. It's a shame – she's doing well. But Pani Krawcik will tutor her, and there's a decent finishing school she can attend, where they'll polish off some of our tomboy's rough edges."

"You mean she won't matriculate?"

"We'll have to see how things go."

"But, Pappa, can't you see—"

"I can see that I've neglected my family for too long. Now I've got a second chance, and I don't intend to make the same mistake again. We're going to live in Pabianice – all three of us."

"But Pappa..."

"But nothing, Idka. We're going; that's final."

Ida was red-eyed when she joined Luiza on the terrace.

"He just won't listen; he's being so selfish."

Luiza knew that it was no use trying to reason with Ida in this mood, but after what she judged to be a decent interval, she ventured, "Perhaps it won't be so bad..."

"Not so bad!"

Too soon.

"We know no one in Łódź. I'll be bored out of my

mind, you'll have no education… how can you say not so bad?"

Luiza looked to her left, to where the mill stood, hidden from sight. She really wanted to make Pappa happy. But how could she become an engineer if she did not matriculate? But then, perhaps it no longer mattered, if Zakątek was beyond saving.

Pani Anna arrived the next day; Luiza suspected that Ida had telephoned her. She and Pappa were closeted in his study for a long time. When they called the girls in, Pappa was behind his desk, which had a label tied to one leg, marking it for removal to Pabianice. Pani Anna smiled encouragingly at them from the window seat. For the first time since they had met him in Łódź, their father seemed subdued. Luiza worried that he was suffering a relapse. He glanced at them, then down at the pen in his hands, spiralling the cap off and on as he spoke.

"Well, our good friend has made me see that I have probably been asking too much of you both."

Peering from beneath bushy eyebrows, which were now completely white, he smiled ruefully. "I suppose I did spring this on you rather suddenly," he continued. "And it's true, as Pani Anna says, that I'm going to be extremely busy establishing the business at Pabianice, while still disengaging from Korski and winding up my side of things here. Too busy for proper family life – yet."

He screwed the cap on firmly and placed the pen on the blotter. Over steepled fingers, he regarded them steadily. Luiza sensed that Ida was holding her breath.

"So, I've agreed that we'll leave arrangements as they

are for now. The two of you will continue to live with Pani Anna at the hotel, and Luiza will stay at school until things are settled. You'll both come to Pabianice at weekends – and you, Ida, can stay longer, as you're not at school."

Ida glanced at Pani Anna, who raised her eyebrows and gave an almost imperceptible shake of her head. Luiza knew that their mother's friend had pushed Pappa to the very limit and any further appeal might risk losing all that had been gained. But Pappa must have picked up on the unspoken communication.

With a tired smile he added, "Ida, I appreciate that you'd rather be in Warszawa, and I don't expect either of you to spend time in Łódź until I can spend it there with you. At which time I look forward to meeting a certain engineer. I believe he's called Timorecki?"

Ida's cheeks bloomed pink as she looked beseechingly at Pani Anna, who laughed. "I thought it was time your father knew that your priorities have changed, Ida, to help him understand why you needed time to adjust to the move."

Chapter 27

Spring 1937, Warszawa

*P*appa did not complete the transfer of his business to Pabianice until March of the following year, so Luiza's education benefited from two more terms of school and piano lessons. But the move was finally happening; after Easter, which they were spending at Malinów, they would not come back to Warszawa. Ida did nothing but complain, so Luiza was taken aback, when she returned to the Mazowiecki after her final piano lesson, to find her dancing an exuberant polka around her bedroom.

"Mirek's coming!" she declared. "Pappa's going to meet him at last. Isn't it wonderful, Lou-lou? Come, dance with me."

Having just said farewell to the Abels and anticipating the same with Gosia and Agnieszka tomorrow, Luiza was hardly in the mood. Earlier, the 'last piano lesson of term' tradition had been maintained. Pani Abel had produced

Luiza's favourite *naleśniki z serem*, and Dawid another quiz, but the mood was subdued. They all knew that this time it was more than a simple holiday break.

Before leaving, Luiza had slipped in to see Misza again. He had almost outgrown his cradle, to which only a few of the paper birds were still attached – those that hung beyond his rapidly extending reach. He was fast asleep, thumb in mouth, dark lashes sweeping rosy cheeks. Luiza had brushed her lips lightly over their tight roundness and crept from the room.

Dawid walked her to the tram. Since the incident with the doorman, Luiza had refused to let him take her all the way home. He was promising to visit them if his work took him to Łódź, when suddenly he reached for Luiza's arm and steered her across the street. Glancing over her shoulder, Luiza noticed a group of young men in the military-style tunics she remembered from the university protest. They held placards calling for an urgent fight against the 'Jewish-Communist Conspiracy' and claiming 'Poland for Poles'.

"Camp of National Unity thugs," he said, quietly. "They picket Jewish shops, campaigning for us to lose our civil rights."

He shook his head, and Luiza glimpsed an uncharacteristic moment of despair before, with a smile, he tucked her arm in his. "Come on, I'll walk you to the next stop."

They continued in silence, Luiza's thoughts returning to a snowy afternoon and the crack of bone on iron. Eventually she asked, "Why do they do this?"

When Dawid responded, his tone was flat. "Fear? Ignorance? What does it matter? They always have and they always will – it's only the degree that changes."

Back at the Mazowiecki, Ida's urgent summons to dance shook Luiza out of her despondency. She was soon capering around the furniture until eventually, breathless and giggling, they both collapsed on the bed.

"You know, Lou-lou, there's another reason why Pani Anna persuaded Pappa to spend Easter at Malinów. I'm going to be received into the Catholic church – at last!"

Ida was radiant, Luiza aghast. "But Ida, you can't spring that on Pappa; he'll be so cross."

"It's alright, he knows – actually, he's agreed."

"Really?" Luiza found that hard to believe. And why, she wondered, was this the first she had heard of it? The familiar, corrosive hurt of exclusion churned within her.

"Pani Anna worked her magic again," Ida continued, happily. "She challenged Pappa to act on those liberal values he proclaims. And she pointed out that I'm not a schoolgirl any longer and he needs to respect *my* beliefs. Besides, Mirek is Catholic."

"Oh, Ida, you're so lucky." Luiza sighed.

Her resentment was receding, checked by her sister's uncontrived delight, and finally quashed by her generous reassurance: "Your time will come, chicken. I'm sure he won't make you wait as long – he thinks you're much less flighty than I am."

"Oh, he doesn't," Luiza protested.

"He does, Lou-lou. He thinks I'm only interested in

fashion and dancing. Whereas *you* care about machines."
Ida laughed, planting a kiss on Luiza's forehead. "You've
always had a special bond with him, ever since you played
with that wretched train set in the attic. Whereas I…"

Ida fell silent.

"Whereas you had a special bond with Mama – I know
it, Idka," Luiza said, stroking her sister's arm. "I was so
jealous – I wished I could embroider, so I'd be the one she
wanted at her side."

"No, you didn't." Ida smiled. "You couldn't wait to be
up in the attic or down at the mill. You could never sit still
for a moment."

Luiza sighed. "I know. But later, when Mama was in
her wheelchair, I so wished I could just sit with her like
you did, sewing and chatting, but I didn't know how. And
then it was too late to learn."

Ida covered Luiza's hand with her own. Quietly, she
said, "I miss her so much, Lou-lou. Not to be able to
introduce Mirek to her – it hurts."

Luiza bit her lip and nodded, uncertain of her voice.

The meeting between prospective father- and son-in-law
was a success. In fact, they got on so well that Ida had to
beg them to stop discussing trains. Luiza had met Mirek
before, but she noted again his calming influence on
her volatile sister. They seemed content in each other's
company, Ida turning down party invitations in favour of
time alone with Mirek. And her laugh was different when
Mirek was there. Less brittle and self-conscious, more
genuine.

A few days after Ida's baptism and confirmation in Pani Anna's private chapel, Mirek had to report back for duty. It was finally time for the Wolfers to leave for Pabianice.

The apartment on the tree-lined street felt familiar; furniture from Zakątek filled the rooms and the same pictures hung on the walls. But it was smaller, and the balcony was no substitute for lawns and a lake. And there was no Mono. But Luiza liked Pani Krawcik, who welcomed them warmly. Ida, however, barely acknowledged the friendly housekeeper and showed no interest at all in their new home. She was preoccupied to an extent that alarmed Luiza. After a few days a sudden, urgent appointment called her to Warszawa. Searching for a misplaced blouse after she had gone, Luiza discovered that her sister's wardrobe was empty, and it dawned on her that Ida would only ever be a visitor here.

It was also clear that Pappa was as much taken up with work as ever. For all his good intentions, he was rarely at home and the science and mathematics tuition he had promised failed to materialise. French lessons with Pani Krawcik went ahead, but Luiza still had a lot of time on her hands and no friends to spend it with. There were cafés, museums and cinemas a mere tram-ride away in Łódź, but they held little appeal without company. Empty weeks stretched ahead of her until September, when she would enrol on a typing and bookkeeping course at The Academy. So, when Aunt Ludmila's invitation to Riga arrived, it was a welcome deliverance.

Chapter 28

May 1937, Riga

The weather was fine, and Luiza walked by the sea every day. She had been to Riga before, after Mama died. But that was in winter. In spring, she could see why, when Uncle Herbert retired, they had chosen to return to the town they had in lived as newly-weds, before he was sent to Petrograd to guard the Tzar. Luiza pestered Aunt Ludmila for tales of their life in the Russian capital before 1917, especially those involving Mama and Pappa. Her parents had stayed with her aunt and uncle while Pappa studied at the Polytechnical University, and from Aunt Ludmila's accounts of grand balls and sleigh rides, Luiza formed a picture of a carefree, debonair couple, very much in love; she held it close.

On her way to the seafront each morning, she collected Aunt Rysia's dog. Arthritic Ferdi had died, but Mama's younger sister also lived in Riga and had a dachshund – a bright little bitch called Bruni.

While Luiza paddled, Bruni barked at the waves to scare them from the shore. When they rolled back in, she skittered up the beach in panic. Luiza took off, racing the breeze along the beach, with Bruni yapping delightedly at her heels. When she could run no more, Luiza sprawled on the sand, and the dachshund was all over her in an instant, licking her face and pricking her bare legs with sharp little claws. Above them was a sky of deep, uninterrupted blue, marked only by a shallow hump of moon that had not yet been rubbed out by the morning sun.

Aunt Rysia, blonde like Uncle Rafi, served a substantial breakfast on Luiza's return. Her appetite sharpened by the sea air, she filled white rolls with ham and cheese and helped herself to tomato and chive salad while her aunt chatted. Her daughter, Luiza's cousin Vera, was a couple of years older than Ida and rarely emerged from her bedroom before mid-morning, while her son, Paweł, was away at Wilno University. Aunt Rysia had frequently stayed at the villa in Saska Kępa and had taken Luiza to her first art gallery and first play.

"They've almost finished the new National Museum. Next year we'll have to make a special trip to Warszawa together, Lou-lou, for the opening."

Before Luiza could respond, Uncle Ryszard, who managed a Polish bank in the Latvian capital, growled from behind his newspaper, "Government of the Colonels, my foot - more like Government of the Imbeciles. Just look at this," he barked, slapping the paper. "Unemployment in the countryside is catastrophic. They'll have a full-blown strike on their hands if they go in this heavy-handed. Killing unarmed peasants, I ask you? Can't they see they need to invest in the rural economy – where else will we get our food?"

Uncle Ryszard's outburst had a familiar ring to it; he and her father had similar political views, whereas Uncle Herbert shared his deceased brother-in-law's military perspective. It meant that their arguments echoed uncannily those she used to hear between Pappa and Uncle Rafi.

Vera and Luiza were going to the cinema that evening, to see *Modern Times*. They were still laughing at Chaplin's antics when they arrived at Aunt Ludmila's. It was Friday, which was bridge night, so the girls made for the salon. But it appeared that the rubber had stalled.

"Oh, come *on*, Herbert, there's *Colonel* Beck running foreign policy, and *Marshal* Rydz-Śmigły looking after the home front. Camp of National Unity, indeed. It's so far to the right that the only possible unity is with the fascists. We need economists and businessmen in government, not just military has-beens who are still fighting an outdated war of independence."

Uncle Herbert scanned the fan of cards in one hand while he drummed the fingers of the other on the green baize of the card table. He was bald, apart from a thin, grey fringe at the back of his head, while Uncle Ryszard had a full head of thick, wavy hair, the glossy brown only faintly peppered with grey. Its sheen brought to Luiza's mind Wojtek's magnificent chestnut, Prince. Beneath his fine mane, however, Uncle Ryszard's face was scarlet as he finished his speech and took a long swig of beer. Aunt

Rysia was trying to catch his eye, and Luiza suspected that he was deliberately avoiding her.

Aunt Ludmila seemed relieved to see Luiza and Vera, who shook her finger at her father and admonished him, "Really, Pappa, behave! It's no good at all for your blood pressure, getting so worked up."

"How was the film?" Aunt Ludmila attempted, before Uncle Herbert interrupted, quietly, but they all listened.

"I don't believe fighting for our independence is outdated. We have powerful neighbours on either side and the best we can do is stay neutral and protect our sovereignty. Of course, the economy is important, but what good is the Polish economy without the Polish nation? We four can remember what it was like to be Polish when there was no Poland on the map. We need to defend our country, and who better to do that than the military?"

Having concluded, without raising his voice or his eyes, Uncle Herbert now placed his cards face down on the baize and stood.

"Come, let's eat, and I want to hear all about this funny little fellow with the cane and the silly walk," he exhorted, placing an arm around each of his nieces.

All too soon, Luiza's time in Riga was over, but in Pabianice little had changed. Ida was still in Warszawa, while Pappa spent all his time at the mill. At the end of a French lesson, Pani Krawcik made a suggestion. "Luiza, shall we conduct our next lesson in town? We could combine it with a visit to the Museum of Art and tackle the appropriate vocabulary."

The Museum at Plac Wolności had opened quite recently and was dedicated to modern art, with exhibits that stretched Luiza's artistic perception. Pani Krawick interpreted the many examples of Cubism and Surrealism for her, mainly in French. And she introduced her to the colourful, abstract paintings of Władysław Strzemiński, a friend of hers and the Museum's main initiator.

"He's the founder of one of the lesser known 'isms' – Unism, which is about how art can organise life, and he hoped this collection would bring together all the various strands of modern art."

Over the weeks, the pair repeated these excursions and Pani Krawcik suggested that Luiza address her as Mathilde. Łodź began to feel more welcoming as they attended concerts, plays and poetry readings, as well as visiting galleries.

For Luiza's fifteenth birthday, at the end of July, Pappa joined them at the Museum of Art. It was his first visit and afterwards, over their pre-theatre snack, he expressed his astonishment. "Who'd have thought there was so much going on in the unconscious mind? These surrealists certainly see things I don't. And," he added, with a mischievous gleam in his eye, "I have to say, I'm rather glad I don't. I'm not sure I could sleep at night if my dreams were filled with such spectres."

"But surely that's what art is about? Giving us windows into worlds that are not the everyday?" suggested Pani Krawcik.

"Oh, but I'm quite happy with the everyday, thank you. Remember I'm an engineer. I don't have the imagination

– or the time – for such flights of fancy," teased Pappa, waving his hand in the air expressively and sending a piece of his bread roll flying onto Pani Krawcik's plate.

"Oh, forgive me," Pappa apologised, embarrassed.

"Please, don't worry," Pani Krawcik laughed. "I think you've just created a perfect piece of Dada-ist performance art: Comedy forged by the everyday meeting the unexpected."

Pappa, beaming, fondled his moustache and mused, "Well, who'd have thought it? Seems I'm an artist after all, eh Lou-lou? And all these years I've believed myself to be no more than a clumsy engineer. But I just can't keep up with all these '-isms.'"

Luiza smiled at her father, delighted to hear him so playful. And he was beginning to fill out his waistcoat, too. The slice of chocolate torte he was tucking into was helping.

"Pappa," she said, aiming her fork at his plate (she had finished the cheesecake she had chosen). "Next time, we should go to the Municipal Art Gallery. That's full of figurative art – Polish painters like Jozef Kowner and Zygmunt Szreter. Their style is more post-Impressionist – still lives, street scenes, portraits. You'd like them. I have to say," looking sheepishly at Pani Krawcik, "*Madame, je les préfère à l'avant-garde. L'autre convient bien comme défi intellectuel, mais je préférerais un paysage sur mon mur – c'est plus reposant.*"

Pani Krawcik, nodding, affirmed, "*Je comprends bien, ma fille.*"

Pappa clapped his hands. "*Merveilleux!* I think that exhausts my French. But I'm impressed – the lessons are obviously going well. We must work on the maths and science, Lou-lou."

Luiza raised her eyebrows at her father, and he lifted his hands in submission. "I know, I know. It's my fault, but things will soon be more settled and I'll make the time. Now, if we're to get to the theatre for curtain-up, we'd better get going." He signalled for the bill.

"So, more edification in store tonight, eh? When you said we were seeing *The Undivine Comedy*, I was looking forward to an evening of laughter. But I read the review in yesterday's paper, and it seems it's about the class struggle. If you're hoping to introduce me to another '-ism', I'm afraid you're too late, Pani Krawick. Lou-lou will tell you, I had too close a shave with communism twenty years ago, and I'm unlikely to be converted now."

Pappa scanned the bill the waiter brought and folded some notes under the clip on the salver. Then he rose and pulled out Pani Krawcik's chair, offering her his arm as they left the restaurant.

Chapter 29

August 1937, Malinów

*L*uiza was spending August at Malinów while Ida was in Nieśwież with Mirek, visiting his family before he started his job in Toruń. There was much anxiety among landowners about the impact on the harvest of the Peasant Strike (the one that Uncle Ryszard had predicted), so Luiza offered to help. After a few hot, tiring and prickly days spent gathering and binding sheaves behind the reaping machine, she was relieved when the strike failed to spread, and Waldemar decided that he could manage without her.

At lunch one Saturday, Pani Anna suggested they go to the local fête, but Luiza was looking forward to her second ride of the day.

"Oh, do keep me company, dear, I'm sure you'll enjoy it," urged Pani Anna, "There are lots of activities, and lots of young people – it'll be fun."

When she still looked doubtful, Pani Anna added, "How about you drive us in the trap?"

Luiza immediately felt better disposed to the outing and went to change. She chose a red-and-white dress that enhanced her tan.

The bay pony trotted smartly along the lanes. When they reached the small town, Luiza steered him behind the church. There she tethered him, as they did on Sundays. Today, though, the field beyond was alive with noise and colour.

Babcias in flower-patterned head scarves, shawls crossed over their chests, sat on stools. In aprons stretched between their knees, or nested in straw on the grass in front of them, were brown eggs and creamy pats of butter and curd cheese. Stubby, mottled cucumbers were displayed alongside bunches of radishes and dill. Small, green apples lay in a purple stain spreading from mounds of glistening berries.

Beyond the country-women, wooden stalls were erected, with rainbows of kilims piled high on counters and boldly bloomed scarves draped along spars. Behind these, a wooden platform served as a dance floor, where young men and women in white shirts, black waistcoats and bright, striped trousers and skirts moved energetically to the scrape of a fiddle. Its vigorous rasp was punctuated with the spirited stamps and cries of what Luiza identified as an *Oberek*.

Tadeusz Zielinski, Ida's unrequited admirer, appeared with his sister, Dorota, to bear Luiza away, Pani Anna smiling and shooing her on. They passed between stalls of merchandise to the other side of the dance floor, where kiosks housed games of hoopla and 'guess the weight'. Beyond these a length of rope lay on the ground, with a group of girls collecting at one end and boys at the other.

"Come on," called Dorota, towing Luiza behind her, while Tadeusz headed for the other end.

"Heave-ho!" went the cry, as the rope lifted from the ground to be pulled taut above a white line chalked in the grass. The girls were quickly hauled towards it, until the boys suddenly released their grip and sent them tumbling backwards. Giggling, they reassembled. The boys repeated their trick, and the girls grew more dishevelled while the boys laughed harder. But as they were pulled towards the white mark for the third time, the girls let go first, clapping and whooping as the boys' line toppled. Luiza noticed a well-built, dark-haired young man eyeing her as he brushed down his trousers and tucked in his shirt. She held his gaze for a moment, before turning to link arms with Dorota and stroll back towards the kiosks.

At the hoopla stall, Luiza aimed for a small carved pot. She missed twice and was on her final hoop.

"A bit more to the left," said a voice so close to her ear that she could feel the speaker's breath. Turning, she faced the dark-haired boy from the tug-of-war.

"I have no trouble taking aim with a shotgun," she announced, coolly.

He smiled and inclined his head, reaching for her hand. "May I?"

Luiza surrendered the hoop and moved out of the way. The ring spun through the air before settling lazily around the wooden pot. The stall holder handed it to the boy, who passed it to Luiza with a bow.

"Thank you," she said, placing it in her shoulder bag.

"Will you use it for hairpins?" he enquired.

"I haven't decided."

The two girls drifted to a kilim stall, where Luiza shook out a vivid green-and-red patterned rug. Her fingers rubbed the coarse weave while Dorota whispered, "That was Karol Wyczyński. His family owns an estate near Żychlin. Don't look now, but he's over by the flower stall and he's watching you."

Casually, Luiza glanced over. The dark-haired boy was with a smaller, fair-haired lad, and they were both watching her. She swept her gaze back to the kilim and asked the price, before moving on to the next kiosk while Dorota continued her whispered commentary.

"He's studying agriculture in Warszawa. His friend is a student, too. He's visiting and he's called Wacek."

"Hey, you two!" Tadeusz put an arm around each and steered them to the dance floor.

"Let's see if you dance better than you haul rope."

He swung them onto the platform before jumping up himself. The fiddler was tuning up for a *Krakowiak* as the boys and girls gathered on opposite sides, the original dancers having disappeared, together with their costumes. Now the platform was filling with young people in their holiday best.

The boys went first, their high jumps and loud stamps following the fiddler's rhythm as they strutted in front of the girls. Then, with arms held high and skirts lifting as they spun, the girls drove them back. The tempo increased and some of the boys executed handstands or backflips. Wacek, the blonde student, crouched Cossack-style, raising his legs to the furious rhythm while the others clapped and stamped in time. Finally, he leapt up with a yell and disappeared into the crowd of young men.

Now the girls surged forward again, shaking their fingers at the boys and skipping and spinning furiously. The fiddler reached his climax, a sustained long scream of a note, before diving into a minor key and taking up the stately metre of a romantic *Kujawiak*. Sweating and dishevelled, a wave of boys engulfed the breathless girls. Karol Wyczyński stood in front of Luiza, trying for a gallant bow, his efforts sabotaged by the jostling crowd. Pushed against her, he smiled apologetically, and she felt his hand at her waist. The other grasped her right hand and they began to turn, Karol manoeuvring them into a space as the couples spread out.

"Luiza Wolfer," he murmured into her hair, "I'm very pleased to meet you."

Luiza pulled back to look up at him directly. "And you are?" She would not give him the satisfaction of knowing that she had found out.

He brought the hand he held to his lips and announced, "Karol Wyczyński, at your service." His eyes were a pale brown, flecked with gold. For a moment, Luiza could think of nothing to say.

"So, how did you become such a hoopla expert?" she asked, recovering herself. She tried to maintain her reserve while acutely aware of twin points of heat where he was touching her. Her right hand and the small of her back burned, but she kept her eyes fixed on his and resisted the impulse to look away.

"Oh, I've been coming to the fête since I was a kid. I haven't seen you here before, though."

"No, it's my first time. I'm staying with friends nearby."

"Perhaps I could visit you?"

Luiza shrugged. "Perhaps."

He did not attempt further conversation, but he was a good dancer, and Luiza relaxed as he guided her around the floor. When the fiddler anticipated the final notes of the *Kujawiak*, he held her closer. She was aware of a catch in her breathing and a wave of disappointment that this would soon be over.

She looked around for Dorota and Tadeusz but could see neither. When she told Karol she had to go, he did not immediately release her hand.

"I believe there's a tennis court at Malinów?"

Luiza nodded.

"Then may I challenge you to a match?"

That smile again. Luiza felt flustered and needed to put some distance between them, but he was still holding her hand.

"I… I'll have to ask my host," she gabbled. Karol brushed the back of her hand with his lips before releasing it.

"Of course, let's find her."

Together they walked back towards the church, Luiza spotting Pani Anna in a group of women seated at a table in the refreshment area. When they reached her chair,

Karol bowed and Pani Anna felt for the glasses that hung around her neck and peered up at him curiously.

"Pani Grudzinska, my name is Karol Wyczyński. I've had the pleasure of dancing with your house guest, and I was hoping you might allow me to continue our acquaintance on your tennis court?"

Pani Anna smiled broadly. "But of course. Come tomorrow afternoon."

"Tomorrow afternoon," he repeated, "I look forward to it."

"Charming. Utterly charming," Pani Anna beamed. Luiza shook the reins and clucked at the pony. She could still feel the imprint of Karol's hand on her waist, the softness of his lips on her hand. She was filled with elation and trepidation in equal measure, to the exclusion of all sensible thought.

She had no appetite the next day. Having changed for tennis, she picked up a book but found that she could not connect the words. The sound of hooves drew her to the window, to see Karol Wyczyński trotting up the drive on a tall chestnut with four white socks. The handle of his tennis racket poked out of the knapsack on his back. Luiza felt her heart race but stopped herself from running downstairs, waiting for Magda to announce her visitor.

Karol was stroking the chestnut's nose when she went down. He smiled and she nodded, holding her racquet with both hands to avoid his kissing one of them.

"We'll take your horse to the stable."

"Thank you. And I'll need to change."

He emerged from the tack room in white shorts, spinning his racquet. His legs were muscular and tanned.

"Now, where's the court?"

Luiza did not enjoy the match. Karol was a much better player than she was, which was annoying. He was also patiently solicitous of improving her game, which was intensely irritating.

"Alright!" she snapped, as he vaulted the net for the third time to correct her stance for the serve. Karol held up his hands in submission and jumped back. Her serve went over the line again. She was relieved when Magda appeared with a jug of lemonade.

Together they sat on the bench at the side of the court, Luiza acutely aware of how small the distance was between their bare knees. Karol chatted easily about films (he loved Westerns and his favourite actors were Gene Autry and John Wayne) and horses (the chestnut was called Whisky and always shied at motor cars) and she gradually relaxed.

"When can we play again?" Karol asked. Her hand was in his, his head lowered for the kiss, his gold-flecked eyes raised to hers in enquiry, "Tomorrow?"

Nonplussed, Luiza nodded and her face grew hot at the moist pressure of his lips on the back of her hand. At last, he raised his head and met her eyes again, with that look she found so unsettling. He mounted Whisky, the saddle creaking as he settled into it.

"No, wait." She would not make it so easy for him. "I have a dress-fitting in Żychlin tomorrow. Come on Tuesday."

Karol nodded, pressing his heels to Whisky's flanks. The chestnut took off down the drive at an easy canter. Before disappearing where the track wound to the left, Karol looked back and saluted. Luiza was reminded of Wojtek on Prince, vanishing into the copse at the top of Pan Rubacz's field. She grimaced at the thought of her hopeless crush, aged twelve. Three years on, how different were the circumstances. This time, she felt increasingly confident, it was she who was the object of passion. She smiled. Karol might lack a Clark Gable dimple, but his eyes more than made up for it.

On Tuesday afternoon he drove up in a two-seater trap, already dressed in his tennis whites. Luiza had had a quiet word with Magda, who brought the refreshments much sooner than she had on Sunday. She also brought an invitation from Pani Anna, for Karol to stay for tea.

The table was laid beneath the beech tree on the edge of the lawn. Grażyna was fully occupied, protecting the embroidered tablecloth from a tide of chocolate that threatened to overflow Roman's plate; the two-year-old was using both hands to cram a piece of torte into his mouth. While Luiza concentrated on her own slice and hoped her mouth was not smeared, Pani Anna presided over the samovar and Waldemar quizzed Karol.

"How did you manage the harvest? Were you hit by the strike?"

"No, thank heaven. But they've had a hard time in the south – I heard they even tried to block food supplies getting into towns."

"Until the police changed their softly-softly approach and fired a few shots…"

"Roman, no!" Grażyna was out of her chair. "Oh, Karol, I'm so sorry."

Roman had slid from his seat to emerge between Karol's legs. The toddler gazed curiously at the visitor, a chubby, chocolate-stained hand planted on either leg of Karol's spotless shorts. Pushing his smudged face into Karol's lap, he rubbed it from side to side while Karol stared, aghast. They were all struck dumb. At last, Grażyna grabbed her son. She held him at arm's length as she hurried towards the house, calling back apologies.

Luiza swallowed a giggle, and Pani Anna left the samovar in order to help her guest. Approaching purposefully, a napkin in hand, she let it hover uncertainly above the affected area of Karol's shorts. Her obvious discomfort ruptured Luiza's grip on her laughter. With an explosive snort, she dissolved into helpless tears of mirth. A flash of irritation crossed Karol's face, but it swiftly resolved into amusement and he smiled good-naturedly as Luiza did her best to recover.

"Oh, I'm sorry," she hiccupped, "It's just…" Her explanation was lost in further giggles.

Pani Anna shook the napkin at her. "For goodness' sake, pull yourself together, Lou-lou. Poor Karol. He can't possibly go home like this. Waldemar, get the poor boy something of yours to change into. Karol, you'll leave those here for laundering."

Waldemar, who was also laughing, led him away. Pani Anna waited until they were out of earshot. "Honestly, Lou-lou, you could have shown the poor boy some sympathy."

Luiza bowed her head in contrition, but the picture of Pani Anna, her hand poised irresolutely above Karol's lap, would not go away. Her shoulders shook.

"Lou-lou!"

"Oh, I'm sorry, Pani Anna, it's just… your face!"

"MY face?"

"Yes, when you were about to dab at the stain on Karol's shorts, you looked… confused?"

For a moment, Pani Anna's expression remained stern, before the skin around her eyes crinkled and her mouth softened.

"Oh dear!" she exclaimed, using the napkin to dab her eyes. "Oh dear, yes, well, I was at a bit of a loss."

Luiza snorted again, and the two of them convulsed with laughter.

Chapter 30

Autumn 1937, Pabianice

*L*uiza rode Rumi over to Karol's home to deliver his freshly laundered shorts. They did not play tennis again that summer, but they went riding and to the cinema in Żychlin. But soon it was September and time for Karol to return to Warszawa and Luiza to Pabianice and the next stage of her education.

The Academy was nothing like school; there was no uniform for a start. Thanks to her Warszawa dressmaker, Luiza was stylish enough for the fashionable clique and was included on cinema outings and invited to a few parties. For a while, playing the role that had always been Ida's was a pleasurable novelty for her. But none of her new friends rode, nor did they show any interest in the cultural interests that Mathilde Krawcik had shown her. Their prime concerns were clothes and boys.

On the former, Luiza's appearance scored highly, but

with no interest in fashion analysis, she soon fell short. And she did not offer Karol for approval on the latter because her feelings for him were still unclear.

He wrote several times a week and complained that her own letters were not so regular. If only she could have shared with Gosia and Agnieszka the delicious tingle of his touch, but also her irritation at his extreme attentiveness. They would understand this ambivalence. While a handsome, devoted boyfriend was cause for celebration, he could not possibly compete with their proven female friendship. But her new companions considered an ardent suitor the only desirable relationship. Luiza knew that her currency would be wildly enhanced if she revealed his existence and she toyed with letting his name drop casually. But she could not face the rapt interrogation that would follow. She longed for the casual hilarity of the Musketeers and started to avoid the clique until, eventually, their invitations dried up.

Of the subjects she studied, she enjoyed typing, perhaps because it involved mechanics. When there were twelve girls hammering away at twelve Continental machines, the noise almost matched that of the engine shed at Zakątek. She was dextrous with her fingers, despite her clumsiness with needle and thread, and it was satisfying to spool out a neat, correctly typed sheet at the end of an exercise.

Double-entry bookkeeping, on the other hand, was tedious. At least, so she thought at first, mainly because of its connection with Pani Aurelia. But as time went on and her columns added up, she found the logic and the quantifiable outcomes rewarding. They made a refreshing change from the indeterminate conclusions involved in art. She still visited galleries with Mathilde Krawcik, but while she was now much better informed, she was less certain of her own direction and rarely painted now.

Seated at her dressing table, Luiza regarded her face in the mirror and compared herself, as ever, with her sister. Her eyes were still Ida's and, consequently, Mama's. "The colour of the Baltic in winter," she remembered Pappa saying. Ida's hair was now as dark as her own, and she had cut the weighty length off years ago. Now it waved gently about her face, a single curl falling artlessly over her forehead. Luiza's was still cropped into a more practical bob and her face still broader. Her features seemed more distinct, where Ida's were soft. Her nose was sharper, her cheekbones higher, her expression more concentrated. She sighed, feeling in the carved wooden pot that Karol had won on the hoopla stall for a hairgrip. Clipping back her fringe and applying cold cream to her face, she glanced at the sheet of paper beside the jar: his latest letter.

She wished she could feel as certain as Karol did. His words, scribbled untidily in black ink, described plans for their life together on the Żychlin estate, once he had completed his studies and his national service was done. She would be eighteen then and they could marry. Luiza knew that it would be a life she was suited to: horses, hunting, countryside, all the things she loved best. And she would not be far from Pappa, which was important, because there was no telling where Ida would be. Her sister would have to follow Mirek wherever the railway took him. But if it was such a good life, and she only had three years to wait for it to begin, why did she not feel excited? What else did she want?

She could not shake the thought that there was more to discover, more places to see, more people to meet. Karol was not the problem – she liked him a lot. He was fun to be with, so long as they avoided the tennis court. And the thrill she experienced at the touch of his hands and his lips, especially when they wandered beyond her waist, was delicious. But did she love him? He loved her – he said it in every letter. But how could he be so sure? Would she recognise love if she felt it? And what about her dreams of becoming an engineer?

Pappa had promised that, in a couple of years, she could travel with him to Manchester in England, to the annual textile manufacturers' conference. She would be his assistant. The prospect filled her with an excitement she did not feel when she imagined life on Karol's estate. Reaching for a tissue, her glance fell on another sheet of paper. The ink was blue, and the writing smaller and neater than Karol's. Wiping her face, Luiza sighed again. What should she do about Wacek? If she told Karol that his friend wrote, almost daily, declaring undying love for her, Karol would kill him. She had written to Wacek, stating clearly that he must stop. Yet the letters kept coming, and now he was proposing to visit her.

Chapter 31

August 1938, Malinów

They were in the hall, the stained glass on either side of the front door rendering the sunlight in pastel lozenges on the pale marble floor. Luiza stood next to Pappa, who glanced repeatedly at his watch. Pani Anna, on Pappa's other side, steered it back into his waistcoat pocket.

Magda, the maid, gasped and Pani Anna clapped her hands to her mouth as Ida floated down the stairs. Her face was radiant behind a thin veil of net that fell from a pale blue, pill box hat. Her coat, with its wide lapels, was the same colour. Cut to fit, without buttons, it revealed the darker blue brocade of Ida's dress. Her sheer stockings matched the dress and showed off slim calves above cream and navy, low-heeled court shoes.

Ida had designed her wedding costume herself and overseen its assembly with hawk-eyed attention to detail.

Luiza had lived through each painstaking stitch, staying with Pani Anna while their outfits were made. Hers also had a buttonless coat, but loose-fitting, worn over a cream taffeta blouse and a brown silk crepe, pleated skirt. She had even managed to insert a pair of tan brogues, which Ida grudgingly agreed went with the outfit.

In an unprecedented reversal, while they were in Warszawa it was Luiza who went out and Ida who stayed in. She was busy embroidering her trousseau and waiting for phone calls from Toruń. But Luiza was reluctant to miss any opportunity to catch up with Gosia and Agnieszka. And there was Karol. He was in the middle of exams but still wanted to meet up.

Pani Anna insisted that he brought Luiza home by nine ("I'm sure I can trust you, young man, but she's in my charge."). It was a credit to Karol's charm that she allowed Luiza out unchaperoned. Recognising the precarious nature of this trust, he made sure they were always through the revolving doors of the Mazowiecki three minutes before the ormolu grandfather clock next to the reception desk chimed the hour, allowing enough time to deliver Luiza to the first-floor apartment before her curfew.

He usually came in with her and entertained Ida and Pani Anna with energetic re-enactments of the shoot-outs from whichever Western they had seen. Today, however, at Luiza's insistence the feature had been Zarah Leander's latest, *Habanera*. So now Karol was rumbling his way through a cruel approximation of *Du Kannst Es Nicht Wissen*.

"She sounds nothing like that," Luiza protested. She was a fan of the German star and her unusually deep voice.

"But Lou-lou," laughed Ida, "you have to admit, she does drone a bit."

"I like the way she sings. Anyway, we've seen enough of your films, Karol, so there's no need to be so rude about my choice."

"But you love horses and gunfights."

"I know. But whenever we see a film that isn't a Western, you always pull it apart."

"Only because you women like such mawkish rubbish," Karol parried and threw up his arms, feigning the need to protect his head from an anticipated onslaught by indignant females.

While Ida launched a spirited defence of the romantic imperative and Pani Anna laughed, Luiza remained silent. She was pondering the fact that Karol, when they were on their own, behaved in precisely the sentimental manner that he dismissed on screen. And, when he had ridiculed the insanely jealous husband in *History Is Made at Night*, could he not see how closely it echoed his own behaviour over Wacek?

Karol's blonde friend never did visit her in Pabianice, but he wrote incessantly, even after she returned his letters unopened. In the end, Luiza had told Karol. While she knew he would be angry, she had never thought he would challenge Wacek to a duel, for heaven's sake!

"How could he?" fumed Karol. "How dare he?"

His hand, holding the letter, shook as he read Wacek's words.

"I'll kill him!"

Luiza pleaded with him to calm down. It was fortunate

that Wacek had yet to arrive in Żychlin for Easter, or the duel might have taken place. As it was, Karol sent the challenge via a friend in Warszawa, who reported that Wacek moved out of the rooms they shared the very next day. Luiza received no more letters, and Wacek's name was never again mentioned.

Once exams were over, Karol began his National Service, so Luiza had not seen him since May. He wrote amusingly about his fellow draftees and of his delight that he was to serve with the cavalry. But Luiza thought his declarations of love were less ardent. And his letters were certainly less frequent, though this could be because he had less time now. She was unsure whether she felt disappointment or relief.

Watching Ida and Mirek at the wedding breakfast, she tried to determine whether she missed Karol. Noticing how the newly-weds' hands constantly sought each other, even while speaking to others, she envied their affinity, the common purpose of their joint adventure. While she enjoyed Karol's attention, and was roused by his touch, she could never quite shed the sense of being an observer at their encounters. Each time they parted she invariably felt lighter, as if now she could relax and be herself once more. She was certain that all Ida felt at parting from Mirek was loss. But now there need be no partings; after a short honeymoon in the lakes of the Mazury, they would be together in Toruń.

The bride and groom left after the meal, in a scarlet, two-seater Alfa Romeo borrowed from a friend of Mirek's. Luiza stood on the front steps between Pappa and Pani

Anna, waving until all that remained was the dust whipped up by the wire-spoked wheels and the distant roar of the engine.

Chapter 32

February 1939, Toruń

O nce they had settled in, Luiza visited the newly-weds. They had rented a small apartment in the home of a Jewish family who were distantly related to the Abels. Pani Kopkrowska doted on Ida, popping up to the attic flat most days with a dish of *kugel* or a freshly baked *babka*.

"She thinks I'm too thin," laughed Ida, "Come on, Lou-lou – help me out and eat some."

Luiza loved visiting. Unlike with Pani Anna, or with her aunts in Riga, in Toruń she felt properly grown-up, staying with her married sister, with no supervising adult.

It was early February, and snow lay thick on the ground. Ida had invited her to spend Carnival with them, and on the first Saturday of her stay, there was a sleigh party. Twelve of them crammed into two horse-drawn sleighs. Snuggled deep in furs and blankets, they arrived at an old mansion a few kilometres out of town, tumbling into the warmth of a large hall. A fire blazed in the huge fireplace at one end and a long table groaned under platters of food at the other. A maid circulated with a tray of brimming champagne coupes, as a man with a severely receding hairline, in a velvet smoking jacket, raised a toast.

"To the twentieth century – and kicking you all out after dinner!"

"Just you try," challenged one of Mirek's friends, amid laughter.

"Watch me," countered the balding young man, whom Ida had identified in a whisper as Maks. "His father was a cousin of Prince Korecki."

Mirek's father managed the Korecki estate in Nieśwież.

"In our Second Republic," Maks continued, signalling for the maid to top up his glass, "I'm no longer under any obligation to indulge you freeloaders. My poor ancestors may have had to let yours eat them out of house and home, but times have changed. So, make the most of what's on the table because it's all you're getting."

He raised his glass. "To the Republic!"

Having joined in the toast, his guests surged towards the table. Luiza helped herself to a steaming bowl of *bigos* and found a chair. A thickset man who had arrived in the other sleigh took the seat next to her.

"Hello, I'm Jerzy."

Luiza was caught with a mouthful of *bigos* too hot to swallow and could feel her face grow red. Diplomatically, Jerzy turned to the man on his other side. By the time he turned back, Luiza was dousing her scalded mouth with champagne. Jerzy forked up some stew and made an exaggerated show of blowing on it.

"So, you're the beautiful Pani Timorecka's sister. And just as beautiful, if I may say."

Luiza felt her face redden further. Annoyed, she refused to remain at a disadvantage in this conversation. The man was good-looking, with a shock of dark hair framing a square face. But he was old, as were all Mirek's friends, and he reminded her uncomfortably of Wojtek.

"Yes, I'm Ida's sister," she said, regarding Jerzy levelly. "But I'm certainly not as beautiful. And I don't care for flattery."

Jerzy's smile faded, but a moment later he chuckled. "Well, then I certainly shan't engage in it, Pani Timorecka's sister."

"Luiza Wolfer." She held out her hand. As Jerzy took it, Luiza swung his down into a handshake, leaving his lips touching empty space. "Pleased to meet you."

Jerzy straightened and adjusted his grip to a firm clasp, the corners of his mouth twitching. But he maintained a serious tone as he replied, "Jerzy Wolkowski, at your service."

"Actually, Pan Wolkowski, you may be of service. Can you explain what our host meant, about his ancestors?"

"Ah, the custom used to be that guests would turn up unannounced during Carnival and stay on – it could be for days – until they grew bored and moved on to the next poor host. But most of us have jobs now. Besides, we're a lot better behaved these days."

A hand with scarlet nails appeared on Jerzy's shoulder.

"Darling, I hope *you're* behaving."

The woman wore her blonde waves swept back from her face, Carole Lombard-style, and her lipstick matched her nails.

"Jerzy, I need your assistance in a dispute. So sorry to interrupt, dear."

The crimson smile she directed at Luiza did not reach her hazel eyes. Jerzy shrugged ruefully as he got up. "See you back at Anatol's, Pani Luiza Wolfer," he said with a wink, and followed the woman to the other end of the table. Luiza turned her attention to their host, who had taken the seat opposite her and was talking to a tall young woman, whom Ida had earlier identified as Roza. She was the only female engineer in Mirek's team, a fact that had sparked Luiza's interest.

"Oh, come on, Hitler repeated only last month that there's been no change in their attitude to Poland. He said as much to Beck. They've honoured the non-aggression pact for five years – why stop now?"

Maks took another swig of champagne and beckoned the maid with the tray. Roza replied, "Because the Corridor is an affront to German nationalism." She placed a hand over her glass as the maid proffered the bottle. "The Nazis won't put up with being cut off from East Prussia indefinitely, just so Poland can retain access to the sea. Think what Hitler's done to Austria and the Sudetenland. What's going to stop him doing the same here?"

Piqued, Maks slurred, "Because they'd be fools to set themselves against the Polish military machine. Just let them try."

Roza smiled coldly. "As you pointed out earlier, this is the twentieth century. The Germans have tanks and aeroplanes."

She glanced over at Luiza, as if looking for support. Luiza smiled weakly but said nothing. She wanted to ask Roza how she had come to be an engineer, but a conversation would mean introductions, and Roza would hear her German surname. Luiza could not bear that this impressive woman might suspect her of disloyalty to Poland.

Later, at Anatol's apartment, the lights were dimmed and the gramophone played sultry jazz. There was no food, but there was plenty of vodka and it did not take long for Ida to assume the role of supervising adult.

"Mirek, we need to take Lou-lou home. Anyway, I'm tired."

Mirek knocked back a shot and looked regretfully at a passing bottle, before heading for the bedroom to extract their coats from the pile. Outside, the three of them linked arms for the walk home. The hard-packed snow creaked beneath their boots and the air was crisp, the sky strewn with stars. Mirek began to croon Albert Harris's latest hit, 'A Small Bunch of Violets', and Ida swung them into waltz-time, until Luiza peeled off to let the pair dance together to the door of the Kopkrowski house. She applauded their final twirl, then dived past to race them up the stairs.

There were no more sleigh parties, but there were dances and the Carnival market and, on Fat Thursday, just before she left, there were the traditional doughnuts. But Luiza delighted most in the time she and Ida spent together while Mirek was at work. It was a novelty to shop for food, stopping for coffee and cake in the old town square. Luiza was surprised at how competent a cook Ida had become. Together they recalled meals Pani Marysia had served at Zakątek and set about recreating their favourites. Sometimes they took in a matinee at the cinema, but most afternoons Ida sat with her embroidery and Luiza played through Mirek's record collection on the Phillips portable player while they talked. These were relaxed, untroubled conversations; Pappa was settled, Ida content, and Luiza looking forward to accompanying Pappa to Manchester in the autumn. She had hopes that the visit might provide the opportunity to re-introduce her plan to become an engineer.

The sisters spoke mainly of their mother. Luiza's jealousy and guilt had receded. She recalled their childhood in mellow sepia, now, the sharp definition of loss that used to overlay her recollections had at last faded.

On the day Luiza left, Ida walked her to the station. Mirek had dropped off her case earlier, on his way to work. While a porter stowed it in the overhead rack, Luiza hung out of the window to kiss her sister farewell. Ida was pale, but her eyes were bright as she whispered in Luiza's ear. She pulled back to stare at Ida, who nodded, her face alight with happiness. The train began to move and Luiza continued to grin in her direction even after Ida was lost in a surging eddy of steam. When she sat down and peeled off her gloves, the woman opposite raised an enquiring eyebrow and Luiza realised that she was still smiling.

"It's my sister," she explained. "She just told me... I'm going to be an aunt."

"I'm not at all sure it's the right thing to do," said Ida, pulling her damp dress away from her pronounced bump and using her magazine as a fan. "I'm sure she's exaggerating the threat, just to get me in her clutches. Oh dear – how will I survive Pani Timorecka? You must come to Nieśwież soon, Lou-lou – promise you will."

"I promise," laughed Luiza. "I'll be with you in no time, and I won't let Mirek's mother boss you around."

She peered out of the carriage window at the sound of a whistle. This time it was Ida who was leaving, and instead of February snow, there was an August heatwave to contend with. Ida's train was en route from Toruń to Łódź, where she would see Pappa, before travelling on to Warszawa and then east to Nieśwież for her confinement. Luiza, at Malinów for the month, had taken advantage of the train's halt at Kutno to catch a few minutes with her sister. But now the guard was signalling.

She hugged Ida and jumped down to the platform. Her sister leant out of the window as the train began to move, closing her eyes for a moment to enjoy the breeze as the train gathered speed. She opened them again to grin at Luiza and wave furiously. Luiza watched her gloved hand until it disappeared. She turned back along the platform to collect Rumi, looking forward to the ride home. Once they were out of town, there was a good stretch of pasture for a gallop.

Walking the horse through traffic, she wondered

whether the danger from Hitler really was sufficient to merit Pani Timorecka's insistence that Ida travel east to have the baby. The groom's mother had driven poor Pani Anna to distraction last year, trying to dictate the wedding preparations from Nieśwież. It took all the diplomacy she could muster from years of dealing with demanding hotel guests to avoid a major confrontation. As ever, Pappa was preoccupied with work and remained unaware of the difficulties. Or so Luiza had thought, until Ida later confided that Pappa had cautioned her, the night before the ceremony, to "Beware of marrying the mother, as well as the man."

"Never move to Nieśwież, whatever you do, Idka," he had admonished. "And don't let Mirek accept a posting within two hundred kilometres of the place."

Yet, since Mirek had been called up to report to his former military unit, Pappa was suddenly in favour of Ida having the baby there. It was certainly a lot farther from the border with Germany than either Pabianice or Toruń.

The town was behind them, and stubble fields stretched as far as the horizon. Luiza urged Rumi forward. Shaking the nagging worry from her head, she gave herself over to the thrill of speed and the deliciously cooling breeze.

Chapter 33

3 September 1939,
A country road between Malinów and Pabianice

*L*uiza rolled over and looked up at clear blue sky. The screaming Stukas had gone, but her ears were still ringing. She scrambled to peer out of the ditch and could just make out the five planes in the distance. They seemed innocent now, like geese in their arrow formation.

She brushed the dirt from her dress before turning to the old lady, who was moaning softly. Luiza helped her up and handed her the flowered kerchief that had slipped from her head. The *babcia* fumbled beneath her chin, until Luiza gently pushed her shaking fingers aside and tied the greasy ends herself. Without warning, the woman let out a loud wail and sank back onto the earth, scrabbling wildly.

"Here, is this what you're looking for?" Spotting a glint of silver in the dusty soil, Luiza retrieved a large crucifix attached to a set of horn rosary beads. The old woman seized it, kissing Luiza's hand and muttering prayers of thanks.

Once more, Luiza pulled her to her feet and managed to manoeuvre her out of the ditch back onto the road. Their fellow passengers, equally dusty and dishevelled, were emerging from the ditch on the other side, the driver shaking his head at the holes that peppered his bus.

"At least they didn't hit the engine," he consoled himself and ushered them back on board.

Two young men, who had earlier told Luiza that they were on their way to join up and send the Germans packing, joked, "Poor shots, those Krauts. Five Stukas and they can't even take out a bus." But their bluster did not convince, and nobody laughed.

Luiza wondered if she would ever laugh again. It was hard to believe that only two days ago she had been looking forward to the first partridge shoot of the season. And then going to Nieśwież, to meet her new niece or nephew, due at the beginning of October. And after that, to England with Pappa for the trade fair in Manchester.

But on Friday everything had changed. Out early with Rumi, the loud buzzing of a low-flying plane had spooked the mare. Struggling to bring her under control, Luiza made out black crosses flanked with white – Luftwaffe. She had taken the most direct route back, jumping the ha-ha onto the grass and swerving Rumi to a halt by the terrace, where Pani Anna and Waldemar were having breakfast.

"Good gracious, Lou-lou, you can't ride over the lawn—" Pani Anna broke off her scolding, "What's wrong?"

"The Germans are here; it was a German plane!"

Neither Pani Anna nor her son showed any sign of comprehension. Then distant gunfire confirmed Luiza's words and Waldemar rose hastily.

"I'll see what I can find out. Luiza, take that poor horse to the stables and make sure she's properly rubbed down. Mama, please find Grażyna."

On her return from the stables, Luiza followed the sound of voices to Waldemar's office. Bogdan, the dairyman, was nursing a glass of brandy in hands that shook, while Waldemar sat at his desk with head bowed. In an unsteady voice, Pani Anna updated Luiza. "The gunfire was an attack at Kutno station. Bogdan had just got the churns onto the train – thank God no one was hurt."

"We had to dive for cover," said Bogdan, making the sign of the cross and gulping more brandy. "There was milk everywhere — they strafed the line, the locomotive…"

At noon the household gathered in the salon. Waldemar had the walnut doors of the wireless cabinet open as he fiddled with dials. Eventually, President Mościcki's voice cut through the static.

"Early this morning Germany launched a military offensive against our country. We deplore this act of aggression, and together we will defend the freedom and independence of Poland. I urge you to stand united with our army, which will respond to the aggressors in kind. We have requested assistance from our allies, France and Great Britain. The entire Polish nation, blessed by God, will march to victory."

"Dear God," murmured Pani Anna, "we're at war."

Her son, his face set, stood behind Grażyna, who had Roman on her lap. It was as if they were posed for a commemorative photograph. The restless little boy wriggled to get down, but his mother held him tight, kissing his blonde head.

Bogdan was near the door, turning his cap in his hands, with Magda white-faced beside him. Luiza thought of Pappa; she should telephone him. Eventually, Pani Anna broke the silence.

"All we can do now is pray, which is what I'm going to do. You're welcome to join me."

She left the room and everyone except Waldemar followed, processing in silence along the wide corridor to the chapel, where they all knelt. While Grażyna tried to hush Roman's piping enquiries, Pani Anna recited the first of the sorrowful mysteries of the rosary. One by one they joined in, even the toddler. Sitting on his heels, he wound a set of rosary beads around his fingers and chirruped to the rhythm of the prayer, as Pani Anna led them through all five mysteries.

Grażyna left first, leading her son by the hand, then Magda with Bogdan. Dipping their fingers in the *benetier* of holy water by the door, they made repeated signs of the cross. Eventually, Pani Anna rose stiffly from her knees and Luiza followed her. In the corridor, she asked, "May I telephone Pappa? I need to know he's alright."

"Of course, dear, let's do that now. He'll want to know that you're safe, too; in fact, I'm surprised he hasn't telephoned."

The reason for Pappa's silence was soon apparent: The

line was dead. Luiza had never felt so alone. She had to fight back tears before she could ask, "What about Ida and the baby?"

Pani Anna patted her shoulder. "Ida will be perfectly alright, dear. The Germans will never get that far east. You, of course, should be with your father, but it's much too dangerous to travel. We'll have to wait until we can be sure to get you home safely."

Gathered around the wireless again that evening, they learnt that a German warship had fired on Westerplatte Fort in Gdańsk that morning, before the Luftwaffe bombed Warszawa. Meanwhile, German troops marched into Poland from the south and the west, as Stukas cleared a path for them. Luiza tried to remember where she had heard that Poland's military spending in recent years was less than 2 per cent of Germany's. Pappa had always advocated spending on the economy, not arms. Could he have been wrong, and Uncle Rafi right?

By Sunday, there was still no news from Pappa, and Waldemar recommended that Luiza head home. Pani Anna seemed upset, but did not object. Luiza suspected that her son was keen to distance his family from her German surname.

So here she was, dragging herself and the poor old *babcia* out of a ditch for the third time, and still nowhere near home, seven hours into a journey that should have taken only three. The first time Stukas had dropped out of the sky, the passengers had been confident that a civilian bus would not be targeted and had watched the planes hold their course with mounting disbelief. When the driver finally stamped on the brake and yelled at them to take cover, they threw themselves into the nearest ditch just as a hail of bullets raked the road. After that, the driver wanted to detour to a nearby army camp to pick up a military escort, but a well-dressed male passenger argued that this would make them even more of a target, convincing the driver to leave the main highway and stick to back roads. Yet still they were pursued, even on these country lanes. It was a miracle no one was hit.

When the driver finally dropped Luiza in Pabianice, she looked down at her bare feet in surprise, trying to remember when she had last seen her shoes. She was suddenly impossibly tired. Hoisting her case, she set off for the apartment on Ulica Kościuszki and rang the bell. Mathilde Krawcik's anxious face appeared in the crack of the chained door, but she flung it wide the moment she recognised Luiza.

"Thank God you're alive!"

Together they rocked and sobbed, arms wrapped tightly around each other. Eventually, Mathilde released Luiza and picked up her case, closing the door behind them and replacing the chain. Luiza stood in the hall, unable to take another step.

"Where's Pappa?"

Mathilde looked away for a moment. When she turned back, her features were calmly composed, but Luiza felt a cold fear spread from the pit of her stomach.

"Mathilde – please – what is it? Where is he?"

"*Ma chère*, you're not to worry; he'll be fine. But Pan Wolfer's in hospital."

Luiza felt her legs give way, and she sat down heavily on one of the high-backed chairs by the hall table. Since they had listened to President Mościcki's words on Friday, a terror she had resisted naming had gripped her, but now it overwhelmed her. Poland was at war with Germany. Pappa was German, even though he had been a Polish citizen for decades.

"Was he attacked?" Luiza whispered.

Mathilde hesitated before replying, "Yes, but not by his employees. They were from another mill."

Luiza rose, but the older woman pushed her gently back into the chair.

"Not now, *ma chère*, you're exhausted. And the curfew – you can't go out now. Tomorrow you'll see him, but now you must sleep."

Luiza sank back, her face in her hands. When she looked up again, her eyes held a desperate appeal. "Mathilde, are you frightened?"

Pani Krawcik paused before answering, "I was, but not now. Today the French and the British declared war on Germany. We're not alone anymore."

Chapter 34

September 1939, Pabianice

*E*arly the next morning, Luiza caught the tram to the clinic in Łódź. She thought she had prepared herself for the worst, but Pappa's appearance was a shock. One side of his face was badly cut and bruised, the eye discoloured and swollen shut. His right arm was in a sling, and he flinched when she hugged him.

"Lou-lou, thank God," he murmured into her hair. "I was so worried."

"You were worried?" she countered, determined not to cry. "At least I haven't ended up in hospital looking like I've gone twenty rounds with Antoni Czortek!"

Pappa winced as he chuckled. "It looks worse than it is."

"Really?" Luiza was scanning the notes at the foot of the bed. "What's this about kidney damage?"

"They're not sure, it's possible. But don't worry, I'll heal."

"But who did it, Pappa? Who beat you up like this?"

"It's just fear and ignorance on the part of some hotheads. There's no point in getting upset over a few idiots. We still have so many friends – and we have each other. And soon," winking with his good eye, "we'll have another little one. Have you heard anything from your sister?"

"No, the lines are down. Pani Anna says the Germans will never reach that far east, so Ida is safe. Do you think she is, Pappa?"

"I'm not sure it's the Germans who are Ida's problem."

"What do you mean?"

"Hitler and Stalin agreed not to fight each other, but I'll wager that carving up Poland between them was part of their agreement. He may decry imperial Russia, but Stalin wouldn't say no to getting the old territories back."

"Oh, Pappa – what will happen to Ida? And the baby?"

Suddenly, her father looked exhausted. Easing himself back on his pillows, he closed his eyes.

"Pappa?" Luiza ventured, uneasily.

He reached to pat her hand. "I'm sure she'll be fine, Lou-lou. Mirek's family will make sure of that. They're well connected, with his father working for Prince Korecki. They'll take good care of their grandchild and its mother, so don't worry. Now, let me get some sleep so these old bones can heal."

Luiza stayed for a while. Her father's breathing was shallow, and the hand resting on hers fluttered. Gently, she slid it onto the sheet and tiptoed from the room.

On the tram home, Luiza allowed her anger to

percolate. Her helplessness fed the brew. Wishing she had one of the guns from Malinów with her, she allowed herself the solace of an imagined confrontation, where the cowardly bullies who had attacked Pappa grovelled as she took aim. But the unavoidable truth was that she had been far away and unable to protect him. And she was even further from Ida. Their small family was fragmented, and Luiza felt desolate, powerless. They were being buffeted by the decisions of others. Her anger towards the men who had beaten Pappa shifted to Hitler. Without him, none of this would be happening. As she focused her hatred on the zealous little man with his ridiculous moustache, her sense of impotence diminished. She still had a choice: She would not let him destroy her family. They would survive.

But a few nights later, in the cellar with Mathilde Krawcik and their neighbours, Luiza felt a lot less certain that she could determine the outcome of this war.

Each apartment had its own storage cage down here; in the candlelight, their bars projected disquieting footage onto the whitewashed walls. Discarded chairs and trunks radiated macabre shapes within the distorted grid pattern, while fearsome shadows loomed each time someone shifted in their quest for a comfortable position on the stone floor. Meanwhile, the artillery bombardment at street level provided a relentless soundtrack that could not be tuned out; there was no rhythm to the staccato bursts and no regularity to the deafening crunches that lifted the shifting shadows on the wall in unison, the nervous occupants of the cellar jumping with each sudden crash.

It was close to midday before they emerged, wiping

coal dust and cobwebs from their clothes and stretching chilled, cramped limbs. The silence rang eerily in ears grown accustomed to constant noise, and it was a while before Luiza could discern new sounds. Eventually, she registered a steady rumble punctuated by regular creaks and insistent squeaks. It came from the end of their street and only made sense when, from the apartment balcony, she looked towards Zamkowa, the main route running east to west. A steady stream of carts and bicycles, piled high with bundles of furniture and even geese and chickens, was rolling past the intersection. Men and women, old and young, with children of all ages, pushed and pulled at wayward wheels. Others propped up mountains of belongings against a threatened avalanche.

That evening, she and Mathilde were trying to decipher the truth behind the reassuring announcements on the radio when a loud knock brought them both into the hall. Luiza opened the door to four Polish infantry officers.

"Pani, excuse us, please."

It was the tall one in front who spoke, but all four clicked their heels and saluted smartly and somewhat incongruously, given their torn and dusty uniforms.

"We need somewhere to stay and wondered if you might have room? We've been separated from our battalion by the German advance and plan to re-join them at first light, after we get some rest."

Mathilde hesitated, but Luiza thought of Karol, who could so easily be in the same position. "Of course, you're welcome. I'm not sure we have four beds to spare, but we'll see what we can do."

Relief flooded their faces, and she realised how young they were. One in particular, who had a spray of freckles across his broad nose, was not much older than she was.

Mathilde went to prepare food and Luiza showed them into Pappa's study while she sorted bedding. On her return she found them poring over a map. The young lieutenant looked up and their eyes met; he blushed.

"May I use the bathroom?" he asked.

"Of course, second on the right."

By the time he re-joined them in the dining room, his friends were tucking into Pani Krawcik's spread as if they had not eaten for days, which was quite possibly the case. But the freckled lieutenant barely ate. While the others compared their favourite dishes, as if stowing away familiar comforts to brace themselves against what was to come, he said nothing and steadfastly avoided looking in Luiza's direction.

After supper, the four of them returned to the study. Minutes later, the major re-entered the dining room, where Luiza was helping Mathilde clear up.

"Apologies, Pani, for the trouble we've put you to, but our plans have changed. We've decided it's best to move on under cover of darkness, so we won't be availing ourselves any further of your hospitality. Thank you." He was correct and courteous, but the warmth of his earlier reminiscences about his grandmother's *pierogi* was gone.

As they filed out, each touched his cap and sketched a bow, but not one of them smiled, not even the freckled lieutenant. The door closed and Luiza stood in the hall, perplexed and hurt. Suddenly, she slapped her forehead and ran to the bathroom. Above the towel rail hung one of Mama's beautifully embroidered samplers, the words embedded in stitching so fine it looked like mosaic. She had sewn this for Pappa when they were first married, and he claimed that the sight of it always fortified him for the day ahead: *'Guten Morgen'*. No wonder they had left so abruptly.

Thoughtfully, Luiza went to her bedroom and removed a passport from the dressing table. She examined the green cover of the *Reisepass*, emblazoned with a squared-off eagle atop a swastika. Placing it in her skirt pocket, she left the apartment. The curfew was in force, so she opened the street door with care, peering to right and left before sneaking out.

Keeping to the shadows along Świętego Jana, she came to the bridge and leant over the parapet. The full moon was reflected in the sluggish river. She held out the passport and inhaled sharply before releasing it. It dropped into the viscid flow with barely a ripple.

"I'm not German," she said aloud. "I'm Polish. I am Polish."

Chapter 35

17 September 1939, Pabianice

"Pappa, you were right!"

Her father was sitting up in bed with a breakfast tray. He had been released from the clinic a few days ago and was under orders to rest. It was two weeks since Luiza had left Malinów, one week since the Germans occupied Łódź, and they had still not heard from Ida. As usual, Luiza had been to the kiosk on the corner for Pappa's paper, but today's headline had transformed the unease that had been her constant companion for the past fortnight into full-blown alarm.

"It's happened; Stalin's invaded. Oh, Pappa, what will happen to Ida now?"

Her father was scanning the front page.

"And the baby?" Luiza's voice shook with the effort of control. "Oh, the poor baby."

"The baby will be fine," Pappa said firmly. "Ida, too. Do

you seriously think Pani Timorecka would let any harm come to them?"

Luiza gave a watery smile.

"It would be a brave Bolshevik who crossed Ida's mother-in-law," Pappa continued, tucking a stray lock behind Luiza's ear and tilting her chin until she returned his gaze. With a wink he shooed her away, "Now leave me in peace with my paper, Lou-lou."

In his study she lifted the heavy black receiver from its cradle. For the umpteenth time she requested the number of the Korecki estate from the operator, only to be told, yet again, that the lines were down. She sat on at Pappa's desk, noting the creep of gold on the dusty leaves of the plane tree outside the window. Autumn was coming. There had been a crisp bite to the air on her walk to the kiosk and that shocking headline. She clenched her jaw against tears that threatened. What right did she have to cry when she was safe with Pappa? Not only was Ida alone, but she was now at the mercy of Communists... It was because of them that poor Aunt Ludmila could never have children. A posse of Bolsheviks had caught up with her and the other officers' wives as they fled Petrograd in 1917.

Her aunt had disclosed this painful memory as they strolled on the beach in Riga.

"At least I'm alive, Lou-lou. Others weren't so lucky."

She was staring out to sea, where the late afternoon sun sparkled to such blinding effect that Luiza had to shield her eyes. But Aunt Ludmila's unflinching gaze was fixed somewhere beyond the horizon, on a past horror still resonating down the years.

"Dear God, protect Ida and the baby from harm," Luiza prayed. She needed a distraction. In the kitchen, Mathilde Krawcik was slicing windfalls for apple fritters and welcomed an extra pair of hands.

Ten days later, Warszawa fell to the Germans. While Poland defended its capital, there had still been hope. But with its surrender, defeat and occupation were inescapable. Luiza wondered if Karol was among the 140,000 Polish troops taken prisoner. Had the soldiers who sought sanctuary with her – then taken flight because of Mama's German sampler – made it to Warszawa? Were they dead or were they prisoners? And what about Mirek?

Chapter 36

December 1939, Pabianice

*P*appa was back at work long before winter set in, and on an evening a few weeks before Christmas, his papers were spread over the card table in the salon. It was the only room where a stove was lit, now that fuel was so hard to come by. Luiza and Mathilde were there, too, half-heartedly sorting through a box of decorations. Luiza could muster no enthusiasm for festivities, but it was important to demonstrate to the occupying force that they would not allow them to curtail their lives.

When the doorbell rang, all three looked up. There had been no heavy footsteps or banging of doors, so it was unlikely to be Germans. But it was well after nine and too close to curfew for a social call.

Pappa grimaced as he rose, his injuries still playing up. He signalled for Luiza and Pani Krawcik to stay where they were, but they still followed him into the hall. Guardedly, he opened the front door and peered through the small chink afforded by the chain.

"How may I help you, Pani?" he asked politely. Luiza stepped to his side to inspect the visitor for herself. Smart cuffs peeped incongruously from beneath shawls that were layered, *babcia*-style. A snow-crusted headscarf cowled the woman's head, and her laced boots were scuffed, slush patching the leather dark.

When she pushed the scarf from her face there was a pause before Pappa exclaimed, "Idka? Can it be you?" Fumbling to release the chain, he drew the woman into the hall, then hurriedly secured the door again.

"Ida!" Luiza's cry pierced the silence and all three turned on her, hissing "Ssshhh." She clamped her hands to her mouth, then threw herself at her sister and held her tight. Pappa eventually pulled her away to allow Mathilde Krawcik to assist with unravelling damp cloth.

Ida was soon in the salon, furnished with a bowl of soup. Luiza sat on the carpet, leaning against her sister's knees, while Pappa angled his chair as close to his elder daughter as possible. Pani Krawcik, having provided food, had tactfully withdrawn.

With each spoonful, Ida's pallid face and blue lips edged closer to their natural colour. While she ate, they gave her their news. Pappa minimised his injuries, and Luiza downplayed the bus journey from Malinów. Its dangers were diminished, anyway, in the light of Ida's six-hundred-kilometre odyssey through two zones of occupation. They told her of the bombardment, which ended in the fall of Łódź, the trail of refugees going east to escape the Germans, only to head west again as the Bolsheviks advanced. Ida nodded and it occurred to Luiza that her sister had travelled the same route.

At last, Ida put down the bowl and sat back and Luiza, unable to contain herself any longer, posed the question that had been hanging in the air from the moment she arrived.

"Idka, what about the baby?"

Ida's face broke into a smile and a flash of her familiar, vivid self emerged from this pale wraith. "Little Mirek – he's an angel. Look, I have a picture."

Grandfather and aunt crowded in to scrutinise the photograph. Wide-eyed, with ears that stuck out comically, a square-faced baby stared back at them.

"When was he born?"

Ida's smile lingered as she gazed at her son, "October 5th." She tucked the photograph back in the breast pocket of her jacket. "I was so worried when the pains started – there was no midwife, no way to get to the hospital. So Pani Timorecka sent to the castle for help. The younger Korecki son, he's a medical student. And he was there, thank God. He delivered Little Mirek."

Reflecting on her son's arrival, Ida's face grew lambent. Luiza was reluctant to cast a shadow, so held back and it was Pappa who enquired further. "But where is your baby now, Idka? Why have you left him? And what about your husband?"

The light faded from Ida's strained face and her eyes welled. "Oh, Pappa, Mirek's missing in action – there was a telegram. I haven't heard from him since September.

He couldn't say where he was, but he wrote about a hotel renowned for its excellent service. I think it was code for the Mazowiecki, meaning he was in Warszawa. But then Warszawa fell and he never replied to my letter about Little Mirek – he may not even know he has a son. How can I even be sure that Little Mirek still has a father?"

Ida crumpled, shaken by great, shuddering sobs. Luiza folded her arms around her sister. Without her many shawls, she felt insubstantial.

Smoothing his worried frown into an encouraging smile, Pappa grasped one of Ida's hands. "Come, now, Idka, we must all pray and hope for the best and you, my dear, must look after yourself and your son, until Mirek's return. But dearest girl," Pappa's tone grew more tentative, "I still don't understand why you're here and not with Little Mirek? Why would you put yourself in such danger?"

Ida took the handkerchief that Pappa proffered and her sobs slowly subsided. Luiza sat back on her heels and waited.

"I just couldn't bear it any longer, the not knowing. It's been tearing me apart, worrying about you and Lou-lou. And being so terrified about Mirek. I have no idea how to find him, but at least I knew where to look for you."

She blew her nose and her voice rose perilously as she continued, "I just couldn't stay there any longer, Pappa; Mirek's mother made it impossible!"

Ida shot Pappa a look of appeal, before dropping her eyes to the handkerchief she wove around her fingers.

"She kept taking Little Mirek from me, so I could 'rest'. But I wasn't tired! She wouldn't leave me alone with him –

everything I did was wrong. She said she was worried he wasn't safe with me because I'm 'highly strung'. Oh Pappa," Ida's eyes were full of entreaty. "I'd never harm Little Mirek. I'm a good mother. But she even started taking him into her room for the night.

"I told her I had to know that you and Lou-lou were safe and I wanted you to meet your grandson, but she wouldn't let me bring him. She said I should go, if that's what I wanted, but under no circumstances could I take Little Mirek."

Pappa nodded slowly, "I can see why she'd be worried about a baby being taken on such a dangerous journey, Ida. I wouldn't have been happy about that myself."

"I know, Pappa, I was desperate, or I'd never have considered it. But I just couldn't cope anymore," her voice had escalated again, but now it suddenly reduced to a whisper, "Oh, I miss my baby."

It seemed that Ida's tears were spent. She simply rocked and whimpered, which Luiza found even more distressing. She tried to still her sister by enfolding her in her arms again, but Ida's body was unyielding and Luiza had to back away. With a reassuring squeeze of her shoulder, Pappa gestured for her to go.

Getting ready for bed, Luiza acknowledged, reluctantly, that this alien sister frightened her. She had so longed to see Ida, to know that she was safe, but she had to admit that her previous state of anguished uncertainty almost seemed preferable. At least then she could find occasional respite in comforting visions of Ida nestled lovingly with her baby. Now she was faced with an Ida she barely recognised, while the tiny nephew she had yet to meet was abandoned amidst who knew what dangers.

Luiza turned to the Madonna on her bedside table but found that she could not formulate a prayer. Should she ask for Ida to retrace her hazardous journey to be reunited with her son? Could she even get there, with each day taking them deeper into winter. And even if she did manage to get back, what might she find?

In the end, Luiza left it to the sad-eyed woman and simply begged her, as she did every night, to keep her sister and the baby safe.

Ida stayed in bed the next day. Luiza tried to make her eat, but she lay unresponsive, facing the wall. It was Mathilde Krawcik who succeeded, sitting with her hour after hour, patiently chivvying, a mouthful at a time. Finally, on the fourth morning after her arrival, Ida rapped on Luiza's door and entered. Her face was no longer pinched, and her smile had lost the haunted absence of that first evening. There was even a glimmer of mischief in her demand.

"Come on, Lou-lou, get up and find me some clothes that don't make me look like a gamekeeper. If I'd known that one day I'd have to borrow from your wardrobe, I'd have insisted you refine your style."

The improvement continued, though there was a brittleness to her sister's good mood, an unnatural shrillness to her high spirits. Luiza sensed that Ida's apparent recovery was putting Pappa on edge as much as it did her. And that, like her, he was unable to escape the conviction that Ida should really be in Nieśwież.

Chapter 37

December 1939, Pabianice

Their subdued, depleted Christmas over, Luiza was alone when the bell rang. Pappa and Ida had gone for a walk, while Mathilde was visiting friends. These days, the doorbell initiated dread rather than anticipation, so it was with misgivings that she opened the door, only to have her fears confirmed by a man in field grey. As she took in the squared-off eagle perched on a swastika that spread its wings over the soldier's right breast, the clicking of heels drew her gaze to his gleaming boots.

"Oberleutnant Helfer at your service, Pani. I am to be billeted in your apartment."

He spoke in halting Polish, his tone almost apologetic. Surprised by the absence of bombast, Luiza glanced at his face, which was thin and clean-shaven, wire-rimmed glasses resting on a long nose. His eyes would have been unremarkable, were it not for the startling length of the pale, straight lashes that swept down, cow-like, when he blinked, which he did frequently. Luiza was struck by the bewildering thought that this Oberleutnant was nervous.

"Oh, we had no notice, I didn't know..." she stammered in confusion.

"No, of course. Apologies – Christmas, you know, communications have been lax – but the records show that three people live here, in a four-bedroom apartment. As I'm sure you're aware we, of necessity, requisition all available living space."

"Yes, but my sister arrived unexpectedly and is currently using the fourth bedroom."

"Ah." Oberleutnant Helfer blinked rapidly as he shifted his duffle bag from his shoulder to the floor. "I see the problem. Unfortunately, the room where I was billeted has been requisitioned for a senior officer and I cannot return. Nor would I wish to make a request to be allocated elsewhere, as this would inevitably, *ahem*, raise questions about registered occupants."

Luiza breathed in sharply. The Oberleutnant's manner remained mild, but there was an unmistakeable threat, however reluctant, in his words. Instinctively, she sought to disarm and found herself speaking German.

"No, of course. My sister is just visiting, and we can easily rearrange things. We would certainly not wish to cause any trouble."

Oberleutnant Helfer was blinking rapidly again. His mouth, which had opened in disbelief, now curved upwards in delight.

"You speak excellent…" he began, but at that moment the street door opened, and laughter accompanied footsteps climbing the stairs. Both the Oberleutnant and Luiza looked towards the landing, to see Pappa and Ida emerge. They fell silent at the sight of the German officer. Luiza explained hurriedly, in German, "This is Oberleutnant Helfer. He's to be billeted with us. I said that Ida is only here temporarily and can easily move into my room."

Pappa inclined his head in agreement, "Naturally, Oberleutnant Helfer, this will not be a problem."

The officer nodded in return, declaring, "It appears that I have found the most exceptional accommodation. How is it that you speak such excellent German – all of you?" He ended with a quizzical consideration of Ida, who had not yet spoken, but who rewarded him with a dazzling smile as she replied, "Yes, all of us. My father has lived in Poland most of his life, but he was born in Saxony and brought us up to speak his mother tongue. Now, Oberleutnant, we must not stand on Prussian ceremony any longer. It's time to show you Polish hospitality. Please do come in."

"I had, of course, noted the German surname. But since you're not on the Volkslist, I assumed it was an historical anomaly."

They were seated in the salon, drinking tea and eating the last of the small *piernik* that Pani Krawcik had contrived to make with hoarded sugar, cocoa and ginger. At least, Oberleutnant Helfer was eating the last slice, while the three Wolfers chased crumbs around their plates to keep their guest company.

"No, of course we're not on the Volkslist," began Luiza, indignant that they should be linked with the fawning Volksdeutsche, but Ida interrupted in a tone set to mollify.

"Our father took Polish nationality a long time ago, and he and my sister only recently moved to this part of Poland. We've never before lived anywhere with so many ethnic Germans to identify with. Besides, we can't be classed as Volksdeutsche because we all hold German passports."

Luiza shifted uncomfortably at this. Ida continued to smile at the Oberleutnant as she offered him more tea. With a shake of his head he rose from his chair, announcing that he wished to retire.

"I'm most grateful that you were able to make the room available at such short notice."

"But of course. As we said, I'm only visiting – it's really no trouble."

"Then I will wish you all a good evening." On his way out he paused, his hand on the doorknob. "I wonder if I might invite you to celebrate *Sylvester* with me?"

The family were silent, dumbfounded at this unexpected and unwelcome invitation. Ida was the first to regain her composure. "How kind of you. Unfortunately, as I'll be leaving immediately after, we'd planned a quiet, family evening at home."

"Exactly as I'd hoped. It's an unforgiveable presumption, I know, to invite you to a celebration in your own home. But, if you'd allow me, I can supply all that's necessary. And it would be so much more *gemütlich* here than in some impersonal restaurant. I always prefer to spend *Sylvester* at home."

The Oberleutnant was blinking again, and his voice registered appeal rather than command. Luiza was surprised by an urge to comply with his request, an impulse that sat uneasily with the strong antipathy to all things German that she had felt since the invasion.

Once he had left the room, the three of them regarded each other uncertainly. Eventually, Pappa shrugged as he pursued the last grains of *piernik* on his plate.

"At least it means we'll eat well on *Sylvester*," he said in Polish and licked his finger. "Poor Pani Krawcik needn't worry about creating another festive meal out of thin air. But Idka," he added, putting down his plate, "what did you mean about leaving immediately after New Year?"

Calmly, Ida replied, "I must get back to my baby; it's not right that we're apart. And there may be news of Mirek – any communication would be sent to Nieśwież. But the important thing is to be reunited with my son and then, if there's still no word from his father, I'll bring him back here."

Luiza gasped. "Seriously, Idka? You'll come with the baby? How will you manage that? What about Pani Timorecka?"

Ida smiled. The tremulous woman who had appeared on their doorstep had vanished, as had the excitable one who replaced her. Luiza now recognised the sister on whom she had relied in the dark days after Uncle Rafi's death and amid the worst worries about Pappa.

Formidable, intransigent Ida, who could plausibly make the arduous journey east and return with her baby.

Pappa spoke again. "Idka, I think it's right that you return to Little Mirek, but it will be difficult. We must consider how to get you there safely. Any travel plans beyond that will have to wait."

Ida inclined her head, but Luiza noted the set to her jaw and knew that her sister's mind was made up.

They spent an unexpectedly pleasant *Sylvester*. Oberleutnant Helfer turned out to be an excellent pianist. Mama's instrument, which Luiza had scarcely touched since the move to Pabianice, responded sweetly, if slightly out of tune, as the German accompanied himself singing Schubert *lieder* in a pleasant tenor.

They feasted on cheeses and cold meats and caviar. Even the bread, finely milled with none of the husks and sawdust they had grown accustomed to, was delicious. Especially when spread with more butter than they had seen in the last three months.

For dessert there was a hazelnut torte covered in whipped cream and, to wash it all down, a bottle of Henkell champagne. Conversation was politely stilted at first, then Luiza and the Oberleutnant discovered a mutual admiration for Zarah Leander. And when Pappa shared his childhood recollections of his birthplace, it turned out that the Oberleutnant's grandmother had also been born in Crimmitschau. Gustav (as he insisted they call him) blinked less as the evening went on. With Pani Krawcik he reminisced about a holiday in Paris, but it was obvious that the person he most wished to engage was the least forthcoming. Having eaten, Ida became absorbed in her embroidery.

As midnight approached, Pappa threw open the window. Discordant chimes rang out the last decade and welcomed in 1940; lights flickered in the sky to the faint accompaniment of hisses and bangs from German fireworks. As they wished each other happy new year, the awkwardness of the situation reasserted itself. All were aware that, for four of them, such happiness entailed something very different from the aspirations of the fifth. Providing a welcome excuse for the evening to end, Ida announced, "I have to be up very early tomorrow to get on my way."

In fact, Ida did not leave the next day. Once Gustav Helfer understood her plans, he insisted that he ensure her safe passage, at least as far as German jurisdiction extended.

"I can't possibly let you make your own way. The weather's atrocious and the situation is by no means stable. There are always staff cars going east – I can find a seat for you in one of them. And I'll get travel warrants for you in German and in Russian."

Preparations took several days, but at last Luiza stood with her father at the street door, watching Ida walk up Ulica Kościuszki with Oberleutnant Helfer, his gloved hand hovering at her elbow in case she slipped. As they disappeared around the corner, Luiza repeated to herself the words that Ida had whispered as she hugged her goodbye: "I'll be back as soon as I can, with Little Mirek – it won't be long before you meet your nephew, I promise."

Chapter 38

May 1940, Łódz

*I*t seemed to Luiza that the cherry blossom was even more flamboyant this May, as if to challenge the ugliness beyond the trees. From where she stood, the jubilant froth almost obscured the meanness of the fence, but Luiza wondered how it felt to view this rosy extravaganza from within its bounds.

The wire had gone up last month, but Luiza never thought they would actually seal it. She had been bringing food and medicine into the ghetto since February without a problem. She simply carried a jacket on the pretext of visiting a tailor.

Pappa had done business with Pan Frenkel and Pan Majer for years, but Luiza had rarely met them before Łódz turned into Litzmannstadt. Now she regularly visited the single, cramped room the two families shared, in circumstances that clearly embarrassed them, and her, acutely. The food she brought was purchased with Pappa's money, but Pani Majer required pills for a stomach ulcer, and the Frenkel's youngest was diabetic, so Luiza took in food and warm clothes and brought out rings and necklaces to fund the medicines.

In her handbag now there was a bottle of pills and two phials of insulin, but no way to get them in. When a gust of wind showered her with pink petals, she brushed them from her sleeve and turned back, defeated.

"Pani Wolfer!"

Luiza spun round. The urgent whisper came again, "Over here."

Scanning the fence, Luiza located the boy on the other side, crouched by a broken wall. It was Frenkel's eldest – Pappa had attended his Bar Mitzvah last summer.

"Pani, please – the medicine," he hissed. "Push it through the wire."

Luiza stepped onto the grass, but a couple appeared further down the path, so she diverted to the nearest bench. The man and woman passed by, wrapped in each other's arms, and Luiza waited for her heart to stop racing. She checked the path in both directions and was about to try again when she spotted a pair of field-grey uniforms coming the other way. The soldiers parted to allow the unwitting couple to pass between them, reuniting on the path with laughter and coarse gestures. Luiza busied herself with the contents of her handbag as the soldiers approached. She forced down the bubble of rage that rose in her at their lewd offers to help her find what she had lost, refusing to let on that she understood what they said.

Eventually they moved on, discussing as they went what Polish women had in common with cows.

Luiza counted to ten before scanning the path again. Quickly, she crossed the grass and pushed the small bottles through the wire. Turning back to the path, she caught a flash of movement in her peripheral vision. When she looked again, the boy had gone.

Climbing the stairs to the apartment Luiza prayed, as always, that a letter from Ida would be waiting on the hall table. She closed her eyes as she opened the door, willing the letter into being before she opened them.

There had been no news since Ida left – nearly five months of waiting. Life had settled into a surprisingly humdrum routine, given that their home was occupied by the enemy. Luiza knew they were fortunate to have courteous Gustav billeted with them, generously supplementing their rations with his own. Friends of Mathilde Krawcik had been assigned an officer who gave them nothing, yet insisted they all eat together. While he tucked into the meal that Mathilde's friend had cooked with the German's privileged ingredients, the family, too hungry to make their own sparse plate last the duration of their guest's three courses, watched. And the officer had requisitioned the salon for his exclusive use, as well as taking over the master bedroom. When Luiza thought of the Frenkels and the Majers, behind that fence, and wondered how the Abels were faring in Warszawa, she felt shame at her own discontent. In truth, her life was barely affected by the tragedy unfurling about her. Her nation might be in crisis, but what she predominantly endured was tedium.

Pabianice had only ever been tolerable, she now realised, because she was not here all the time. Visits to Warszawa, Toruń and Malinów had been such frequent interruptions that she had never really built a life here. Karol had been an absorbing distraction, too. She prayed for his safety when she remembered, which was less and less frequently as the months passed. She felt guilty that she did not worry more about him, but Ida took up all available heartache.

Luiza was lonely. Even with Gustav's contributions, supplying regular meals took a lot of queueing and bartering, which left Mathilde Krawcik no time for outings. Besides, their favourite works of art had been declared 'degenerate' and replaced with social realist images promoting Aryan superiority. These, insisted Mathilde, were truly degenerate; Luiza simply found them alarming.

Pappa was always at the mill, where Luiza often accompanied him. At first it was because she feared another attack, but the mood had shifted since one of the men had apologised for his part in the assault. Luiza knew that Pappa's employees appreciated that, unlike their neighbour, Lukas Vogel, Hugo Wolfer eschewed the Volksdeutsche. Before the war Vogel had cut an unremarkable figure, but now he strutted around in the yellow uniform of a Nazi administrator. And his daughter, who was a couple of years younger than Luiza, kept trying to recruit her to the Hitler-Jugend. Luiza shuddered inwardly each time she saw the girl in her white blouse and dark blue neckerchief. She was forever on her way to some parade or gymnastics display, proudly showing off her latest badge while boasting about the superior rations her family could claim.

On the other hand, Pappa's workers owed their jobs to his German connection. Without it, the business would have been taken over or shut down.

At the mill, Luiza typed Pappa's letters and helped with the bookkeeping. It made her feel useful. And she visited the factory floor, which was like stepping back into childhood, thrilling to the rhythm of the machinery, infected by Pappa's enthusiasm. She longed to discuss how they might still achieve her dream of becoming an engineer, but it seemed insensitive to raise this while Ida's fate was unknown. Luiza was sure that Pappa's first and last waking thought was of Ida, just as hers was, yet they rarely even spoke her name. As time passed without news, it became more difficult to admit to the constant worry, as if voicing it might make the worst come true.

There was something else that Luiza found impossible to mention: her shame at their association with the enemy. She wondered whether Oberleutnant Helfer would treat them with such decency if they were mere Poles – Untermenschen. Would he share his rations with them? Would he have helped Ida?

It always came back to Ida. How could Luiza get on with her own life when she had no idea how, or if, her sister was getting on with hers?

She closed the door and opened her eyes. There was a letter on the hall table. She held her breath. The cream envelope did not bear Ida's distinctive hand, yet the old-fashioned cursive was familiar. A moment of despondency gave way to elation and Luiza smiled as she exhaled. She had not heard from Aunt Ludmila since before the invasion.

Chapter 39

June 1940, Poznań

The journey took most of the day and at first nobody in the carriage spoke. Everyone was wary, cautioned by the posters admonishing vigilance. *Beware that stranger – he may be a spy. It's always safest to Keep Schtum.* The only conversation was among the scattering of German soldiers. But as time and kilometres passed, food and purposes of travel were shared – even with the soldiers, though Luiza was careful not to reveal that she spoke German. The journey seemed remarkably normal, with people travelling for business, or visiting family, just as she was. It was hard to remember what was going on behind the fence in Łódz when everyday life ticked on like this.

Both Aunt Ludmila, looking older and thinner, and Aunt Rysia, as blonde and elegant as ever, were at the station to meet her. Together with an excited dachshund.

When Luiza crouched to greet Bruni, though, she looked up at Aunt Rysia in confusion.

"Poor Bruni," said her aunt, "we lost her – distemper. This is Tommi."

Luiza had no time to mourn Bruni's passing with Tommi wriggling around her ankles. It was hard to avoid stepping on him as she hugged her mother's sisters.

"Oh, it's so good to see you," she exclaimed, clinging to both her aunts. In their embrace she felt the uncertainties of recent months recede; a quiet assurance suffused her, the absence of which had defined these ten months of occupation.

"Come, let's get you home, Lou-lou," chivvied Aunt Ludmila, threading her arm through Luiza's. Aunt Rysia was trying to control Tommi, who seemed unduly interested in Luiza's case.

"What have you got in there?" laughed her younger aunt. "Sausages?"

"Well," grinned Luiza, "Now that you mention it…"

In the dining room of the spacious apartment her aunts shared with their husbands and her cousin Vera, the salami, supplied by Oberleutnant Helfer, was loudly appreciated.

"Goodness, Lou-lou, I'd forgotten what real meat tastes like." Uncle Ryszard's mouth was full, his eyes closed, and Luiza watched with satisfaction as each bite of salami and fine rye bread (also provided by Gustav) was savoured.

"Mmm, and isn't bread that's not all grit and sawdust completely delicious?" murmured Aunt Ludmila. Aunt Rysia slapped her husband's hand as he reached for another slice of salami.

"Enough! Leave some for Vera. You'll get indigestion, gobbling like that."

"Where is Vera?" asked Luiza.

"At work," said Aunt Rysia with a frown. "She's volunteering at the hospital. It's so brave of her, but I can't help worrying – she sees such unpleasant things."

"War's hardly about sightseeing," Uncle Herbert remonstrated, but Aunt Ludmila placed a hand on his.

"Of course it isn't," retorted Aunt Rysia, indignantly, "But Vera's German is excellent, she could be working in an office. Then I could relax. It's bad enough that her brother's in the thick of it, without having to worry about Vera, too."

Uncle Herbert snorted. "Far better she's among regular soldiers in hospital than the SS in an office. Surely you can't want her working for the enemy?"

Pointedly, Aunt Ludmila cleared her throat. "As you well know, Herbert, we chose our enemy – German rather than Bolshevik – and left Riga to escape those murderers. We agreed to be pragmatic, so now you must stop being provocative. We're lucky to have this large apartment, but it will soon shrink if we don't all make an effort to get along."

"Of course, dearest," sighed Uncle Herbert, peering meekly from beneath bushy grey eyebrows. "Rysia, I apologise. I'm just as proud of Vera as of Paweł. And no news is good news in his regard, I'm sure, my dear."

Aunt Rysia nodded stiffly, and Uncle Ryszard stroked her shoulder. Luiza thought of Karol and wondered, irrationally, whether he and Paweł might be somewhere together – perhaps Mirek, too. Then she remembered the freckled lieutenant who had sought sanctuary in Pabianice with his three companions. Where were they all?

There was no answer to that question, so instead she asked, "How did you get here from Riga? It must have been awful. The refugees coming through Pabianice looked completely done in."

Aunt Ludmila nodded. "Poor wretches, we passed them on the road. We were fortunate – we had Ryszard's car. Then, when we could get no more fuel, we were able to buy train tickets. We almost came to Łódz, but that train was delayed, and Rysia said she'd always wanted to see Poznań. But we were extremely lucky to get this apartment."

"Yes, it's lovely," Luiza agreed as she examined the room properly. There was nothing she recognised from Riga, but what could they have brought with them? Yet the room was fully furnished, with all necessary tableware, down to embroidered napkins and ivory-handled cake forks. On one wall hung a large family portrait: a seated elderly couple with what looked like their son and daughter-in-law standing behind them, and four children, ranging from a toddler to a boy who brought to mind the Frenkel's eldest. A chill crept up Luiza's spine. She glanced at Aunt Ludmila, who held her eye.

"We were very lucky," repeated her aunt. "The apartment was promised to an SS Obersturmbannführer, but his wife didn't want to live so close to the zoo – apparently she's afraid of animals. Herbert turned up at just the right moment. Otherwise, it would have gone to some other SS officer."

"Herbert turned up at just the right time with a German surname and a pocket full of our jewels," interjected Aunt Rysia.

"So, you've no idea where they are?" Luiza's gaze had returned to the portrait. She found herself thinking of Isaak Abel's Pissaro and wondering who was enjoying its effervescent colours.

"Oh, we have a good idea," said Aunt Ludmila, wearily. "But we'll take good care of their home. When they return, they'll find it just as they left it."

The next morning, Luiza got up early to take Tommi out. They walked to the Zoological Gardens. It was cool but bright, with the promise of another cloudless, early summer's day. She tried playing with the dog – hide-and-seek among the rhododendrons, their pink and lilac blooms beginning to turn limp and brown – but he was a less adventurous character than Bruni. Without salami to distract him, he was happy to trot at her heels as they wove among the acid-yellow laburnums. Luiza remembered running by the sea with Bruni and her spirits lifted as they had then – there was something about walking with a dog. She was calculating whether Mono could still be alive, when an incongruous sound intruded, taking her instantly back to Zakątek on the day that Janek had driven home Pappa's new lorry. They followed the sound of the klaxon beyond the trees, to where the animal enclosures began, and there it was again. Not a vehicle but an elephant! Luiza grinned, delighted by such unpredictable jubilance in the midst of war and destruction. She willed it to trumpet again, but instead there was an unearthly howl that made her scalp prickle. A wolf? Luiza felt a moment's sympathy for the Obersturmbannführer's wife.

Scraping the thinnest film of butter onto bread with the texture of compacted sawdust, Luiza felt virtuous. She was leaving the fine rye for the others. She thought of Aunt Rysia's lavish breakfasts in Riga and her mouth watered. Yet some things were unchanged: Uncle Ryszard's commentary on the news was just as vigorous, while Uncle Herbert still grunted and growled from behind his paper. Since the worst had happened, though, the two men appeared to have buried their differences and were equally glum about despatches from France.

"First the British get driven back to the sea, and now Paris has fallen. Good Lord, is there no stopping Hitler?"

"He's off to a good start," opined Uncle Herbert, "but he'll get too cocky and think he can take on the Bolsheviks, too. That will be his downfall, mark my words."

"But Stalin's his buddy."

"Pah, once Hitler gets tired of chasing the Brits across the Channel, he won't be able to resist the challenge in the east. But if Napoleon couldn't do it, Hitler certainly won't."

Panicking, Luiza blurted, "But if Germany declares war on Russia, how will Ida ever get home?"

Uncle Herbert met Aunt Ludmila's disapproving stare and turned a reassuring smile on Luiza. "Oh, it won't be any time soon, my dear. Ida will be back long before then."

Luiza was sorting Aunt Ludmila's embroidery silks

into a rainbow progression of shades when Vera entered, bleary-eyed and yawning, her blonde hair unbrushed.

"Lou-lou! I'd forgotten you were here. How wonderful to see you," she exclaimed, and hugged her cousin close. "Oh, and even better now that I see what you've brought."

She tucked in, answering Luiza's questions between greedy mouthfuls.

"Oh, it's not so bad – Mama likes to worry. All I really do is wash bedpans and give bed-baths.

"To German soldiers?"

Vera looked up. "They're just men, Lou-lou."

"I know." Luiza sighed.

"I do it for them in the hope that someone is doing the same for our boys."

Luiza sighed. "I hope you're right. But where are our boys? Ida hasn't heard from Mirek, nor you from Paweł. Karol's vanished, too. I wrote to Pani Anna, asking if his family had any news, but she hasn't replied."

"Well, you can't rely on the post these days, you know that."

"But we're in the same Reich District and everything's working with German efficiency here. It's different with Ida – of course there are problems with communication from the Soviet zone. But Pani Anna… Did you know I was at Malinów on September 1st? It felt like the Grudzinskis couldn't be shot of their friend with a German name fast enough." With a wry smile, she added, "Of course, if Pani Anna had got her way, she'd have shared that name. I bet she's relieved now that Pappa didn't marry her."

Vera shrugged. "I think it's more complicated. Even

though the signs were clearly there, the invasion still came as a shock – nobody wanted to believe it would happen, and there was a lot of knee-jerk reaction."

"Yes," Luiza agreed, "poor Pappa got beaten up by some of his workforce."

Vera looked up. "Really? Is Uncle alright?"

"He's fine now – one of them even apologised."

"You see what I mean?" Vera placed discs of salami neatly on a second slice of bread. "Pani Anna probably feels guilty now about rushing you away."

"To be fair, it was Waldemar who had more of a problem with me being there. I'm just searching for a reason why she hasn't been in touch."

"It could be anything. Perhaps she's unwell? Or just very busy – doesn't she have a hotel in Warszawa? She may not even be at Malinów."

Luiza nodded thoughtfully, trying to decide which of two blues was closer to indigo. "You're right. Perhaps I should write to the Mazowiecki."

"Right then," pronounced Vera, standing and shaking crumbs from her napkin onto her plate. "I'm going to get dressed and then I'm going to show my little cousin round Poznań. I'm off today, so we have all the time in the world!"

Chapter 40

September 1940, Pabianice

Surprised to hear laughter, Luiza glanced in the mirror and smoothed her skirt. She had been making the most of the late September sunshine, strolling by the river before the evening chill that presaged autumn set in. In the dining room she found her father in the company of two men in Wehrmacht uniform. They were passing round a bottle of schnapps and an album lay open on the table. One of the soldiers pointed at a photograph. "That's where my father worked. He'd be tickled pink to see me having a drink with the boss's son."

Pappa looked up as the door clicked shut behind Luiza and grinned broadly. Luiza could not recall when she had last seen him so happy.

"Lou-lou!" he exclaimed, spreading his arms in welcome. "Come and meet Friedrich and Johannes.

Gentlemen, I'm delighted to introduce my younger daughter, Luiza."

Both soldiers stood and echoed each other's polite '*gnädiges Fräulein*'. Luiza smiled back. Pappa was still beaming.

"Just imagine, Lou-lou, Friedrich and Johannes are from Crimmitschau. On the tram back from Łódz, I overheard these two gentlemen and thought to myself, 'if that's not a Saxon accent, I don't know what is'. As it turns out, not only are they from Saxony, but they're from the town where I was born! What are the chances, eh?"

Pappa looked so delighted that Luiza felt grateful to the men who were the cause of such joy.

"But that's wonderful. Let me get you something to eat with that schnapps."

"It's already taken care of. They're staying for supper. Pani Krawcik's preparing it now."

Over the course of the meal, however, the mood darkened. Luiza doubted that even the second bottle of schnapps would have so loosened the soldiers' tongues had an officer been present. But Oberleutnant Helfer was away.

"It's shocking, what we're doing to the Poles."

"None of us wants to be here. But what choice do we have?"

"This isn't soldiering, it's butchery. It's all down to the blasted SS (excuse me, Fraulein)."

"The SS and the bloody Fuhrer," muttered Johannes, and then seemed startled that he had spoken aloud.

Pappa nodded. "We're no supporters of national

socialism, my friend, and it warms my heart to hear you say this. It shows that all is not lost."

Luiza pleated her napkin as she pondered their words. These Germans clearly hated Hitler and yet were colluding in his tyranny. Did they have a choice? It must be terribly dangerous to refuse. But if enough Germans took a stand, surely the Nazis would be finished? Yet would she herself be brave enough to do that? Throwing her passport in the river seemed a feeble gesture in comparison.

As if he could read her mind, after showing Friedrich and Johannes out, Pappa moved his chair closer to hers and took her hand.

"You're ashamed to have a German father."

It was a statement, not a question, and Luiza was too stunned to deny it.

"I understand. I'm ashamed of what my people are doing. But, as you've seen, not all Germans agree with it."

"Yet they still do it."

Luiza scrubbed the back of her hand across her eyes, but they were filling too fast to blot the tears away. Pappa shook out his handkerchief and gave it to her with a sigh.

"If I were younger, perhaps – I hope - I would take a stand. But at my age, all I can do is not join in. And try to keep my family safe."

He paused, before adding, "I'm sorry, Lou-lou."

Luiza saw that his eyes were wet, and she passed the handkerchief back. He blew his nose.

"You have nothing to be sorry for, Pappa. You don't flounce around in a silly uniform, and you haven't replaced your Polish employees with Volksdeutsche. That's taking a stand. It's just… I feel ashamed of our German blood, and I've never felt ashamed of who I am before."

"And you mustn't now! German blood is nothing to be ashamed of – those were good Germans you met this evening, and there's another sharing our home."

"I know. Oh, Pappa, it feels so awful, though. What's going to happen? It's as if the future's been stolen. Sometimes everything feels completely hopeless."

Pappa stroked her hand. "You're so young, Lou-lou. It's hard to believe now, but this war will end."

"But, what about…?" Luiza hesitated.

"Ida?" Pappa interjected, gently.

Luiza nodded, her eyes filling with tears again. He really could read her mind.

"I don't know, Lou-lou." He looked wrung out. The evening's ebullience had drained away and Luiza wondered if she would ever see him laugh again.

"My dear child, all we can do is pray."

And Luiza did. That night, and every night, she knelt before the icon on her bedside table and begged the scarred black Madonna for guidance.

"Blessed Mary, show me what to do. Give me the strength to get through this, to support Pappa and Ida. Blessed Virgin, please send news of Ida."

Chapter 41

March 1941, Pabianice

"Yes, I understand. This afternoon at five, in the dining room of the Europejski. I'll be there." Her father replaced the receiver but did not release his grip. His face was chalk white.

"Pappa, what is it?" Luiza left the letter she was typing and went to stand behind her father, her hands on his shoulders. She lowered her face until her cheek touched his.

"Who was that, Pappa? It was about Ida, wasn't it?"

At the mention of her sister's name, her father seemed to reassemble himself. Brushing her cheek with his moustache, he made to rise from his chair. Luiza stepped back to give him space, but he sank down again, his palms still braced on the wooden arms. Luiza moved to the other side of his desk and, facing him, tried again. "Pappa, please. Who was that?"

He gave a shake of his head, as if to clear it. When he spoke, his words were deliberate, as if trying to make sense of each as it emerged. "She said she has news of Ida – she has a letter from her."

"You're meeting her? She'll give you Ida's letter? What's her name? Can I come?"

Pappa met Luiza's eyes with a weary smile.

"I'm meeting her this afternoon, and I'll make sure I get the letter. She called herself Pani Malczewska. And no," he added, shaking his head, "you can't come, Lou-lou."

"But…"

"No." Pappa held up a hand. "I'm going alone. But I'll tell you everything on my return, I promise. Now, can you please finish that letter? I must sign it before I catch my train. I'll have to call for a car; there's no time for the tram."

Luiza struggled to concentrate. She had to re-type the final page with Pappa peering over her shoulder, repeatedly screwing and unscrewing the cap of his fountain pen. When she finally rolled the sheet out of the Olympia, he scrawled his signature and hurried out.

That evening, Luiza waited in the salon. With Gustav on leave in Germany, his enhanced fuel ration was not available, so she wrapped herself in a blanket. At some point she must have fallen asleep, because when she woke, chilled and stiff, Mathilde Krawcik was drawing back the curtains. It was morning.

She could not face breakfast, nor could she bear to leave her look-out by the window. She did not know if Pappa would come home or go straight to the office.

Should she walk to Bauer and Lande? She wondered for the hundredth time why he had not telephoned.

Then someone turned the corner onto Ulica Kościuszki. Luiza tore down the stairs and into the street, where rain pummelled her face. She splashed in a puddle and realised she was still wearing slippers. They flapped treacherously as she ran, so she shook them off. By the time she reached her father, one of her big toes had burst through her inadequate darning.

Pappa was pale, and he ignored her questions as he pulled her under his umbrella and steered her back to the apartment.

"Yes, I know I promised to tell you everything, but not a word until you're warm and dry. Your teeth are chattering, Lou-lou. Get out of those wet things, for heaven's sake. Your filthy stockings are soaking Pani Krawcik's clean floor!"

Exasperated, Luiza went to change. When she found her father in the dining room, she was in clean clothes, but her hair still dripped down her collar. Pappa was drinking coffee and playing with a slice of bread. Luiza sat down opposite and shook her head at his offer of coffee.

"Just tell me what happened, Pappa. Please."

Her father sighed before pushing his plate away. "Well, I met 'Pani Malczewska' in the Europejski dining room as arranged. And she gave me 'Ida's letter.'"

"Why do you say it like that, Pappa? Do you have it? Can I see it?"

Pappa reached inside his waistcoat and handed Luiza a folded piece of paper. Luiza opened it carefully and read aloud: "Please listen to Pani Malczewska. She is a friend and can help me." Luiza looked up. "But this isn't Ida's writing. Who wrote it?"

Pappa sighed again, then shrugged, his eyes unfocused.

Luiza read on. "I was bringing the baby back to you, but I was shot by a Soviet border patrol." She gasped. Frantically, she turned over the page, but there was no more.

"Shot! Is she alright? What's happened to the baby? This Pani Malczewska – what did she tell you?"

Pappa was looking down at his nails as he ran his thumb backwards and forwards across them. "She said that she met Ida in prison," he responded without looking up.

"In prison? But why isn't Ida in hospital, if she was shot?"

Pappa met her eyes for a moment, before continuing to examine his nails. Luiza was shocked by his look of desolation. He continued in the same quiet monotone.

"The Bolsheviks think Ida's a spy. Pani Malczewska knows people who can get her out. But to do that, Pani Malczewska wanted $150."

"Dollars?"

Luiza put the letter on the table and looked from it to her father. Tapping the paper, she asked, "Whose writing did Pani Malczewska say this is?"

"Pani Malczewska maintained that Ida had written it. She said it wasn't surprising that her writing has changed after what she's been through. And she insisted that I could have my daughter back if I paid $150. When I pointed out that possession of foreign currency is a capital offence, she suggested that, 'with my contacts', I should have no difficulty finding it and, besides, surely my daughter was worth it?"

His elbows on the table, Pappa rested his forehead on his hands.

"What about Little Mirek? Is he alright?"

"She didn't say." Pappa looked up. "But she did say that she worried for my daughter's sanity if she had to stay in prison."

Luiza's hands flew to her mouth. "Oh, no, poor Idka."

Pappa appeared to be staring at something beyond her. With an effort, Luiza controlled her panic and asked softly, "Pappa, what happened?"

Her father looked at her directly, and this time he held her gaze. She was again dismayed by the depth of despair in his eyes.

"What happened is that I excused myself. But instead of going to the cloakroom, I made a telephone call."

Luiza waited. Eventually she asked, "Who did you call, Pappa?"

"The Gestapo."

Luiza had been leaning across the table towards her father, but now she pulled back abruptly and stared at him, appalled. Eventually she spoke, her tone querulous, "Why? Why would you do that?"

Pappa's eyes were still fixed on hers, and he spoke forcefully. "Because, in Nazi-occupied Poland, possession of foreign currency carries a death sentence. Because I don't believe that Pani Malczewska is Polish, at all. Because, however desperate I am to recover one daughter, I cannot risk leaving the other unprotected."

His eyes glistened. As he fumbled for a handkerchief, a single tear rolled down his cheek. Luiza looked away, trying to make sense of what she was hearing.

"What happened, then?" she asked. When there was no reply, she turned back. Pappa had composed himself. He went on, "Two Gestapo officers arrived. Pani Malczewska tried to run, but they arrested her and took her away."

"Took her away? Where to? What will happen to her?"

"She'll be questioned and then they'll decide what to do with her."

"But…"

"Lou-lou, listen. I didn't trust that woman. She's not a friend to Ida – I believe her purpose in contacting me was something else entirely. If I had done as she'd asked, I could have been shot! Even if I hadn't been caught, I'm certain that Ida would not have been returned to us."

Luiza looked down at her hands. Pappa reached for them across the table. After a moment, she leant forward and placed them in his.

"Do you trust me, Lou-lou?"

"Of course, I trust you, Pappa," she exclaimed. "Of course, I do. It's just… to call the Gestapo! Couldn't you simply have left the hotel?"

Her father nodded thoughtfully. "I could," he agreed. "Perhaps that would have been a more honourable course of action. But my priority is finding my daughter."

"But how can reporting Pani Malczewska to the Gestapo help you do that?"

Hugo let go her hands and sat back. Grimacing, he kneaded the back of his neck, turning his head from side to side.

"By doing the Germans a service, I'm hoping they'll feel more inclined to help me."

"Lou-lou! Is that you?"

From where her father stood, at the door to their apartment, his voice spilled down the stone steps to Luiza. She let the heavy street door swing shut behind her and stared up at the unprecedented sight of Pappa hanging over the wrought iron balustrade on their landing. His face was flushed, his ebbing white hair caught in a shocked halo by the rays that filtered through the domed rooflight three floors above.

"Hurry, Lou-lou! I've been waiting for you. I've had a call!"

Infected by his urgency, Luiza took the steps two at a time. For a moment Pappa appeared baffled by her swift arrival, glancing back down to the foyer before seizing her wrist and drawing her into the apartment.

"I had a telephone call," he repeated, as she removed her jacket and laid her gloves on the hall table. A contrary impulse made her move slowly and with deliberation, as if to counter her father's unusual discomposure. She picked at some blossom snagged in the rough tweed of her skirt, distracted by the thought that a whole year had passed since the wall had gone up around the ghetto. She had posted the phials through the wire in the usual place this afternoon but, for the first time, the Frenkel boy had not appeared. She followed her father into the salon.

"From German-Soviet liaison in Warszawa," Pappa went on, pacing from the unlit stove to the window and back again. Luiza rolled the petals between her fingers and wondered why the boy had not come. Would they find the medicine?

"Lou-lou! Are you listening?" Pappa had stopped pacing and was standing in front of her, his hands clasped as if beseeching her attention. "It's about your sister."

Luiza's stomach lurched with the familiar cold weight of worry. She swallowed hard and musings about the Frenkels and Majers evaporated, leaving only the dizzying void that was Ida. In a voice so calm that she could not believe it came from her, she asked, "What did they say?"

"That her release has been agreed."

Pappa beamed and Luiza floated from the chair into his embrace. She found that she was sobbing. Pappa patted her back and stroked her hair, muttering endearments he had not used since she was a child. In time, they both sat down and Luiza asked, tentatively, "Did they explain anything?"

Neither of them had mentioned the woman at the Europejski since his return from Warszawa. Luiza had repeatedly fought to interrupt, but never completely halted, a train of thought that led to a dark and fearful place. Pappa had remained withdrawn, his eyes veiled, his appetite diminished.

"Did they say anything about Pani Malczewska?"

Pappa looked out of the window. At last, he spoke. "It seems that I was right not to trust her. She was already known to the German authorities by a number of pseudonyms. She's Russian and specialises in foreign currency acquisition for whoever will pay the highest price. The officer who telephoned said that their assumption is that Ida came to the attention of a criminal network in prison, who thought they could use her to access funds, via my contacts. They employed Pani Malczewska to initiate proceedings."

"And did the officer say what's happened to her?" Luiza asked.

"The officer expressed the Reich's sincere gratitude," Pappa said, dully. "He confirmed that she was a criminal they had been after for some time, and that, as such, she has been executed."

Luiza gasped and a tremor shook her whole being. Pappa regarded her. For a moment his eyes displayed a profound misery that she found acutely unsettling, before they grew shrouded once more, and he continued tonelessly, "The Soviet authorities, desiring to express their gratitude for my part in the capture of this criminal, have agreed to release Ida from prison, into the care of her mother-in-law. She'll have to report to the police regularly, though. She's still under suspicion."

"She's not coming home?"

Pappa shook his head. He appeared to have aged in the time they had been sitting there. "She was caught trying to leave the Soviet zone, for a purpose they believe was espionage."

"Ida a spy? But how on earth…?"

Pappa shook his head, wearily. "They won't explain further. But Ida and the child will be allowed to stay in Nieśwież. They will be safe there."

"So, little Mirek is with her? Oh, thank goodness for that. But how will she cope with Pani Timorecka – you remember what Ida said about her?"

Pappa pushed himself out of his seat and walked to the door. With his hand on the doorknob he spoke, his back to Luiza. And there was ice in his words.

"I imagine that life with Pani Timorecka will be infinitely preferable to life in a Bolshevik prison. Perhaps if Ida had appreciated just what she has in Nieśwież, she would not so recklessly have placed herself and her child in danger. Nor made others face impossible choices."

Luiza remained at the table, struggling to come to terms with her emotions. She acknowledged relief that Ida and her son were safe. But where was the joy that should accompany such news? The familiar, oppressive weight had not lifted, although its source had changed. She now felt burdened by Pani Malczewska's fate. That, and her father's grim demeanour.

Chapter 42

Summer 1941, Pabianice

*n*early a month had passed. Pappa's hands had developed a tremor. He was pale and subdued, and reminded Luiza of the time after the accident at Zakątek. Even Gustav noticed. The Oberleutnant was frequently away these days, but he ensured a regular supply of ingredients for Pappa's favourite dishes.

After supper one evening, Pappa broke his silence. "I've had a message from Isaak Abel."

Luiza, who had been clearing the table, sat back down. "Are they alright? Have they left Warszawa?"

"They're in the ghetto."

"No!" Luiza's eyes filled with tears. "Oh, I so hoped they'd gone to America. Why wouldn't Dawid go?"

Pappa regarded her. "I think you know why, Lou-lou. He's a man of principle, a brave man."

"But the others? Misza? They wouldn't leave without Dawid – shouldn't he have done it for them?"

Pappa sighed. "Who are we to judge?" After a pause he continued, "Isaak asks for my help – for the child."

"For Misza? What's wrong with him?"

Pappa studied her again. "He's sick – starving. They all are, but Isaak says he would never ask for help for them – he knows how dangerous it is. But, for the child's sake, he's asking – they're desperate."

"What can we do? How can we help? I haven't seen the Frenkels and Majers for over a year. I can't imagine it's any easier to get into the ghetto in Warszawa."

"Isaak's message came through Pan Bielski…"

"Gosia's father? Does he know the Abels? Gosia never said."

"He doesn't. But he does know others in the ghetto. He and his wife both treated Jewish patients long after other dentists stopped. He says there's a way in. He's in touch with a network that's helping Jews and he said they could get you in. Not me – I'd stand out too much, he said. But you, you could go unnoticed. But it's dangerous, Lou-lou. Really dangerous. I can't ask you to do it. I can only tell you what he said."

Luiza stared at her father. "Of course, I'll do it! The Abels were always so kind to me. You know how they welcomed me into their home – I loved going there. I want to help."

Pappa smiled. For the first time since that meeting in Warszawa. It was a sad smile, but it warmed Luiza's heart.

"My brave Lou-lou. God bless you and keep you safe. I believe you have more courage than your old father."

"Don't say that, Pappa. Pan Bielski made it clear – you can't do it, but I can."

Pappa smiled again, this time with a hint of the old twinkle in his eye. He tugged his waistcoat, where it hung loose at his waist.

"He said that a portly man would look out of place. And he feared I might get stuck in a tunnel. But then, he hasn't seen me recently."

He let go of the waistcoat and took Luiza's hand. Looking at her intently, he said, "If you really want to do it, Lou-lou, you must go as soon as possible – time is short. You can stay with the Bielskis and you'll be told what to do."

Luiza had not been to Warszawa since the occupation, and the damage appalled her. She had to skirt piles of rubble on streets where whole houses were missing. Of those that still stood, some bore bullet holes, others lacked walls. A charred stench hung in the air, sometimes displaced by something worse. Yesterday, when she and Gosia were on their way to a café to meet Agnieszka, happily anticipating the reunion of the Three Musketeers, something warm and foul-smelling had rained on her. Shock gave way to nausea as she realised that it was the contents of a chamber pot, casually tipped out of a window. They had to return to Gosia's for her to wash her hair and change.

The eventual reunion was disappointing. Agnieszka was engaged to be married, and her conversation revolved around the silk required for her dress. Luiza was outraged when she asked her to use her 'German connections' to procure it.

"What German connections?"

"Well, your father – he's German, isn't he?"

"No, he's not!" Luiza almost shouted. "He's Polish – we're Polish."

"Alright, alright, keep your hair on," huffed Agnieszka. "I just thought you might be able to help, that's all.'

"Well, I can't. And anyway, how can you possibly worry about a wedding dress in the midst of all this?" Luiza waved her hand in the direction of a velvet-swagged window, through which the ruined building opposite was visible.

Agnieszka shrugged. "Life goes on, you know."

"Not for everyone, it doesn't," Luiza began, but Gosia dug her elbow hard into Luiza's hip. "Remember, Agnieszka never used to come into Jewish shops with us," she had warned, on their way to the café. "I'm not sure we can trust her with the real reason for your visit – it's not worth the risk."

Now Agnieszka spooned up the last of her ice cream and gathered her gloves and handbag, before sliding herself along the bench seat and out of the alcove. Standing across the table from them, she checked her face in the mirror of her powder compact and wiped her little finger across the corners of her mouth. Snapping the compact shut, she threw Luiza a frosty smile.

"All for one and one for all, I don't think," she said, before turning on her heel. Luiza and Gosia watched in silence. An SS officer had just entered and he held the door open for her, clicking his gleaming heels and raising an arm.

"Heil Hitler," he intoned.

"Heil Hitler," Agnieszka replied with a smile as she exited to the street.

The house on Ulica Żelazna was undamaged. Luiza rang the bell twice, as instructed, and waited. Behind her, running down the middle of the street, was the ghetto fence. The houses on this side of Żelazna faced it, while the houses on the other side were behind it. She pulled her headscarf lower on her forehead and adjusted the weight of the basket. It was heavy with bags of millet and buckwheat, two loaves of Gustav's fine rye and their entire month's ration of butter. Gosia's mother had warned her to disguise its weight so as not to draw attention, so Luiza had gritted her teeth as it dug into the crook of her arm and tried to walk without leaning over to balance the load.

A woman not much older than Luiza opened the door.

"I was told you have some curtains you no longer need."

"Yes, come in and I'll show you. There are some other things you may be interested in, too," the woman said, glancing up and down the street. Satisfied, she stepped back for Luiza to enter. "Follow me, and don't dawdle. Looking at curtains doesn't take all day."

She led Luiza to the end of a corridor, where she rapped on a door before opening it and nodding her through. Luiza found herself at the top of a narrow staircase. She moved the basket to her other arm, so that she could grasp the handrail, and descended with care. What light there was came through a small, dirty window set high in the wall – presumably at ground level outside. She heard a sound from the far corner of the cellar. The top half of a man was visible, framed in a low arch in the wall. He beckoned her over, took the basket and disappeared. Peering through the arch, Luiza could see that the man was standing on ground that sloped steeply downwards. He held her basket in one hand, a flashlight in the other.

"Come on," he said. "No time to lose."

Luiza sat on the ledge and lowered herself gingerly. She took a few steps, finding that she had to bend her head as the ceiling lowered. Following the man's receding back, she soon had to crouch lower. She marvelled at the pace at which he moved, bent over like that, toting her heavy basket. Her back and her thighs began to ache. It might be easier to crawl, but the smell from the wet – in places waterlogged – ground, made her reluctant to place her hands on it. She wished she had worn trousers, but Gosia's mother had insisted that she must not stand out.

Just when she thought she could go no further, the gradient changed and Luiza found herself going uphill. The man had stopped. He turned to her with his finger to his lips, before switching off the torch. In the darkness Luiza heard a scratching sound. Her skin crawled at the thought of rats, until she identified a regular rhythm to the sound – a signal of some kind. A fainter scratch came in reply and the man's silhouette was revealed as light leaked through an opening hatch. The man clambered through, then held out his hand to pull her up.

They were in a cellar just like the one they had left. Another woman, who could have been the sister of the girl in the house on Żelazna, eyed her suspiciously and asked what her business was.

"I need to get this to the Abel family on Nowolipki, number 20."

Luiza gestured towards the basket that the man had set on the floor. The woman drew back the cloth and checked the contents.

"Go through there and up the stairs," she said, pointing at the cellar door. "Out the gateway, turn right. After you've crossed Smocza, number 20 will be on your right. But be quick. He won't wait for you more than twenty minutes."

Luiza glanced at the man, then at her watch.

"You'll have to leave that here," said the woman, holding out her hand.

"But how will I know when to return?" asked Luiza, panicked.

"Just make your delivery and come straight back. If you're seen wearing a watch in here, you'll arouse suspicion."

Luiza took off her watch and gave it to the woman, then hoisted the basket and made for the door.

Misza must be five now, but it was hard to believe. His eyes appeared huge in his shrunken face, and he seemed both younger and, incongruously, much older. In spite of the stuffy room, he was covered with a blanket. Beneath it, his small chest rose and fell rapidly, his lips opening and closing to the same desperate rhythm in their urgent quest for oxygen. His unblinking gaze never left Luiza.

Pani Abel's soft contours, which had pressed so

comfortingly against Luiza on the piano stool, were gone. Her black dress, rusty with wear, hung loose. Her silver wings were yellowed and the rest of her hair was coarsely threaded with grey. Her hands were empty of their jewelled rings. Only a gold band remained.

Pan Abel's rosy cheeks were shrivelled; beneath his yarmulke his luxuriant white curls had faded and frayed. He rose unsteadily to greet Luiza, but Elsa quickly guided him back to his chair and he sank down gratefully. It was the only chair in the room. There was a double bed, and the pallet on the floor on which Misza lay. And what looked like a pile of rags on the floor along one of the bare walls. The plaster was scuffed and cracked. Not a single picture was hung, and there was no rug on the wooden floor.

Dawid had taken the heavy basket from her. His corduroy trousers were a greasy, indeterminate grey. His hair was long, as was his unexpected beard. He no longer looked like a movie star. He and Elsa were both thinner, but her dark hair still tumbled about her face and she still hooked it behind her ear impatiently. She regarded Luiza with a smile and her eyes flashed warmth and gratitude. She was the first to speak.

"Thank you," she said.

Luiza spread her arms helplessly. "It's so little… it's nothing."

"It's by no means nothing." Dawid's voice took her back to their last conversation, when he had steered her away from the fascist thugs. She remembered his words: "It's always been the same, and it always will be. It's just the degree that changes." But surely, he could never have imagined this degree. If he had, he would have taken his family to America. Surely.

Pani Abel was already buttering a slice of bread. She gave it to Elsa, who sat on the pallet and propped Misza against her. Breaking off a small piece, she held it to the little boy's mouth. His eyes were still fixed on Luiza, and his mouth seemed too occupied with breathing to eat. Luiza felt tears well up. She could not bear this, and suddenly she was terrified that she would be stuck here, unable to pass back to the other side.

"I'm sorry, I must go. They said I must be quick – he won't wait."

She looked around the miserable room, took in again the faces of the family who had always welcomed her so warmly. They smiled at her. Even here. Even Misza. She had to get out.

"Sorry," she muttered. "I'm sorry," she repeated, louder. She turned to walk back to the door and was startled to find it immediately behind her. She had taken no more than one step into the room; she had simply stood and stared. Ashamed, she turned back. They were still smiling. "It's too late," she thought. "I'm too late."

She could think of no honest words that would counter the hopelessness of the wretched room, so repeated, "I'm sorry," and turned to go. In the doorway she turned back again. "Goodbye," she said.

She thought she would never displace that image of the Abels. But then, on 22 June, Germany broke the non-aggression pact and attacked the Soviet Union, and Ida

once more took up all available concern. Luiza called
Nieśwież and, at last, there was an answer. But it was far
from reassuring.

"…kind Russian came to warn… won't leave suspects
alive… she's hiding… farm…"

The line crackled and swallowed words, but Luiza
understood enough of what Pani Timorecka was saying
to feel frightened. Of course, the Soviets would not leave
behind spies who might aid the enemy.

"The baby?" Luiza asked, "Is he alright?"

"… angel… with me…"

"What about Mirek? Any news?"

"… no… not…"

There was a series of clicks, then the line went dead.
Luiza replaced the receiver and went back to her own
desk. Pappa was in Warszawa, so she would have to wait
to see what he made of this. She tried to get on with her
work, but the columns swam and the numbers refused to
tally. Eventually she gave up and set off for home in the
sunshine, pausing at the kiosk where her eyes were drawn
to the headline: *Army of the Fatherland conquers Wilno –
European crusade against Bolshevism marches on to Minsk.*

The Germans would pass Nieśwież on their way to
Minsk, so it was only a matter of days. Could Ida stay
hidden until they arrived? How had it come to this, Luiza
wondered, that she found herself urging the German army
on?

As she opened the front door she glanced reflexively
at the hall table, even though she knew there could be no
letter from Ida; how could she write if she were in hiding?

Suddenly, the full import of Pani Timorecka's words struck home: If the Bolsheviks found her, Ida would be shot. Luiza's legs buckled and she found herself on her knees. She reached for a chair to pull herself up, then rested her elbows on the seat instead. Clasping her hands together, she closed her eyes in prayer.

Chapter 43

December 1941, Pabianice

"Uncle Georg looks just like you, Pappa – only without the moustache."

The photograph showed a man seated behind a desk. Luiza handed the small, scalloped square back and took another. This one featured the same man in a garden, standing between a short, plump woman wearing a dirndl, her hair pulled back in a bun, and a younger, taller woman, also in a dirndl.

"So, that's your aunt Gretchen, and your cousin, Helga. She's the same age as Ida."

They fell silent. Helga might be the same age but, unlike Ida, she was safely at home with her father. As was Luiza. The pair were currently huddled by the stove in the salon, Christmas decorations abandoned at their feet. Luiza had just brought the box up from the cellar when Pappa blew in, ruddy-faced and mantled in snow. He had been away for nearly three weeks, having made the decision to visit his brother while at a textile exhibition in Vienna the previous month. "It's over thirty years since I last saw him – who knows when I'll be in Austria again?" was his reasoning for travelling a further two hundred kilometres south of the capital. Now he was expounding on the beauty of the landscape around Luneberg, a pretty alpine town nestling beneath the Lavanttal Alps of Carinthia. It sounded delightful, but Luiza wondered why Pappa was quite so taken. And then she understood.

"But I don't want to leave Poland, Pappa. I won't leave you. Why on earth should I go and stay with people I've never met?"

"Because they're family, and you'll be safer there than here."

"But I'm perfectly safe here! It's over two years since the Germans came, and look at me – nothing's happened. I'm not leaving, Pappa. That's final."

She expected the argument to escalate, but Pappa merely brandished another photograph. "Can you really see a likeness? I thought I caught a glimpse of your grandmother in Helga. Ida's always reminded me of my mother."

They sat on companionably, finding solace in glimpses of the familiar that brought Ida closer.

They had lived with the unspeakable dread that she might have been shot until a letter finally arrived in August. Relief, however, was short-lived. Yes, Ida was alive, but Little Mirek had disappeared. When Bolsheviks searched the house, just as Pani Timorecka's 'kind Russian' had warned, they could not find their suspect so took her son instead. Ida had come out of hiding to learn that his distraught grandmother had been unable to save Little Mirek from being swept up in the Soviet retreat.

Luiza had thought that nothing could be worse than waiting to hear whether Ida had been shot. Yet her sister's letters since August charted such a devastating deterioration in her mental state that it was just as worrying. Pani Timorecka had also written, and it was evident that the mutual loss of their sons, far from bringing the two women together as Pappa had ventured might happen, had in fact poisoned their relationship further. Each clearly blamed the other for Little Mirek's abduction. It could be argued that this, at least, was logical, given that Ida's actions had led to her son's vulnerability, and that he was in his grandmother's care when he was taken. Less rationally, however, they each also held the other responsible for Mirek being 'missing in action'. Luiza and Pappa tried to persuade Ida to leave the pernicious atmosphere of the Timorecki house, but their requests for her to come home seemed only to increase her hysteria. She clung to the desperate hope that Little Mirek might find his way back to Nieśwież, while they lived in fear that she might set out eastward to recover the toddler herself.

Luiza focused on the photograph in her hand; was that a hint of Ida in Helga's equivocal regard? How could one cousin be carefree, the other bereft? One sister untroubled, the other devastated? Such were the challenges she put to the scar-faced Madonna each night and blamed the lack of response on her own inability to hear rather than the Virgin's inadequacy.

Five months later, on a mild, May evening, Luiza hung out of a train window as Pappa faded into the dusk. When she could no longer make him out, she turned back to the empty compartment and eyed her suitcase, which the porter had hoisted onto the luggage rack. On the label was written: Luneberg, Carinthia, Austria.

It was the arrival of the summons that had given Pappa the leverage he needed. They knew it was coming – Gustav had warned them. Mired in the Russian winter on the Eastern Front, early in 1942 the Nazis extended their trawl for labour throughout the occupied territories and commanded Polish youth to toil in German industry. When Luiza's order came, Pappa had reassured, "No need to worry; you have a German passport."

Luiza's admission that she had thrown it in the river did not evoke the fury she had anticipated. Instead, Pappa was silent for some time. Eventually he commented, mildly, "It's fortunate, then, that your sick aunt in Austria needs someone to look after her." And it was fortunate that they had Gustav to help with travel documents.

The seats on either side of the compartment had already been made up into four bunks, leaving nowhere to sit, so Luiza slipped off her shoes and climbed up beneath her case. While her heart ached with leaving Pappa, she could not deny a fizz of excitement; she was setting off for the unknown, embarking on her own adventure. The novelty of the experience had edged Ida to the periphery of her concerns, but now a sliver of guilt pierced her conscience: She had almost forgotten her nightly plea for Little Mirek's safe return. Closing her eyes, she directed a fervent prayer to the Virgin, begging for her nephew's protection and her sister's steadfastness. Over the months, Ida's communications had calmed from the extreme agitation of last year, yet their bleak despondency was possibly even more chilling. At least she no longer wrote of rescue missions to the Soviet Union, but she still refused to leave Nieśwież.

Luiza's thoughts followed a familiar trajectory, contemplating not only her sister's suffering, but that of so many others. Her memory of the Abels' abject misery surfaced, along with her many arguments with Pappa. She had been determined to take more supplies into the ghetto, but her father would not allow it; the risk was too great. Then there were the Frenkels and Majers. When she had last gone with insulin to the perimeter fence, sunlight had reflected on something in the grass on the other side. Her last delivery had not been picked up. Since January thousands had been moved out of the Łódź ghetto. It seemed likely that Pappa's friends were among them.

As ever, Luiza came up against this inexplicable injustice: While others seemed doomed, she had been given a means of escape. It was an insoluble conundrum which she regularly placed before Our Lady. Recently, she believed she had caught the whisper of a response. Or perhaps it was just what she hoped for. Nevertheless, a voice in her head directed, 'Seize your opportunities. Do not waste what you are given', and Luiza's thoughts wound back to Luneberg and its tantalising possibilities.

With her mind so busy, she had not expected to sleep. But she reckoned without the soothing rhythm of the train. She woke only once, when the door slid open at Katowice to admit two passengers. In the light from the corridor, she made out a woman with a young girl. When the announcement that they would soon be arriving in Vienna roused her next morning, their bunks were already empty.

From the North Terminal, Luiza took a taxi to the Südbahnhof. The route swung round the Ring, its classical buildings widely spaced among greenery splashed with pink and white blossom and blowsy purple rhododendron blooms. Her train was at the platform and a cloud of steam billowed along its length. The porter had just heaved her case aboard when the carriage lurched, and they were on their way to Graz.

Once clear of the suburbs, lush meadows rolled past the window. When she left the compartment to use the WC, she could make out distant alps to the west. She remained in the corridor for a while, mesmerised by the shifting horizon as shadowy peaks rose and fell away. These were her first mountains, and their uncharted promise thrilled her.

When she returned, she had a companion. A woman she judged her senior by about fifteen years sat opposite, elegantly dressed in a tailored jacket of the green, felted material Luiza had already noted was popular in Austria. A grey hat with a fan-shaped, iridescent feather in its green band sat aslant dark curls. The woman uncrossed long, silk-sheathed legs and leant forward, her hand extended. Luiza was uncomfortably aware of her own bare legs; stockings were hard to come by in Pabianice.

"Good morning. I do hope you won't mind my joining you. My companion along the corridor simply would not be parted from his pipe – I could barely see the window for smoke. I'm Elena." The woman flashed a smile which revealed white, slightly overlapping teeth. Luiza shook the gloved hand and responded, "Luiza."

They sat back. Aware she was being observed, Luiza examined the contents of her handbag.

"I couldn't help noticing the address on your suitcase," Elena commented. "You're travelling to Luneberg?"

Luiza nodded while inserting her ticket in a different pocket, as if that had all along been the purpose of her rummage.

"What a happy coincidence. It's where I'm going. In fact, it's where I live."

"Really?" Curiosity supplanted self-consciousness and unleashed a torrent of questions about their destination.

"Well, that was quite an entrance."

Aunt Gretchen was smiling, but Luiza sensed a hidden barb.

"Here's me, living in Luneberg all my life and never once given a lift by a Von Burg. And there's you, Luiza, turning up in their car before you've even set foot in town."

The plan had been for Luiza to take the bus from Graz to Luneberg, arriving at her uncle's late in the evening.

Instead, Countess Elena Von Burg, as Luiza now knew her travelling companion to be, had insisted on giving her a lift. So Luiza had doubly surprised the Wolfer household, arriving early and in a gleaming Mercedes, her case conveyed to the door by a chauffeur in livery.

Nothing at Uncle Georg's was quite as Luiza had expected. Although Aunt Gretchen's infirmity had been concocted to avoid Luiza being sent to a labour camp, she had still expected to be of some service to her aunt. Yet whatever she did was met with disapproval. Whether it was picking beans or peeling potatoes, Aunt Gretchen would enquire whether this was how it was done in Poland and require Luiza to adopt a more refined technique. Her aunt came from Switzerland, and Luiza remembered that Pappa had alluded to his sister-in-law's 'Swiss precision'.

Meanwhile, she soon realised that Uncle Georg's initial familiarity, as a trimmer, more economical version of her expansive father, was superficial. Her uncle's smile switched on and off at his mouth and failed to crinkle his eyes the way Pappa's did. He was perfectly pleasant but radiated no warmth. And he was always formal, even with his wife and daughter. For the most part, though, he ignored his wife. Aunt Gretchen clearly irritated him; on occasion he exploded and slammed out of the room, sometimes not reappearing for a day or two. As time went on, Luiza noticed a pattern to these outbursts. Tensions were particularly heightened at lunchtime on Thursdays. Uncle Georg had an office in the town hall, but he came home for lunch every day. Conversation at the table was often stilted, but on Thursdays Aunt

Gretchen's overwrought attempts to plug the silences grew particularly obsessive.

"The plums weren't as good last year, but then the cherries were excellent. Weren't they, Helga?"

Her daughter nodded.

"Look, you can tell by the colour," continued Aunt Gretchen, holding up a spoonful of plum juice and letting it drain back into her bowl. Luiza was reminded, disconcertingly, of urine.

"But then, the year before the plums were exceptional and we got so few cherries. I wonder how they'll be this year. So much blossom, but you can't always count on that, can you, Helga?"

Luiza's hapless cousin shook her head. Aunt Gretchen rarely addressed her husband.

"We'll have the cherry compote this evening. It's better than the plum. Oh, no... oh well, we'll have it tomorrow, then."

Uncle Georg pushed back his chair so energetically that it teetered on its hind legs and threatened to topple. There was a breathless moment before it righted itself, with a reverberating thud, on the parquet.

"For God's sake, have it tonight, but can you just stop whittering on about it?"

Luiza tried to spoon her compote silently in the hush that followed her uncle's exit, but she soon made her excuses and left.

Outside, early summer resonated, crystalline and uplifting. Ahead rose towering, white-capped peaks. Her path led through emerald meadows strewn with dazzling clusters of pink and blue and yellow and white. As she walked, she breathed deeply to exchange the stultifying atmosphere of the house for alpine air, while reflecting on the scene she had just witnessed. It dawned on her that Uncle Georg was never at home on Thursday evenings. Neither did he appear at breakfast on Fridays.

Luiza escaped outdoors whenever she could. The mountains lent a vital charge to the landscape and rendered her energised and keen to explore. She wished she had use of a horse so she could travel further afield. Sometimes Helga walked with her, but they shared none of the closeness that Luiza had found with her cousin Vera. Conversation with Helga did not flow. Luiza did not like to bring up the apparent tension between her aunt and uncle, but she did think Helga might be curious about life in Poland and share a familial anxiety about Ida. Yet her cousin asked no questions. Even when Luiza received a letter from Pappa, Helga never enquired as to her uncle's news.

Those were the days Luiza felt most home sick. Seeing Pappa's rounded hand, she pictured him at his desk and felt the distance between them keenly. She always scanned the pages for Ida's name before settling down to read. Usually it appeared just once, confirming that the situation remained unchanged. But then a letter arrived in which Ida's name punctuated the pages. Her sister had finally come to Pabianice, as they had long hoped she would. But while her father claimed this as good news, Luiza could tell that he was alarmed. Far from easing his anxiety, it was clear that Ida in person was cause for even greater concern than in absentia.

Luiza wondered wildly if she should go home to help. But she knew it would be madness. If she were sent to a labour camp, Pappa's problems would only get worse. She told her hosts that her sister had finally turned up, hoping to explore how such a longed-for development could be so problematic. Her aunt and uncle expressed relief that Ida and Pappa were reunited. The desired conclusion had been achieved, and they seemed unable, or unwilling, to interrogate further.

So, as usual, Luiza opened her heart to the wooden Madonna, but also to the gilded Virgin in Luneberg's fantastically ornate Catholic church. Then an invitation, the first of many, was delivered by the same chauffeur who had driven her from Graz. Countess Elena proposed that Luiza join a party at their hunting lodge, perched high on the Saualm. And soon Luiza had a friend with whom to share her unease.

The Von Burgs' well-stocked stable was an essential part of these weekends. Guests rode all day, with races across alpine meadows in which the young newcomer was frequently placed. They lunched at mountain farms on black bread and salty butter, sour cheese and peppery smoked sausage, all served on wooden platters and washed down with cloudy cider. On the way home their saddlebags bulged. Supplies in the shops were strictly rationed, so farmers were making a killing on the black market.

Sometimes it was just Luiza and Elena. Then they strapped bedrolls to their saddles and pretended to be cowboys, sleeping out under the stars. Lying side by side, they told each other about their lives. Elena was born in Italy and had come to Austria fifteen years ago, to marry the Count. They had two children: a boy of twelve and a girl who was eight. Both were blonde, curly-haired imps, who ran wild throughout summer at the lodge, encouraged by Elena. "They'll spend enough of their lives behaving decorously," she explained.

She was Luiza's age when she first arrived in Luneberg. Perhaps it was their mutual 'foreignness' that made it easy for Luiza to confide in her. Elena was clearly shocked by Ida's tragedy. She was warmly solicitous, and Luiza even told her of the fatal consequence of Pappa reporting the Russian spy to the SS, something she had never admitted to anyone. But Elena simply squeezed her hand. "These are evil times, Luiza. No one should be forced to make such a choice."

Aunt Gretchen was pleased with the butter and bacon Luiza brought back from the mountain farms and praised the Von Burgs' charity to a refugee from benighted Poland. In town, though, she defined her niece's relationship with the Countess as friendship, not charity. She emphasised this particularly when visiting her sister's family.

While Uncle Georg was a municipal engineer, Aunt Gretchen's more glamorous sister, Heidi, had married a pharmacist, like their Swiss father. Jakob was enterprising and ambitious and had expanded the business inherited from his father-in-law. Their daughters were attractive and vivacious and did not want for suitors, while Helga, who took after her more stolid mother, was yet to be courted. Perhaps the fact that her Polish niece spent time with nobility had reset the balance for Aunt Gretchen.

Chapter 44

December 1942, Luneberg

*L*uiza stood in the middle of the room, taking a moment to scan surfaces, before setting the photograph from Ida's wedding on the chest of drawers. Ida and Mirek watched her abstractedly, their attention borrowed briefly from one another. Pappa grinned broadly while Pani Anna studied him sideways. Luiza herself stood slightly removed from the group. Next to the wedding picture she placed the icon of Our Lady of Częstochowa. Then, having arranged the final items on the dressing table, she hid her suitcase beneath the bed and surveyed the room – her room. Satisfied, she counted out her first week's rent from the envelope containing her wages.

Since the pretext for her coming to Luneberg was to look after Aunt Gretchen, she had not been able to look for work at first. But almost six months on, with an

improvement in her aunt's health plausible, a friend of
Uncle Georg's, who ran the bank in Luneberg, had agreed
to try her out as a cashier. Her bookkeeping experience
meant that she was quick with figures, but she also proved
to be good with customers and he soon offered her a
permanent position. Hugely relieved that she was no
longer dependent on her family, Luiza had moved into
town to board at Frau Doktor Lechner's.

Now she sat in the chair by the window to consider her
options. For the first time in her life, she did not have to fit in
with anybody else. She could do exactly as she wanted. But
perhaps not quite yet, she thought with a sigh. Pulling on
her coat, she felt in the pocket for her ration book. On top of
rent, her landlady required her tenant's meagre sugar, meat
and butter allowance. A fleeting memory of a mountain
farmer's laden wooden platter made Luiza's mouth water,
but it would be summer before she sampled those again.
She glanced at her watch. If the queues were not too long,
she could still make Benediction at St Markus.

A few days later, Helga turned up with a letter from
Pappa. It must have crossed the one Luiza had sent with
her new address. She offered her cousin tea (pitiably
weak, the leaves re-used for the umpteenth time) and they
chatted easily. Away from home, Helga was more relaxed.
She sat in the chair (Luiza perched on the bed) and
inspected the room approvingly. She asked about Luiza's
job and what she did when she was not at the bank. When
Luiza mentioned a cinema trip with a colleague, Maria,
Helga looked so wistful that Luiza made a note to invite
her cousin on their next outing.

After she left, Luiza opened the letter with misgivings; in the months since Ida had been in Pabianice, her condition had not improved. Each time Pappa wrote, Luiza felt more concerned for them both. From the first line it was clear that a crisis point had been reached, because Pappa had contacted Pani Anna. Luiza paused; her own letters to both Malinów and Warszawa had gone unanswered. She had prayed to Our Lady for understanding and acceptance, but it still hurt. Pani Anna had been there when Mama was not. And then she, too, had disappeared. After all their families had shared, could she not see beyond a surname?

Reading on, Luiza had to swallow hard, for Pani Anna had not rejected them. She had answered Pappa's call and travelled to Pabianice. She had even taken Ida back to Malinów. Then why had she ignored Luiza? Did she care more about Ida? Or simply consider that Ida's need was greater? Or maybe the fact that her sister no longer had a German surname make a difference? Luiza immediately regretted this thought and sent up a quick prayer for forgiveness.

Poor Pappa. She should have been there to help. Perhaps together they could have handled Ida. Yet maybe it was for the best that she was with Pani Anna. Their mother's friend had always known how to pacify her sister. At least, she had before Ida lost her husband and her child. Could even Pani Anna soothe her now? She read on, and it became clear that she could not.

Ida had not settled at Malinów. In fact, she had been so disruptive that she had been admitted to a nearby psychiatric clinic. The news shocked Luiza. She felt winded, as if from a blow to the stomach. Was her sister mad? Luiza had only the vaguest notions of psychiatric treatment, disturbing images involving straitjackets. How could they abandon Ida to this?

Forcing herself to finish the letter, she was reassured that Ida was not mad but suffering a nervous breakdown. A strict regime of rest and medication was prescribed. Pappa had visited and reported that she was already calmer. And Pani Anna had promised to look in frequently. Really, Pappa insisted, they should think of Ida as enjoying a rest cure at a sanatorium. It was undoubtedly the best place for her. She would soon be back to her old self and then she would come home.

Luiza held on to his reassurance and tried to quash her own discomfiting doubts: Unless circumstances changed, surely Ida would relapse? Little Mirek's continued absence would place her under the same unbearable strain. Luiza was overcome by a need to hold her sister, to share her pain. She longed to go home. But Pappa had foreseen this and ended his letter with a specific admonishment against even contemplating such a foolhardy act.

Besides, she had a job now. She could not simply take off – she had responsibilities here, a life here. An independent life. She realised that she had not felt homesick for some time – until this moment, when her heart felt seared. But she knew that there was nothing she could do, and after a while, the pain grew less. She felt callous, yet she reasoned that her best course was to get on with her life here. To seize the opportunities given. Meanwhile, she would pray for Ida and for Pappa.

Luiza spent Christmas at Uncle Georg's, mostly missing Pappa and Ida. For New Year, though, she was at the lodge on the Saualpe. This was her new life, and it was wonderful. Before, in her dealings with Elena's friends, however welcome they made her, she still felt junior. But now that she was an independent, working woman, she had achieved adulthood and acquired confidence. Even the Count no longer intimidated her. As they watched the fireworks in the valley below and toasted 1943, she remembered doing the same for 1940, the first *Sylvester* of the war. She had been a child then. So much had happened since.

The first day of 1943 was also her first time on skis. The party left the lodge on foot before dawn, having barely slept. Carrying their skis, they climbed at first by torchlight. It took nearly seven hours and in places the snow came up to her waist. But as soon as they reached the top of the run, Luiza forgot how wet and tired she was. With her spirits revived, she barely registered the instructions from various members of the party as she pointed her skis downhill. Only Elena's 'let your body take you' penetrated before she pushed off.

The descent lasted less than a sixth of the time their arduous climb had taken, yet it was overwhelmingly exhilarating. Cutting through crisp blue air between crystal-bedecked pines, her skis skimmed immaculate slopes. She took a few tumbles, but her landings were soft, in deep powder, and having extricated herself, she set off again eagerly. When she came to a triumphant halt at the bottom, she was delighted to discover that she was not the last. She would no longer resent winter for limiting riding opportunities, because this was a match for the most thrilling gallop.

By early April, the thaw had begun in Luneberg, but the Saualm was still clad entirely in white and she would ski again on Sunday. Elena was meeting her after work tomorrow to drive up to the lodge. On her way to the bank, Luiza's thoughts were already on the mountain slopes, while her eyes guided her boots over icy pavements. She mounted a doorstep to avoid a glassy patch and was almost knocked over by a man exiting the building. She had to grab his sleeve to steady herself and began her apologies before looking up. When she did, her hand loosened its grip.

"Uncle Georg?"

"Luiza."

With a curt nod, her uncle turned towards the town hall. Beyond it lay his house. This was not his route to work. And then it occurred to her that it was Friday. The one day of the week when Uncle Georg was never at breakfast. She stepped carefully into the street to look up at the building and caught a movement in a window on the first floor. A fleeting impression of blonde curls and red lips. They disappeared so swiftly behind the lace curtains that Luiza wondered whether she had imagined them.

"But I assumed you knew," Maria said. It was their coffee break. Not that they had coffee, just the ersatz stuff that someone said was made from acorns. Luiza grimaced as she sipped. Perhaps it would be more palatable with sugar, but her ration went to her landlady. Having related her surprise encounter with Uncle Georg to Maria, she was still absorbing her friend's revelation.

"A mistress? Uncle Georg? Does Aunt Gretchen know?"

"Of course. It's not an uncommon arrangement, you know."

Luiza took another sip. At least it was hot.

"What do you mean?"

"Well, some women, once they reach a certain age… it's just easier if their husbands go elsewhere to have their needs met."

"But what about Helga? Does she know?"

"Oh, I should think so. I believe it's been going on a while."

Luiza swirled her cup thoughtfully. "It certainly explains Uncle Georg's absences." She drained the murky liquid before concluding, "Aunt Gretchen may know, but I don't think she's happy about it."

She caught Maria's eye. Her friend smirked and ventured, mischievously, "Perhaps it's still the lesser of two evils, though?"

Luiza did not react. The news that her uncle kept a mistress had genuinely shocked her. She wondered whether Pappa knew. And then she wondered whether, had Mama lived, her parents might have come to a similar arrangement. Surely not. She could not imagine any of Pappa's friends doing this. Life here was somehow more calculated than in Poland. Little was left to chance. Even though the war was barely noticeable here – apart from rationing – life still felt more martial than in Poland,

where there were Nazi uniforms on every street. Luneberg
had no military presence, yet it was more regimented.

Maria regarded her with a raised eyebrow and an
impish smile.

"Don't," admonished Luiza. "It's really not at all funny."

"Perhaps just a tiny bit? When you picture your
respectable uncle's Thursday night routine?"

Luiza tried not to imagine Uncle Georg in the throes
of his weekly routine. But the more she tried, the more
vivid the image grew. Soon the two of them were giggling
convulsively as tears streamed down their cheeks. Herr
Weiss, the senior cashier, came in for his break and peered
at them disapprovingly. Biting their lips and wiping their
eyes, they left him to enjoy his ersatz coffee in peace. Luiza
reflected that she had not laughed like this since she was a
Musketeer. Perhaps she was not yet completely grown up.

Chapter 45

Spring 1943, Luneberg

One of Luiza's first acts of independence after moving to Frau Doktor Lechner's was to take instruction in the Catholic faith. It felt peculiar, yet liberating, to make this decision entirely on her own. Her family here were Lutheran, but she did not need their permission. She did not even need Pappa's, though she wrote to tell him.

On weekends when she was not at the mountain lodge, she usually went to her uncle's for lunch after Sunday Mass. On the first such occasion after their doorstep encounter, she was reluctant to leave the baroque splendour of St Markus after Mass ended. She was not looking forward to the meeting; it was bound to be awkward.

Yet Uncle Georg was as blandly pleasant as ever. If he was not embarrassed, then why should Luiza feel flustered? She determined not to, and her visits from then on were less dutiful and more enjoyable. If her uncle could hold his head up, then she certainly could.

Conversation loosened. Luiza entertained them with her adventures in the mountains and with tales from the banking hall (she was careful to protect confidentiality – it was a small town). Family tensions only renewed when Helga said that she would like a job, too; while a refugee from Poland needed to work for a living, it seemed that a well brought up Austrian girl did not.

By mid-May, snow remained only on the highest slopes, so the Von Burgs and their guests could ride up to the farms again. Luiza was relieved; there had been days when all she had for lunch was a slice of bread and a wrinkly apple. She took eggs and speck to Aunt Gretchen and was rewarded with *Bauernfrühstück*, when her aunt added her offerings to a pan of fried potatoes and created the most delicious meal Luiza had eaten in a long while.

It was a whole year since Luiza had arrived in Luneberg. She had friends and a good job. Even Helga had grown closer. And she had been accepted into the Catholic church. She was as devoted as ever to the Virgin, but receiving Communion had deepened her relationship with the Son. Now she was as likely to petition Him to protect her family as she was His Mother, but she also remembered to give thanks. Because she felt truly happy. And then the telegram arrived.

It was from Pani Krawcik. *He is very weak but there is no need to worry yet a letter will follow.* Luiza blamed herself. If she had remained vigilant, Pappa would not have had a stroke. She could not forget seeing Mama, so shockingly twisted. Could Pappa speak? Would he need a wheelchair? She must go to him – she had been unable to save Mama, but she would save him.

Uncle Georg agreed that Luiza should go, but she needed travel documents. He promised to acquire them, though it would take a few days. At least the letter should have arrived by then. But the next day there was a second telegram: *Condition deteriorated greatly Luiza come immediately.*

Now Uncle Georg offered to go with her. The travel permit was issued the following day, but just as they were leaving, a third telegram arrived: *Condition hopeless when will you be here.*

It was fortunate that Uncle Georg accompanied her; Luiza was too dazed to navigate the journey alone. She followed meekly from bus to train in Graz and looked blindly out of the window all the way to Vienna. There was no sleeping compartment left on the Łódź train, so they sat up all night. Uncle Georg nodded off, while Luiza recited the Rosary, over and over.

When they arrived in Łódź, though, she took over. She guided them onto the Pabianice tram, where Uncle Georg found a seat while Luiza remained standing in the morning crush. As she stared at the back of someone's newspaper, the urgent buzz of anxiety that had filled her head since the first telegram suddenly fell silent. The words were printed in bold and bordered in black: *Hugo Ryszard Wolfer, Textile Engineer, born Crimmitschau 25/06/1879, died Pabianice 08/06/1943.* Today was June 9th. She was too late.

Pani Anna led Ida to the graveside, where the sisters each gathered a handful of earth to toss onto the polished lid. This time, Luiza knew it was true. Pappa was dead. She had kissed his waxen face and held his chill hand. She knew that her loving, exasperating, irreplaceable father would never again pull her into a breath-stopping hug. Never again raise a bushy, quizzical eyebrow. Never again indulge in a rum baba. Luiza felt hollow.

With an effort, she turned to Ida, only to be shocked anew by her pallor. Perhaps it was the stark contrast with her mourning dress, but her sister appeared translucent. It was her eyes Luiza found most distressing, though. Dull and unfocused, their vital energy was extinguished. She took Ida's unresponsive hand and held it to her cheek. Pappa was gone and this husk of her sister was all that she had.

Uncle Georg left the next day. He had been such a help, dealing with official matters and winding up Pappa's business. And he had done his best to console her. But his embrace was constrained, and they were both relieved when it ended.

Pani Anna left, too. She had brought Ida from the clinic but did not offer to return her. Nothing was said, but Luiza sensed that their mother's friend's involvement was at an end. With Pappa gone, they could not afford the clinic, anyway. And with Pappa gone, perhaps there was no longer any reason for Pani Anna to invest in their family. It was up to Luiza alone to take care of Ida; she would have to come to Luneberg.

Gustav did all he could. According to Pani Krawcik, he had called in a senior German doctor as soon as Pappa became ill. But now, he informed them apologetically, two German officers would be moving into the apartment with him, so they should make sure to take anything they wanted. Looking around at the pictures and furniture she had known all her life, Luiza wondered how she could take it with her. Where would they put it? The only home she had was her room at Frau Doktor Lechner's. In the end, she wrapped a few dishes from Mama's favourite dinner service in their suitcases, and Gustav promised to send on the picture of the stag that had always hung in the salon. It made her happy to think of Gustav playing Mama's piano. He would make sure their things were treated with respect.

She worried about Mathilde Krawcik. Gustav had asked her to stay on as housekeeper, but she had turned him down. "He's a nice boy – one of the good Germans. But I cannot work for three of them. You're not to worry, though, I'll find something. It's your sister who's your concern."

They both looked at Ida, who stood alone by the window, gaunt in black and unnaturally still. Luiza went over to explain their plans and tried to meet her sister's gaze, but Ida looked past her.

Gustav arranged a car to take them to the station. As they were leaving, Luiza turned back for a last look. Sunlight poured into the hall through the salon's open door, as it had the first time they saw the apartment. Pappa was so alive with plans for his new venture then, and now he was gone. She took in the hall table and the Persian rug, which she remembered from Zakątek. She was leaving behind all that had ever meant home. She took Ida's hand and led her down the familiar staircase for the last time.

In the three months since they had been back in Luneberg, Luiza sometimes felt hopeful. There were signs of improvement. Ida had taken up her needle again and Aunt Gretchen was delighted with the tablecloth her niece had worked for her. It was surprising to Luiza that Ida seemed at ease with their exacting aunt; the two pottered around the kitchen and garden amicably. And it was reassuring that her sister was occupied while Luiza was at the bank. Weekends were more difficult. Elena encouraged Luiza to bring Ida to the hunting lodge, but her once gregarious sister seemed overwhelmed by the guests and the activities and retreated to her room. She sometimes came out for walks, and then the pellucid landscape worked its magic. Her eyes recovered their lustre, her cheeks grew less sallow.

They tried a trip to the cinema with Maria and Helga, but it was a disaster. Luiza thought a comedy was a safe choice, but it featured a small boy and Ida pushed her way out of their row and run all the way back to Frau Doktor Lechner's.

Her landlady was understanding about the extra lodger, as long as Luiza supplemented her rations. But it would be a problem once winter set in. Meanwhile, the strain was beginning to show. Luiza's room, for all the pride she took in it, was not large, and sharing the single bed meant that neither sister slept well. Though Luiza doubted it was the bed that kept Ida awake. Whenever she looked, her sister was staring at the ceiling.

On an afternoon in early October, Luiza was surprised to find her waiting outside the bank. And more surprised when Ida smiled and linked an arm in hers. They set off in the opposite direction from home and were soon out of town, the slope of the Saualm ahead. The leaves were turning, a sprinkling of red and gold among the pines, and Luiza felt the familiar rush of well-being from the mountains. Ida also breathed deeply. "I can see why you love it here, Lou-lou," she said. "It's beautiful." She squeezed her sister's arm and led her to a bench at the side of the path.

"I'm so pleased that you're happy here, Lou-lou. That you feel at home. But I don't."

Luiza stared at her, suddenly panicked at what was to come. Ida laughed – really laughed. It was an eternity since Luiza had heard that sound.

"Don't look like that, Lou-lou! You're always worrying about me – you have to stop."

Luiza considered how best to respond. If she argued, she might lose this glimpse of the old Ida. How could she reassure her without frightening her off?

"I know I'm a worry to you all," Ida continued. "You've done your best to look after me. And you've succeeded. Look at me – I'm a picture of health." She laughed again, and Luiza wondered whether the miracle she prayed for had finally occurred.

"But Lou-lou, I need to be back in Poland. I'm much too far away."

She paused, and the clear focus that had so encouraged Luiza was gone. Now she saw something other than the alpine view in front of her.

"It's Little Mirek's birthday today. He's four."

Luiza's eyes filled, and she gripped her sister's hands, full of remorse. "Oh Idka, I'm so sorry, I should have remembered… I feel terrible. Poor Little Mirek – and you, Idka – poor you, I can't imagine…"

Ida stopped her with a finger on her lips. "This is the second of my baby's birthdays that I've missed, and I can't miss another. I have to find him, Lou-lou."

"But how, Idka? How can you possibly find him?

Luiza still had no idea how Ida intended to find her son, but she had been unable to dissuade her from leaving. Uncle Georg, too, had tried his best. But Ida, no longer vague and disengaged, was resolute. At least she had agreed to stay with Aunt Ludmila and Aunt Rysia in Poznań, initially, and plan her search with their help.

They took the bus to Graz together. On the platform, the sisters embraced. Luiza could not hold back her tears but Ida, dry-eyed, seemed impatient to begin her quest. She withdrew first, to step up into the train. Through the window, Luiza saw her smile, briefly, before facing forward. Hurrying beside the train, she willed Ida to look her way again. But her sister's gaze was fixed on Little Mirek.

Chapter 46

December 1955, Singapore

*J*ack's at the workshop and the twins are at school. Amah's out, too, shopping. It's time to open the letter.

She retrieves it from the bureau and picks up Pappa's silver letter opener – one of her few mementos. She pauses. Prayer has sustained her thus far and allowed her to hope. But what if the letter confirms that it's all been in vain? Is her faith strong enough for that? Can she bear the truth?

Settling herself on a chair, she strokes her belly and remembers Ida's last postcard: *The war has been hard. I can no longer laugh or cry.* No mention of the child. It was dated June 1947 – the month after Luiza married Jack. While her sister's life dwindled, her own expanded, brimming so full of love and family, friends and travel, that sometimes she forgot all about Ida.

Now she lets her mind wander, populating the twelve years since her sister took the train from Graz. The following summer, in 1944, Luiza met Ortwin. She was infatuated with the handsome doctor. When he asked her to marry him, it was as though her life had found its natural conclusion. So, when Aunt Ludmila, fleeing west from Poznań ahead of the anticipated Soviet advance, wrote that Ida refused to come with them, she didn't let herself consider the consequences for her sister. Ortwin filled her life and her thoughts and left no room for unease.

It was that awful night before Christmas in 1944, when the Americans mistakenly bombed the camp near Luneberg, killing nearly fifty British and French prisoners. That was when he asked her to be his wife. Saying yes to Ortwin was a commitment to life, to a future. A rejection of the misery of war.

Not that she should complain. She was blessed when Pappa sent her to Luneberg. He gifted her the freedom of the mountains, the chance of a fulfilling job, of love, of life. There were times when the bombs had fallen much too close; she had known fear. Hunger, too. But she had not been hurt; she had not starved. Her war could have been so different. It could have been Ida's. And when it was all over, she was safely out of Poland, away from the chaos of the Soviet landgrab. Saved by Pappa, and then by Jack. Without him, she would be in Argentina now. Yet here she is, with Jack and the twins. And soon this baby, too. Luck has been with her all the way. Did she plunder Ida's share?

She thought of Ortwin again. He was a bear of a man, so different from lean, athletic Jack. But the difference was more than physical. She glances at the bookcase, at the small, leather-bound volume of poems by Schiller that Ortwin gave her. On the flyleaf, in his looping letters, was the dedication: *with my undying love*. Jack knows about the book. It's a talisman of their shared history.

She trusts Jack. He would never break his word. Ortwin's words were as fine as Schiller's, but they were false.

They'd already set their wedding date when Helga told her. She remembers with shame that she suspected her cousin was lying. That she wanted to destroy Luiza's happiness because no one had yet chosen her. But it was true, Ortwin was sleeping with one of the nurses at the hospital – had been since before their engagement. Luiza returned the ring, refused to see him and sent his letters back unopened. But he would not give up. In the end, she had to look him in the eye and tell him what she thought of him.

She took Helga along for support. Afterwards, walking home, they stopped to watch a man taking a beautiful horse over some jumps. When he trotted over to ask, in broken German, whether the Frauleins would like a go, a wave of his arm included them both in the invitation. But he was looking at Luiza. And anyway, Helga had never been on a horse.

His blue eyes were the same shade as Pappa's. He made the offer tentatively, with none of Ortwin's self-assured bombast. When Luiza replied that his horse was very fine and she would love to give him a try, he seemed confused – his German really was limited. So, she simply smiled and nodded, and he grinned. There was no mounting block, but he linked his hands for her to step up, and soon she was putting the big chestnut through his paces. She had not given a thought to her outfit, but her skirt was wide enough to tuck beneath her thighs, so she hoped she was not presenting too shocking a spectacle. No doubt Helga would let her know, afterwards.

They soared over the jumps – the horse had such a strong launch. Eventually, reluctantly, she handed back the reins and repeated, with gestures that she hoped the man would understand, that it was a very fine horse. It seemed he did. With a smile he stroked the burnished neck while the chestnut nuzzled the pocket of his breeches. The man pulled out an apple and offered it to Luiza. Her first thought was that it was a gift for her. Thank goodness she realised it was for the horse. Mexico, he was saying. So that was his name. She held the fruit to Mexico's muzzle and laughed as his whiskery lips tickled her palm.

She thanked the man again and turned to Helga to continue their walk. But he soon caught up with them and asked if she would come riding with him. It seemed that he could bring a horse for her. With a lot of gesticulating, they arranged to meet after work. He knew where the bank was.

Helga commented that she had barely finished with one sweetheart and now she had found another. But it was Mexico Luiza had fallen for. She did not even know the man's name.

Mexico. Such a magnificent horse. But how could she not have realised? Even when the man told her his name she had not suspected. The horses were Hungarian – left behind in the rush to escape the advancing Allies – so she assumed he must be Hungarian, too. Of course, that made no sense, but why would she question this marvellous opportunity that had landed in her lap? She had not ridden for ages.

It was her own fault. When she fell for Ortwin, she deserted her friends and allowed herself to become absorbed into his crowd. He had come to the lodge on the Saualm early on, but he was not keen on the outdoors, didn't ride. And there was tension between him and Elena, which it was easier to avoid. She had given up so much for Ortwin, seduced by the security he offered. With both Pappa and Ida gone, she was adrift, and Ortwin anchored her – even if it was at a distance from her friends. At least she still saw Maria at work. Poor Maria. She had her own Ortwin, that British officer who promised to leave his wife but never did.

Luiza recalls the clatter of hooves on cobblestones. She had already changed and was waiting outside the bank. The man was riding Mexico and leading a grey mare. She was pretty, but Luiza wanted to ride the chestnut again.

And she did. It was the first of many such afternoons. They rode till sunset, even though the poor man was tortured with hay fever – she had never heard anyone sneeze so loudly. Their conversation was limited, yet she felt easy with him, so when he invited her to the cinema, she agreed. Partly for fear that he might take his horses and go if she didn't, but also because she knew that she would not mind sitting next to him in the dark.

And then, when the time came, she looked out from her room at Frau Doktor Lechner's and saw a British uniform. She could not possibly be seen with him. Girls who went with Tommies were 'chocolate girls', doing it for nylons and confectionery. Uncle Georg would never forgive her.

So, she'd stepped back from the window and left him standing there. It must have been nearly two hours before she went down – after dark, so as not to be seen. Yet he was still waiting. And the way he smiled when he saw her. No recrimination, just sheer delight. There was a kindness, a decency to Jack and she decided that night that Uncle Georg would just have to come to terms with his niece courting a British soldier.

And Jack had won him over. Aunt Gretchen, too. They were married less than a year after they first met. They might have waited – given Jack's disgruntled father time to come round to the idea of a foreign daughter-in-law – if Luiza had not been ordered to report to a displaced persons' camp near Munich. From there, she was to be relocated to Argentina. But Jack immediately appealed to his commanding officer. And because she had been translating for the occupying force, whose interpreters did not speak Russian or Polish, while she could render both into German for their military courts, the Major requested an extension to her stay in Luneberg. It gave them enough time to organise the wedding, and once she was a British citizen, no one could deport her. Yet another blessing.

She looks at the letter again. Did Ida pay the price for all her good fortune? She cannot put it off any longer. She has to face the truth.

As she opens the envelope, a photograph falls out. It's a boy in his late teens. Luiza remembers Ida showing her that first picture of Mirek, the one Luiza advised her not to show Pappa. The boy in this photograph challenges the camera with the same confidence. He has the same high forehead and broad face, the same flirtatious smile.

The letter is from Mirek's brother-in-law – Luiza can't remember if she even knew that Mirek had a sister. A friend of his heard a Red Cross appeal on the radio, asking for news of Ida and Mirosław Timorecki. He contacted the station and got her address.

I am happy to inform you that your nephew, Mirek Timorecki, 16, is well. He is currently living with his aunt and myself, here in Łódź, to attend school. Previously, he lived with his father in Toruń. Sadly, his mother is no longer alive…

A trapdoor opens and Luiza plummets through. She scrabbles for something to stop her fall, but down, down she goes. She's never known such despair, never felt so completely alone. All those prayers. She glances at the icon on the sideboard. Did you not hear them? Why? Why?

The letter trembles with her hand. She longs for the time before she opened it, when she still had hope.

She doesn't know how long she's been sitting there. Amah pokes her head round the door. "Lunch soon, Missy?" Luiza nods, though she feels nauseous. How will she face the twins when they burst through the door. And Jack?

The letter in her hand barely flutters now. There are more words for her to read. The ink is blotched in places, where Mirek's brother-in-law's pen snagged on the coarse paper's uneven surface.

It was my mother-in-law who found your nephew in an orphanage in 1947. I believe your sister was also looking for him – a family near Żychlin, the Grudzinskis, told us that Ida turned up there a few years ago. They said she had been searching everywhere for her child, but she was unwell in her mind and she went away again. No one knows where. The Red Cross has confirmed, though, that she is deceased. Sadly, my mother-in-law has also died.

Your nephew, Mirek, is keen to learn more of his mother's family and would like to write to you. Please let me know if he may.

The photograph lies in her lap, half hidden by her belly. Just one eye is visible, only half the boy's mouth. Its upturn is familiar, and the direct gaze from the single eye seems enigmatic rather than bold. Little Mirek. As much Ida's boy as Mirek's. And he's alive. She looks at the icon again, the mother she turned to when she lost her own. *I understand*, she thinks.

Chapter 47

February 1966, Kent, England

*A*ll those letters. All those parcels, filled with food and clothes and sent to a place that used to be home. Once so familiar, it was where she belonged. But now it feels alien – sinister. A place of secrets, Soviet and godless. Luiza shudders.

She looks around the living room, registers the carved standard lamp from Singapore, the cabinet full of gleaming shooting trophies from Berlin – Jack's and hers. This is home now. This semi-detached box on a housing estate. Jack knows it's not what she came from, and she knows he feels bad about that. But she's content. Life is simple here, uncomplicated by shifting borders and threats of occupation. This island nation is so confident in its watertight boundary, so secure in its identity.

It's not been easy since Jack left the army. She'd never had to do housework before. That vacuum cleaner row –

she can smile about it now, but for the first few months, England was as shockingly alien as Poland is now. Trying to navigate the role of housewife without her ready-made, army support network, the three children at school all day and Jack at work and stressed by his first ever job out of uniform. She'd felt desperate. But slowly they've built a life for themselves, a community through the church, and she recognises, though she doubts she'll ever fully understand, the under-stated humour and the reserve of the English. It's been tough, but nothing like… her eyes are drawn to the icon of the scar-faced Madonna that hangs on the wall above the sideboard. It's larger than the one she still keeps by her bedside. She feels she should offer thanks, but she can't. All she can think of are the wasted years. And the eternal question repeats itself: "Why?"

No answer is forthcoming, because there is none. What possible justification could there be? Her fingers holding the letter don't seem to be part of her. When she plucked the coarse blue envelope from the door mat, she was expecting just another of their deliberate steps towards each other, nephew and aunt drawing closer while simultaneously emphasising the distance between them. But this has blown apart their carefully constructed relationship and made a mockery of her gratitude for Mirek, her consolation for Ida's loss. What a cruel delusion.

She wishes she could share Mirek's frenzied elation, the joy of discovery that's evident from his slanted, tightly packed lines – crammed as if he feared running out of space. It's so different from his customary, neatly spaced script. But she feels no joy; she just feels cheated.

She makes herself read it again.

Dearest Aunty,

I have the most amazing news. You will not believe it when I tell you – I still scarcely believe it myself. But I will start at the beginning…

November 1965 – Central Poland

Mirek lowers his newspaper. He hadn't noticed the women get on. Last time he looked, the seats opposite were empty, and since then he's been absorbed in the report on milk production in Podlaskie – his dairy placement at agricultural college was on a collective farm there. There are two of them, plumply middle-aged and neatly dressed, sitting across from him and chatting animatedly about… hospital-visiting? Do-gooders, obviously. But how did they penetrate his concentration? What did they say to distract him from such innovative cost-efficiency measures?

Idka. Unusual, but not unknown, so why…?

Such a fine needlewoman, did you see that embroidered tablecloth?

There are two things he's always known about his mother. Since Aunt Luiza made contact he's learnt more, but from his father, and even his grandmother, who was always reluctant to speak of her, he knew her pet name, and how beautifully she sewed.

"Excuse me," he ventures.

The women pause.

"I couldn't help overhearing," he continues, "You spoke of Idka? And that she's a fine embroiderer?"

Perplexed, they both nod.

"I just wondered, where did you meet her?"

It must have been five years since he began his search for his mother's grave. After he married, when the first of their two girls arrived, he'd felt the need for a solid connection with the absence from his life that Aunt Luiza had given a shape to. Brought up by his grandmother until her health started to fail, and then a short time with his father and stepmother in Toruń before high school in Łódź, where he'd lived with his father's sister, he only knew his Timorecki side. But when Aunt Luiza made contact, she revealed the unacknowledged half of his inheritance. She'd sent photographs – his mother was beautiful and so stylish – and brought her vivacious sister to life in the stories that filled her letters. He'd got to know his grandfather, too. Not the one who died defending his master from the Soviets, but the one who invented the wound dressing that he himself had used during military service. She'd painted a picture of a life that was unimaginable in the drab uniformity of communist Poland, a privileged life that went against everything he'd been taught. Before all the loss and the tragedy, there'd been colour and adventure. And there'd been love. Aunt Luiza made him understand how much his mother loved him. She had died searching for him; it was only right that he should find her grave. Yet he hasn't. Again and again, all he's met are dead ends.

Barely ninety minutes after quizzing the two women, Mirek is approaching the hospital entrance. He'd left the train at the next stop and caught the first one back, alighting at Gostynin, where the women had got on. As he walks down the long drive, the building appears to glow, the pale sun of the winter afternoon reflected in its many windows.

The receptionist tells him to wait, and he sits impatiently on an uncomfortable metal chair in the drafty hall. There's a strong smell of disinfectant, but it doesn't quite mask an underlying dankness, which grows stronger as he follows the woman sent to fetch him through a succession of doors that slam shut behind them. He supposes she's a nurse; they pass others, men and women, wearing the same white coat. He struggles to measure his stride to the nurse's, resisting the urge to push her aside that is fuelled by adrenalin-spiked expectation.

She turns through a door to the side of a corridor, and he follows her onto a ward – about twenty iron bedsteads with matching coverlets, some of them stretched over recumbent shapes. At the end, beneath a window, a large table and some chairs. The occupants of the empty beds are gathered here, some in night clothes, some doing jigsaws or knitting, some simply sitting and rocking. A low keening comes from one woman, whose chair is angled towards the trees beyond the window. Beyond her, on a chair pushed close to the window to glean the last of the daylight, sits a woman whose lank, dark hair is neatly clasped at her neck. Her head bowed, her eyes follow the needle she plies deftly, repeatedly piercing the linen stretched tight on the hoop she holds in her other hand, drawing the vivid red thread through again and again. As

Mirek comes closer, he makes out nascent poppies amid yellow cornstalks and spears of green.

The nurse bends to retrieve a fallen piece of jigsaw and calls, "Idka, you're a lucky girl today – here's another visitor."

Reflexively, the woman looks up, but her gaze is empty.

"Only this time, it's a gentleman caller, Idka," the nurse adds with a smirk.

Clouded, blue-green eyes (the colour of the Baltic in winter, thinks Mirek) come to rest on him. Slowly they clear. The woman rises, her embroidery falling to the floor. She surges towards him and fills his arms. Her thin body shaking, she sobs. "Mirek, my Mirek, you didn't die. You were missing so long I nearly gave up. But you're alive, you're here. Now we can find Little Mirek together."

Everyone says I look like my father, Auntie, but I didn't really believe it till then. The nurse told me to go with it, not to try to explain things straight away. So over time, with one of the doctors, we've slowly told her the truth – that her husband died – though not in the war – and that I'm Little Mirek. But I'm still not sure she understands. Sometimes she seems to, but then she'll get agitated and tell me we must go and look for our son.

I'm taking Ewa and the little ones to visit Mama at the weekend. I hope that will help her grasp things. And I've told the doctor that we want her to come and live with us. He says it may be possible, in time. But we mustn't rush things.

Oh, Auntie, isn't it unbelievable? And wonderful? I have my mama, you have your sister. She isn't dead!

I'll write again soon and let you know how things are progressing. I haven't told her about you yet – the doctor says we mustn't burden her with too much information. But when she's living with us, you must visit.

Luiza folds the letter. *Ida isn't dead.* She feels years of mourning recede. Along with the sense of being cheated that was so strong when she first read the letter. If she hadn't been granted Mirek, he would never have found Ida. And now she'll have the chance to live with her son. She'll return to life. When she's well enough, Luiza will write to her. They'll tell of their lives, their memories, their children – in Ida's case, grandchildren. Her sister and their shared past will be restored to her. And one day, when she feels brave enough and they can afford it, she'll travel to Poland and they'll hold each other again.

Chapter 48

June 1971, Poland

*L*uiza shifts on the cracked, red vinyl seat. Painfully, she peels away one thigh, then the other, and attempts to smooth the creases from her damp shirt-dress. The window's open, which means that her pre-departure visit to the hairdresser was in vain. No amount of hairspray could withstand this, but the alternative is unbearable. It's summer, yet the heating is on.

Positioning herself for optimum ventilation, she closes her eyes against the monotonous plain that stretches as far as she can see beyond the smut-smeared glass. It appeared soon after the train left the stark Warszawa suburbs. A seemingly random configuration of blocks of flats has eaten into the woods and fields she remembers. Apparently still under construction, their unclad walls reveal concrete ribs. Yet the washing lining the balconies, and the Syrenas and Polski Fiats parked in the wasteland beneath, point to established habitation. She wonders at life in an unfinished home that is already crumbling and remembers the earth floors and dark rooms of the cottages in Zapole. Would Pan Cholowa be happier on the eighth floor of one of these blocks? With running water, heating, electric light? Where would he meet his neighbours for a smoke and a grumble? Where would he grow his vegetables?

The train screeches and jolts as it slows down. It startles her awake. Gdańsk. She's never been this far north in Poland. Yes, she swam in the Baltic, but that was in Latvia; this will be her first glimpse of the Polish coast. Three hours to go; Kołobrzeg is still two hundred kilometres west. She ponders the irony that all that remains of Hugo Wolfer's family is meeting in what used to be part of the homeland he foreswore. The seaside town where Mirek lives was Kolberg before the War. What would Pappa, who celebrated Poland's re-emergence in 1918, think of Poland post-1945? His chosen homeland shifted westward, her eastern territories swallowed by the Soviet Union.

It seems to Luiza that the whole of Poland has been consumed by the relentless and joyless Soviet enterprise, though. Since landing in Warszawa six hours ago, nothing about the profusion of grey concrete and tired, shabby people has resonated with the memories she's cherished for thirty years. Now, as the train gathers speed out of the station, affording Luiza a glimpse of glistening water between the soaring cranes and towering hulls of the shipyard, she frets that the memory she guarded most zealously might be about to fragment in the same way.

She must have dozed again. The sun is low in the sky, scattered clouds are edged in pink. Above the phosphorescent sea hangs the faint imprint of a crescent moon. A young man has taken the seat opposite. He's about the age of her own sons. His hair, like theirs is long, and he's wearing the universal uniform of youth: jeans and T-shirt. But his jeans are carefully pressed, a crease knifing its way down the front of the extravagant flares. She smiles at what her daughter would say about ironed jeans. The young man smiles back.

"How long still to Kołobrzeg?"

"It's the next station – just another ten minutes or so. Pani is here on holiday?"

"I'm here for…" Luiza hesitates. "For a reunion."

"Ah, Pani comes from the West to meet Polish relatives."

He switches to English to assert, "Pani speaks very good Polish," and nods, as if confirming his opinion.

"I should hope so!" Luiza exclaims in Polish. "I was born here."

The young man looks taken aback.

"I apologise, Pani, but you speak with an accent."

It's Luiza's turn to be taken aback. "Really? What kind of accent?"

"Oh, not strong, but it's there. Are you from America?"

"England."

The boy reverts to English with a grin. "Ah, The Beatles, Manchester United, The Rolling Stones."

Luiza smiles and continues in English, "And how is it you speak such good English? Did you learn at school?"

The boy grimaces. "School? Of course not. In school they teach only Russian." He spits the words.

"Then, where… how?" asks Luiza with interest.

"Oh, it is because the sister of my grandfather, she lives in America – in Chicago – and she sends me the language tapes: Teach Yourself English. They work, yes?"

"They certainly do – or rather YOU work." Luiza laughs.

"Ah, here is Kołobrzeg," says the boy, in Polish.

Luiza starts with alarm. She'd meant to go to the toilet, apply powder and lipstick, comb her hair. She scrabbles through her bag for her compact, but the train is pulling to a halt. She gives up and reaches for her suitcase.

"Please, Pani, allow me."

The young man takes her case from the rack and beckons her to follow him. He opens the door and alights, placing the case on the platform before helping her down the steep step. Before relinquishing her hand, he kisses it.

"I hope Pani enjoys her reunion," he says, and jumps back up. He pulls the door shut and waves. Luiza waves back, still feeling the imprint of his lips on the back of her hand. The sensation sweeps her back through the decades. She remembers Karol, whom she hasn't thought of in years. She remembers galloping Rumi over the autumn stubble and watching her mother waltz into the salon bearing her coffee tray aloft. She remembers Pappa, his waistcoat straining to contain his belly, a Habana cigar in his hand. She remembers Uncle Rafi racing across the lawn in Pappa's sagging swimming costume. Gone, all are gone. She remembers Ida, radiant on her wedding day, laughing on Mirek's arm.

"Lou-lou?"

Luiza turns. Dark, lank hair frames the woman's lined face. Her lips are unpainted, barely visible between toothless gums. But her eyes are alight. Her eyes are Ida's.

"Oh, Lou-lou – haven't we grown old?"

Epilogue

I grew up knowing that my mother lost her mother when she was nine. I grew up knowing that this motherless Lutheran child then found comfort in the icons of Catholic Poland and a replacement mother in the virgin with the chubby baby on her knee. I grew up hearing the reverential tone that accompanied the name Alis: the glamorous older sister, poised and perfect in the black-and white-photos with the crinkled cream edges. I grew up knowing my mother was the tomboy, encouraged by a father who had hoped for a son.

Part of me revelled in the tales of her childhood in pre-war Poland: The house with the trees and the lake; the mill down a lane that was knee-deep in mud in the winter and choked in dust in summer. The shooting parties and the horses; the handmade shoes and gloves. The deranged nanny who placed a snake in my six-year-old mother's bed; the pranks my mother and her sister played on student interns at their father's mill.

But the spellbinding accounts of salt in the sugar bowl and ritual Easter Monday soakings by local boys came at a cost: frequent pious references to God's mother filling the void left by the loss of her own, delivered in a tone charged with virtuous self-pity. How these allusions to her bereavement and its sanctimonious resolution rankled. The exoticism of my mother's early life, which stood in such sharp contrast with my own suburban 1960s upbringing, remained beguiling, but I grew resistant to the implicit demand for compassion for this girl who rode the ponies I longed for and enjoyed the pleasures a wealthy, indulgent father could provide.

As I grew older, the stories grew darker: industrial sabotage; a bus strafed by German Stukas; brave, compassionate sorties into the ghetto. All as Alis slowly faded from the foreground.

I found it hard to think of my mother as a sister. Hers was a redoubtable and unallied sovereignty. She was strong-willed and manipulative; so was I. She bent circumstances to her will; I stood firm. My father, always mild with me, his only daughter, adored his wife and was fiercely protective of her. I believe he was painfully conscious that he could not provide the material comfort she had grown up with, nor the status she had once known. In our many and bitter arguments during my teenage years, he always sided with my mother, even when I sensed his rational self was on my side. My mother was not given to compromise; how did she ever rub along with a sister?

I was ten when the letter that pitched Alis back centre stage landed on the doormat. My mother, who had never sought Polish contacts since arriving in England five years previously, began to make Polish friends and serve Polish dishes. In 1971, my mother returned to Poland for the first time in thirty years. She asked me to go with her, but I felt no desire to peek behind the menacing might of the Iron Curtain. A diet of spy movies and a convent education, which placed communism firmly in the devil's camp, had instilled a fear that inoculated me against any curiosity about half my heritage.

It was only post-degree and post-PGCE, with the terrors of teaching practice behind me and no wish to face the cruelty of thirteen-year-old girls again any time soon, that I finally visited Poland. In 1979, the Iron Curtain had not yet been tweaked aside by Solidarity, yet a year as a 'student of Polish heritage' in Kraków seemed infinitely preferable to standing at the front of a London classroom. I learnt Polish language and history and recognised that my romantic notion of having a Slavic soul was misplaced. In England I had played up the esotericism of my provenance; in Poland I became 100 per cent British, having found myself in a place where the entire population was capable of driving me to distraction just as my mother did. It seemed that all Poles knew, instinctively, what I should do, eat, think...

However, most of them were – just like my mother – kind and loyal and generous. Travelling by train meant offers of shared food and invitations to stay from complete strangers. Many became friends, and I remained in touch when I returned to London. During the 1980s and '90s, I returned to Poland frequently to chart, as a journalist, the dramatic lurches from Solidarność to martial law and then Glasnost.

And as I came to understand my mother's homeland, I came to realise that hers was a story that deserved to be told. I returned to Poland with my mother. We visited the places where she had lived. We survived a four-week road trip in a beat-up old tank of a Mercedes. There were many screaming matches over directions (this was pre-satnav, although my mother continued to give directions into her nineties, contradicting the satnav she had insisted on buying me). But I came home with a full notebook, fired up and determined to write.

Then my son was born.

I returned to the manuscript when he was sixteen. I despaired of the purple prose, and the structure was decidedly off. The many, extraordinary coincidences screamed: unbelievable! The historical context required for these lives lived during some of the twentieth century's most significant events was turgid. I tried again. I attended a selection of creative writing courses. I fictionalised it. Then I memoir-ised it. Then I fictionalised it again.

What I finally deliver here is a combination of contextual memoir and historical framework, transposing scenes from a narrative that I have lived with for decades. It is a story that throws open yet another window on how the Second World War blew families apart and left them scattered in its aftermath. It is the story of two sisters whose lives diverged dramatically.

I have changed names, created or conflated some characters, fictionalised around the known events, but the coincidences – even the most unlikely – are genuine. Life *is* stranger than fiction.

My mother is now dead. She lived to ninety-two. We argued almost to the end. But by then I had learnt that being a sister was at the heart of her indomitable will. It was the secret of her survival.

Acknowledgements

inding Ida has been decades in the making, with extensive support along the way. Too many to list individually, but family and friends who have read and fed back on its various incarnations, you know who you are, and you have my eternal gratitude. Not only for editorial assessments, but for unflagging belief in and support for the project. There were times when I thought I would never get this past the finish line; you must have had the same doubts, but you never let on!

I will, however, name my son, Esa, whose long-awaited arrival interrupted the process, but who eventually kickstarted it in a different direction. His query as to whether anybody outside our family would be interested forced a realisation that, if he could be sceptical that such a remarkable story was of wider interest, I was clearly not getting it right. He sparked a serious re-appraisal of my approach, culminating in this publication, which I sincerely hope will be of general interest.

The change in approach led to creative writing courses at City Lit (thank you, Jonathan Barnes), The Arvon Foundation (Jane Harris, your encouragement was invaluable) and mentoring from The Literary Consultancy (thank you, Anna South). And thanks to all at The Book Guild who guided this novel from my head to the bookshelf.

My Polish cousin, Staś ("Little Mirek"), is a big part of this story. With the passage of time, accounts develop and diverge. The one told here is based on my mother's memories; the filling in of any blanks is the product of my own research and imagination. I hope Staś will be tolerant of my surmises.

My final and greatest thanks go to my mother, Irena Burgess. I'm sorry I didn't get this finished in time for you to read it, Mum. But I hope that those who do will recognise the redoubtable, unique sister you were.

*M*arya Burgess's BBC career spanned almost 40 years, reporting for *Woman's Hour* and *PM*, producing *All in the Mind* and *For One Night Only*, and finally curating *The Listening Project* in partnership with the British Library. Over the years, Marya has attempted to tell her mother's remarkable story, but it was only after moving to rural Scotland that *Finding Ida* finally took shape.